Dear Jane

CW00552615

The final book in the

Highbury Trilogy

inspired by Jane Austen's 'Emma'

Allie Cresswell

Author photograph © Tim Newell

Cover image from an artwork by Mike Shayler www.scruffmonkeyart.co.uk based on an original work by Colin Bradley www.colinbradleyart.com

Graphic design by Rebecca Watson Design
www.rebeccawatsondesign.co.uk

This book is dedicated

to my fellow-writer, encourager

and dear friend

Becky.

Volume One

Prologue

Our story begins in Highbury, a thriving, populous village in Surrey. Donwell Abbey was by far the largest and most majestic house to be found there, but its situation a mile or so from the village itself, and the youthful age of Squire George Knightley, with his natural diffidence and unassuming gentility, meant that Hartfield, a comparatively new mansion much closer to the High Street, was generally considered to be the premier property. Its occupants, Mr Woodhouse—a widower—and his young daughters certainly thought themselves the cream of Highbury society and Mr Knightley was too affable a man to contradict them. General and Mrs Bramhall occupied a house called Randalls—a very pretty property as equidistant from Highbury to the west as Hartfield was to the east. These three, with the very recent addition of Mr—formerly Captain—Weston formed the principal set in the little town.

It behoves us to say a little more in respect of Mr Weston. The Westons had been Highbury people for two or three generations, having risen significantly in wealth and consequence from their origins in a trade which, while respectable, was still a trade. Mr Weston, having an adventurous spirit and being possessed of a solid education and a small independence from a distant relative, had chosen not to involve himself in the family affair but had enlisted in the militia and travelled extensively both in England and further afield. He had married, very well, a wealthy young lady of a prominent Yorkshire family. Miss Churchill's brother and sister-in-law had not approved the match but Miss Churchill's character was not one to defer to any person whose ideas were not in accordance with her own. The marriage had not been happy and had an unhappy termination in the death of Mrs Weston when her little boy Frank was but two years of age. Mr Weston being comparatively poor, and Mr and Mrs Churchill being childless, it had been agreed that they should rear the motherless child and that he should, in due course, become their heir. The consequences for Frank and the effect on his character is part of this narrative's object to discover. Suffice it to say at this juncture that Mr Weston had, immediately upon the matter of Frank's management being settled between himself and the Churchills, quit the militia and taken himself to London, there to involve himself in the family business. He had accomplished this with no very small degree of success over a period of eight or nine years and at the commencement of our story found himself moderately prosperous on the proceeds of his industry and able to take a less active role. This being so he had determined to return to Highbury. That he enjoyed the society of the first families in the place was a result of his own novelty to them, his genial character, gentlemanlike manner and a sense that, though long absent himself, his family association with the locale earned him that entitlement.[i]

Of agreeable—if a degree or two lower ranking—families in Highbury there were many; the vicar, Mr Paling, his wife and children were held in high esteem. Mr Perry the apothecary was a very pleasant man and hosted card parties for gentlemen that were well-attended. Mrs Goddard was universally popular, a widow lady who ran a school for little girls. The Coles, though risen from trade, were almost genteel enough to be included in the same superior tier as the Knightleys and the Woodhouses and now most ambitiously aspired to it; after all, if Mr Weston could be encompassed in it, why not they? But, somehow, they did not sit quite comfortably there. The Palings and the Perrys comprised their more natural circle.

One other family it is necessary to mention.[ii] Mrs Bates and her daughter had at one time occupied the place that Mr Woodhouse and his daughters now inhabited—not their mansion but their position in the social hierarchy. Her husband had been the vicar of the parish but his death and his family's failure to provide for his widow had reduced her from the comfort of the pleasant old vicarage to a suite of rooms above the local grocer's shop. What very small income she received, her rent and the cost of an annual allowance of coal, came from sources unnamed but suspected, by her at least, to be the squire of Donwell, with whose family of old she had particular and tender ties.

Mrs Bates—at this time aged as close to sixty as makes no difference—was loved and respected by all, a friend to the humblest cottar and the squire of Donwell and to every type and degree of person in between. She was gentle of character, wise and kind, but sorrows coming fast on each other's heels had caused her to be increasingly quiet, and perhaps a little melancholy. The latest of these had been the death of her second daughter, Jane. The addition of a little granddaughter to the accommodations above the grocer's had been bittersweet; little Jane was a delight in every way; a thoughtful, considerate girl, very intelligent, pretty and well-mannered. But she provided an extra mouth to feed, feet to be shod, an education and a future in life to be secured. Love alone—and Mrs Bates lavished *that* upon her foundling child—could not supply all that would be necessary. Thankfully, help had come in the shape of Colonel and Mrs Campbell. The colonel had reason to be beholden to Jane's father and was minded to enfold Jane in the shelter of his commodious wing where she would provide companionship for his own little girl. All that could be done in the way of education, accomplishment and affectionate up-bringing he offered to do, but beyond that he could not provide; a dowry, specifically, was beyond his power, likewise any competency that would enable Jane to live independently. He would equip her to make her own way. She would be a governess—one whose first-rate talents and exceptional gentility would recommend her to the most superior families in noble houses— but a governess, nonetheless. With no better, alternative course at hand, Mrs Bates had agreed to the colonel's proposition and as our story begins the day of Jane's departure to the colonel's house in London was fast approaching.[iii]

One more burden did Mrs Bates carry—her surviving daughter. Miss Bates was popular in Highbury, anxious to please and to be pleased with everything, even that which was not perhaps very pleasing. She tended to erratic behaviour and a general lack of good sense but was well-meaning. Her errors were small, silly ones, quickly forgiven. But she was a talker, speaking mainly nonsense, platitudes and irrelevancies but occasionally revealing what should have remained private. She described in detail what could easily be seen, and listed the interminable minutiae of the last ten things she had heard, done, seen, or thought that were usually of no interest to anyone. She was tolerated for her mother's sake and because of her own essentially kind nature, a figure of fun, perhaps but not one who could be endured for any length of time. Mrs Bates herself had lately affected deafness as a means of shutting out her daughter's relentless, empty diatribe. Hetty was a confirmed spinster; how could *her* future security be assured?

'And so, Jane,' said Emma Woodhouse, 'you will come no more to Hartfield to play with my dolls. You are going to the Campbells' to stay always, and will not come back to Highbury. I suppose Rowena Campbell has not so many toys and books as me? Nor half so many dolls?'

Jane Fairfax looked up from where she sat on the nursery floor. Emma occupied the only chair in the room and looked down from it at her little visitor with some considerable air of superiority. It was always so when Jane was sent to play at Hartfield. Although the girls were of an age—almost nine—Jane was always made to feel younger, inferior and certainly poorer. She *was* poorer—there was no denying it—thirty thousand pounds poorer than Miss Woodhouse. But she was not younger and decidedly she was not inferior by any meaningful measure, being brighter, more accomplished and arguably prettier than Miss Woodhouse of Hartfield. Jane did not reply at once, unsure as to which of Emma's inaccurate statements she ought to contradict. Or whether she ought to contradict any—Miss Emma Woodhouse disliked being told she was wrong.

At last, she said, 'Miss Rowena has some very nice dolls, but you are right, they are not so numerous as yours. Of books she has a great many, *and,*' because she felt she ought to defend her little friend Rowena, and Miss Woodhouse should not be allowed to have things all her own way, 'most of hers she has read.'

'I thought not,' Emma said, disregarding Jane's second comment, 'not so numerous as mine, and not so nice, I expect. But still,' she smiled very sweetly, 'more than you have at home, and so I suppose you will be pleased to go, and leave your grandmamma and aunt?'

Jane considered. 'I am not unhappy to go to the Campbells. I have been going there since I was five or six, and feel very at home at their house. They treat me very kindly. But as for being happy to leave Grandmamma and Aunt Hetty, no, of course, I shall miss them very much.'

'Naturally the Campbells treat you kindly,' Emma replied. 'Papa says a young lady in your situation should always be treated kindly. The Bible says we must be kind to orphans. I suppose you will stay in the attic and wear all Miss Campbell's hand-me-down clothes and be required to clean the fire-grates and do all their mending.'

'*That* does not sound very kind,' Jane said. 'It sounds more like *Cendrillon*[iv] to me. Rowena is not an ugly step-sister!'

Miss Woodhouse settled an unruly flounce on her dress. 'Perhaps she is not absolutely ugly, but she is not pretty.[v] I have heard that her nose is decidedly snub and her hair is only a very dowdy brown. My nose is aquiline—Miss Taylor says that artists throughout the ages have idealised the aquiline nose in their paintings. But if *I* had a snub nose and a plain face I would not like someone with nicer features coming to live with me, and yours *are* quite nice, Jane. If I were Rowena Campbell, I might well shut you up in the attic.'

Jane could easily believe it. She looked down and pretended great interest in adjusting the bonnet of the doll she was holding. It was

Alicia, one of the five or six dolls she was permitted to play with at Hartfield. The others—Emma's special dolls—were put out of reach on the occasion of Jane's visits, whether by Emma herself, or the maid, or Emma's governess, Jane did not know. She *did* know that it was not an aquiline but a Greek nose—like hers—which was the artist's ideal, and could cite examples too. Mrs Goddard had a great many interesting books with pictures by the great artists and Jane had perused them on her frequent visits to the school. But she knew that Emma would either refute her examples or run crying to Miss Taylor; argument with Miss Woodhouse was futile. She did wonder though, about little Rowena Campbell—shy, mousy and awkward. Would she really welcome Jane as her constant companion with all the inevitable comparison that would necessarily ensue? Jane could not help her pleasing looks or her quick wit but she would be mortified if they made Rowena Campbell unhappy.

She was much too sensible to be frightened by Emma Woodhouse's lurid allusions but she did not like the idea of being pitied—by the Campbells or anyone else. The words 'charity case' had been murmured in her hearing; she was to be felt sorry for because her mama and papa had died and she had only her grandmamma and aunt to take care of her who could barely afford to do so. She was a burden who had been placed on their frail and inadequate shoulders and was now to be transferred to the Campbells' much more substantial ones. It might be done kindly, with infinite gentleness, but so it was; it was her lot.

Jane sighed. 'I am very thankful to the Campbells,' she said.

'Of course, you are thankful,' Emma said complacently. 'Those who are the recipients of others' benevolence *must* be thankful and show their thankfulness by not expecting more than they receive. *That* is presumption.'

Beyond the window the sounds of Emma's elder sister Isabella larking around with John Knightley rose up from the shrubbery. Isabella was fifteen years old. John was seventeen[vi] and soon to go up to Cambridge. Jane wondered if George—who must now be addressed as Mr Knightley—was also about the Hartfield grounds. He had just returned from Cambridge and taken up the duties of squire at Donwell. He ought to have been a grand and intimidating personage to someone of Jane's age and reduced circumstances but somehow the kindness of his eye and the gentleness of his speech made Jane feel that he was a friend. *He* did not pity her. *He* did not feel sorry for her and her poverty was of no matter to him; he liked her for herself. This carried great weight with her. She would rather spend her time with him than with Miss Woodhouse, but it was always assumed the two girls were great friends and they were bundled off to the nursery together while Mrs Bates and Miss Bates took refreshment with Emma's father. She was expected to be a good guest. That, too, was her lot. So now she said, 'Your dolls' house is far superior to Rowena's. I would like it very much if you would be so kind as to show me the furniture again, Miss Woodhouse.'

That night, after Aunt Hetty had heard her prayers and tucked her into bed, Jane said, 'I am a very lucky girl, am I not, Aunt, to be invited to the Campbells' house.'

'Indeed, you are, Jane dear,' Hetty said, 'and you must always be conscious of your good fortune and show your gratitude to the Campbells.'

'How should I show it, Aunt? I cannot always be thanking them. They will get tired of hearing it.'

'Well,' Hetty considered, 'I do not know if one can ever say thank you too often, so long, of course, as one *is* thankful. I count my blessings every day and am sometimes overwhelmed by how numerous and abundant they are! Yes, indeed I am Jane. When one is given much, one has much to be thankful for and the thank-yous will just come pouring out of me! Perhaps I tire people with them? I had not considered. No, I do not think you can voice your thanks too frequently. But if I may give you a little advice on this question, Jane, it would be that you should not *presume*. The Campbells are such liberal, generous people. They intend to treat you quite on a level with Rowena; nothing that is provided to her is to be withheld from you and it will *seem* to the outside world that you are another daughter to them. But, Jane, you are not, and you would be deceiving yourself if you ever made the mistake of believing that you were. What you receive from them is due to their goodness, not your deserts and there *will* come a time after which the Campbells' goodwill will cease. You must accept the termination of their favour just as you accept its commencement—with grace and gratitude.'

'Yes, Aunt.'

'There's a good girl. Now go to sleep. The colonel comes tomorrow with the coach very early and you must be up, and ready and not keep him waiting.'

The journey from Highbury to that part of London where the Campbells resided was no more than a dozen miles, an easy road with no requirement for passenger or horse to stop. But the colonel, in his great consideration and pre-eminent desire to make much of Jane, had frequently called upon the coachman to halt that he might show Jane the sights along the way; the Royal estates of Richmond and Kew, the river bank at Hammersmith. A journey of some two hours had therefore become four by the time the colonel's carriage pulled up outside their house in Bute Square. No sooner had Jane descended than Rowena was on the steps to greet her. She was dressed—as always—very prettily, but no amount of ribbon could disguise the fact that Rowena Campbell was not a pretty child; a small mouth beneath a nose that Miss Woodhouse might very well label snub but that we will call retroussé, brown eyes neither finely shaped nor of such a lustre as to compensate, a low forehead and hair of such brownness as might be found on a sparrow's wing. But what she lacked in beauty Rowena Campbell certainly made up for in nature. She was of a sweet disposition, very kind and gentle-mannered, but shy, keeping to the shelter of her mama's skirts and loath to speak, especially in unfamiliar company. Her intellect was not of the sharpest and she found her lessons hard, but she was most earnest to do well and did not lack diligence. Jane she loved with an affection that was warm and full of disinterested admiration, fully recognising her friend's superior beauty and understanding without feeling the least taint of resentment or envy.

Now she took Jane's hand and drew her into the warmth of the hall. 'We are to have no lessons today, Jane, in celebration of your arrival. When Willis has gone over your things and seen what … what little additions or improvements might be needed, Mama will send for the dressmaker and you shall be measured for whatever you may require. Then we are to go to the river, if it does not rain. Miss Blossom says we may collect such leaves, nuts and twigs as we find to make a collage. Shall that not be nice?'

'Indeed, it will, Rowena,' said Jane, although to tell the truth the early hour of her departure from Highbury and the exigencies of the journey had rather fatigued her. She would rather have spent the remainder of the day by the nursery fire with a book. 'I have messages from my grandmamma and aunt for your mama. Is she at home?'

'Not at present; she visits a friend. But we are to dine with Mama and Papa today—another treat to celebrate your coming to us. You will see her then. Let us go upstairs in the meanwhile. I have something to show you.'

The Campbells' house was substantial but rather cluttered with mementoes from their travels—evocative, no doubt, to them who had climbed the Gilbraltan rock, wandered the lemon groves of the Canaries and bartered in the bazaars of Constantinople, but oddly eclectic to the untraveled. By now Jane was quite used to the elephant's foot, the be-tasselled African javelin, the Egyptian death-mask and the fixed snarls and glass-eyed stares of various mysterious creatures brought home from foreign climes. She followed Rowena up the sweeping staircase, along the elegant landing and up again to the nursery apartments where a new chamber had been made ready for the girls.

'Mama says we are too big for the nursery now—or that the nursery is too small for us! Either way she has decided that we shall sleep in this room now. How do you like it, Jane? The window overlooks the square, you see? And there are two of everything—one for you and one for me.'

'It is … very nice indeed,' Jane said, looking around the room that was large, even with the duplicates of furniture. She had spent her whole life sharing not just a room but a bed, at first with her mama and then with her aunt Hetty, who was bony and tended to jerk and thrash around in her sleep. Their bedroom, although the larger of the two provided in Mrs Bates' apartment above the grocer's shop, had been less than a quarter of the size of this one. 'I shall not know what to do with all this space,' Jane admitted. 'My things will not need half these drawers.'

'But they will do, after a while,' Rowena said, her eyes shining with pleasure. 'I wanted to know which bed you would prefer, Jane. This one by the window, or the other, in the corner. I have not slept in either. I wanted you to have your choice.'

The bed by the window was certainly to be preferred. It would enjoy the morning light and the refreshment of the breeze when the weather was warm, but it was also closer to the fireplace. The other bed was beyond the door, far from the fire and rather closed in by a large press.

'I shall take the bed in the corner, please,' Jane said, walking across the room and perching on the counterpane, 'that is, if *you* do not prefer it.'

Rowena was too honest and naive to suspect any calculation on Jane's part and happily agreed to take the better bed. Then they were called downstairs.

Mrs Campbell was a homely, practical woman without airs of any kind but having that degree of natural sympathy and kindness that recommended her wherever she went. Now she drew Jane into the warmth of her embrace, instinctively understanding how such a great change in Jane's circumstances might overwhelm her.

'My dear Jane,' she said, 'how delighted we are to have you here with us. I hope you like the arrangements we have made upstairs. The colonel says he left your grandmamma and aunt in excellent health but I know that does not mean you will be easy about them. If you find you feel the least homesick, uncomfortable or distressed in any way you are to come directly to me. To come to us for a holiday is one thing but to come to us, as you have done, as a settled thing, is quite another. I understand it will take some getting used to. You shall write to them every week—or more often if you desire—and they shall write to you. *That* will help you bear your separation and it is the ardent hope of the colonel and myself that you will soon feel as thoroughly at home here, as secure and comfortable as … well, as Rowena does.'

Jane nestled into the crook of Mrs Campbell's arm and felt as though she might weep. Mrs Campbell was such a warm and comfortable body, so very motherly and considerate. Her goodness—and the colonel's— was almost too much. She felt humbled by it and perhaps a little guilty. The house in Bute Square was so luxurious; fires burned in every room, the carpets were deep, the curtains very lavish, the furniture mingled just that combination of elegance and comfort that is always to be desired. It could not help but create comparisons in Jane's mind. Her grandmamma's rooms were eminently respectable but so very confined. Their poverty was evidenced in the threadbare rugs and sagging upholstery and in the sounds that rose from the shop below. How could it be fair that she should enjoy all the open-handed Campbells had in their power to bestow while they—her grandmamma and aunt— should be left to struggle on, counting out their daily ration of coal and subsisting on the kindness of their neighbours? The alteration was hard to accustom herself to. Indeed, Jane reminded herself, she must not become accustomed to it, since it could not last indefinitely.

'Thank you, Mrs Campbell,' she said now. 'I am most grateful to you.'

'Now, Jane dear,' Mrs Campbell went on, 'I have asked the dressmaker to come and take your measurements. Willis has had the tiniest peek into your valise and it seems that just a very few additions to your wardrobe are needed to equip you for life in London. It is quite different, you know, to life in the country, and what is perfect *there* will not serve *here*. I would not cast the least aspersion on your grandmamma's provision; you are amply provided for in *almost* every respect.'

But it seemed to Jane that the inadequacies of her wardrobe were legion. A walking outfit, a riding habit, dresses for the afternoon and pinafores for the school room were ordered along with undergarments, stockings and more footwear that Jane believed it would be possible to make use of.

'What need shall I have of dancing slippers?' she enquired at one point.

'We are to have dancing lessons,' Rowena said. 'I am sure I shall be very clumsy but *you* will dance delightfully Jane.'

'As two novices you are sure to progress at the same pace,' Mrs Campbell said equitably.

'An art master has been engaged also. And wait until I show you the stables! Two ponies, both so sweet-tempered, with such soft mouths. I shall call mine Cherub, but I have not chosen which. *You* shall choose the one you like best. And Miss Blossom will instruct us in the pianoforte,' Rowena went on breathlessly, eager to reveal the full panoply of good things to be laid at Jane's feet.

'I am sure it is all too much,' Jane said, with a trembling lip.

Mrs Campbell clapped her hands. 'Thank you, that will be all for today,' she said. The seamstress and her assistant began bundling up the fabric samples they had brought. The shoemaker collected his patterns. All were ushered from the room with great dispatch. 'This has all taken much too long and you girls have not had your excursion to the riverbank,' Mrs Campbell said. 'Miss Blossom will scold me. She is most insistent that her charges have a proper quantity of air and exercise each day. Go and get your wraps, girls.'

That night, a little while after Nanny had removed the candles, Rowena slipped across the room and climbed into bed beside Jane.

'You do not mind, Jane, do you?' she whispered. 'I know it is but the wind in the chimney that makes that moaning noise and the tapping on the window is only the rain. But when I am by myself, I do fancy such things—such strange and terrifying things. When I slept in the nursery, I was not afraid because Nanny was there.'

'No, I do not mind,' Jane replied, making room on the pillow for Rowena's head, 'and if Nanny rebukes us we can tell her that you came to comfort me, because I was homesick and cried. It is only a little untruth.'

Only a little untruth indeed. As Jane had settled herself in the high, spacious bed she had been thinking about the floors below her in the house in Bute Square, the many splendid rooms, the library of books, the elegant dining room and the two drawing rooms. She had imagined the dance and art classes—what pleasure they would be! Her own pony! The pianoforte lessons and the new dresses—what could be more delightful? It seemed like a dream—it *was* a dream indeed, and one from which she must one day wake to face the harshness of day. She wondered if any amount of velvet, any number of wax candles, any indulgent hours of reading could soften that sharp transition. Could the bitterness of the medicine that had to be swallowed be offset by sugar tasted in advance? Or would the sugar simply make the bitterness worse? She did not know. But she did begin to feel very wistful about Highbury's little cobbled street and the homely rooms above the grocer's shop. She had not cried, but she had longed most ardently to be back there.

'Oh Jane,' sighed Rowena, without a suspicion of her friend's melancholy feelings, 'how glad I am that you are come.'

Enscombe was a large house standing alone on the periphery of a broad-stretched Yorkshire moor. It was very imposing without being the least beautiful; old grey granite, very weathered; flat, utilitarian façades, a multiplicity of windows that managed to look blank and blind. No light shone from within and only the barest smudge of grey against the rain-laden clouds suggested a fire somewhere inside.

The last of the January snows lay on the moorland scrub. Black pools of peaty water shimmered with ice. The land stretched for mile upon mile; grey and featureless and unspeakably bleak. The way to Enscombe was long, straight and unmarked by tree or fence; only the coachman's long familiarity with the way kept the horses on the narrow track, the carriage and its single occupant from foundering in the boggy pools or gravel pits that bordered it either side.

At last, the carriage pulled up on the gravel forecourt of Enscombe. The ancient doorway opened just enough for a manservant to come out. He descended the short flight of steps and opened the carriage door. 'Good afternoon Mr Frank.'

The boy who stepped out of the carriage was about eleven or twelve years of age, with curly hair and an agreeable face. 'Hello, Monks,' he replied, cheerfully enough. 'I didn't expect to see you so soon. What's happened? Is my aunt unwell?'

In fact, Frank Weston had only been back at school about a fortnight before being summoned to the headmaster's office and told he was to return home. He was to pack all his belongings. It was not certain if, or when, he would re-join his school fellows. 'You are required at home, Weston,' was the headmaster's only explanation.

Monks began to supervise the removal of the trunks from the rear of the carriage. 'Mrs Churchill is in the library, Mr Frank. I believe tea has just been served.'

Frank ran up the steps and pushed his way through the door, whose hinges got stiffer and less accommodating with every year.

'I declare,' the young man muttered to himself with a wry smile, 'one day this door won't open at all and we'll all be imprisoned in Enscombe until we die of cold and starvation.'

The hall was large, chill and bare of furniture save a hard chair on which Monks or his deputy was permitted to sit during the hours of the night watch. Frank Weston crossed it quickly and made for a long, gloomy passageway that took him deep into the interior of the house. He passed half a dozen doors on either side, all closed, and a gallery beneath a high, glass atrium where marble statuary and enormous artworks were shrouded in sheeting. His footsteps rang and echoed as he walked, duplicating themselves five, ten, a dozen times. As a small child he had enjoyed this illusion, running up and down and shouting so that his little voice and stamping feet became a regiment in full battle cry. Of course, his aunt had not liked it. He had been reprimanded often on account of being too noisy, too energetic, but that had not stopped him.

'You are your mother's son,' his aunt had said, as though this were a bad thing, 'undisciplined, wilful and wild. Monks, you must teach Mr Frank his manners.'

Monks had beaten him, but not hard.

Afterwards Frank had smiled at his aunt. 'Thank you, Aunt. But I think I am also my father's son.'

'Too true,' she had agreed. 'It remains to be seen whether your defiance manages to grind your irrepressible good humour into submission, or vice versa.'

Frank Weston recalled this episode as he traversed the corridors of Enscombe. The occasional flickering lamp pushed back the shadows. Cold seeped from the walls and the floor, un-checked by carpet, curtain, wall-hanging or rug. At last, he came to the door he sought, knocked gently and waited. Presently a thin shard of voice called, 'Enter,' and he went inside.

The room was comparatively warm; a fire burned in the grate and some dozen or so lamps illuminated the towering shelves of books, reflecting the room back in the tall, crazed windows. What light there had been during the day had faded. 'Good afternoon, Aunt Churchill,' Frank said, crossing the room and placing a kiss on the cheek of the lady who sat before the fire. 'The day has turned to night. Shall I ring the bell and ask for the curtains to be closed? I suppose Uncle Churchill is in the estate office. Mmm. Tea cakes. May I have some?'

Mrs Churchill inclined her head and Frank helped himself from the plate. 'I must say,' he said, through crumbs, 'I didn't expect to be home again until Easter. What has happened? Frazer Minor said that probably the Churchill estate has been swallowed up in debt and my school fees hadn't been paid. *Have* they?'

'Of course, they have, Frank. I wish you would sit down. Will you have some tea? You have not enquired after my health.'

'Yes, tea, please, Aunt. I *have* been sitting down! For hours and hours. A fellow needs to move around, you know, or he seizes up.' Frank sat down, however, and accepted the cup Mrs Churchill passed him. He dreaded asking after his aunt's health as there was always a litany of ailments and complaints but he could not avoid doing so now. 'How *are* you Aunt? I hope I find you … improved.' 'Well' was never a word to be used in association with Mrs Churchill.

'Signally *not* improved, indeed much worse,' Mrs Churchill grizzled. 'Doctor Whimberry writes me off as a lost cause. Sundry aches, a tremor that is marked particularly in the morning and renders me almost incapable of holding a cup to my lips. The headache is my permanent companion. He has bled me until I have no blood left to drain and still sees no amelioration to my condition. I believe my veins have all-but collapsed. I do not know what keeps me alive.'

'What does he do with the blood?' asked Frank with the ghoulishness common to boys of his age.

'Frank, that is an inappropriate speculation,' his aunt snapped, although perhaps realising that the topic was not suitable for a child. 'Whenever people relate anything regarding their health you ought to show sympathy and concern but by no means pursue details.'

'Forgive me, Aunt. I feel very sorry for you and am most concerned.'

Mrs Churchill looked mollified. 'Thank you. Yes, that is most satisfactory. And then you might offer a little compliment as to their stoicism, if you feel it apposite. Of course, not everyone suffers with such fortitude as I. There are invalids who bore one rigid with a catalogue of their supposed ailments. Thankfully, *I* am not amongst them.'

There was a pregnant pause. At last Frank said, 'Indeed, Aunt, you suffer bravely.'

Mrs Churchill looked almost pleased. 'You may have another tea cake, if you wish.'

Frank took advantage of the temporary shift in her humour to ask, 'So why have I been sent for? It was rather inconvenient, I don't mind telling you. I was to play in the school eleven on Saturday. Is Papa quite well?'

Frank was used to seeing his father some once or twice a year, when his uncle Churchill took him to London to visit the tailor. Frank was fond of his father and would have liked to have seen him more often, but had accepted that Mr Weston's business, his own schooling and his aunt's uncertain health precluded it.

'Your papa writes to tell me he has removed to his place of origin.'

'And where is that?' Frank enquired.

'A place called Highbury. It is in Surrey; it is no surprise he never mentioned the place to you, or his connection with it. It is a humdrum little town without elegance or éclat of any kind; quite rustic and impossibly shabby. One imagines yokels,' Mrs Churchill gave a shudder. 'His family lived there. They were in trade. They *are* in trade, indeed and your father concerns himself with the matter.'

'Oh,' said Frank, speculatively, 'and … I am to join him there? To learn the business in my turn?'

Mrs Churchill clutched her throat. 'Emphatically *not,* Frank. You are a gentleman. You will not sully your hands with so contemptible a concern. No, your returning from school has no relevance to your father's return to Highbury. What I am going to tell you now was resolved after your mother died and now the time has come when that resolve should be fully acted upon. You are old enough to understand it, I think. In fact, I thought you old enough some years ago but, as usual, I was over-ruled.'

Frank suppressed a smile at this idea.

Mrs Churchill curled her lip, creating a vinegary expression habitual with her. 'It would be wrong to say your father has renounced you. He is fond of you, I will allow him so much, and as a fond father he saw that *we* can do more for you than he can. We have no children, you know. Your mother's portion was substantial but nothing to the size of the Churchill capital as a whole. Your father has next to nothing on his own account. It was agreed that your uncle and I would have the management of you—*that* much, I conjecture, you will have realised. What you will not have apprehended is that on your coming of age you are to adopt our name and, in due course, inherit the Churchill estate. On such terms your father relinquished you. It is for your own good, *he* saw that. What could he offer you in comparison?'

Frank thought his father could offer a great deal; excellent companionship, friendly understanding and very liberal notions about of the amount of cake it was good for a boy to consume. 'I am very fond of Papa,' Frank mumbled, 'I hope I shall still see him … from time to time.'

'Yes, yes,' Mrs Churchill waved an impatient hand, '*that* arrangement must continue, I suppose. But your schooling will not. That is, it will not continue as it has done. The fact of the matter is simply this, Frank; I find I cannot do without you. Thus far I have sacrificed you to your education but you can have no notion of what it has cost me. I have *suffered*,' she passed her hand before her eyes, 'oh! untold pangs. No mother could have suffered more than I have. Your being at school has *almost* been the death of me, Frank. Dr Whimberry has long been urging me to bring you home. *He* says you are essential to my well-being. But I refused, naturally. It is simply not in my nature to be selfish. However, just after Christmas we heard of an excellent tutor just released from his duties at Blenheim. He has been preparing your cousin for Oxford but a little local difficulty has meant that the Marquis of Blandford has gone abroad for a time. Your uncle has secured the man's services and he arrived a few days ago. So, from henceforth you will take your lessons here, in this very room. I shall remove myself to the east drawing room. It is draughty and the fire smokes—it will be meat and drink to my rheumatism—but I do so happily in the knowledge that these resources,' she indicated the books, maps and curios that lined the shelves, 'shall be opened to you.'

'And what about my uncle?' In Frank's remembrance this room had been his uncle's domain. He was always to be found here until his aunt decided that it was too good a room for his exclusive use and that she had better claim to it, its turkey rug being thicker, the curtains better lined and the fire in some way hotter than those in the drawing room she had inhabited previously. 'Will he not wish to return to the library?'

'Oh,' Mrs Churchill waved an imperious arm, 'he finds the outdoors more conducive. He is always out with the dogs or toiling in that weather-beaten excuse for a garden. I declare he would sleep in the glasshouses if I allowed it. No, Frank, you will take your lessons here with Mr Tunnock. I have had a suite of rooms prepared for him on the first floor adjacent to yours. If I had my own son, it is exactly what I would have done. I could not have sent *him* to school and I am determined to treat you as though you were my own.' Mrs Churchill sat back in her chair and folded her hands in her lap. 'Yes,' she said, through half-closed eyes, 'if I *do* live you will have the great satisfaction of knowing that it was your company that has prolonged my life. When you are not at your studies you will be my constant companion. You may read to me when the weather is inclement, and when it is fine we will drive together. Will not that be most pleasant?'

'Yes, Aunt,' said Frank, but very doubtfully. He sat in silence as he assimilated all his aunt had said, until her drooping lids indicated that she slept.

Nevertheless, Frank said, very quietly, 'Excuse me, Aunt, I think I will go and see to my things,' before he crept from the room, as Mrs Churchill was a notoriously light sleeper and had been known to feign sleep in order to overhear what people said about her when they thought she was not listening.

He made his way through the desolate passageways of Enscombe, mounted a stone stairway and came to the door of his rooms. Monks had delivered his luggage and a maid was in the process of unpacking for him.

'Thank you,' Frank said, 'I think I would like you to leave those until later, please.'

The maid bobbed a curtsey and left the room. Frank sank down on the rug before the fire which, thankfully, had been kindled in the grate, and considered this sudden and unwelcome reversal in his circumstances. To inherit the untold wealth of the Churchill estate would be an agreeable thing, he supposed. What idea Frank had of money was comparative. Frazer Minor, whose father was an earl, had more. Beacon, whose father was a bishop, had less. Featherstone, who was a scholarship boy, had none at all. Frank had been content to be ranked comfortably between Frazer Minor and Beacon, but on the whole had preferred the company of Featherstone and had been more than happy to share the contents of his tuck parcels with him. Frank understood that money was an advantage to be desired but not coveted; a benefit there was much pleasure in sharing. Certainly, to inherit, in due course, the acres of moor around Enscombe, the farms and copses in the wold, the horses and carriages, all that was the *visible* evidence of his uncle's wealth—all excepting Enscombe itself which, Frank determined there and then, he would raze to the ground as soon as possible—would be a very wonderful thing. He presumed there was more that existed *invisibly*, but that was harder to comprehend and so he did not think of it. Even so, with such a prospect as he *could* imagine, he was fortunate, even blessed. But, oh, the price to be paid!

Frank put his head in his hands. The glimmer of the prize to be his one day was all-but obliterated by the stony path he must walk to claim it. He would miss school, the rough and tumble of the dormitory, the lessons—that were sometimes dull but occasionally illuminating. The food at school was good, plentiful and of a type calculated to satisfy the boys' relentless appetites. It was certainly preferable to the table at Enscombe which was, in comparison, quite frugal—Frank had not infrequently been forced to raid the pantry for supplementary sustenance. These things would be a loss but there was one aspect of his aunt's announcement that seemed to Frank to be a greater evil. He supposed, from now on, that as their heir his course in life would be prescribed by the Churchills. They would dictate his acquaintance, his leisure pursuits, his education and his travels. This tutor—Tunnock— would, no doubt, be a crusty old professor unearthed from a catacomb who spoke Greek as an amusing, pleasant diversion from speaking Latin. *He* would not allow the kinds of high jinks Frank enjoyed at school; all would be solemnity, grind and cramming. A profession, should he wish for one, would be denied him. He would not be allowed to enlist, as his father had done; he was doomed to be a gentleman. It seemed likely that the Churchills would even choose his wife! The prospect was insupportable—to be so constrained, so regulated, tethered like a horse to a treadmill. By the time his uncle died Frank might be an old man himself, easily forty years of age. What good would money and land be to him then, with all his youth wasted away in subservience to the caprices of his aunt?

Frank looked about him. His room at Enscombe was not terribly austere; it had been his mother's before she married, he had been told. Beyond his window the rain fell and the wind howled across the moor, quite as bleak and desolate as Frank's own feelings. Perhaps he ought to run away? How far could Highbury be? He could beg his father to relent … Frank had all the determination and courage of his mother. A solitary trek to Surrey held more of excitement than fear and what he lacked in experience he more than made up for in charisma—he could charm his way into or out of most situations. He stood uncertainly in the middle of the room, considering what he might need for the journey. He was determined that the Churchills would not have things all their own way. He would have some control of his own destiny.

The door resounded with a confident knock and opened to admit a tall young man Frank had never seen before. He was dressed neatly enough in clerical black but a thick head of dark unruly curls and a bright glint in his merry eyes belied the sobriety of his dress. He strode quickly across the room, his hand extended. 'Churchill, I presume (for so I am instructed to address you)? Pleased to meet you. I'm Tunnock, your tutor.'

'How do you do sir,' Frank said, almost in spite of himself, 'I must say, you're not what I expected.'

'No? Ah, you have a fire,' Mr Tunnock said. He turned to it and warmed his hands. 'No such luxury in my room. I'm half starved. I've already written to my mother, asking her to send thicker shirts and drawers. I don't hear the dinner bell yet—what time *do* your uncle and aunt dine? Whatever time it is, I don't think I can wait. Why don't you show me the way to the kitchens? I bet *you* can persuade the cook to give us something, can't you?'

Frank smiled, his plans for escape abandoned although his resolve to resist the absolute sway of his aunt was not. 'Yes, sir. I believe I can.'

Chapter One

Three years passed. They wrought much change in our protagonists but little in Highbury. Advent hymns mutated seamlessly into Christmas carols, dun ploughed land greened imperceptibly into spring wheat, old potatoes were replaced by new. The years crept around in Highbury, a slowly turning wheel.

Now, it being May, Miss Bates lifted the lid of a serving dish to discover asparagus spears and early peas. 'Oh Mother, how lovely,' she said. 'I must run down to Abbey Mill Farm and thank Mrs Martin for I am sure she has sent these to us. Her asparagus is always up first, you know. How kind of her to let us have some. Perhaps you will accompany me. No? It is a very pleasant day. We will not need to by Donwell proper if you do not wish it. Although I must say that I do not at all comprehend your aversion to the place. So good as the old squire was to us! I would expect you to have the fondest memories. Oh, very well, do not frown at me like that. Let me cut you some of this pie. Just a small slice, Mother, you really must. There—it is such a small portion I think even Mr Woodhouse could not object to it. Tomorrow is Tuesday,' (raising her voice), 'Tuesday, Mother, and we shall hear from Jane!' She resumed her natural speaking voice to continue, 'I do not know why you do not hear me, for Mrs Cole speaks no louder than I and you hear *her* perfectly. Yes, so tomorrow we shall hear from Jane. I shall get up very early and go to the post office although I know the coach does not arrive until ten. But I am always too excited to wait! We shall hear about their visit to the theatre. I wonder what the play was. Do you suppose they had a box? We may get news concerning Jane's summer visit. Here is May upon us and she normally comes for June, does she not? But as yet there has been no word. It is a pity, for I am sure Miss Emma is avid to know when dear Jane will be back amongst us and if we *had* word I could mention it this evening. The Woodhouses are to dine at the vicarage with the Knightleys and *we* are to take tea afterwards. Shall that not be extremely pleasant? Of course, it is none of my concern but if I am to give an opinion, *I* think Miss Emma a little young for dinner parties. I am sure the Campbells do not take Jane or Rowena when they dine from home. I suppose Mr Weston will be of the party—he usually is. I shall be delighted to meet Mr Weston at the vicarage for he is a most agreeable man. Quite a favourite with our Jane, I recall—*our* Jane, you know Mother, not *dear* Jane, although, to be sure, *our* Jane was also *very* dear—but that is a long time ago.vii Ah! How the time flies! So, as I was saying, we are to take tea at the vicarage and it would have provided the perfect opportunity to mention to Miss Emma ... however, we have *not* heard and so I shall hold my tongue on the subject. One would not wish to convey *wrong* information. I believe Patty's pastry improves. What do you think? It is still a little heavy, is it not? But better than last week. I declare I had indigestion all night long after those turnovers she served. Thank heavens we did not offer one to Mrs Cole when she called. I thought I would have to apply to Mr Perry for a remedy but the peppermint tea you suggested was all I needed. Oh!' (half standing so that she could see out of the window), 'there *is* Mr Perry. I shall just open the casement a little and say but a very few words. No, do not worry Mother, I shall only open it a *very* little and there will be no draught. Mr Perry! Mr Perry! How do you do? Yes, very well I thank you. We shall hear from Jane tomorrow. Yes! Indeed, it hardly seems a week since the last letter but Mother and I do quite count on them, you know. We always say that we do not feel the week can quite begin until we have heard from dear Jane! How does Mrs Perry? I am delighted to hear it. Do ask her to step in tomorrow. She is always so good as to wish to hear Jane's news. How are all the little Perrys? That is excellent indeed. And what about little Lucy's boil? Oh! Quite healed! That is very good. Good day to you Mr Perry! There, Mother,' (closing the window), 'I told you I would say only a very few words. Mr Perry is very good, an excellent neighbour. It seems rude to let him pass without seeing how he does. Mrs Perry will call tomorrow, I have no doubt of it. Shall I help you to more of this pie? No, I don't think I will partake either. Hermia's hospitality will make good our deficiency here; she serves ample bread and butter with tea, does she not? And the nicest cake? Sometimes I am able to slip an extra slice into my reticule. Nobody ever notices! I do it very discreetly, only once I did drop it and that was quite awkward but Hermia's pug ate it and so the incident passed off. Mr John Knightley is home from Cambridge! He has gained his degree and is to go into the law! I saw Mr Knightley today—as proud as a peacock—such an affectionate brother—and who can blame him? It is a very great thing. He is to go into the chambers of … but I forget the names now, a long string of them! I will ring for Patty to clear if you are finished. Will you drop a hint to her about the pastry? It is rolled too thick, I believe, and insufficiently cooked. Not that I know a thing about it. You know I have no hand for pastry at all! But I do enjoy asparagus; the season is all too brief. I will walk down to Abbey Mill Farm directly. It is a pity you will not come … but no, very well, we will consider the topic closed. There will be plenty of time for me to get there and back before we must dress. Mr Knightley offered his carriage but I said it would not be necessary. So very considerate as he is! But the evenings are lighter now and it is a pleasant walk to the vicarage, is it not? We will enjoy the exercise. Ah, Mother, well that was very nice. I do enjoy a quiet chat over dinner. Here is Patty to clear and I will get my shawl.'

Chapter Two

Since Mrs Bates' residency there, Highbury vicarage had been altered. The drawing room had been enlarged by the removal of a partition wall between it and the morning room, and new French doors added. Mrs Bates could never enter without lamenting the changes—such a cosy and comfortable house as it had been when *she* was mistress of it—but naturally she never voiced her reservations. This evening, in deference to Mr Woodhouse, the French doors were tightly closed and a fire burned in the fireplace. He could not abide the least suspicion of a draught so although the evening was very fine, without any hint of breeze, and the vicarage garden particularly lovely, everyone was confined to the indoors in accordance with his particular preferences. A chair was placed for Mrs Bates and the backgammon board brought forward and put between them.

'Excellent Mrs Bates,' said Mr Woodhouse. 'I hope you will indulge me. I do enjoy a game of backgammon and no one plays with such cleverness as you. I had the board and pieces brought over especially. I know that Mr Paling does not play. Chess is his game. Ah! I am afraid it is too protracted for me. To begin a game of chess I would have to come quite two hours earlier! I do not like late hours, you know Mrs Bates. I like to be home by nine o'clock, or earlier, if it can be done without giving offense.'

This fact was so well known to Mrs Bates—well known to everyone in the room, indeed—that she made no reply, but began to arrange the pieces on the board.

In a quieter voice, and leaning close to Mrs Bates, Mr Woodhouse added, 'I would not wish to give offense *here*, such unobjectionable people, the Palings.'

Mr George Knightley stood by a far window—well away from the fire—and turned the pages of an atlas for Miss Emma Woodhouse. 'Good evening Miss Bates,' he said as that lady entered the room, and to pre-empt the protracted monologue usually attendant upon her arriving anywhere, added, 'won't you join us? Emma, move to one side to make room for Miss Bates on the window seat. I am just putting Miss Emma right on a question of geography,' he said. 'I cannot let her go on in her mistaken belief that the Peak District is in Wales.'

'Goodness me now, Miss Woodhouse,' Miss Bates said, settling herself happily on the seat, 'that would be a lamentable error to make if one were travelling in that direction. Upon my word! To set out for the one and arrive at the other! What a pickle!'

Mr Knightley pointed to the atlas. 'Look, Emma,' he said, 'the Brecon Beacons, the Cambrians, the Snowdon Massif—all in Wales, but not the Pennines.'

Miss Emma pouted and folded her arms. 'It does not matter where they are, since I have not been to them,' she said.

'Jane has been,' Miss Bates said, 'to both, if I am not mistaken. The colonel and Mrs Campbell are so very assiduous in their care. Jane has been all over! Lyme, which is in Dorset, you know, and Derbyshire,' she looked a little uncertain, 'that, I think, is in the Pennines, is it not Mr Knightley?'

Emma gave a little snort of laughter. Mr Knightley moved his foot and pressed the toe of her slipper with it. 'One certainly could not traverse one without touching the other,' he said. 'I am very pleased to hear that Miss Fairfax is being given such opportunities. If I had my way *all* young ladies,' with a significant glance at Emma, 'would benefit in similar fashion. Young ladies can become very insular when they remain in one place.'

'Oh! Jane is exposed to a wide range of places,' Miss Bates cried, 'and experiences, too: the theatre and exhibitions of curiosities. She wrote of a menagerie … let me think … perhaps last December. I shall have to go and re-read her letters. I keep them all, you know Mr Knightley. I have them all in a box, right from the very first. One a week for three years that is … oh! Ever so many! My box is quite full, you can imagine!'

'Emma, how many letters might Miss Bates have? Can you calculate? I am sure Miss Taylor has taught you arithmetic.'

'Oh,' said Emma, 'she attempts it, but I am always able to divert her on to more interesting subjects.'

'She ought to be firmer with you,' Mr Knightley said with a frown, closing the atlas and restoring it to a shelf.

'Girls have no need of arithmetic,' Emma declared.

'Girls who are seamstresses or cooks use arithmetic,' Mr Knightley chided. He indicated the maid who at that moment brought in the supper. 'Susan Bright used arithmetic just now when she cut up that cake. How else could she have made twelve such equal slices?'

'I shall never need to sew clothes or cook,' Emma said archly. 'We have Searle to cut our cake. If I were ever likely to sink so low, I suppose I should have to learn, but that is a distant prospect.'

'Jane can add things up in her head as quick as lightning,' Miss Bates said. 'She has her own allowance, you know. The Campbells encourage both the girls to keep their own accounts. She has a little pocketbook with the figures written in such neat columns; shillings and pence, of course. The allowance does not stretch to pounds; that would be too much.' She gave a little trill of laughter, to show the absurdity of such a notion. 'Nobody expects it. Jane does not expect it. She does not expect anything! They are so very good.'

'As to a shilling here or there,' Emma arched her eyebrows, 'for a person like Jane Fairfax, I quite see the necessity, but it is of no moment to *me*. I know there are twenty shillings to a pound but I would have to multiply that by thirty thou ...'

'Emma!' Mr Knightley said sharply, 'that is a vulgar and disgusting observation. Go and sit with your sister. Miss Bates and I can converse more pleasantly without you.'

Emma slipped off the seat, 'Very well,' she said grumpily. 'I will leave *you* to deliver a piece of news that I am sure will interest Miss Bates very much.'

She crossed the room to where her sister sat with Mr John Knightley and Mr Paling. Isabella Woodhouse was by this time almost nineteen years of age, a well-enough looking girl but with none of the beauty that promised to develop in her younger sister. She was perhaps something older than her years in manner and character. The burdens of taking on, at only twelve years of age, the management of the household, her sister and—more onerous than either—her father, following the death of Mrs Woodhouse, had suppressed her natural youthfulness. Without the calm and reasonable influence of her late mother, Isabella had become, like her father, something of a worrier, preyed upon by large anxieties about small things and afraid of disasters most unlikely to occur. She had just become engaged to Mr John Knightley—*this* was the news to which Emma had referred. They had promised themselves to each other as very young people, before John Knightley's going up to Cambridge, and his returning now—with an auspicious career in prospect and every probability of making a success of himself—Mr Woodhouse had consented, most reluctantly, to the match. Not that he had reservations about John Knightley—*he* was an unexceptionable young man; a little gruff of manner, perhaps, not altogether assiduous in the matters of tightly fastened casements and apt to close doors very abruptly, but otherwise a most agreeable son-in-law. It was marriage itself to which Mr Woodhouse objected and in particular the great changes that it brought. In this case a very great change indeed; Isabella would remove to London. His suggestion that John Knightley travel the sixteen or so miles each day to his chambers had been laughingly rejected. No, they must take a house in London and Isabella would go there and keep house for him, a lamentable change, poor Isabella would find it very frightening. The air in London was known to be noxious. If they must go, they must find a house in an area where the air was tolerable. It was certain that no apothecary even approaching Mr Perry's excellence would be available.

Isabella trembled very much at the prospect of leaving Highbury and her father but her confidence in John was absolute. 'I have learned a great deal in the way of household management and the supervision of servants,' she was saying as Emma joined the little group, 'as a result of running my father's house for so long. I have the keys, you know. Searle comes to me for her orders and I keep everything just so. My father does like a well-regulated household and I am sure John will find me quite competent.'

'I have no doubt of it,' Mr Paling replied. 'My Hermia was the same—as the oldest girl, you know, she had deputised for her mother in ever so many ways. An older daughter is quite the best choice Mr Knightley. I congratulate you most heartily.'

John Knightley looked very pleased and pressed Isabella's hand, 'I am sure you will manage everything beautifully my dear. Any woman's touch, you know, for me, will be a novelty. I have no recollection of my mother. George and I have dragged ourselves up. I daresay we are half savage.'

'That is no very kind reflection on Mrs Sparks,' Isabella said. 'She did her best with you.'

'Yes,' John agreed, chastened, 'she was kind.'

'The Sparkses have retired to the coast, I believe?' Mr Paling enquired.

'Yes, a place in Norfolk.'

Mr Paling and John Knightley talked on; Norfolk's game and the opportunities for sea-fishing interested John Knightley more than they did Mr Paling but the reverend was used to drawing people out on topics of their choice.

Isabella turned to Emma and said, 'When I am married, Emma, you will have to take over household affairs for Papa. Miss Taylor will assist you, unless he thinks to employ a housekeeper. Indeed, I think that might be best, for you are very young to take on such a burden.'

'I am the same age that *you* were,' Emma replied stoutly. 'I am sure I can do no worse than you and may do a great deal better. I shall encourage a great deal more cake, for a start.' She eyed the cake that Mrs Paling now dispensed to her guests. 'Papa is too frugal. Stewed fruit without custard or cream is not my idea of a dessert. We shall have syllabub at least twice a week, candied fruits, jellies and *mille-feuille* and every kind of cake that exists in the whole world.'

'Papa will have an apoplexy if you even suggest it,' Isabella said. 'Look how he makes Mrs Paling pare down his slice of cake to a quarter of its size. It will be just so many crumbs on the plate if he is not careful.'

'Miss Bates will take the remainder, though. It is well known that she pilfers food from parties. It will not go to waste.'

'Poor Miss Bates. She is ridiculous, of course. But she must be hungry, poor soul. Have you ever wondered what that might be like, Emma?'

Emma shook her head. 'No, for even when Papa is very parsimonious in carving the joint I know where Searle keeps the left-overs and go and help myself. Papa never notices anything when he is engrossed in his button collection. I would not allow myself to be hungry. I would never consent to be poor, like the Bateses.'

'One does not consent to be poor, Emma. It is a situation in life that one finds oneself in.'

'If one marries a poor man, one consents to be poor,' Emma said.

'John is not a poor man,' Isabella re-joined, 'but,' with a doe-like glance at him, 'if he were, I would still be his wife.'

'In your case it would make no difference, since *you* are rich. Here comes Miss Bates. She moves to be nearer the cake. I will sit somewhere else Isabella. I have had a sufficiency of Miss Jane Fairfax to last me the entire evening.'

'Miss Woodhouse,' exclaimed Miss Bates, 'and Mr John Knightley! Mr George Knightley has just informed me of your happy news. Congratulations! I could not be more delighted for you. Wait until I tell Jane. I shall write to her tomorrow. She remembers you both most fondly in her letters and always enquires after you both. We shall hear from her tomorrow. Tuesday is her day, you know—that is, Tuesday is *our* day. She writes on Monday and the letter reaches us on Tuesday. Or sometimes Wednesday—but that is rare. She is such a regular correspondent except once, when she had the measles. Then she did not write for three weeks and Mother and I were so concerned. I almost took coach to London to enquire, for I knew there must be something seriously amiss for her not to write. But then we heard from Mrs Campbell, and although we were very anxious—my mother, you can imagine, was extremely worried, and I was too, measles can be so very serious—our minds were to some degree put at rest. And so, you are to be married. August, I believe, is to be the month? That is a pity, for Jane, if she visits, generally does so in June. She will miss it. Not but that I will write in great detail, you can be sure. Oh! Mrs Paling. Really, are you sure? That does seem to be a very large portion … thank you. Always so good. Your cook has such a light hand with sponge. I wish she could instruct our Patty. The pastry at dinner today … but I do not complain, not a bit of it, for we are so very fortunate. And Mrs Martin sent the first season's asparagus, which was very nice, and so kind. Mr John Knightley, I do not think you heard me say, for you were engaged in conversation with Mr Paling and I would not interrupt …' and Miss Bates went on to reprise the whole of her soliloquy to Mr John Knightley.

'Mr Weston is in London on business,' Mrs Paling said to Mr George Knightley. 'He was sorry not to be able to join us.'

'He is still required to travel a great deal,' Mr Knightley said. 'From his account of it his brothers let the business slip most abominably. There is much ground to make up. To give him credit, he *has* made up a good deal. But for a man in Weston's situation, I think it no bad thing. He needs to keep busy.'

'Mr Weston's situation?'

'Oh yes. Well, you know, he misses his son.'

'Ah, Frank. Of course. He must be—what?—Thirteen or so now?'

'Fourteen, I think, and doing very well by all accounts. Weston would like him to come to Highbury but the Churchills will not hear of it.'

'I wonder why?'

'They are jealous of Frank—they would keep him all to themselves. And then I gather the aunt is unwell. Weston thinks it spleen and caprice; she is a selfish, bitter woman.'

'Constant illness can wear away anyone's good nature,' Hermia Paling suggested, diplomatically.

'To hear Weston's account Mrs Churchill never had any,' Mr Knightley laughed. 'But I am glad on another head that Weston is away.'

'Oh?'

'Yes. General Bramhall tells me he is to quit Randalls. His wife's health has deteriorated to such a degree that he feels she requires closer supervision. Mrs Cropley found her last week wandering some distance from home in a state of undress. I do not know if you have observed any great alteration in her competency?'

'She *has* seemed somewhat confused of late. There was a certain incongruity in her conversation on Sunday; she made reference to her mama who, I am almost certain, cannot still be living,' Mrs Paling said. 'It must concern the general a great deal.'

'Indeed, it does. They go to stay with their daughter for a while and in the meantime Randalls is to be let. Weston, I know, has always desired to own the place and would no doubt take the opportunity to offer General Bramhall a fair price. But I know such a venture would be beyond Weston's means at present. It is better that the matter be settled in his absence or I fear he might over-stretch himself.'

'The Bramhalls are very worthy people, they will be missed,' Mrs Paling said, 'but I am certain the new incumbents at Randalls will be made welcome. Highbury is such a friendly town.'

'And so,' said George Knightley later that evening as he walked home to Donwell Abbey with his brother, 'the news of your engagement will have reached Kingston by morning. Miss Bates can be relied upon to save us the inconvenience of disseminating the information ourselves.'

John smiled. 'She is a dear, warm-hearted soul, very ready to enter into the felicitations of others even though she has had so few experiences of them herself. Nevertheless, I would rather spend fifteen minutes with her than thirty; if she complimented Mrs Paling on the cake once she must have done so a dozen times.'

'It *was* good cake,' George observed.

'All cake is good, if it comes to that, and Mrs Paling's cook certainly need not be ashamed of hers, but to hear Miss Bates on the topic you would think it was ambrosia.'

'She had observed the spare slices, of course, and I have no doubt she took them home with her one way or another,' George replied. 'I must speak to William Larkins. Perhaps I ought to increase their stipend. I do not think Mr Sparks did so for the whole of his time at Donwell and there is no doubt that costs *are* rising.'

'Ah, brother,' John sighed, 'you are a better squire than I would have been. I would not have been sufficiently discerning to have judged which impecunious widow lady to assist. If Mrs Bates then why not Mrs Tremble, or old Mrs Stokes? But I fear my altruism would not have encompassed *any*.'

'Our father began the business with Mrs Bates,' George said, 'I simply carried it on. Mrs Tremble lives with her son who is a skilled stone mason and earns a regular wage. Mrs Stokes has the income from the Crown; Abdy merely manages it for her, you know.'

'Is there anyone in Donwell or Highbury parish whose business you do *not* know?'

George considered for a moment. 'No,' he said at last, 'I don't believe so.'

They walked in silence down the moonlit drive, past a copse and round the periphery of an enclosed area of parkland until Donwell Abbey came into view. It looked splendid, benign and reassuringly stalwart but also exceedingly large—so many rooms were shrouded and unused; the entirety of one wing was shut up altogether and most of another visited only periodically by the maids for the purposes of dusting. The loneliness of George's situation struck John with some forcefulness. For a man as young and naturally gregarious as George, Donwell must be forlorn indeed.

'You must bring a wife home before long, George,' John burst out, clapping his brother on the back. 'Why don't you take yourself to Bath or Cheltenham for a while in the autumn? Or to London at least? When I am established my first object will be to make the acquaintance of pleasant fellows with marriageable sisters. Do you require just good family, or fortune also?'

George considered. '*Some* fortune would be advantageous, I will own to you John. Our cousin Sparks maintained the estate diligently but he made no improvements that would increase its yield. Abel Larkins could by no means convince him to plant timber—if he had done so in '81 it would be halfway to maturity by now—and the quarry has been untouched these thirteen years because he would not repair the cottages. *They* are only so much stone and rubble themselves, now. He has let the cattle breed indiscriminately ...'

The brothers walked on, John but half attending George's litany of Donwell's problems. He was no farmer and certainly no diplomat—both qualities required by a successful squire. He was to go into the law, a profession more suited to his impatient, somewhat opinionated character.

Chapter Three

August came, and John Knightley and Miss Isabella Woodhouse were married in the little parish church. It was a joyful occasion, with plentiful satin if parsimonious quantities of cake—Mr Woodhouse's doing; there *was* cake, but he dissuaded everyone from having any. Miss Taylor wept happy tears, Mr Woodhouse sad ones, Miss Emma Woodhouse glad ones—for she had the keys to the house in her reticule at last and stood poised to take her place as the *de facto* head of the Hartfield establishment.

It was agreed that the match had every hope of happiness. The couple's fondness for each other had been a settled thing for some years, their engagement and marriage long expected. Highbury people were constitutionally opposed to anything sudden, a surprise or secret. They liked to see and predict a thing long before it took place and it was quite a matter for amiable dispute amongst the wedding guests as to which of them had prophesied *this* first. Mrs Cropley said she had seen something between the two as early as the year before Mr John Knightley went up to Cambridge. Mrs Hopley stated her suspicions had dated from some years before that. Miss Taylor thought there had been a moment, once, in the Hartfield garden, when John Knightley had helped Miss Isabella Woodhouse down from a tree—she could not have been more than ten or eleven years of age. Mr George Knightley blithely threw in that he had seen it coming from the first moment John had seen Miss

Woodhouse in her cradle, 'He was four years old and declared the baby the ugliest thing he had ever seen.'

But, all jesting aside, Highbury liked the openness and the predictability of the Knightley -Woodhouse alliance. They approved of the equality of the parties—their families inhabited the same sphere and were intimate. Neither money nor manners were wanting on either side. The tempers of the two young people were well matched—the decided opinions of the one were allowed for by the easy, malleable mind of the other. They invited no strangers to carp or criticise, to stand aloof or to be too familiar. It was a pity that the young people must leave Highbury, but there it was. They had taken a house in Brunswick Square, an area known for its wholesome air and proximity to a reputable apothecary.

True to his word John Knightley soon began to seek out superior families with marriageable females and several times George Knightley was invited to stay and dine in Brunswick Square in order to ascertain if there were any on show who could attract his interest. On the whole he found them dull. One or two were quite beautiful but had no conversation. Some were conversable but had not that style of beauty that appealed to him. Some were proud and cold, others silly. One, the French ward of an eminent man of law, was very lovely but spoke no English. Another, who had beauty and elegance and just that degree of wit that Mr Knightley found amusing, confessed to him privately that she was secretly engaged to a man of whom her papa would not approve.

'John, I pray you will desist in your efforts to find me a wife,' Mr Knightley told his brother at last. 'I am spending so much time away from Donwell that William Larkins is beginning to get jealous. Isabella's cook has not a wide repertoire—I fear I cannot face her fricassee again without some months' respite. To cap it all, I have not seen a single lady who suits me. You had better let me lapse into confirmed bachelorhood. *You* will not be behindhand in providing an heir for Donwell and I am perfectly content with my dogs for company.'

General Bramhall had quit Randalls the previous month, his departure delayed by half a day on the discovery that Mrs Bramhall was not to be found in any room of the house or in the grounds; certainly not in the coach where she had been firmly placed and told to remain with her pet poodle and caged parakeet. She had been found at last by the river—quite as far away as Mrs Goddard's school. The poodle had been located in Mrs Martin's kennels—where her spaniel bitch would produce, some weeks later, a litter of strangely woolly puppies. The parakeet was never found at all; Mrs Bramhall had set it free. There was a strange and poignant irony in her gesture, for she herself was to be taken to her daughter's remote country residence, a house surrounded by very high walls, with locked gates and a vigilant staff whose remit it was to curb her recent propensity for wandering—she would never enjoy another moment of solitude or freedom again.

Randalls lay untenanted for the whole of the following year. As Mr Knightley had predicted, Mr Weston did try most earnestly to accrue the funds to purchase it, but it could not be managed and he gave up the scheme for the time being. His son Frank, at that time, claimed his whole attention. The boy was by now just fifteen years of age. His education remained in the charge of Mr Tunnock despite repeated attempts to persuade Mrs Churchill that the boy would be better served, and happier, at school. She was deaf to their entreaties, however—she must have Frank with her; he was indispensable to her health and well-being. Nothing would be denied him in the way of books, horses or sports. He was free to wander at will in the estate and the nearby market town. He might invite whomsoever he pleased to Enscombe providing of course they were of respectable connection and could withstand the bleakness of the house's situation and the frugality of its hospitality.

Frank had struggled on under his aunt's interdictions. To do him justice he had taken ample advantage of Mr Tunnock's excellent teaching and had progressed well in his studies; he was probably better informed on the humanities, more competent in Greek and Latin and had a sounder understanding of arithmetic than most boys his age. He spent as much time as possible in the outdoors, on the moors and along the riverbanks of his uncle's estate. He rode, shot, hunted and fished with competence and flair. He courted the society of those neighbours who had a spark of kindness about them, whose halls rang with laughter and where the pleasanter things in life were not rationed. Such was the geography of the area that these houses were far-flung—he might have to ride for an hour or more to spend an amusing hour in company with families who had young people of his age. Mrs Churchill grudgingly approved these connections. For Frank's sake she returned their hospitality as frequently as her health and good manners dictated and if the families quailed when an invitation embossed with the Churchill insignia arrived, and looked out their thickest chemises and warmest wraps, she had no suspicion of it.

Frank also associated with people of a lower order about whose existence Mrs Churchill had not the least suspicion and, if she had, of whom she would have disapproved with a vengeance. This included a pair of brothers, gamekeepers, who lived a wonderfully disordered bachelor existence knee-deep in dogs in a ramshackle cottage in the Enscombe woods. Frank patrolled the copses and coverts with them for glorious hours, and returned to their cottage to kick off his boots and roast his feet before a roaring fire, to eat pie without the aid of cutlery and drink beer from an earthenware mug, and be regaled with stories of waywardness and wenching until night came on and drove him home. He was befriended also by an ostler, a scarred ex-militiaman. He was employed part-time at the local inn, had a keen eye for horse flesh and acted as tipster and bookmaker for those with money to lose on the racecourse. He took Frank on regular jaunts to various racecourses all unbeknownst to his aunt, and introduced him to his younger sister, a pretty girl, very amenable, who was maid of all work at the inn.

These illicit distractions alleviated Frank's boredom and sense of entrapment to some considerable degree. In addition, in league with Mr Churchill, Mr Tunnock ensured that their curriculum dictated some portion of the year be spent away from Enscombe. The object of this scheme was a sort of holiday for Frank, a release from the carping neediness of his aunt and the austerity of Enscombe and an opportunity for him to meet with his father—although naturally *this* element of the excursion was always kept veiled from Mrs Churchill's knowledge. She lamented very much the necessity of the expedition, sometimes frightened them by determining to go with them and on more than one occasion made her health a reason for them to abandon it altogether— she was much too ill to be able to spare Frank, even for such an important thing as his education. But, on the whole, she grudgingly allowed it, on the strict condition that they travel by private conveyance, stay only at the best inns, mix with no riff-raff and by no means go within fifteen miles of Highbury. So, on the pretence of geological surveys, historical research or architectural study Mr Tunnock and Frank Churchill made their annual way to London where a chance encounter with Mr Weston had been arranged. Mr Weston looked forward to these occasions with great anticipation, his mind filled with how Frank might have grown, what he might have learned, how his character might have continued to form itself in the months since their last being together. Mr Tunnock always found it convenient to call upon sundry acquaintances while he was in the city and so had adopted the habit of melting away, leaving Frank and Mr Weston to converse, explore and dine alone.

Their rendezvous was generally at Mr Weston's club, and on the occasion of which we now speak, one grey morning in April, Mr Weston was there in good time, waiting under the portico, his hat in one hand and his umbrella in the other. He gazed anxiously down the street, trying to make out his son's figure amongst the crowds that thronged the pavements, eager not to miss one second of the pleasure or the pride of looking upon him. But at last he saw, not Frank, but only Mr Tunnock, hurrying down the thoroughfare towards him, looking very agitated indeed, unshaved, his clothes flung on anyhow.

'Frank is gone,' Mr Tunnock gasped, when he had met Mr Weston halfway up the steps. 'I woke this morning and knocked, as we had agreed, and his bed was empty. His valet says he waited until two for Frank to come in last night, but there being no sign of him he had taken to his bed at last.'

'So, Frank has been gone since last night?' Mr Weston said, stricken with anxiety.

'Yes, sir. We arrived at Marylebone at about six and dined almost immediately. Then Frank said he felt restless and would take a few turns in the street. We agreed what time we would take breakfast and I ordered it from the innkeeper. I said I would knock on Frank's door on my way to the breakfast parlour and we said goodnight. It was not late but I had some letters to write.' Mr Tunnock clutched at his stock. His face was white with shock, his eyes quite wild. Even as he spoke, he looked about him, hoping to see Frank emerge from the crowds that milled about. 'Oh sir,' he concluded, turning back to Mr Weston, 'what can have become of him? You do not suppose ... thieves, an assault? Oh! My mind is in turmoil. That he may have come to some harm ...'

Mr Weston suffered similar anxiety but his older and wiser head remained calm. He took Mr Tunnock into his club and ordered food and brandy, 'For you will not have eaten the breakfast you ordered and no one can think clearly on an empty stomach,' he said. 'Frank is a clever lad, and well-made, for his age. Although he is but fifteen, he might well pass for older. He is quick-witted and agile. If he were to be set-upon I think he would give good account of himself, would he not?'

Mr Tunnock nodded. 'He has been sparring with Mowbray, the smith's boy. He is a foot taller than Frank and half as heavy again, but Frank bests him every time.'

'There you are, then. And Frank is charming—he could talk himself out of most scrapes. If he were in trouble, he would recommend himself to anyone upon whom he called for aid. Of course, we will make enquiries and we will search the vicinity of your lodgings. But my instinct is that Frank has met with no accident. Tell me, what was his mood yesterday? Did he seem distracted?'

Mr Tunnock chewed and swallowed the last morsel of his bacon chop before replying, 'In point of fact he was in rather a bad humour. We almost quarrelled. He was intent upon attending the races at Ascot but I vetoed the scheme—there is no knowing who we might have encountered and if rumour of our being there had found its way back to Enscombe …'

'You did quite right to refuse,' Mr Weston said. 'It is one thing for you to deviate from your itinerary to meet *me,* quietly, discreetly, but to be seen in public so very far from your avowed program of study would be quite another. I wonder that Frank even wished to attend a race meeting. Has he done so before?'

Mr Tunnock considered, and coloured. He knew of Frank's association with the ostler—though not with the ostler's sister—and suspected Frank had made forays further afield than the far side of the moors or the market town. 'I think he might have,' he stammered at last.

'There we are, then,' Mr Weston said, rising and reaching for his hat. 'If you have finished your breakfast we will return to Marylebone and search the nearby streets with great care. If we find no trace of Frank we will ride to Ascot. It is a two-day meet, is it not? Whatever—or whoever—Frank was so anxious to see yesterday will still be there today.'

It proved to be just as Mr Weston had conjectured. There being no sign of Frank in the environs of the inn, and no reports of anyone wounded or apprehended, they rode to Ascot as quickly as two hired nags could take them. They made their way to the enclosures behind the stands, where the horses were prepared for the races. Lines of temporary stables, scruffy tents, caravans and stalls supplied accommodation and sustenance for the jockeys, ostlers, farriers and muck-boys, a far cry from the elegant provision made for the ladies and gentlemen who mingled in the stylish marquees beside the track. The place was busy. One race had just concluded, the sweat-coated runners were trotted round a make-shift ménage to relax their muscles, blankets thrown across their backs. Boys ran with barrows of hay and buckets of water. The owner and trainer of the winning horse congratulated each other with loud guffaws. Meanwhile the runners for the next race were being brought out. Tense-jawed jockeys slapped their horse's necks. Everything was bustle and noise, a confusion of faces and men hurrying about their business. Mr Tunnock and Mr Weston wandered amongst it all until Mr Tunnock spied a face he knew.

'You there,' he called. A man turned his scarred face, started in recognition and then slid his eyes away. 'No, do not walk away,' Mr Tunnock cried, taking the man by the sleeve. 'I know you, I think. You work at the inn near Enscombe. What do you here?'

'I 'ave care of a gentleman's filly,' the man said with sullen defiance. 'She is to be in t' next race but one. I take 'er to all 'er races, sir. 'er owner trusts no one but me to 'ave t'andling of 'er.'

'I do not doubt your skill. But tell me, have you seen the young master from Enscombe?'

The man denied it vehemently, but his eyes glanced towards a covered wagon that was set alongside a lean-to stable across the improvised yard. The rear of the wagon was lowered and upon it sat a young woman in a dirty dress with hair very much disordered and rather fuller of hay than was quite fashionable. With her sat Frank Churchill.

Frank started very violently upon seeing his tutor and his father, blushed red, but stood up and squared his shoulders as they approached. To his credit, he made no effort to run, or to distance himself from his companion, indeed he held out his hand to her and assisted her from the back of the cart. 'Father, Tunnock,' he said, his voice tight but perfectly steady, 'I did not expect to see you here. How do you do?'

'*We* do very well, Frank,' his father said, his mouth twitching only a little in his happiness at seeing Frank alive and well, and in wry understanding of the nature of his son's escapade, 'only we have been a little concerned about *your* well-being.'

Frank looked at Mr Tunnock. 'You did not see my note?' he asked, genuinely aghast.

Mr Tunnock shook his head.

'I left a note propped upon the mantel in my room. I did not wish to cause you concern but you see I had most pressing business here at Ascot and, as you would not come with me yesterday, I found it necessary to come alone today.'

'I was so dismayed to see your bed unslept in that I did not think to examine the rest of the room,' Mr Tunnock admitted.

'You came last night, I believe, Frank,' Mr Weston said with a reproachful frown.

'I set off last night, but arrived early this morning. It is quite a walk from Marylebone.'

'You *walked?*'

'Yes,' Frank said proudly, 'I did.'

Mr Weston was lost in a mixture of anger and admiration for his son. More than half of him wanted to slap the lad on the back for his courage and resourcefulness, but the other half wanted to give him a sound whipping. He had no opportunity of resolving this dilemma before Frank went on, 'In point of fact, Father, I am glad you are here. It was my intention of bringing Miss Lovat to town with us yesterday so that I could present her to you today.' He looked to his companion and saw her, perhaps, with less of the rosy tint of his former vision. Her gown was unspeakably dirty, her patens very knocked about, her hands rough with work. The slight caste in her left eye, which had seemed so coy and appealing in the half light of the stable the previous night, now gave her a somewhat deranged aspect. 'Of course,' he said, more hesitantly than before, 'I would have allowed her the opportunity to prepare herself—a dressmaker, milliner and so on.'

'A bath?' Mr Tunnock suggested.

'Naturally,' Frank agreed, and now he really did begin to see the impossibility of his position. But he had cast his lot and, in all honour, he could not now retreat from it. He lifted his chin and looked his father in the eye. 'You do not see her here in her best light sir, but I assure you, she is a splendid girl and, in short, it is my intention, when I attain my majority, to make her my wife.'

Frank's words fell like a stone into the little pool of shock and awkwardness that surrounded them. Beyond it, men rushed about, horses whinnied and stamped and the farrier's hammer tapped a relentless beat. The girl beside Frank simpered and said coquettishly, 'Oh, *Frank*! You're so gallant,' and slipped her hand into his.

Just then her brother let out a piercing whistle from the other side of the ménage. 'Fan!' he shouted, 'fetch 'er bridle! Tis time to saddle 'er up.'

Mr Weston made a deep bow. 'Miss Lovat,' he said, with exquisite formality, 'it is a great pleasure to make your acquaintance, but I see we keep you from your duties.' He handed her his card. 'I do myself the great honour of asking you to call on me when you are next in town,' he said.

Miss Lovat took the card and squinted at it without the least comprehension of what was written upon it before tucking it into the bosom of her dress. 'Charmed I'm sure,' she said before hurrying off to attend her brother.

Mr Weston took Frank's arm and led him gently away.

'I shall not see her again, shall I Father?' Frank said in a voice very low and miserable.

'Of course, you shall, if you wish it Frank,' Mr Weston said affectionately. 'I shall not prevent it. You have sufficient of your mother's spirit in you for me to know it is quite useless for me to stand in your way. But I think, if you consider, you will find that while Miss

Lovat is no doubt a very splendid young lady, she has not quite those qualities you would choose for your wife.'

They sauntered through the crowds. Mr Tunnock had fallen a few steps behind them and so father and son spoke in confidence.

'I liked her because she was kind and affectionate,' Frank said at last. 'I get so little in that way at Enscombe, Father.'

'I know, my boy,' Mr Weston said, and pressed Frank's arm against his side. 'Your mother would have doted on you, if she had lived, and perhaps we could have provided some sisters for your comfort, but it was not to be.'

'If you married again, Father, I would have the love of a step-mother. I would come and live with you, if you would have me.'

'I had not considered marrying again, Frank,' Mr Weston admitted, 'but if ever I did, you would be most welcome. You are welcome *now*, but your aunt is against it.'

'She is against everything that is comfortable and pleasant,' Frank grumbled.

'She would certainly be against you deriving any comfort and pleasure whatsoever from Miss Lovat,' Mr Weston said with a smile. 'Perhaps *that* was part of the attraction you felt for the young lady?'

'Perhaps it was,' Frank agreed, a little cheered. But the lifting of his spirits was of short duration. 'It is a great honour to be my uncle's heir,' he said soberly. 'I know I will have wealth and consequence that I have done nothing to deserve. They are generous as far as material things are concerned but—oh, Father—my aunt's caprice is such a heavy price to pay. I am sure my uncle feels it as keenly as I. She can never be pleased. Everything is too hot or too cold, too soon or too late, too little or too much. She is a martyr to her ailments but what they are no one can discover. She has seen a hundred medical men and not one of them has arrived at a diagnosis she is prepared to accept—or with *any* diagnosis, in some cases. I am the worst afflicted—whatever ails *her* means that *I* cannot be spared. If you knew the meets I have missed, the dinners I have left uneaten, the parties I never arrived at. There is so little diversion in Yorkshire but, due to my aunt's ill health, I regularly miss the very few entertainments that are available.'

'I am sorry for it, Frank. I wish I could provide for you so that you were not under obligation to the Churchills. Perhaps I might, in time. The business is beginning to yield fruit …'

'Oh, I am too far on with it to give up now,' Frank sighed. 'And what if my leaving her really did kill her, as she says it would? How could I live with my conscience afterwards?'

They had come to the inn in the high street where Mr Weston and Mr Tunnock had stabled their horses.

'We must find you a mount to return to town,' Mr Weston said, 'unless you would rather remain here?'

Frank laughed. 'Half a night spent on a stable floor was quite sufficient, thank you. A hot bath and a comfortable bed will cure me of my heartache, I believe. Poor Fanny. I have used her ill.'

Mr Weston looked benevolently on his son. 'I shall see Miss Lovat is recompensed, if she calls on me,' he said. 'I do not think she is the kind of girl who really expects to be the mistress of Enscombe, Frank, but it does credit to your honour that you were prepared to put her there. You must be famished. Let us go inside and see what fare the landlord has to offer us, while Mr Tunnock makes the arrangements about the horses.'

Later, as they rode back to London, Mr Weston said, 'It seems to me, Frank, that you have been managing matters at Enscombe quite admirably, with fortitude and also with some resourcefulness. I am the last man to recommend any subterfuge or double dealing but if you *can* arrange some diversions for yourself away from your aunt's eye, you should continue to do so. What she does not see need not trouble her. You might see it as a kindness to her, to protect her from what will cause her unnecessary alarm. You can confide in your uncle; indeed, I counsel you to do so—*he* will understand your need to try your independence. And before long you will be going up to Oxford, will you not?'

'He could pass the entrance examinations tomorrow without any difficulty,' Mr Tunnock averred.

'Mrs Churchill is yet to sanction my going up,' Frank said dolefully, 'but I will think on what you have said, Father. I am not a child now. It is not right that I should be utterly under my aunt's rule so long as honour and duty are satisfied. Where she is intractable, I must be ingenious.'

'And I will write more frequently, and contrive more frequent meetings,' Mr Weston promised. But his heart was heavy when he separated from Frank the next day, and for the next few months he laboured under a heavy burden of guilt and concern for the life he had sentenced his son to live.

At the same time, he did, with half an eye, begin to look about him. He had never entertained the notion of marrying again but Frank's suggestion remained with him. Certainly, he would not aspire to a lady of high standing, nor of wealth. Inequalities of that nature had soured his first marriage. He would rather be the recipient than the supplier of gratitude. But a gentlewoman, a comfortable lady who could be a mother to Frank and a solace to himself—that might not be a very bad thing. His eye lit at first upon Mrs Goddard. She was a widow, of about his own age—which was at that time just forty—manifestly a very motherly and caring lady. But she would certainly not relinquish her school and he did not like to think that Frank would have to compete with a dozen little girls. No, Mrs Goddard would not do. Miss Bates? He gave a shudder—too talkative and too bony—*she* would be impossible. The only other suitable unmarried lady Highbury had to offer was Miss Woodhouse's governess, Miss Taylor. Now *there* was a strong possibility. In person she was pleasing, and the ideal age— perhaps five or six and twenty. To be sure she could not be released from her duties at Hartfield for some time, but that did not matter; he was in no particular hurry. She had no family that he knew of. This he saw as a positive advantage—no one knew better than he the dreadful burden of unsympathetic family connections. He decided that he would by slow—by very slow—degrees become better acquainted with Miss Anne Taylor.

Chapter Four

Three years more passed by. Time can bring about much change in anyone but with very young ladies—as with very old ones—the change is perhaps more evident. Miss Jane Fairfax and Miss Rowena Campbell were now almost fifteen years of age; certainly, they were no longer children even if they were not quite women; they were taller, their figures fuller, their characters almost fixed, their minds more completely formed. Rowena had ceased to cross the bedroom to share the comfort of Jane's proximity in the night. She was still afraid of the dark but had schooled herself to think her fears very silly. Probably there was nothing in the dark that could not be clearly seen in the light and, being seen, recognised. She was, she told herself very sternly, too sensible to give way to childish fancies. Any supposed malevolence, perceived chill breath or imagined cry could only be the product of her fevered fears and if not, well then, Jane would feel it and Jane would oppose it with all the courage of her rational mind and the whole fortitude of her indomitable heart. While Jane was near, Rowena need fear nothing.

Jane was happily and comfortably established in Bute Square, the strangeness and homesickness she had felt at first having long since evaporated. She was accustomed to the dresses, the outings, the treats and wonders that attended her every day—accustomed to them, but not inured. Her early resolution to regard all the advantages the Campbells provided as delightful privileges had held fast. She saw them as an enchanting walk through green pastures before the vertiginous ascent of an arduous mountain that must be scaled. In the meantime, she felt loved and valued. No sisters could be closer than she and Rowena, no daughter more precious than she was to the Campbells. The Campbells' fondness for her was as equal to their affection for their own daughter as made no difference. Indeed, many observers and some acquaintances held the belief that Jane was their own, legitimate off-spring and the Campbells made no effort to disabuse them. What was the need, when to all intents and purposes, it was so?

To all intents and purposes save one. The colonel continued in his reluctant determination that beyond an excellent education, a wide range of accomplishments, good guidance and elegant companionship in her youth he could offer Jane nothing. His income was good—more than good while he remained in service at the War Office—but his capital was modest and would provide for only one daughter's dowry; he must give Rowena the benefit of the whole of it. From pangs of guilt and misgiving on this matter the colonel had long since ceased to suffer; Jane already promised to be a beauty, with a figure tending to just that degree of plumpness that is always pleasing, hair a very unusual shade of auburn and eyes that were fine and full of intelligent fire. The governess reported excellent progress in all subjects. The dancing master spoke in raptures of the lightness of her step and elegance of her bearing. The art master, music and deportment teachers gave similarly enthusiastic account; Jane was on her way to being a superior young lady in every way. Add to this that she was modest, thoughtful and kind and the colonel was in no doubt that she would in the fullness of time attract offers of marriage from unexceptionable young men, scions of great families and inheritors of influential titles if only he could see his way to placing her within their orbit. She might be groomed to become a governess but the probability of her ever having to take up that post seemed small. No, the colonel did not reproach himself—he had done and would continue to do all that could be done for Jane and to her would accrue all the success, fortune, position and happiness of his glad generosity.

For his own daughter he could not say as much. Rowena was a timid wren beside the bravado and brighter plumage of Jane—this in spite of Jane's own eager and disinterested efforts to bring the quieter girl forward. Rowena had no more vociferous advocate, no more earnest encourager than Jane. Whatever Jane's success it was always turned to Rowena's account; Rowena's forbearance in listening patient hour by hour had enabled Jane to master a tricky piece of music. Rowena's dogged determination at her lessons had inspired Jane to greater heights of achievement. Rowena's generosity in lending a brooch had perfected Jane's dress. Jane would hear no praise but must attribute it to her friend's goodness. It made her dearer than ever. But in truth Rowena was a heavy-handed, blundering musician; she had no ear for music and her singing voice was commensurately discordant. She was a stolid, uninspiring artist and an indifferent dancer. Her stitching was clumsy and her retention in lessons usually of short duration. She was hesitant in conversation and shy of strangers. Her looks were dowdy. She could not equal, let alone surpass her friend on any measure of comparison— she was a sweet-natured, shy but unremarkable little girl. She would need her father's protection in the future; a very attractive dowry to secure a husband or sufficient capital to provide an independence for as long as she might remain single.

Thus ran Colonel Campbell's thoughts on the matter when he was at liberty to pursue them, but this indulgence was not often granted to him as his time was very much taken up at the War Office where the lords in authority found him an indispensable assistance. Many of *them* had never worn a uniform let alone stepped upon a battlefield in the entirety of their lives; *they* had no notion of the realities of combat, the hardships of the troops or the exigencies of supply. The colonel's contribution prevented daily catastrophe in the way of requisitions for ordnance incompatible with any weapon in the arsenal, foods that would perish before they reached the quartermaster, uniforms that were uncomfortable and impractical in battle and maps rendered illegible by the least quantity of rain. He was naturally much appreciated, but much required, and his duties kept him often from home. Lord Knox was the gentleman who most often occupied the colonel's time, required his advice and bombarded him with reports and lists for his urgent perusal. Lord Knox was one of the chief men at the War Office, extremely willing but not very able to direct military affairs with efficiency and expediency. He had come to rely very heavily on Colonel Campbell's experience as well as on his good nature. Many excellent directives that had originated with Colonel Campbell had been attributed to Lord Knox and it was not unusual for muddle-headed, useless or incendiary commands on the point of being issued from Lord Knox's department to be countermanded at the last possible minute by Colonel Campbell's timely intervention.

Therefore, it was not very surprising for Lord Knox to say one day, 'Lady Knox is eager to know your wife, Colonel. Bring her to Knoxbury in June, if you are at liberty, and the children too. You have children, I think?'

Lord Knox was a thin, small-structured man closer to sixty than to fifty years of age, with a high, nasal voice and very poor eyesight for which he wore thick spectacles—or, he was supposed to wear them, but was more likely to lose them under piles of documents or in his coat pockets. He searched for them absent-mindedly now, patting down his frock coat and rummaging in the drawer of his desk.

'I am much obliged to you, sir,' the colonel replied, passing Lord Knox his spectacles from where they lay on the mantel of the room they used as an office, 'Mrs Campbell will be delighted. Yes, we have two girls at home.'

'Capital,' Lord Knox squeaked. 'Girls! Susan will like that! Our grandchildren are all boys. Bring them for a few weeks. Her mother usually graces us with a visit and unfortunately her presence casts a considerable pall on things. It is a pity. Knoxbury is pleasant in June. There is fishing and tennis and croquet if you like it. We will be a family party—Lady Knox likes to have her grandchildren about her in the summertime—they alleviate the malign influence of Lady Sowerby. I cannot abide the dowager. Mrs Campbell will not mind her, I hope?'

'No indeed, sir, Emily finds herself very much at home amongst all manner of company—it is a gift of hers. She will enjoy it very much, sir, and it will be an amusing start to the holiday for our girls; we go to Worthing, you know, for July and August.'

The colonel had forgotten that June was the month usually set aside for Jane's visit to Highbury but Mrs Campbell soon reminded him of it when he informed her of their invitation.

'She can as well go in July or August can she not? I would not like to offend Lord Knox by declining his offer and I am sure Rowena will not like to go without Jane. There will be a whole platoon of Knoxes there—they are very well connected, you know. Their acquaintance can do nothing but good for our girls.'

'I will write to the Bateses,' Mrs Campbell said. 'We have not fixed on a date for Jane's holiday so I suppose they have made no particular plans as yet although, bless their hearts, they are always so very eager to see her. I believe they live the whole year through in anticipation of nothing but Jane's visit to Highbury.'

'There is no reason why they could not come here,' the colonel remarked, easing his feet from his boots, 'if they miss her so much. I would not object to them as house guests, if you think they would like it. Or they could join us at Worthing, perhaps. I have taken a house quite large enough to accommodate them.'

Mrs Campbell hesitated. The Bateses were worthy people, the old lady very genteel and quiet, the younger lively and amusing if somewhat erratic. But she did not think she wished to share her holiday with them and she was not sure that Jane would like it particularly. Jane always wrote to her grandmother and aunt on Monday and the letter was naturally shown to Mrs Campbell before it was despatched. It seemed to Mrs Campbell that Jane drew rather a veil over the situation in Bute Square, referring to 'comfort' but never detailing to any degree the luxuries they enjoyed. She might, for example, mention a visit to the theatre without specifying that they had travelled there by private conveyance or occupied a box. More than half her page was taken up with enquiry after acquaintance in Highbury and responses to her aunt's remarks, directing attention there rather than dwelling on Bute Square.

'I think Jane would not wish to make so very apparent to her family the great difference between our situation and theirs,' she said, settling a footstool beneath the colonel's feet, 'which their coming here or joining us at the seaside would surely do.'

'Very well, my dear, do not invite them. But see if Jane can be spared for June.'

A letter was duly sent and a reply received. Of course, Miss Bates wrote, they would miss Jane's company, had been quite counting the weeks until June should come, were most eager to see her and to enfold her once more into the bosom of their little family. All of Highbury was as avid and impatient as possible to renew its acquaintance with her. Miss Emma Woodhouse, in particular, had expressed the warmth of her anticipation, Mrs Cole had gone so far as … &c. &c., a long list of Highbury inhabitants scarce able to eat or sleep until Jane should be amongst them. But at last Miss Bates was generous in her readiness for Jane to partake of Lord Knox's hospitality and renounced all claim to her until July or August or later, whatever suited the Campbells' convenience. 'On *one* head,' she concluded, 'I am happy to postpone Jane's visit and would respectfully suggest August as an alternative. It is quite certain that Mr Frank Churchill will visit his father here in late August, on his way to a tour of the southwest. If anyone excites more interest and affection in Highbury in general than Jane—not *here,* of course, in our home no one is or ever could be more interesting or more affectionately loved—it is Mr Churchill who, like Jane, was so fortunate as to attract the kindness of superior friends and be brought up away from the locality. And yet they are both considered very thoroughly to be Highbury people, as though they had lived here all their lives! Is that not strange? And yet it is indisputably so. Mr Churchill has not visited his father thus far—I believe they meet in London—but we are absolutely assured of him for two weeks at the end of August. It goes without saying that Mr Weston will like to introduce Jane to his son. Of course Jane resides with you and is quite one of your family, due to your great goodness and generosity, for which mother and I give daily thanks, you can be sure, and always will do so, remembering you in our prayers and in our conversation—we never can express the fullness of our gratitude—still she is precious and indescribably dear *here,* in our little home and in Highbury generally, and no occasion of such momentousness as the coming of Mr Frank Churchill could seem quite complete without Jane's presence.'

'We will go to Knoxbury for June, then,' Colonel Campbell said, when he had been given a precis of the contents of the letter. 'Jane shall come to Worthing with us for the month of July, and then depart for Highbury at the beginning of August.'

Mrs Campbell informed the girls of their summer itinerary at breakfast the following morning. It wanted just a few days until June. 'We have so little time to prepare our wardrobe,' she said, with a degree of anxious distraction that was not usual with her. 'The colonel tells me that it will be an informal, family party at Knoxbury—we must hope our sprigged muslins will pass muster for there is no time to have new made up. I shall have to ask Miss Blossom to suspend your lessons—I will need her for sewing. Your petticoats must be let down, Jane, for you are a full three inches taller since last year, and your stockings are all through at the toe, Rowena—your new shoes required new lasts, so much have your feet grown! In the meantime, I think you had better sort through your pencils and paint boxes—it may be that you are required to amuse yourselves for much of the time. If you wish to re-trim your summer bonnets, Willis will assist you. Practice your pieces—you may be asked to play for the company. If you would be so good as to keep out of everyone's way for the next few days, I think we may be able to get ourselves into some state of readiness.' She looked down at her half-eaten breakfast. 'I have no time for this. I must consult Miss Blossom without delay. Rowena, please ring the bell and ask Lottie to clear the table, if you have finished. Good morning, girls.'

Jane and Rowena remained at the table. Rowena looked pale and her lip trembled as she said, 'I cannot play for the company at Knoxbury. You will have to do it Jane. You know you are so much better than me.'

'You play those country airs very nicely,' Jane replied, moving her seat to come closer to Rowena. 'We will go over them together this morning. And perhaps we might try some duets. We will *both* feel happier if we play side-by-side.'

Rowena looked a little more sanguine. 'I might play if you sing,' she said, 'so long as the melody is very simple. When *you* sing nobody looks at the accompanist, and perhaps the pianoforte will be in a far corner …'

'I think it very likely we will not be called upon at all,' Jane declared. 'Lady Knox will prefer her own grandchildren to exhibit and we will encourage them to do so, if they are of our age. If they are older there will be no question but that they will take precedence over us. If they are smaller, we can befriend them and direct them in little tableaux and recitals, which will amuse the adults without requiring us to show ourselves at all. So, you see, Rowena dear, you must not trouble yourself. I hope we can take some long walks and look about us. We must take our butterfly nets and our flower press. Will it not be interesting to compare the botany thereabout with what we find here?'

Thus Jane assuaged her friend's anxieties by replacing them with pleasing anticipation of activities that she knew would be agreeable, and the days passed in pleasant preparation and eagerness for the visit to come.

Chapter Five

Knoxbury was a large country house of modern construction, very comfortable, built within the grounds of an older and now ruined residence, the remains of which formed a pretty, romantic folly surrounded by a carefully managed wilderness some distance from the new house. There was a well-stocked library, a music room, cosy window seats for confidential chat and a dining room that seemed always to have some manner of temptation within; soft, sweet rolls, exotic fruit, cake and a bottomless jug of elderflower cordial. The girls were assigned a large and sunny room with a view over the gardens and told to enjoy themselves, explore, eat and drink whatever they liked.

'You are to consider yourselves quite at home my dears,' said Lady Knox as she showed them where they could put their clothes. 'Punctuality at mealtimes is all I require—I *will* insist on it even though *some* put my requirements at nought—and that you do not tease Bess.' Bess was an ancient and rather odorous spaniel that followed Lady Knox everywhere she went. 'If you wish to play with puppies there are plenty of them in the kennels, but Bess is beyond such frivolities; I am afraid she can be cantankerous. She is not the only one in the household with that affliction but you will discover that for yourselves, no doubt, before the day is done.' With this rather cryptic remark Lady Knox went away.

'I wonder whom she can mean,' Rowena said, clutching Jane's hand.

'I cannot tell,' Jane replied, 'but who will be irritable with *us,* when we are so newly come that we have not had opportunity to give offense to anyone.'

'*You* will never give offense, Jane, but I am so liable to say the wrong thing, or to be unable to utter a syllable, which is often worse.'

'Nonsense, dear,' Jane re-joined, 'you are as mild and unobjectionable as a new-born babe. Now, shall we lay our dresses out? They may have creased in the trunk.'

The family, at their first meeting in the drawing room before dinner, seemed pleasant and easy. The girls made their curtseys to Lord Knox, his daughter Mrs Dixon and her husband, and their four sons of whom the oldest was perhaps seventeen years of age, the youngest ten. Rowena trembled at them—they were big, rumbustious boys, high-spirited, with strong Irish brogues. Jane met them with equanimity, telling herself that, after the formalities of introduction, they would not be much inclined to take notice of two girls who could not climb trees, ride ponies or swing on the rope across the river. They would dutifully partner Rowena and Jane at any dancing that might take place, pass the butter at breakfast and otherwise leave the two girls to their own devices.

Lord Knox was a liberal host, genial and happy to see his guests enjoy themselves. Quick to discern Rowena's interest in flora and fauna, he directed her to the natural history shelves in the library and a large case of butterflies in one of the galleries.

'I shall show you the beehives, if you like, my dear,' he whinnied, 'they are very busy just now—we might see the queen. How would you like that?'

'Very much sir,' Rowena replied in a voice quaking with awe.

'Capital!' Lord Knox cried, clapping his hands. 'One of the boys—I forget which,' he waved towards his grandsons gathered round a tray of canapés, 'one of them is interested in botany. It might be Patrick—he's the second. He's to have his father's farm in County Wicklow, in due course. I call it a farm. Baly-Craig is the Dixon country seat, but there is excellent grazing country thereabouts—prize cows abound. Patrick interests himself in it. I'll get him to show you the best spots for catching butterflies.' But observing Rowena's stricken expression at this suggestion he moved away, saying only, 'In due course, my dear. No urgency, not the least in the world,' and breaking into a snatch of song in a cheerful but discordant, falsetto.

Lady Knox was an easy hostess, as plump as her husband was thin, her loud, low voice the perfect counterpoint to his high, shrill tone. She had no airs and few graces and sat now with her dress thrown on anyhow and stalks of hay in her hair. In truth she was happier in her garden than her drawing room and happiest of all at the stables where she kept a number of valuable breeding horses and a pack of spaniels.

'You boys,' she shouted now, 'don't eat all the canapés! Offer them round, for goodness' sake! The two young ladies have had no chance at them and *will* have none, if you carry on as you have begun. Hugh! Show your brothers the example.'

The tallest boy lifted the tray and crossed the room to where Jane and Rowena sat on a low settee. 'Good evening again,' he said with a pleasant smile, bowing and offering the tray. 'I am Hugh. We were introduced just now but I doubt not you have forgotten all our names already, as, indeed, I have forgotten yours.'

Rowena blushed scarlet. Jane said, 'This is Rowena Campbell and I am Jane.'

'Ah yes. Miss Campbell and Miss Jane,' said Hugh, bowing again. 'Please forgive our greediness,' he looked shamefacedly at the tray, 'there is but a paltry choice remaining to you. Shall I send for more?'

'Not on our account, sir,' Jane said, declining the tray even though she did feel quite hungry, 'I am sure dinner will be served directly.'

Hugh Dixon smiled again and raised a knowing eyebrow. 'Grandmamma likes meals served very punctually,' he said in a confiding tone, 'but there are others who are less particular. We will not be called through for a good half hour yet. Are you sure you will not take something to sustain you?' He proffered the tray again. 'The canapés,' he said, in a low voice, 'are here to assuage our appetites while we wait …'

But the two young ladies shook their heads again and he withdrew. Across the room his parents stood in conversation with Colonel and Mrs Campbell. Mrs Dixon—Lord and Lady Knox's daughter—was a very elegantly dressed lady, more in her mother's image than her father's, very happy to be back at home from Ireland and disposed to be delighted with everything that was not Irish, which included the Campbells. Her husband was a tall, very hale gentleman, every inch the

Irish country squire with a broad, weather-beaten forehead and arresting blue eyes under bristly brows. His manners, perhaps, were not altogether refined but genially bluff, his laugh loud and immoderate.

The other guest at Knoxbury, and the one for whom dinner was now delayed, was the Dowager Lady Sowerby, Lady Knox's mother, and it was she alone who was to sound a carping and disagreeable note in the otherwise blithe symphony of the holiday. She was a bitter and disappointed woman, having lost her husband to find that he had lost their fortune and from being obliged to give up every appurtenance to her position apart from her name which, because of *his* disgrace, had become more of a burden than a blessing. She had no son on whom she could foist the shrivelled remnants of their tainted family honour or the bloated obligations of their debt and this added to her chagrin. She divided her year between her three daughters, a female Lear, her disgruntled malevolence quite as burdensome as a hundred riotous knights, and the summer months were the ones she habitually imposed herself upon the family at Knoxbury.

That no one at Knoxbury had any great affection for her was apparent from the first. When at last she made her stately entrance into the drawing room, leaning on the arm of a footman, Lord Knox and the Dixons greeted her coolly, her great grandsons kissed her whiskery cheek with evident reluctance. She was an extremely aged lady, very splendidly dressed, lustrous with the diamonds that she had managed to keep from her creditors' grasp. Her hair was abundant, very becomingly arranged and altogether artificial. Her wrinkled face was hardly enhanced by a lavish and not very skilfully applied layer of powder and rouge in a style prevalent with fashionable ladies fifty years previously.

'Mama,' said Lady Knox, surveying the old lady with a critical eye. 'Have you emptied your jewel box? You quite dazzle me.' She fingered her own necklace, a rope of glossy pearls, and threw a significant glance at Mrs Campbell, who wore no ornaments at all. 'It may well be that I am out of step with current fashion,' she observed, 'but I think it is not quite polite to outshine so very significantly one's hostess and all one's fellow guests.'

'I pay no heed to fashion,' the lady sniped. She looked witheringly at the company. 'I have been waiting this half hour or more for some gentleman to come to my dressing room to escort me,' she said. 'I am the last person to require any ceremony—who am I, these days, to presume to such a thing? But I would have thought that here, amongst family, *someone* would have known what was due.'

'Mama, you know we sent Hugh up twice but your maid said you were not ready,' Lady Knox said with a sigh. 'Now you are come, perhaps we might dine? I am sure if we do not do so soon these boys will start eating each other.'

'Nonsense,' carped her mother, taking a seat in a large armchair. 'Gentlemen should learn self-discipline—they must not be at the mercy of their appetites or we will all return to savagery. I think I may take a glass of Canary wine and a biscuit. The walk from my chamber has exhausted me. I do not know why you insist on accommodating me at such a great distance from the drawing room, Susan. I must say it does not make one feel altogether welcome. Perhaps you would rather bundle me away in an attic?'

'Or in the old house?' one of the boys said in a low voice, referring to the derelict ruin across the park. His brothers snorted with suppressed laughter.

'Yes, indeed,' said Lady Sowerby, whose hearing was sharp. '*There* I could cause no inconvenience at all.'

'Mama, your suite is the largest the house has to offer, with the best views over the parks,' Lady Knox said testily. 'Ernest and I have vacated it, as we do every year, for your particular comfort. Well, if we are to starve a little longer, let me introduce our other guests that you may petrify them completely with your peculiar charm.'

Lord Knox waved at a footman, who took up a decanter and began to replenish glasses. The butler slunk from the room to inform the cook that dinner should be delayed by a further half an hour.

Lady Knox brought forth Colonel and Mrs Campbell, and then Jane and Rowena, 'Colonel Augustus Campbell, who assists Ernest so ably at the War Office, his wife Mrs Emily Campbell and their girls, Jane and Rowena. May I present my mother, the Dowager Lady Sowerby? Let me warn you at once, she is vinegarish.'

The colonel bowed and said something gallant. The ladies curtseyed and Mrs Campbell put on her most amiable and winning countenance. Lady Sowerby inclined her head by a fraction but otherwise ignored them both 'Girls!' she cried, squinting through her pince-nez at Jane and Rowena, '*you* will make no very interesting companions for my Irish rabble, unless you are marriageable? Is *that* why you have come? Set your caps at Hugh, do you?'

It was hard to say whether the girls or Hugh Dixon found this suggestion the most embarrassing; they all blushed

'Ma'am,' said Mrs Campbell, stepping forward hastily, 'the girls are not fifteen years of age.'

'And so?' Lady Sowerby replied, with a degree of insolence which was astonishing, '*I* was betrothed at fifteen and married a year later. Young ladies can afford to waste no time in putting themselves before eligible gentlemen, particularly if they aspire to fortune and position—and what young lady of sense and taste would *not?* Hugh will be a catch; he will inherit his father's acres in Wicklow. He may have Knox's also, since he has no son, although he will not have the title. The other boys will do nicely too, I'll be bound. Their father has a considerable fortune, though he is plain Mister and a pretty plain mister to boot! I wanted Dolly to hold out for someone titled, but my feelings were ignored. She went for the money.'

'Ma'am, forgive me but I feel I must correct you, if you hold such a mistaken notion,' Colonel Campbell said warmly. 'I refute the idea that we came to Knoxbury with any such low or conniving motive. We came simply at the kind invitation of Lord and Lady Knox.'

'And *I* refute the idea that Dorothy considered my fortune of the least importance when she agreed to be my wife,' Mr Dixon blustered. 'Ours was a match of love. And may I say also that since I *am* in the room it is hardly polite of you to speak of me as though I were absent.'

'Oh, sir. Are you here?' Lady Sowerby said, peering towards the fireplace, 'I had not observed. Very good, you think that, if it pleases you, but Knox had more sense; he would not have allowed his daughter to fall in love with an impecunious man.'

'As to falling in love,' Mrs Dixon said, glancing fondly at her husband, 'who can prevent anyone from doing so?'

'A sound thrashing can be most persuasive,' Lady Sowerby said.

'Papa would not have dreamed of lifting a hand to me,' Mrs Dixon cried.

'Indeed. And look at the result,' Lady Sowerby crowed.

'Madam,' Lord Knox said firmly, 'I hardly think this conversation suitable. You embarrass the young people.'

'Well, let me look at you,' Lady Sowerby said, ignoring her son in law and beckoning Jane and Rowena forward. She looked each up and down with minute attention. 'I know something about young ladies,' she said at last, 'I have not brought up three of my own to be ignorant of their manipulative ways, tantrums and tricks, and I think I am a good judge of quality, too. Hum. Most unlike,' she said. 'One has got all the other's share of beauty.' She gave Jane a piercing look. 'You have more beauty in your little finger than your sister has in her whole person. But has *she* got all of *your* wit? I wonder if you think you have the better of the bargain. Well, looks are a very great thing when you are young, but an old woman with no beauty and no wit is a sad creature indeed.'

'You would know,' muttered Mr Dixon, 'insufferable old crone.' He gathered his sons to him and distracted them from Jane and Rowena's discomfort by pointing at something through the window.

Jane glanced at Mrs Campbell. Patently Lady Sowerby had misunderstood her position in the family. It was not uncommon— generally a slight hint from Mrs Campbell or the Colonel was enough to set matters straight. But the Campbells were not minded to give Lady Sowerby the benefit of a timely word and when Jane followed their glance, she knew why. Rowena's eyes were fixed on the carpet at her feet, her hands trembled as she clasped them tightly before her. A tear fell from her eye and landed with a splash on the toe of her slipper. Jane reached out and took Rowena's hand tenderly.

'We believe our girls equally blessed in both, ma'am. We make no comparison.' Mrs Campbell said stiffly, putting one arm around each of them.

'Comparisons are odious,' Lady Knox agreed, giving her mother a sharp look.

'You are blind, then,' Lady Sowerby remarked, giving no indication of having heard her daughter. 'But *I* shall be the judge of it. You will both play and sing after dinner, and recite some verse. A competition, what say you?'

Rowena looked aghast at Mrs Campbell. 'Oh, mama, I cannot … Please do not …'

'Come, come now,' Lady Sowerby said with a cackle, 'I conjecture you spend your days with music teachers and the like. What for, if not for this? A girl must be ready to display her accomplishments, must she not? The boys will ride their ponies for you, and shoot their arrows and all manner of derring-do to exhibit *their* prowess? How will you answer them, if not in musical proficiency and song?'

'We ride and shoot for our own entertainment, Great-Grandmamma,' Patrick, the second Dixon boy, said bravely. 'These young ladies have no need to exert themselves for our benefit.' He threw Rowena a look loaded with sympathy and kindness.

'They will exert themselves for *mine,* then,' Lady Sowerby replied. 'I insist on being entertained and I will satisfy myself as to these girls' merits. It may well be for your benefit, young sir. You would not wish to have a wife, be she ever so beautiful, if she is as vacuous and dull as an empty room when *this* one,' she waved a claw-like hand at Rowena, 'could be all wit and cleverness beneath that dowdy exterior.'

'You will excuse us, ma'am,' Mrs Campbell said. 'The girls are tired after their journey and will retire as soon as we have dined.' She guided Jane and Rowena to another part of the room. The colonel followed, leaving Lord and Lady Knox as Lady Sowerby's sole attendants.

'So, mama, you have managed to alienate the entire room in only a quarter of an hour,' Lady Knox hissed. 'I declare you grow more irascible with every year. Do my sisters permit such behaviour before their guests?'

'Oh, they never entertain when I am with them,' Lady Sowerby said. 'It is delightful of you, to provide such sport.'

'You will curb your interference, madam,' Lord Knox said, but his command was met with an insolent glare.

'Now, we will dine,' Lady Knox said, moving Bess from her lap and standing up. 'Ernest, you will take Mrs Campbell in. Colonel Campbell, will you be so kind as to give my daughter your arm? Hugh, Patrick, you may escort these young ladies. Mr Dixon and I will hand Lady Sowerby in, if we can bring ourselves not to bundle her into the closet on the way past.'

She grappled her mother from her seat, Mr Dixon lending his willing if not very gentle aid. 'I ask you as a great favour to me to leave those two young ladies alone,' Lady Knox said with great emphasis as they made their way to the dining room. 'You have reduced one quite to tears.'

'She must be a silly, lily-livered thing, then. So much the better that the boys should see it at once, do you not agree with me, Mr Dixon? You would not wish to see your boys marry a spineless wife?'

'Upon my word, ma'am, I assure you my boys are very far from thinking of anything beyond their roast mutton and apple tart.'

'I am quite of their mind. Really, Susan, you allow your servants too much lassitude. They must not be allowed to serve meals at their own convenience. I hope the cook remembers that I cannot tolerate green vegetables. If you think me offensive *now* you have not seen me under the influence of brassicas.'

As she had promised, Mrs Campbell removed Jane and Rowena as soon as the ladies rose from table by sending them to their room, saving them from further exposure to Lady Sowerby's critical gaze. Rowena was deeply distressed, however, and betook herself to Jane's bed once the candle had been snuffed. It took all of Jane's powers to calm her friend's mind until she slipped into a fitful sleep. Jane remained awake, however. It seemed unlikely that they could avoid the ordeal of exhibiting themselves before Lady Sowerby's malicious censure for the entirety of the month designated for their stay. Lady Sowerby was a lady manifestly used to getting her own way, as tenacious as a terrier. For her own part Jane had few qualms. She sang well and played better; she need have nothing to fear. Even if Lady Sowerby despised her efforts the rest of the company would know she did so from mere churlishness; if anyone were to look ridiculous, it would be *her*. But Rowena's performance was likely to bring heavy—and perhaps not altogether unjustified—condemnation from a woman who seemed to have no notion of polite diplomacy. The Knoxes would not pronounce on Rowena harshly but Rowena would judge herself very severely indeed. She, whose confidence was already such a timorous and hesitant thing, would take any criticism very much to heart. It could, Jane considered, quite destroy Rowena to be thus exposed. Jane resolved— notwithstanding how rude it may make her seem, or how much it would detract from her own pleasure—not to sing or play a note while she was at Knoxbury. She would decline with as much grace as possible, she would plead hoarseness, denigrate her competency—she would downright refuse if it came to it—but she would protect her friend from unkind disparagement and unflattering comparison at any cost.

On the following morning the weather was extremely benign: bright sun, a refreshing breeze. Jane woke full of her determination to shield Rowena and to render their stay at Knoxbury as pleasurable as possible for her; she spoke with animation of the delights before them—the meadows, the beehives, the vantage points for sketching—and they descended to breakfast to find their mood further lifted by the news that Lady Sowerby was ill and confined to bed. Although everyone expressed due concern, no one seemed really perturbed and Mr Dixon even declared himself pleased.

'I confess,' he said, heaping ham and eggs upon his plate, 'her absence for a few days will in no way injure *my* enjoyment of Knoxbury. She is a cantankerous old bird and no mistake. I was quite ashamed of her last night, indeed I was.' He glanced up the table to where Rowena nibbled a piece of toast. 'I have told my boys they are not to stand by and watch her torment the young ladies, Campbell.'

'I am glad of it, for Lord Knox and I may well have to return to London for a few days. Matters at the War Office might require our attention. I would not like to leave my girls behind if I thought them vulnerable to any kind of malevolent influence. Indeed, I told Lord Knox last night that we would *all* depart if there was a repetition of last night's outrageous indictments.'

'Rest assured, sir, no one gives the least credence to her. Our hosts are absent from the table but I say nothing in their absence that I would not boldly say in their hearing. Lady Sowerby is vicious and bitter. She would be ridiculous if she were not so cruel. My boys are immune to her, I hope. I recommend you instruct your young ladies to give her no heed.'

With so strong an assurance of the support and compassion of the whole of the rest of the company, the girls' sojourn at Knoxbury progressed pleasantly. The weather continuing kind, windows and doors remained open to the air and sun from morning until well after dusk. The girls strolled around the grounds and picnicked on the lawns. They dipped their fishing nets and even their feet in the slow-moving river that meandered through the park. Beyond the formal gardens there were hay meadows, paddocks and orchards, innumerable opportunities for sketching, flowers for pressing and butterflies for catching. They visited the stables and the kennels, stroking the soft muzzles of gentle horses and holding squirming puppies in their arms. The Dixon boys, as Jane had predicted, were much occupied outdoors, returning to the house filthy and ravenous at the end of each day. In the evenings they included the girls in their parlour games, however and this broke down even Rowena's shyness in the fullness of time. Lady Sowerby's illness lingered and she kept to her room, her indisposition adding materially to the happiness and pleasure of all.

Indeed, she had been all-but forgotten until, some ten days after she had taken to her bed she rose from it, dressed, donned her wig and powder and returned to the drawing room. It happened that on this particular evening Lord and Lady Knox, Mr and Mrs Dixon and the Campbells had been invited to dine at a neighbouring house. The young people had eaten their dinner early and had spent the evening—which was still warm—outdoors playing tennis in the lingering sunshine. Jane and Rowena had been persuaded to try a few strokes; it had been all enjoyment and merriment, informal and agreeable. When twilight came at last they returned laughing to the house and entered the drawing room through the French doors.

'I will call for lights and lemonade,' Hugh Dixon said, 'and then, Connor, you will have to go to bed.' Connor was the youngest Dixon, a stout-hearted little boy very eager to be included in all his bigger brothers' games.

His lower lip began to quiver. 'I do not want to go to bed,' he said, although in truth he was very tired. 'Miss Jane said she would sing to me and she has not done so, yet.'

'It is true,' Jane said with a smile. Connor had earlier tumbled and bruised his knee, and she had promised to sing to him as a distraction from the hurt. 'I did promise the little fellow that I would sing his favourite Irish air.' She had quite forgotten, in all her enjoyment, and in the continued absence of Lady Sowerby, her resolve not to play or sing. She did not recall it now, until a carking voice from the shadows said, 'I am very happy to hear it, for my determination to see if you are more than just a pretty face has not diminished.'

'Oh,' Jane started, the full force of her promise to herself returning. How could she have forgotten? Just then the footman brought lights.

Lady Sowerby sat resplendent in one of the large armchairs, a look of extreme complaisance on her withered, powder-encrusted features. 'I do hope you will oblige me,' she said with an icy smile.

Jane steeled herself. A glance at Rowena strengthened her nerve—*she* was ghastly pale, seeing all-too plainly what would follow Jane's performance. 'I pray you will forgive me, Lady Sowerby,' she began, 'I would prefer not to sing.'

'Oh, but Miss Jane,' young Connor wailed, tears swimming in his eyes, 'you *promised* …'

'What's all this?' Hugh Dixon enquired, coming back into the room.

'Miss Jane said she would sing to me, but now she says she won't,' Connor blubbered.

'Well now *that's* not very sporting,' Hugh said with half a laugh, looking at Jane. Then he saw Lady Sowerby and, to his credit, read at once the entirety of the situation. 'But perhaps Miss Jane is tired,' he suggested, 'I am sure she will sing to you another day.'

'But she promised, she *promised,*' insisted the little boy, becoming more and more agitated.

'Yes, she promised,' Lady Sowerby repeated, revealing her black, broken teeth in a malicious grin.

Jane hesitated, looking from little Connor to Rowena, and then at Lady Sowerby. It would be nothing for her to sing a song or two—an entire opera, if it pleased the old woman—but that she knew that her recital alone would not satisfy. Oh, why had she made such a rash promise to Connor? How could such a resolve as she had taken be so wantonly cast aside for the sake of a wounded knee?

Patrick Dixon, seeing and understanding a little the import of Miss Jane's dilemma from the stricken expression on Miss Rowena's face said, '*I* will sing, Great-Grandmamma, if it will please you.'

'It will *not* please me,' Lady Sowerby snapped. Connor indicated by the volume of his cries that it would not please him either.

'Stop crying, Connor, or I shall have to go and fetch Nanny,' Hugh Dixon said. 'We cannot make young ladies sing for us if they do not wish to.'

'I *will* hear the young ladies,' the dowager concluded adamantly.

Rowena gave a strangled cry of despair.

'I could dance a jig,' said Andrew, the second youngest boy, 'you know that always makes you laugh, Connor.'

But Connor was not to be consoled. The more he cried the more acute Jane's discomfort became and the more fiercely she upbraided herself.

'You must be a heartless young lady to withstand *his* pleas,' Lady Sowerby remarked. 'You are certainly a very insolent one to withstand *mine.*'

The young people had drifted by unspoken accord into a confidential group. 'Oh Jane,' said Rowena in a low voice, 'you will have to sing to her, and then I will play something, and then the ordeal will be over.'

'By no means.' Patrick Dixon hissed. 'We will not put you through any such torment—for I see it *will* be torment to you, although, I must confess, I do not quite see why.'

'When you have heard me play, you will know,' Rowena said brokenly. 'Jane seeks only to protect me. *She* is proficient.'

'Oh, if it is only that,' Patrick Dixon said, 'I am a perfect dunderhead when it comes to anything. Look how inept I was at tennis! But I do not let it concern me. I muddle through.' He leaned towards her and would have taken her hand, but held back from such familiarity. Even so, he said, 'We are friends, here. You need not be afraid.'

'I have not your resilience,' Rowena said. 'However, if you all promise not to laugh at me, I will attempt something.'

'I do fear she will not be satisfied until you perform,' Hugh Dixon said in a low voice. 'She is a tyrant, is she not? Let us get it over with, then Connor will consent to be put to bed. If he carries on in this vein he will make himself sick.'

Rowena nodded her agreement and the whole party moved to the part of the room where the pianoforte stood, leaving Lady Sowerby alone by the empty fireplace.

'Rowena,' Jane almost sobbed. 'I recriminate myself very severely, for having brought this about—the one thing that I was so determined to avoid.'

'It does not matter,' said Rowena dully.

Patrick Dixon lifted the lid of the pianoforte. Hugh Dixon settled the stool. Jane seated herself at the piano, more aware of Rowena's cowed and trembling form than of the notes before her. She played and sang, as flat and lack-lustre a performance as she could manage, deliberately fumbling the notes and pretending to forget the words. It satisfied little Connor, however, who sat next to his brother Andrew and was asleep before half the second verse was through.

Lady Sowerby curled her lip. 'I must say you make no very great effort to entertain. A surly madam indeed, I am quite disgusted with you. You *could* be proficient, if you took the trouble to practice, and your voice has promise. You should exert yourself a great deal more than you do, and mend your manners. Now, let me hear the other. I surmise I have been right all along. *She* will prove to be a nightingale in disguise.'

Very much chastised, and yet not half so much as she felt she deserved, Jane exchanged places with Rowena, who rushed precipitately into her piece. Before half the introductory bars were got through it was apparent to the Dixon boys that Rowena had not exaggerated her lack of prowess and they mobilised in an effort to obfuscate her shame. Hugh stamped across the room to pour lemonade as noisily as possible. Patrick closed the French windows with much banging and wrenching at the handles and then set to work on a disobliging curtain, tugging and wrestling with it until it threatened to come down from its fixings.

When the song began Jane added her voice to Rowena's, singing loudly, to drown out the other girl's tuneless warblings. Andrew got up from the sofa to dance a jig, managing to trip over the rug and knocking a small table over.

'Enough! Enough!' Lady Sowerby shrieked at last, putting her hands over her ears. She threw a withering look at Rowena, who wept quite openly now into her hands. 'You squawk like a seagull, girl, and your playing is execrable. You should never be allowed near a pianoforte again. Oh, stop your snivelling, for pity's sake.' She turned her gimlet gaze on Jane, who stood nearby quite as distraught as Rowena, full of self-castigation, but who had not given way to an outward manifestation of her feelings. 'Well, I see that Miss Jane Campbell is all the treasure the Campbell family has in store—their hopes must rest on you, young lady. Your sister is fit for nothing but a life of retirement, neither use nor ornament. I wonder your parents bring her into society at all.'

'Great-Grandmamma!' Hugh Dixon remonstrated.

'Oh, do not rebuke me, sir,' Lady Sowerby retorted, 'it is for your good that I winkle out these fortune-seekers. If you must take one of these you had better take the beauty. She is churlish, mind, but better that than a dullard.'

The sheer cruelty, as well as the unfairness of the old woman's remarks, ignited a flame of rage in Jane that she could not quench—did not wish to quench. As angry as she was at herself for permitting this situation to come about, Lady Sowerby's venom was insupportable.

'Madam,' said Jane, raising her chin to look the old harridan square in the eye, 'you are mistaken, as well as discourteous and unkind. My name is Jane Fairfax—I am not the Campbells' daughter, merely their ward. The Campbells treasure Rowena as highly and as affectionately as possible and hold her in the highest esteem, as do I and all people of discrimination who are fortunate enough to come within her orbit. That *you* are ignorant of her excellent qualities does not mean she is not abundantly blessed with them; she is the purest-hearted, gentlest and most selfless person it is possible to imagine. But I am not surprised by your blindness, since you are without the least shred of humanity, taste or charity. I doubt *you* would recognise the glory of the archangel Gabriel if he were to appear here before us. Lastly, to reiterate what you have already been told, my guardians came to Knoxbury without the least thought or intention towards any kind of alliance beyond what is compatible with good manners and cordial acquaintance. Now I wish you goodnight.' She took Rowena by the arm and the two walked from the room. The Dixons followed closely behind, Hugh carrying his youngest brother in his arms, leaving Lady Sowerby speechless with affront in her solitary state.

Chapter Six

The following morning the girls' breakfast was served in their room. 'There is great commotion downstairs, my ladies, and the mistress sends her compliments and requests you remain upstairs until called for,' said the maid as she laid out coffee, baked goods and boiled eggs.

'Oh Rowena, I have shamed the colonel and Mrs Campbell,' Jane said, stricken and afraid. 'Of course, Lord and Lady Knox will take Lady Sowerby's part. I shall be sent away.' Naturally she had intended to speak to Mrs Campbell at the earliest opportunity, to lay out, as clearly and disinterestedly as possible, the events of the night before. She had been ready to apologise to Lord and Lady Knox, to own that she had spoken in temper and in pain words that, with proper reflection, it had been ill-advised and discourteous to utter. She might even have brought herself to speak words of contrition to Lady Sowerby if *she* would show herself capable of the smallest paring of kindness.

'You will never be sent away while there is breath in me to prevent it,' Rowena avowed, holding Jane tightly to her.

'I should not have spoken as I did.'

'Who could have kept silent, with such provocation,' Rowena said, recalling, but not admitting, that *she* had not uttered one word in her own defence, or in Jane's. 'The Dixons will vouch for us. Mr Hugh Dixon called his great-grandmother a tyrant. She behaved—Oh! I will never forget the look of utter scorn in her eyes, the derision in her voice. And her words! Indeed, she is quite right. I am fit for nothing …' Rowena broke down in tears once more, a condition that had assailed her on and off throughout the night.

Below them, in the dining room, there was in train a scene quite as bad as Jane imagined. Lady Sowerby was in high dudgeon.

'I am insulted to the point of physical pain,' she rasped, writhing in her chair as though impaled upon it. 'I have known no wink of sleep, no moment of respite from agony since last night. I have endured spasm upon spasm. My honour is wounded to such a degree that only if Miss Jane Fairfax is soundly whipped—and that by my own hand—will I feel even slightly mollified.' She fixed the colonel with a narrow-eyed glower, 'You have come to Knoxbury under false pretences, sir. You connived to thrust your penniless dependent—a natural child, no doubt, tainted by low blood—onto my great grandsons. Such presumption! Would you bring us to the gutter? And worse! That other offspring of yours. She is an imbecile. How might the family line have been irretrievably polluted by such a connection! She ought to be shut away in an asylum; she is not fit for the public gaze. How dare you seek to defile our family with these deviants?'

'Madam, I protest,' Colonel Campbell bellowed, in his loudest parade-ground voice. 'You insult my family beyond my capacity to tolerate.' He turned to where Lord Knox stood trembling with rage and shame on the hearth rug. 'Forgive me Knox, but no duty as a guest or a friend can permit me to allow such pernicious allegation, such outrageous calumny as your mother-in-law offers. I will not permit my wife and daughters to suffer it. I will not suffer it myself. By God, sir, if she were a man, I would call her out.'

'And I would be your second,' Lord Knox piped, throwing arrows of ire across the room. 'She is a meddler, sir, an embarrassment. I am … I cannot express my mortification at what she has brought upon our household.'

'She has contravened every law of hospitality,' Lady Knox lamented. 'Your poor girls. If I had known she intended rising from her bed I would never have gone to the Trefoils' dinner last evening.'

'They are *not* his girls,' Lady Sowerby put in. 'One is a changeling. Perhaps they both are. Neither would have brought any credit to us, you can be sure.'

'Madam, enough!' Colonel Campbell shouted. He turned his back on her and addressed himself solely to Lord and Lady Knox. 'Under the circumstances, lamentable as they are, I have no alternative but to quit Knoxbury within the hour. My compliments and thanks to you madam,' he bowed to Lady Knox, 'and to you sir. I trust that this appalling episode will not mar our excellent working relations at the Office.'

He turned to Lady Sowerby, accorded her the slightest, stiffest bow, and left the room.

In compliance with the colonel's decree the Campbell party left Knoxbury an hour later. They spoke little on their way back to Bute Square. Mrs Campbell, who had been spared the full enormity of Lady Sowerby's spite, devoted herself to the care of the two girls. They told her, haltingly, with many tears and, on Jane's part, much self-reproach, enough of their dreadful experience in Knoxbury's drawing room for her to understand it had been extremely distressing.

'She treated you very ill,' Mrs Campbell said when the tale was told. 'I have half a mind to go back there and take her to task. The woman is without heart, utterly devoid of feeling. If I were to meet her again …'

'We would decline to know her,' the colonel said heavily, 'and she would decline to know us. In her opinion *we* are the ones at fault.'

'It is I who have offended,' Jane said with her head hung very low. 'Indeed, I was unconscionably rude to her, my elder and better …'

'By no means your better, Jane,' the colonel interrupted. 'She, with every advantage of age and experience, a titled personage with three daughters of her own, should have acted with a great deal more forbearance than she did towards two young people hardly out of the schoolroom. Even savages have more of the milk of human kindness than she. No, you should not rebuke yourself, Jane. You were provoked. A saint could not have acted better than you did.'

'Indeed,' Rowena put in, 'Jane acted as she did in my defence. If I had practiced more diligently, or just been more impervious to Lady Sowerby's insinuations—Patrick Dixon said *he* paid no heed to her—I wish I could have his resilience. I am too sensitive. I must be braver. I cannot expect Jane to fight my battles for me always.'

They all felt the truth of this statement and it would have been useless as well as specious to contradict it. Jane would not be able to protect Rowena indefinitely; it was the only evil of their situation. They continued on in silence.

The Campbells returned to Bute Square for the remainder of June and then went to Worthing. They spoke aloud no more of the events of Knoxbury but they did all think about them a great deal. The colonel and Mrs Campbell were more alive than ever to the peculiar delicacy and vulnerability of their daughter; as dear as she was to them, she was not a girl abundantly blessed with accomplishments, wit or character such as to ensure her ready acceptance in society. When the time came, she would need a husband most willing to take her beneath his wing, to shelter and encourage her. The provision of a sizeable dowry might be very necessary to secure such a man, whose character would be of far more importance than his capital. They would choose a poor, kind husband for their daughter over a rich, cold one. This being so the impossibility of providing more for Jane than they had originally stipulated became even stronger. She must make her own way buoyed by every grace and accomplishment they could imbue but by not one penny of their capital.

Their situation in Worthing was quiet and rather remote—their lodgings house in a small settlement some distance from the town, down a sandy lane, hard against the dunes. They sought no acquaintance in the hamlet with the very few other families who holidayed there and Jane had plenty of freedom and peace to go over in her mind the entirety of her situation in life, her relations with the Campbells, the duties she owed to them as well as what was due to her Highbury connections. She continued to upbraid herself for allowing Rowena to fall prey to Lady Sowerby's manipulations and wept many bitter tears as she walked on the sands and amongst the dunes, taking herself very severely to task. As she departed in the coach for Highbury for her month with her grandmamma and aunt, she remained in deep contemplation of matters in Bute Square. Throughout her visit the Campbells were more vivid to her than the Coles and Coxes, the Woodhouses and Knightleys, the Westons, Perrys, Palings and Larkins, the Hopleys and Cropleys and all the little girls at Mrs Goddard's school. They all flocked, eager to see her, quite a parade, from morning till night, up and down the narrow stair to the apartment above the grocer's shop. Or at least, if they did not flock quite with the volition of their own eagerness, they came in response to that of Miss Bates, who, with enough eagerness for the whole of Highbury, earnestly and repeatedly invited them that Jane might be looked at and praised and admired and declared to have grown. Jane was as intimately acquainted with every small aspect of their lives as they were themselves. She dutifully enquired after their gout and their grandchildren, their ailments and apple crops, as evidence that though transplanted from their midst, she was still rooted firmly in Highbury soil. The people of Highbury were happy to see her—at least she had come, *she* came every year, which was more—much more—than could be said for Mr Frank Churchill whose promised visit had—again—been cancelled.

Throughout her time in Highbury, as interesting—or as dull—as it might be, the Campbells were never far from Jane's mind. Her conclusion at last was no more or less than it had been at the first; that she must redouble her efforts to promote and encourage Rowena, must move herself even further into the shadows that Rowena might shine the more brightly. She must leave no room for doubt in anyone's mind—much less in her own—of her extremely humble status and poor expectations; that she was a grateful nobody, an insignificant ward, an undeserving beneficiary of the Campbells' great goodness. Added to this was a new resolution: she would guard her tongue. The power of her temper in Knoxbury's drawing room, and the ready stream of invective that had provided itself to her tongue had surprised and unnerved her. She would tame it, allowing her mouth to speak only generalities and platitudes. Henceforth, she would reserve her true opinions for the privacy of her own mind.

Chapter Seven

Three further years passed in Highbury. Miss Emma Woodhouse, now seventeen years of age, had forgotten the time when her father's table had contained too little in the way of cake, as well as other unpleasant childhood reminiscences. In a dim corner of her mind, she felt there had once been distastefulness and criticism; a suggestion that she did not attend to her lessons, read or practice her music as she should; the accusation that her manner was insufferably precocious, and her character wily. She had been caught out in schemes that had the unhappiness or embarrassment of others as their object. There had been talk of punishment—chastisements that would be humiliating and disagreeable—but nothing had come of it. Now, she had influence if she did not exactly have power, she had consequence and nobody would dream of pitying Miss Emma Woodhouse of Hartfield. She had long since given up any pretence of study in the schoolroom; Miss Taylor was her companion and confidante, not her governess. Her situation as the mistress of Hartfield justified any air of superiority in her manner—how could it not, when she was unarguably the first lady in her circle in wealth, in elegance and in importance? And if no one *now* was aware of her cleverness in managing things to her own satisfaction it only showed how justified her early forays had been to foster those skills of astute resourcefulness.

She now had the household so securely under her own sway that any deficiency in Hartfield hospitality was inconceivable. She pandered most diligently to her father's tastes—his gruel was thin and smooth and of that luke-warmness that particularly pleased him—but no one else was expected for a moment to partake of it. For *them* there were platters of thin-cut sandwiches, seedcake and tarts with as much cream as any of them could stomach. She agreed wholeheartedly with her father that such indulgence was bad—but how could the Woodhouses offer less at their card parties than, for example, the Coles offered at theirs? It was unthinkable! The fault, she told him, was not in the offering of such luxuries, but in the consumption of them. If people chose to eat too much cake—and only a very little bit would be too much in Mr Woodhouse's opinion—they had only themselves to blame.

Emma was fortunate; Highbury was a small place with few substantial properties. Mr Knightley, whose wife would have taken immediate precedence over Emma, remained unmarried. Mrs Paling, who was Emma's superior in years, in experience and in judgement, was a quiet, homely woman, very happy in her situation, with no interest in asserting herself socially. Miss Taylor was welcomed as an equal by all who mattered in Highbury. With Mr Weston she was a particular favourite and Mr Knightley spoke highly of her but she was the last person to push herself forward or to attempt to outshine Emma in any way. Randalls—a substantial and architecturally very fine property— remained shut up. No new tenant had come to it who might challenge Miss Woodhouse's eminence and Highbury certainly had not the temerity to offer one—she was uncontested as she might not have been in a more populated or fashionable town.

But in the time of which we now tell, word came that Randalls had been let at last—let to a Mr Philip Mosley and his sister. Highbury was all agog to see them, alive with rumour as to their provenance. Where no facts are known it is natural for interested parties to conjecture them and Highbury gossip supplied the notion that the new tenants at Randalls were Mulattoes, children of a West Indian plantation owner, come to England for the first time. Or, that they were an elderly, superannuated clergyman and his spinster sister. Or that he was a disgraced younger son of a peer and his companion was his mistress who only posed as his sister. They were rich, they were poor, they were respectable, they were reprehensible—every species of speculation was whispered about them as Randalls was opened up, staff engaged, furniture polished and gardens tidied. But the worst of their crimes was that, though the tenancy was signed in March, they did not make good their occupancy of the house until May. Miss Woodhouse, naturally, was very anxious to understand the status and derivation of her new neighbours. She hoped Miss Mosley would be young, timorous and glad to be taken under the wing of the mistress of Hartfield. If she were old, infirm and retiring, that might do just as well. Her greatest fear was that the new tenant at Randalls would be assured, well-travelled, fashionable and haughty, the kind of lady who would see in an instant that Miss Woodhouse was as green and insubstantial as a willow sapling.

Then, in a simple closed carriage and bringing with them but one modest cartload of luggage, they were known to be in residence. Mr Mosley was reported to be a very young gentleman—barely twenty years of age, with a somewhat drooped and depressed demeanour. His sister was several years his senior, very elegant and classically beautiful with extremely refined manners, but decidedly aloof and very superior in air. Emma quailed when she heard it, and put off making her introductory visit on the excuse of a cold.

Mr Knightley, Mr Paling and Mr Weston lost no time in calling upon Mr Mosley. He was invited to dine, to shoot, to play whist at the gentlemen's Thursday whist club, but all offers were declined. Messrs Cole, Coxe and Perry fared no better. Even Mr Woodhouse— Highbury's most gentle, friendly and innocuous gentleman—could not tempt young Mr Mosley from his own fireside; he was impervious to the very compelling inducements of a turn around the Hartfield shrubbery and one of Searle's very soft-boiled eggs. Miss Mosley reportedly sat immobile and silent during the gentlemen's visits, an expression of lofty disdain etched upon her features.

'They decline to be acquainted with us,' Mr Knightley said to Mr Weston one afternoon as they returned from another cordial approach to the tenant at Randalls. '*He* has returned no calls that I know of.'

'A very immature, inexperienced fellow,' Mr Weston agreed. 'Frank has more in his little finger than this man has in his whole person. He seems hardly fit to be out of the schoolroom. As to conversation—I tried politics, literature, architecture and travel—I could make no progress whatsoever. You?'

'I drew a blank on farming. I can categorically say he has no interest in livestock nor in arable, nor milling nor the smithy.'

'You exhausted your repertoire, then!' Mr Weston said, giving his friend a jocular slap on the shoulder. 'I fear I must leave you to contend with their reserve alone, Knightley,' he continued. 'I go to London again tomorrow. It is my time for meeting Frank, you know.'

'Ah, is that so? And you have heard categorically from him that he is to be spared by his aunt? Last year, you know …'

'Yes, I recall. He was prevented at the last minute. No, I have heard today that he and his uncle are on their way. Since the Churchills completed their tour the educational pretexts for Frank's visits to London have been dropped—in fact the tutor has been released from the Churchills' employ. Frank is twenty years of age now—a man. I wished him to go up to Oxford. I believe he wished it too. But Mrs Churchill decided that a tour would be equally beneficial, so that is what occurred. Unfortunately, they could not go to Europe—that, in the circumstances, was impossible—the Hebrides, Wales, Ireland and the most notable cathedral cities had to suffice. Nominally, he has his independence, except that his aunt will not allow him to exercise it. As far as *she* believes the only purpose of their present journey is to visit the tailors so that Frank can be fitted for new suits and shirts. She has no notion that he is to meet me.'

'I do not like the subterfuge of it, if I am candid with you Weston,' Mr Knightley said, hacking at some brambles with his cane. 'A boy—even a grown one—ought to be able to meet his own father if he likes it. Indeed, I think it detrimental if he does not. If he *can* not. I still feel the lack of mine every day.'

Mr Weston put his hand on his friend's arm. 'I am sure you do, George. He would be very proud of you. You walk in his footsteps.'

Mr Knightley smiled sadly, and then shook himself. 'I think we must try another tack with the Mosleys,' he said with enforced brightness. 'I wonder if any of the ladies have called on Miss Mosley yet?'

'Miss Woodhouse has not—she has a cold. I cannot speak for anyone else.'

'They must not delay or it will cause offense. It is not easy to determine who might be our best representative. Miss Woodhouse, I suppose, is our premier lady—although I would not for the world let her hear me say so. But she is so young; for all she might believe herself to be very worldly-wise, like young Mosley she is hardly more than a child. I suspect her cold—she was perfectly well when I saw her last. No doubt she is daunted by Miss Mosley's reputation.'

'Mrs Bates has manners that no one can find objectionable, and a warm, genuine kindness that might do very well,' Mr Weston suggested.

'Oh yes,' Mr Knightley demurred, 'but she rarely stirs abroad without Miss Bates who, I fear …'

'Oh no,' Mr Weston agreed, 'on no account. Not if we ever wish to be admitted to Randalls again.'

'I wonder if we might prevail upon Mrs Paling. She could take her girls. All women—even unmarried ones—love children, do they not?'

'It may well be that the Mosleys have come to Highbury in search of seclusion and retirement. They may wish for no company and seek no society,' Mr Weston speculated.

'Well, as to that, they have come to the wrong place!' Mr Knightley said with a wink.

Mrs Paling did call upon Miss Mosley but she did not take her children with her. It happened that her mother, Mrs Winwood, had invited herself to the vicarage for an extended stay while her husband toured the Holy Land. Mrs Winwood—the reader may dimly recall—was a very stout, self-important and formidable lady whose husband had for a short time ministered to the Highbury flock before being transplanted to the more fertile soil of the archdeaconry. She was not a lady by any means to be put off by conceited reserve or cold looks. She accompanied her daughter to Randalls very determined to glean as much information about the new tenants as possible.

'I'll not be temporised by hoity-toity manners,' she declared as her daughter drove the gig towards Randalls. 'If Miss Mosley hopes to wither us by pride and disdain she must think again. I am disgusted by people who consider themselves too important for common courtesy.'

'We do not know her situation,' said Mrs Paling. 'It may be that she labours under some trouble that we know nothing of.'

The ladies were fortunate to find Miss Mosley alone in the sunny drawing room. She sat very stiffly on an upright chair and held a piece of needlework in her hands. She rose as they were announced, and greeted them with chill formality before gesturing them towards a hard settle not designed to encourage anyone to sit very long upon it. Mrs Winwood launched in with a volley of grandiloquent pronouncements, throwing asunder platitudes and postulated notions, asking questions and largely supplying the answers in an attempt to establish herself as a person who must be deferred to even by the lady of the house. Miss Mosley gave monosyllabic replies or simply a stately nod of her head, offering nothing whatsoever in the way of information. After a quarter of an hour the visitors were as uninformed as to the history, family connections or characters of Mr and Miss Mosley as they had been at the start. They could divine no reason for the Mosleys coming to Highbury and learned nothing of how long they might remain.

At last, even Mrs Winwood's fund of conversational gambits having failed, Mrs Paling gently remarked upon Miss Mosley's mourning costume and her hostess divulged that it was worn following the sudden death of their mother.

'Oh, the death of a parent is a dreadful thing,' Mrs Winwood cried. 'A *sole* parent?' She raised an enquiring eyebrow.

Miss Mosley indicated that her father still lived.

'And you do not stay with *him,* to relieve the burden of his sorrow?' Mrs Winwood's tone was barbed, implying a shocking dereliction of filial duty.

Miss Mosley bridled; the first truly natural, instinctive response she had made.

'Mama,' Mrs Paling said quietly, 'we do not know the circumstances. Perhaps there is some quarrel between the parties.'

Mrs Winwood sniffed, 'I should like to think that *regardless* of the state of relations between me and my daughters, something as grievous as death would supersede any trivial disagreement.'

'Perhaps the disagreement is not trivial,' Miss Mosley retorted.

'Indeed?' Mrs Winwood leaned against the back of the settle with an air of complaisant satisfaction, confident that she had broken the shell of Miss Mosley's reserve at last. 'Then you have my sincerest condolences,

Miss Mosley, and I speak with authority when I say that family rifts are the most heart-breaking things, between mother and daughter or,' she narrowed a speculative eye, 'between father and son?'

A slight widening of Miss Mosley's dark and brooding eye indicated that Mrs Winwood's arrow had hit the mark. With some instinct they could not explain, Mrs Winwood and Mrs Paling remained in attentive and expectant silence. It stretched out between the ladies until at last Miss Mosley said, 'My brother is the youngest of us, and was quite the apple of our mother's eye. He has acted in a way that has displeased our father—very materially and profoundly displeased him. For the better comfort of both, it has been thought convenient to …'

' … to put some distance between them?' Mrs Winwood interposed. 'Ah, well perhaps that is wise; they *say* that distance makes hearts grow fonder …'

'I hope most ardently for reconciliation,' said Mrs Paling feelingly.

'I fear,' Miss Mosley said, icily, 'that no distance they can possibly put between them will induce my father to forgive my brother. You will excuse me if I do not elucidate on private family concerns.'

Mrs Winwood was by no means ready to absolve Miss Mosley or to relinquish the advantage she felt she had gained. 'Is that so? Upon my word, your brother's crime must be serious indeed. He is in disgrace. A financial misdemeanour, perhaps?' she probed. 'Young men these days do run about so, do they not, and … run up debts?' Mrs Winwood paused, to see the effect of her conjecture. 'Or so I believe. I have no sons, Miss Mosley. I have raised seven daughters, but in doing that of course I have had a great deal to do with young men; seven daughters require seven husbands, you know.' She had not met Mr Mosley but her opinion of him had taken a decidedly downward turn. She inferred profligacy, gambling—every hue of pecuniary recklessness. 'Your brother must be a very dissolute young man,' she concluded.

'He most certainly is *not*,' Miss Mosley cried. 'I would not have *that* charge levelled at him. His conduct will have financial consequences, perhaps, but is not in its nature monetary.'

'Ah!' Mrs Winwood crowed, feeling that she had gained another point. 'Your father has cut him off, or threatens to. Well, the parable of the talents teaches us …'

'Mama,' interjected Mrs Paling, to prevent the misapplication of scripture she felt sure was in the offing, 'we do not know the nature of Mr Mosley's error—if there *has* been error—and it is not our place to preach.'

'No, indeed,' Miss Mosley said witheringly.

'You are quite right, Hermia,' Mrs Winwood allowed, 'but,' calculatedly blasé, 'if the quarrel is not over money, what *can* be its cause?'

The Highbury ladies looked enquiringly at Miss Mosley. This time she met their eye with steely determination; she had said enough, more than enough to satisfy these meddling village women.

'I think you said you were but lately returned from the Continent?' Mrs Paling enquired.

'Your mama suggested it and I did not contradict her,' Miss Mosley said. 'In point of fact my brother has been in the Indies. He travelled there via Lisbon.'

'Manners *abroad,* I believe,' Mrs Winwood speculated, 'are quite different from ours. One imagines little more than savages. There is the matter of language—so few foreigners speak English. Perhaps there was a duel?'

'Upon my word, madam, your insinuation could not be further from the fact,' Miss Mosley cried. 'My brother's manners are unexceptionable in any polite society, here or abroad. And he speaks fluent Portuguese. Also French, as a matter of fact, and some Italian.'

'Forgive us, ma'am, we meant no slur on your brother's character,' Mrs Paling said gently. 'He sounds like a very accomplished young man.'

'Indeed, he *is,*' Miss Mosley said, with more softness of feeling than she had yet evidenced. 'He would never get himself into a predicament of *that* sort. I doubt he knows how to fire a pistol. He has certainly never learnt sword-play.'

'Paling found him somewhat depressed in spirits, I think you said Hermia?' Mrs Winwood remarked.

Mrs Paling made a noncommittal sound. Her husband had passed no remark to *her* about Mr Mosley's mood and if he had, she would not have communicated it to her mama.

'He is wracked with guilt, perhaps?' Mrs Winwood probed.

'He has suffered the loss of his dear mama and in some way incurred the displeasure of his papa,' Mrs Paling chided. 'It is hard to imagine what worse afflictions a young man could be subject to. Mr and Miss Mosley deserve our utmost sympathy and prayers.'

'That may be,' her mama said, rising to her feet, 'but if there is anything reprehensible in her brother's character Miss Mosley ought to own it without delay. Some of us have daughters. If the man is guilty of ungentlemanly conduct, we should know it.'

Miss Mosley's infuriated expression implied that Mrs Winwood had at last hit the crux, or close to it, but she steeled herself, and rising, said, 'I think I must bid you good day, ladies. Your inquisition risks giving offense and I have duties about the house.'

Mrs Winwood withdrew, quite satisfied in her own mind that she had uncovered the mystery of the pallid, down-hearted Mr Mosley and his icy sister. As they made their adieus Mrs Paling pressed Miss Mosley's hand and whispered, '*Do* call on me. My mother can easily be got rid of.'

'Mark my words, Hermia,' Mrs Winwood said as the gig left Randalls' sweep, 'that young man has behaved dishonourably towards some young lady. The grief of it sent his mother to her grave and his father's disgust has manifested itself in banishment to Highbury. He will in all likelihood be disinherited. Well, I shall not notice him if he does deign to come into society.'

Chapter Eight

The other ladies of Highbury made their calls on Miss Mosley in quick succession. Miss Woodhouse made a remarkably speedy recovery from her indisposition to do so, the anxiety attendant on meeting Miss Mosley being eclipsed by the idea that Mrs Paling—and, worse, Mrs Winwood—had assumed precedence by calling first. All who met her declared Miss Mosley to be elegant and well-mannered but singularly uncommunicative. She returned no visits but it was made known that the change in air had occasioned some slight malady that kept her, for the time being, at home.

'On the whole,' Emma mused aloud to Mr Knightley, 'I think it is much better to be reticent in asserting oneself into unfamiliar society. Miss Mosley is quite right to take her time. One cannot immediately understand the delicate balance of relations between neighbours. It would be so easy inadvertently to cause offense by misunderstanding the little distinctions that lift one family just slightly above another.'

'I do not think Highbury is very fastidious on that score,' Mr Knightley said. They were, at the time, in the house of Mr and Mrs Cole where a varied representative sample of families was taking tea and playing whist. He looked around the assembled company. 'Everyone here is properly attired, polite and presentable. Who is to tell that one is superior to another?'

Emma thought she could very easily do so. No one wore a frockcoat of equal quality to her papa's and no lady who claimed any degree of social superiority would slurp her tea as Mrs Larkins did, but she forbore to say so as she knew that Mr Knightley would only laugh at her.

'Mrs Winwood is convinced that Mr Mosley is guilty of some very abominable crime towards a young lady,' she said. 'She has warned me against going abroad unchaperoned.' Young Mr Mosley had been seen wandering in the woods and fields adjacent to Randalls, a very dispirited and mournful figure.

'Mrs Winwood has not met Mr Mosley, so far as I am aware,' Mr Knightley said with a note of disapproval. 'Her information about the young man can only be speculation and conjecture. I do not think it is right to blacken his character.'

'She claimed the knowledge came from Miss Mosley, and Mrs Paling did not contradict her,' Emma said.

'I still doubt its accuracy. Young Mosley seems to me to be a mild-mannered gentleman, very young and somewhat green. He does not appear to me to be malevolent. Indeed, if I were to make a guess it would be that *his* heart has been ill-used, rather than the other way. That he is unhappy is very apparent. I am sorry Mrs Winwood has set her face against him. I will try to dissuade her from such harmful innuendo if I can. But this topic is hardly suitable. Let us speak of other things. Do you know that Miss Fairfax will be amongst us before long? I hope that *this year* you will try harder with her, Emma.'

'Oh, is she?' Emma sighed. 'I have escaped her two most recent missives or I suppose I would have known it was imminent.'

'You should not be lax in paying your respects to the Bateses as often as you pass by, Emma,' Mr Knightley advised. 'Mrs Bates is a very good person, compassionate and considered. I find her an excellent confidante—she is a good listener. If you ever needed to confide in a lady ...'

'She is *forced* to be a good listener,' Emma said with a laugh. 'Miss Bates gives one no other option. Look at Mrs Winwood now; craning her neck to gain her daughter's attention. She wishes to be released from her tête-à-tête!'

'As a good guest, then, you should lend her your aid. I will excuse you. I am very pleased that you are so alive to the little hints and signals that, when properly interpreted, can make social occasions pleasant and comfortable for everyone. *You* saw there what I did not. Off you go, Emma, and rescue Mrs Winwood.'

Emma had no option but to do as he asked. She crossed the room and sat beside Miss Bates on the low sofa. 'You will excuse me, Mrs Winwood,' she said when Miss Bates paused in her diatribe to draw breath, 'but Mr Knightley is most desirous of a few moments' conversation with you, if you would be so kind, and,' she said with a sigh, 'I have not had the pleasure of hearing from Miss Bates when we are to expect to have Miss Fairfax's company this year.'

Mrs Winwood said, 'Certainly, Miss Woodhouse,' and relinquished her seat with no very well concealed sigh of relief.

'Oh, Miss Woodhouse,' Miss Bates said, 'you are very kind, indeed you are. And I am so very happy to see that you have completely recovered from your cold. Mother and I were extremely concerned about you. I hope the beef tea we sent was some benefit? Really, there is so little—really nothing at all—which *we* can offer *you* in any way whatsoever, and you are so very good that the flow of kindness is all the other way. That mutton you sent the week before last was so very nice, and Patty stretched it into ever so many meals—such a generous quantity as you provided. I believe that what with pies and stews and cold cuts and turnovers we were eating it all week—for we have no icehouse, you know, no way of keeping things fresh, and whatever we get must be cooked and eaten promptly or … in short … but it was no hardship, none in the least. We both like mutton very much indeed, which was a good thing in this case, was it not?' She allowed herself a modest chuckle at her jest. 'But as I was saying, beef tea is something that mother *can* make, and her receipt has proved beneficial for ever so many people. I do not know how many flasks of it I have carried over the years, and everyone always says that they feel so much better afterwards. Of course I always call to enquire, and to collect the flasks, for one is not so very well supplied that one can afford to … but I digress, for what I really wish to know is whether you *are* now quite recovered, and to answer your kind enquiry about Jane, whose letter, as it happens, this being Wednesday, is to hand, and indeed I have it here, if you would care to look over it. I read it to Mrs Winwood just now. She was kind enough to say how well Jane writes, and indeed she does. When Jane *does* come, we are advised on no account to let her go abroad alone. Mrs Winwood is of the opinion that Mr Mosley is a very dangerous young man. I had no suspicion of it myself. I met him, you know, one day last week. He was in Mr Knightley's pastures and I had gone there to see if the elderflowers were ready, for, as well as beef tea, mother does make very good elderflower cordial. They were too inaccessible, however, but I saw him and he bade me good day quite like any ordinary gentleman, and in fact he did assist me over the stile for my hem had got caught in some brambles there—quite inextricably snagged. I had been there a good quarter of an hour, helplessly pinioned and I had just said to myself, "Hetty, you are in a pickle this time," when there he was. I do not know what I would have done if he had not ... but he was good enough to lend me his assistance and I had no suspicion of him being so very carnal and disreputable. If I had I would not have allowed him to release me, although, I suppose, I might have been there still for no one but me ever walks those paths, I believe! But here I am running on and I have not read you Jane's letter.' She began to rummage for it in her reticule.

'Oh Miss Bates,' Emma cried, 'my father rises from the whist table and I believe our coach is being called for. You must excuse me. You know he detests late hours and will certainly be ready to go home. I must forgo the pleasure of Miss Fairfax's letter until another day. Pray excuse me.' Thus she successfully managed to avoid even the salutation of Miss Fairfax's epistle, let alone its substance, and made her escape without further ado.

'It seems,' said Mr Woodhouse as they rode the short journey back to Hartfield, 'that I have mis-judged the young man at Randalls. Mrs Winwood says he is as black hearted as possible, a miscreant who is not to be trusted within half a mile of any respectable young lady. Emma, my dear, you will not take the gig out again without James or one of the other footmen to accompany you, and you will confine your walks to our own gardens.'

'Yes, Papa,' said Emma, without the least intention of allowing her freedom to be curtailed by any such interdiction. 'I will not set foot beyond Hartfield without Miss Taylor, for you know she has cared for and protected me since childhood and would allow no harm to befall me. It is not unusual for us to be joined in our walks by Mr Weston, so there is an additional safeguard. And for good measure we shall take Tartar with us.' Tartar was an old hound who was supposed to guard Mr Woodhouse's poultry houses but spent more time lying before the kitchen range than at his place in the yard. He was large and cumbersome but without the least particle of ferocity; he would make no very effective protector.

'Very good, Emma,' said Mr Woodhouse, not realising that she had effectively circumvented his interdiction against her leaving the grounds of Hartfield.

'And as to going out in the gig, you know that I cannot until Lady's lameness is cured.'

'No indeed, Emma, you must not, until the swelling is quite gone down. That could cause irreparable harm. Perry has supplied an emollient but he says in the meantime the horse must be rested.'

'I should not dream of putting her in danger, Papa. I shall not drive the gig until her foot is quite healed.'

'There, my dear,' Mr Woodhouse said, patting her hand. 'You are a very good girl.'

And so Mr Mosley's character was besmirched around Highbury, girls kept indoors and mothers righteously appalled at his supposed crimes. Whatever the nature of Miss Mosley's indisposition it did not necessitate the services of Mr Perry, which irritated Highbury regardless of her brother's infamy. If one was ill one ought to call on the local apothecary—not to do so was tantamount to a snub. If Miss Mosley was *not* ill, however, she ought to return her calls. Miss Woodhouse began to feel that Miss Mosley's wisdom in holding back from society had gone on too long; to withhold herself further could only be seen as insolence. Common courtesy dictated that Miss Mosley show herself at the doors of the ladies who had visited her and it decreed most especially that she present herself at Hartfield, the premier address in the district and the home of the foremost lady. In addition, Mrs Winwood's diligence in smearing the reputation of Mr Mosley was beginning to have the opposite effect to that intended. Far from being disgusted and afraid of Mr Mosley, Highbury's young ladies were quite intrigued by him. Miss Woodhouse found herself rather infected by their lurid curiosity.

'He must only go abroad at night, when there is a full moon,' said one of the Misses Coxe in Ford's. 'I imagine him to have a superfluity of hair about the face, and unnaturally pointed teeth.'

'Stupid girl,' her mother scolded, 'I forbid you to have such notions, and especially to voice them aloud. What will Miss Woodhouse think of you?'

Miss Coxe looked askance at Miss Woodhouse where she stood looking over lace trimmings at the counter.

'I wish she would take you under her wing,' her mother went on, loudly. 'She would teach you proper manners and what it is to be a lady.'

Emma pretended not to have heard but she liked the idea of a protégé, some grateful young person to groom and encourage, like a pet. She very much wished to have a particular friend. Miss Taylor, of course, was a friend, a very dear one, but an interesting scheme had suggested itself to Emma a few weeks previously when she and Miss Taylor had been caught in a sudden downpour in Broadway Lane. They had sheltered as best they could beneath the canopy of some overhanging trees, but the rain had been so prodigious that it had looked very much as though they would both be soaked through to their skin. Then Mr Weston had emerged from farmer Mitchell's gate carrying two umbrellas. He himself was as wet as possible, the water quite pouring from the brim of his hat, but he had held out the umbrellas to them. Miss Taylor had looked particularly doused, her bonnet all but disintegrated, its flowers woebegone and drooping and her hair loosed from its chignon and falling over her shoulders. But Mr Weston had been all chivalry, putting up the umbrella for her and holding it aloft, then offering his arm to assist her to safety. Emma had been left more or less to fend her herself but she had not minded too much. The picture of Mr Weston and Miss Taylor arm in arm in the rain had been a prepossessing one, and she had decided on the spot that she would make a match between them.[viii] Miss Taylor was precious to her and her loss would be grievous but the interest of the scheme, the manoeuvrings and intrigue attendant on moving them closer would compensate, and then there would be a vacancy. But Miss Coxe would not do. Oh no, decidedly, Miss Coxe would not do at all, pert and asinine as she was. Mr Knightley would have her befriend Jane Fairfax but that, too, was out of the question.

Chapter Nine

To the Bates' inexpressible pleasure—although Miss Bates did try most earnestly and comprehensively to express hers—Miss Jane Fairfax arrived in Highbury for her annual visit. That she was taller, her figure fuller, her beauty more refined was immediately evident from the moment she stepped down from the coach, and neither her aunt nor her grandmamma could restrain themselves from remarking upon it as they folded her into their embrace. The coachman carried Jane's trunks up the narrow staircase and into the room that Mrs Bates had vacated for the duration of Jane's visit.

'For, you know, it is not right that you should share with me now, Jane,' Miss Bates explained breathlessly when the alteration to their usual arrangement was discovered. 'Mother does not mind. We are both very small and will fit into the bed with no difficulty. If she has need of me in the night—not that she ever does—I will be on hand without the necessity of fiddling with the candle and finding my slippers and dressing gown and crossing the landing. It is a very small landing, to be sure! But, no, you see, you do me the greatest favour in the world by taking the smaller bedroom while you are here. Mother will hear of no other arrangements, will you Mother?'

Mrs Bates opened her mouth to add her assurances to Hetty's but swiftly shut it again as Miss Bates swept the conversation on to the Highbury news.

'Mr Knightley's housekeeper is in the process of re-ordering the pantries. The Donwell pantries, you know, are vast. *I* have been there several times to review the arrangements. Mr Knightley is so good as to think that my opinion counts for something—although I am sure I do not know what! He sends for me on the least pretext and I have had to quite abandon your poor grandmamma for whole afternoons at a time, for, you know, once I am down at the Abbey there are so many claims on me! Is that not something? His housekeeper, Mrs Hodges, is anxious to converse with me and it would be wrong to pass Mrs Larkins' door without stepping inside. I know Mrs Martin would never forgive me if she thought I had been so near to Abbey Mill Farm but not paid my respects. Grandmamma will never go to Donwell you know, that is, she will not go to Donwell Abbey—the house itself. I do not know why. No, it is quite a mystery that she has never explained to me. So she will not come with me but stays here quite alone for hours together while I am away. I do not suppose Mr Knightley realises what a sacrifice it is for her, when he requires me at Donwell. But she does not complain. She does her knitting and sometimes Mrs Cole is so good as to call in. I believe she has sometimes taken herself out for a walk up and down the High Street or even further afield. But now you are come, dear Jane, and she will not be alone if I am from home. Oh! What luxury!' turning to her mother, 'Will it not be a luxury, Mother, to be spared the boredom of your own company? I am sure it shall. So now, Jane, Patty is making tea and we have some very nice Madeira cake that Mrs Perry has sent.'

Jane and Mrs Bates exchanged a look that was full of understanding. Mr Knightley knew what he was about in summoning Miss Bates to Donwell and Jane would in no way impinge on her grandmother's few hours of blessed solitude and quiet. 'I very much enjoy a walk in the Highbury countryside,' she said, 'indeed it is one of the things I look forward to *most*. I am sure Grandmamma will not wish me *always* to be indoors with her.'

Mrs Bates indicated that nothing could be further from her desire. The wholesomeness of fresh air, the benefits of exercise, the splendour of the local scenery—all these were communicated by her decided shake of the head and a hand positively raised in denial.

'Oh, but you cannot walk abroad alone, Jane,' Miss Bates said. 'There is danger. A newcomer to Highbury—a Mr Mosley—he is not to be trusted. He has behaved abominably towards a young lady. He is known to be licentious. His sister keeps watch on him night and day. To be sure *I* met him once and he seemed all courtesy and kindness. I was in one of my scrapes—you know how I do fall into them! I saw nothing about him that alerted me to the least peril, but Mrs Winwood says it is certainly the case and so you must by no means venture out alone.'

'I am sure that this young man cannot be as bad as he is being painted,' Jane said reasonably. 'He would have been detained if he posed such a risk as you suggest.'

'Well, that is a strange thing, Jane, for Mr Knightley is of your opinion,' Miss Bates said. 'Indeed, he has made it his business to call on Mr

Mosley several times. *He* says Mr Mosley is more sinned against than sinning and that the Highbury rumourmongers should hold their tongues. I do not know. Mrs Winwood was quite convinced of his delinquency and has brought many round to her way of thinking. But the Mosleys are reclusive, taciturn people—*that* is beyond dispute. Mother and I went to pay our respects and I declare that if *I* had not filled the silence with conversation we would have sat in utter silence for quarter of an hour. Not that it is any hardship for *me* to talk—I know my own Achilles heel! Thankfully I was able to relate what I knew of Randalls' history—not that it is much. I dimly recall a family living there when we were at the vicarage but it was empty long before your grandpapa passed away. The Bramhalls were there a good few years and I told Miss Mosley about them and particularly about the improvements that had been made before they took possession. It was just before the old squire died. Such a horrible accident. Your mother and grandmamma were in Brighton at the time. Oh Mother, do not fidget. *Here* is your handkerchief. I put it on the table next to your knitting. Tea will be here directly. Miss Mosley seemed not very interested. She admitted to some fine specimens in the shrubbery but that was all she did offer in the way of remark and I must say, having been there, the place is nothing to how it was. The décor was quite shabby. Perhaps that is why the rent is low. If it *is* low! I must not speculate. It is none of my concern. Here is Patty. Thank you, Patty. Put the tray there and I will pour.'

It went without saying that Jane would be taken to visit all those who interested themselves in her welfare. She must be displayed to Mrs Cole, Mrs Perry, Mrs Goddard and Mrs Ford but Hartfield, naturally, was their first port of call. The young ladies spent a mutually unhappy half an hour exchanging enquiries regarding their respective families' health and making observations about the weather before Jane, at Miss Bates' insistence, said a few words about her recent visits to Vauxhall Gardens, Sadler's Wells and Drury Lane. It was delicate. Miss Woodhouse, for all her self-importance, led a sheltered, parochial existence. *She* had never—and possibly *would* never—be able to experience anything similar.

'Colonel and Mrs Campbell certainly do exert themselves on your behalf,' Miss Woodhouse remarked when Jane's brief account had come to a close. 'How *grateful* you must be.'

Jane murmured her agreement.

'Oh indeed,' enthused Miss Bates, 'we cannot express our thanks sufficiently. The Campbells are *so* very good. Only last month they engaged a new maid to attend Jane and Miss Campbell. One maid dedicated to them alone! French, if you please! Can you imagine? It is for the arrangement of their hair, you know, and to assist them with dressing, and to take care of their gowns. Oh! So *many* gowns! For walking and riding, for being at home and for being out! I declare they are out in society every day, or, if they are not, they receive callers at home. Oh! Jane's life in London is quite a whirl! I declare I can hardly keep up with all her engagements! They *had* been served by one of the housemaids—*she* had looked after those things since they came out of the nursery and was a sweet and biddable little thing. But she had no notion of how ladies arrange their hair these days, or of the new line for gowns, or how a kerchief should be properly draped around the neckline. Of course, the new maid has all the new styles to a nicety. The

French, I think, are considered to be in the vanguard of such things. And you see the result! Does not Jane look beautiful? Of course, here, with us, she manages for herself, and does so very becomingly, but with the Campbells everything is done for her, quite as though she were a great lady.'

Miss Woodhouse pressed her lips together. She had had the same maid for ten years or more and she could not answer for the arrangement of her hair or the line of her gown being absolutely à la mode, and as for a kerchief, she did not think she possessed one. Miss Fairfax certainly did look infuriatingly stylish. 'My sister writes of London fashion,' she said, passing over Miss Bates' speech and declining to offer the compliment that it had been designed to wring from her. 'She tells me that no one of taste would think of emulating anything that originated in France. Fashion abroad is extraordinary—quite shocking. I do not think it would be considered altogether polite here in Highbury. There is a saying about silk purses but I cannot recall it just now.'

'Oh, to be sure …' Miss Bates faltered, feeling that some rebuke had been offered but not quite sure what it had been.

Jane felt herself going hot with indignation on her aunt's behalf. 'I fear that we must draw our delightful visit to a close, Aunt,' she said stiffly. 'The dinner hour approaches and Miss Woodhouse will wish to dress.'

Emma was already as dressed for dinner as she would ever be. 'Touché,' she thought to herself with reluctant admiration, 'I suppose I deserved that.'

In the meantime, Miss Bates had rallied herself sufficiently to say, 'We are invited to drink tea at the vicarage this evening. I hope we shall have the pleasure of seeing you there, Miss Woodhouse?'

Emma stiffened—she had not been invited. 'Regrettably I have another engagement this evening,' she said untruthfully.

Chapter Ten

It happened that Mrs Winwood was absent from the vicarage for a short period and Mrs Paling took advantage of her mother being away to prevail upon Miss Mosley and her brother to attend a small, very select evening party. Apart from the Bateses, Mr Knightley was to be the only other guest and the Mosleys had been assured of a cordial reception. It had become all too clear to them that while their failure to return calls, patronise Mr Perry or shop at Fords had caused a certain amount of dismay, rumours about Mr Mosley had added materially to Highbury's dudgeon; people were offended and Mrs Winwood had been so successful in her rumourmongering that some of them were also afraid. Therefore Mrs Paling determined—and Mr Knightley agreed—that a quiet introduction to Highbury society would help to smooth matters out, silence the gossips and put a lie to the fevered insinuations that were rampant concerning Mr Mosley.

When the Bates party arrived at the vicarage Mr and Miss Mosley were yet to arrive—they had been deliberately invited some quarter of an hour later so that there would be time to seat Mrs Bates in a comfortable chair and for Mrs Paling to explain her scheme.

'Ladies,' Mrs Paling began, 'I am glad to have this opportunity to lay matters out to you as honestly and succinctly as I can. Mr Mosley and Miss Mosley have been labouring under the burden of private troubles it is no business of mine—or of anyone—to speculate about. And yet this is *just* what has occurred; half-truths and idle musings have been put abroad, exaggerated and taken as fact. Conjecture about Mr Mosley is rife to the point—in some quarters—of hysteria. One of Mrs Goddard's pupils became so afraid she swooned quite away. It is uncharitable and unchristian as well as ridiculous. To set matters onto a better footing Mr Paling and I, and Mr Knightley, agreed that Highbury has no kinder, more compassionate or right-thinking family than yours. We quite rely upon your natural generosity to make Mr and Miss Mosley feel welcome. No one in Highbury is thought of more highly than you or is more generally popular. If *you* contradict, when you can, any misinformed gossip that might be abroad we can be certain that this silliness will be at an end.'

'If we exert ourselves, the rest of Highbury will follow,' Mr Knightley said.

'For my part I am happy to say Mr Mosley is a polite and unexceptionable young man,' Miss Bates said. 'I always *have* said so. But it is not easy to contradict Mrs Win … those who speak with such decided authority.'

'I believe it is difficult—if not impossible—to judge a person before one is thoroughly acquainted with them,' Jane said quietly.

Mrs Bates smiled her approval.

A little movement in the passageway alerted them to the Mosleys' imminent arrival. The door opened and Miss Mosley walked into the room followed by her brother, and Mr Knightley stepped forward to shake Mr Mosley's hand.

Miss Mosley, seeing Mrs Bates and Miss Bates by the fireplace, approached them directly. 'I offer you my heart-felt apology,' she said, a look of contrition on her face. 'I have not returned your call—I have made *no* calls. My brother and I believed—mistakenly, Mrs Paling thinks—that we were each other's best remedy in our grief and trouble.'

'Oh, Miss Mosley,' cried Miss Bates, 'do not concern yourself for one moment on our account. We are so very happy to see you *now*. I wonder if I might do myself the great honour of presenting my niece. This is Jane. Jane Fairfax. My sister's child. She resides with a Colonel and Mrs Campbell …' Miss Bates drew Miss Mosley down on a sofa between herself and Jane and related, at length and some volume, the entirety of Jane's history. This effectively smoothed over the awkwardness attendant on the Mosleys' arrival. Soon tea was served and not very long after that Miss Mosley could declare herself as thoroughly acquainted with Miss Fairfax's situation as if she had known her for a lifetime.

After tea the doors between the drawing room and the morning room were opened up and Jane was invited to play the pianoforte, something she did with great skill and taste as well as enormous enjoyment—without Rowena present, she could give full rein to her powers.

During tea Mr Paling and Mr Knightley had monopolised most of Mr Mosley's attention, to save him the discomfort and the ladies the immediate awkwardness of direct conversation. He was a tall, slender young man who had not quite gained the breadth of figure or maturity of feature which would characterise his adult appearance some three or four years hence. Nevertheless, he was strikingly good looking; pale complexioned with large, dark eyes, a sensitive mouth and very dark hair. He spoke little but what he did say was eloquently spoken in a quiet, well-modulated tone.

After Jane had sung, he made his way across the room to congratulate her. 'I play a little myself,' he murmured, 'but not half so well as you, and I do not sing at all. I have neither the voice nor the confidence for it. But you sing *very* well Miss Fairfax, if you will allow me to say so.'

'You are very kind, sir. I have had the great good fortune of being the recipient of good teaching, and I have the use of an excellent instrument at home—that is, in Bute Square, where I am so fortunate as to reside with my guardians Colonel and Mrs Campbell.'

'But no teacher—be he ever so good—and not even the most exemplary instrument can make an indifferent player into a superior one,' Mr Mosley remarked. Having overheard the majority of Miss Bates' minute exegesis of Jane's circumstances he felt emboldened to enquire, 'You have no pianoforte to play while you are in Highbury?'

Jane shook her head.

'I will ask my sister to invite you to Randalls,' Mr Mosley offered. 'The instrument there is tolerably good, I think.'

Jane's eyes widened and she caught her breath. It would be a delight to her to practice her music and—if she were truthful—the opportunity to escape the confines of the rooms above the grocer's shop would also be welcome.

But Mr Mosley misconstrued her expression. He took a step backwards. 'You need have no fear of encountering *me*,' he said. 'I spend most of my days out of doors. I walk a great deal.'

'Oh sir, you misapprehend me,' replied Jane with feeling. 'You offer me such an opportunity as I had not looked for. I miss playing exceedingly when I am with my grandmamma and aunt, although,' (lowering her voice a little), 'I would not wish them to know it. They set such store by my visits, and are *so* exceedingly kind. I would not like them to think I lack *anything*.'

Mr Mosley's frown cleared. 'Ah! I understand you completely and,' (leaning a little closer), 'I will be discreet. I thought for a moment … but I see you are not of the general Highbury ilk.'

There was no reply Jane could make to this so she said, 'Where do you walk, sir? Have you climbed up to see Widowbower? It is an ancient copse on the top of one of the hills hereabouts. It is one of my favourite walks. On a clear day the views are exceptional.' She paused before going on, 'There are local anecdotes—very ghoulish and fanciful—but,' she gave him a level look, 'I set no store by those.'

Mr Mosley smiled his understanding and his gratitude. His eye glazed a little but he replied, 'I think I *have* been there, although I did not know its name. One of the trees must have fallen in the winter storms. I sat on it for an hour or more and sketched the view. I like to draw, Miss Fairfax. It calms the mind, although I have an indifferent hand.'

'I have also taken my sketch book there, many times,' Jane said, waving away his self-deprecating remark. 'It would be interesting to compare our renditions.'

The Palings' maid crept into the room to whisper something to her mistress.

'Oh,' Mrs Paling said, a little nonplussed. 'Well, I suppose you had better show her in.'

The maid went out for a moment before announcing Miss Woodhouse.

Emma stepped into the room, took in the company, started very theatrically and said, 'Oh! Forgive me Mrs Paling. I had no notion that you were entertaining company or I would not for the world have intruded. Your maid can give me the small assistance I require. Excuse me. Good evening.' She began to back out of the room, apparently determined to impose herself no further and yet managing very successfully to survey the room to make herself mistress of all that transpired there. So *this* was what had been plotted behind her back! A clandestine introduction of the Mosleys into Highbury society and *she* had been excluded!

'Oh, Miss Woodhouse,' Mrs Paling protested, 'we are all friends here. Pray do not stand on ceremony. What is amiss? How can we help you?'

'The smallest inconvenience, it is really nothing at all,' Emma prevaricated. '*I* was determined to go on but Miss Taylor insisted I call here for aid.'

'What has occurred, Emma?' Mr Knightley asked, stepping forward.

Emma gave a little laugh, 'Just the silliest thing. Miss Taylor and I decided upon an evening stroll. The air is so agreeable, is it not, and my father is so occupied re-cataloguing his button compendium that we thought we could be spared for half an hour. But my lace, you see,' she indicated her foot, where one boot-lace dangled and another had become sheared off, 'there is something amiss with it and I hoped for a piece of string or something to effect a temporary repair ...'

'Come in, come in,' Mr Paling said, motioning Miss Woodhouse towards a seat. 'And let Miss Taylor also be brought in—she must not wait outside in the twilight all alone …'

'Oh, she is *not* alone,' Emma interrupted with a gleeful light in her eye, 'for we encountered Mr Weston on our walk. He is returned from London. I believe he was on his way to Donwell Abbey, Mr Knightley, to see if you were at home.'

'Let them *both* come in then,' Mr Paling revised. He knelt down before Miss Woodhouse and began to remove her boot. 'I can see to this in an instant,' he said, 'if you will allow me.'

And so, her ruse meeting with success, Miss Woodhouse insinuated herself into the Palings' at-home. She sat with extreme complaisance, her foot upon a stool as though it was injured—which of course it was not—as fresh tea was brought for her and while Miss Mosley begged her forgiveness. At last, Mr Mosley was brought forward to be introduced, leaving Jane alone by the pianoforte until Mr Weston entered the room with Miss Taylor.

Emma engaged Mr Mosley in lively, tinkling conversation, her eyes— very bright with pleasure at her cleverness—scrutinised him minutely as she attempted to draw him out. *She* saw no hint of brutishness about him, no wildness of expression or leering quality of speech that could justify the macabre rumours that had been prevalent in Highbury. She congratulated herself very thoroughly on having found out the truth and undertook to quash any suggestion that Mr Mosley was anything other than a perfectly respectable young gentleman. She would notice him, and, what was more, she would do so before the Palings could claim it as their success. If Miss Emma Woodhouse admitted Mr Mosley's acquaintance, who in Highbury would dare to snub him?

Mr Mosley suffered Miss Woodhouse's assault of cordiality with the look of a cornered animal. His quiet conversation with Miss Fairfax had been one thing, *this* was quite another. Mr Paling read the situation very speedily and said, 'Let us go into the gardens, Mosley. The night is very clear. Are you interested in astronomy at all?'

'You must forgive my brother,' said Miss Mosley when the two had disappeared into the gloom of the vicarage garden. 'Neither of us is really fit for society. If you knew how he girded himself even for this agreeable, small and very select party.'

'Oh, and I have intruded upon it unconscionably,' said Miss Woodhouse, fumbling with her boot. 'My lace is quite fixed and there is no reason for me to impose myself further. I quite upbraid myself for my rudeness. Miss Taylor! We must return to Hartfield. Papa will be anxious. Good evening.'

Mr Weston felt no compunction about having joined the party uninvited, certain that he *would* have been included if his being returned from London had been known. He was fresh from his time with Frank and full of his son's praises. 'He has been on a tour of Britain, you know Miss Fairfax,' he said when Miss Taylor and Miss Woodhouse had quit the room. 'He toured quite extensively with his tutor. His aunt and uncle accompanied them—*that* inhibited their travels somewhat. Mrs Churchill cannot abide any degree of privation and she is not a good sailor—I know *that* from personal experience. Frank and Tunnock were able to spend some time away from her in the Lakes, but then she sent word and they had to return before half the peaks they had determined to climb had been conquered. They repaired to Buxton but Frank said it was very dull and Mrs Churchill derived no benefit from the waters, so they continued south-west. Frank very much wished to see Land's End but they got no further than Plymouth before Mrs Churchill found she must turn back. St Michael's Mount and the Scillies had to be quite given up. Frank *wished* to go on but was unable to do so. Ah! He is like me, at that age, and, if I may say so, Miss Fairfax, like your dear mama, who shared my thirst for travel. In the end she journeyed further than I! God rest her soul,' he paused and looked away, momentarily subdued. When he looked up again it was with eyes quite dewy. 'Your mama was … I hope you do not mind my saying … She was a *remarkable* young woman. You have some of her looks. I own to you, whenever I see *you*, I think of *her*. Ah! But …' shaking himself, 'returning to Frank: it is wrong, Miss Fairfax, for a young man in his majority to be so constrained, do you not agree? It disturbs me greatly. Frank wished to read for a degree at University—he is more than able—but the idea was vetoed by his aunt; *she* would not release him. So an extensive tour of the country was suggested as an alternative; equally formative, just as useful in its way, I suppose. But I feel it was not as efficacious as it could have been. To have his aunt and uncle in tow … He should have been able to step into his independence. But there it is. So now Frank must cool his heels and wait … well, it is distasteful to elucidate further. I am sure you understand me. I hope to prevail on Frank to come to Highbury. He is well thought of here—as *you* are— considered quite a native although he has never set foot here in his life! I am surprised you have not encountered him in London for the Churchills are there often, now. You have not, I suppose?'

Jane shook her head. 'I have not had that pleasure.'

'And a pleasure it *would* be,' Mr Weston enthused, 'I hope you will forgive me for saying so. I am biased, of course! But I think even a disinterested observer would say that Frank is a handsome, intelligent and well-mannered young man. He is lively, with something of a mischievous wit. I am sure his aunt disapproves. He is like *his* mama in that, as you are like *yours*.'

'I do not remember my mama,' Jane said quietly. 'Mrs Campbell speaks of her occasionally. She speaks of the late Mrs Weston also, although I do not think they were very well acquainted.'

'She will have told you of Louisa's daring escapade, I suppose. She was engaged to a young rake—not *her* choice, but once again Mrs Churchill had prevailed. He treated her abominably and they parted, but, as is always the case in such matters, Louisa bore the brunt of society's censure. She became untouchable for any eligible young men of family and wealth. The taint of scandal, be it never so deserved, does not wash clean easily Miss Fairfax. It is shocking that rational men and women can be so morally blind, but they *are*. Ah well! I should not judge. It is an ill wind that blows *nobody* any good and so it proved to be for me. *I* knew the truth about Louisa and I had nothing to lose and much to gain in the alliance.'

'Mrs Weston was fortunate.'

Mr Weston considered. 'I will own to you that *she* was not always certain of it. Her family objected to me and threw us both off once we were married. Although she married me freely, I had ample evidence that she resented the rift with her brother for my sake. For a person to marry against the wishes of their family is a great evil, Miss Fairfax. But, on my own account, I considered myself fortunate. Of course, if I had *not* married Louisa Churchill, I might well have married ... but it is fruitless to think of it now. The party is breaking up. It has been a pleasure to converse with you. I must pay my respects to Mrs Bates before Mr Knightley's carriage takes you all away. Good night to you, Miss Fairfax.'

Chapter Eleven

Mr Knightley's need for Miss Bates' advice on the arrangement of his pantry shelves did not diminish. She went to Donwell secure in the knowledge that her mother had Jane to attend to any little needs that might arise in her absence and that Patty had been fully instructed as to the dishes for dinner. If she thought of the ones she had left at home at all—and she scarcely did, so numerous and absorbing were the little things that must be mulled over and decided, tried out, compared and contrasted—she thought of them as quietly reading, knitting or—in her mother's case—snoozing until she should return.

How surprised she would have been to know that almost as soon as the hem of her skirt had brushed the doorstep her mother was out of her chair, Jane standing ready to assist with her shawl and basket. They would be out on the High Street together before Miss Bates had gained the gates to Donwell Abbey's long driveway. Mrs Bates would take a long and circuitous path up and down the street, calling at every shop, greeting every neighbour, happy to have, for once, the opportunity to speak for herself and to hear her friends' accounts without incessant interruption, unnecessary repetition or misinterpretation. Jane would accompany her until the outer limits of the village, when she would walk off by herself into the Highbury countryside.

Usually she met nobody, and this pleased her greatly. She enjoyed the solitude, the opportunity for thoughts to chase themselves at random through her head. The weather remained exceedingly fine—warm sun, a slight breeze—and the fields, woods and hedgerows were at their glorious best. *These,* she told herself, these simple pleasures and natural blessings, were the luxuries that would have to content her in years to come. Occasionally she encountered another—a farmer, a boy employed to scare birds or a milk maid driving the cows home for milking—and would gladly exchange a few words before walking on. She walked with no special object in view, letting pathways entice her as they would, exploring one day a field, another a copse, and she sought no companion. But, since meeting Mr Mosley at Mrs Paling's evening party she did keep half an eye out for a glimpse of his tall, slender figure, the smudge of his dark hair above the intense green of the hedgerow. Knowing that he habitually roved the countryside made it not unlikely that she would at some point encounter him and so it happened that when she came across him balanced on a gate looking intently across a swathe of green wheat, she evidenced no surprise but simply bade him good day.

He had been lost in thought and her voice brought him abruptly from his reverie. His face, when he turned it to her, despite the warmth of the day and the enlivening effect of the ruffling breeze, was pale, his eyes large and unhappy. Dark shadows beneath and creases at the outer corners suggested powerfully the notion that his whole visage had been furrowed with extreme melancholy. Nevertheless, he shook himself, jumped down from the gate and held out his hand.

'Good day, Miss Fairfax,' he said, and she thought she discerned some measure of genuine pleasure at seeing her. He indicated the view over the gate. 'This is a pleasant prospect, is it not? I have my sketchbook here,' he patted a large pocket in his coat, 'and some pencils. I was contemplating attempting it but,' he indicated the gate, 'my seat was somewhat precarious! I think I may well have toppled off.'

'If you will allow me,' Jane said, 'I can show you a place where you may sketch in relative comfort. I have done so myself in years gone by.'

They were standing in a green lane, hedged on either side by hawthorn entwined by dog-rose and wild honeysuckle. Jane motioned that they should proceed through the gate.

'By all means,' Mr Mosley said, showing with a gesture that she should lead the way.

Jane opened the gate and they passed into the field together. They walked along its periphery, up the natural incline of the slope until they came to a little stand of deciduous trees and a semi-circle of boulders that had been dug from the earth in years past and moved to the corner that they would not impede the plough. 'This is the place I meant,' she said, holding her hand out to show the stones, which were flat and smooth and, because of the overhanging canopy of the trees, perfectly shady.

They turned to survey the view that opened out before them.

'I believe this is a better vantage point, also,' Mr Mosley declared. 'Now I can see the church tower in the distance. It will make an excellent focal point for my drawing.'

Jane smiled. 'I will leave you to your work, sir,' she said, preparing to withdraw.

But Mr Mosley said, 'On no account. I pray—if you would be so kind—that you would keep me company for a while. I have had the benefit of so little conversation since I came to Randalls. Indeed, I have been fit for none, I suppose. I blame no one but myself. But I feel …it would comfort me …' He paused and looked away. 'Unless you are expected elsewhere? I would not detain you,' he concluded.

Jane looked at the sky—the sun was still high. 'I think I have an hour yet, before I must return,' she said, lowering herself onto one of the boulders. 'But I shall not bother you with idle chatter. Please get out your sketchbook and begin.'

Mr Mosley did so, and sketched diligently for some half an hour, seeming to be lost in his work except that he did, from time to time, allow his head to turn just a little, did glance at Jane's feet as they rested on the grass, did dare to raise his eyes to her face to see her steady gaze and expression of repose as she looked over the landscape before them.

'There,' he said at last, holding his paper out at arm's length to consider his rendition. 'I think I have enough to serve me. I may try a watercolour.'

'May I look at your other sketches?' Jane asked, holding out her hand.

He passed her the book without hesitation and she leafed through it, seeing views she knew well; cosy farmhouses, the mullions and chimneys of Randalls, architectural features of the church as well as sketches of fallen trees and botanical studies of flowers. Then she came to some pages that were filled with portraits—all of the same young woman. They showed her seated and standing, laughing, resting, reading, reflected in a mirror by candlelight. The pictures were intimate in that there was clearly easiness between the artist and his subject; her eyes looked out of the page with unveiled affection, frankness and trust.

'Ah,' said Mr Mosley with a sigh, 'you have found my pictures of Susannah.'

Jane handed the sketchbook back. 'She is a beautiful young lady,' she remarked.

'She is,' he agreed, but then amended, 'she *was.*'

The look Jane had fleetingly seen on Mr Mosley's face earlier returned to it now—an agonised, contorted expression, bitter with regret. He passed his hand over his face a few times as though to wipe it away.

'She is …' Jane began.

'Oh, no, not *dead,*' Mr Mosley burst out, 'at least, I pray not. But she is destroyed. *I* have destroyed her.' His voice betrayed such recrimination and self-loathing as Jane would not have believed possible.

'Come now,' she said gently, 'surely she will rally. Surely you do not bear the whole burden of blame, if there *is* blame. It is rare, I think, for any situation—be it ever so bleak or hard to bear—to have but *one* single cause. These things come about little by little; a misunderstanding, a word spoken or withheld, in-built prejudice, simple ignorance or a moment of thoughtlessness. These things, comparatively little in themselves, compound upon one another. In the end, who can say which single one was to blame?'

'Oh there *is* blame,' Mr Mosley said warmly. He paused. His eyes roved over the fields before them but saw nothing of them now—he saw only some inner landscape, a scene of error and unfairness and cruelty.

'Perhaps,' he said at last, and his voice was calmer, 'perhaps you are right—you, who know nothing of the matter—have with some innate wisdom and, I suspect, some profound quality of gentleness and kindness, got closer to the truth than I have yet managed.'

Jane said nothing, sensing that to do so would dislodge Mr Mosley's delicate balance on the cusp of some new understanding.

'Would you allow me to tell you about Susannah?' he asked hesitantly.

'I would be happy to hear anything you wish to tell me,' Jane said.

Mr Mosley got up and held out his hand. 'Very well. But we will talk as we walk. I am mindful of your hour, you see. I would not be accused of detaining you beyond your time.'

Jane took his hand and he helped her to her feet.

Mr Mosley's story was not long in the telling and it seemed that it was a tale he had told himself many, many times. As he related it they retraced their steps along the green lane and through the woodlands that brought them back out onto the Highbury Road.

Mr Philip Mosley was the younger son of a busy, well-regarded but only moderately prosperous merchant whose business—the trade and conveyance of goods across the seas—was precarious. He had been well educated, destined to join his father and elder brother in the running of the family business. It was felt that *three* principals, who could, between them, treble the scope, the persuasive powers and the efficiency of one, would transform the enterprise into a notable, successful and very affluent concern. But young Philip Mosley felt disinclined to take part in the trade—for ethical reasons, and due to a strong vocation towards the church. The previous year he had gathered his courage to inform his father of his twofold reasons for resisting the family's plan. *This* was his first crime. His father's anger and disappointment had been extreme but his mother's dismay had given greater cause for the young man to tremble—she had become suddenly and severely ill.

Seeking to make reparation he had agreed to a voyage in pursuit of the business' object, in order to see if he could not reconcile his natural reluctance, which was instinctive and somewhat ideological, to the actuality of the thing. He had taken ship to the West Indies. On board he had become acquainted with a respectable family by the name of Brokenshire; father, mother and daughter. Mr Brokenshire was a chaplain appointed to minister at the newly built Trelawny Parish Church in Falmouth, Jamaica. His wife was a gentle, understanding and motherly soul. The daughter—Susannah—was a rare beauty, blessed with intelligence and wisdom, wit and virtue. Philip had fallen in love. The gentle prompting of the chaplain had strengthened Philip's sense that he was called to serve God and, in his love and kindness, had provided such a stark and unflattering comparison to Philip's father that the young man had begun to feel misused and resentful towards the man who had forced him to turn from his inclination and his vocation. He determined to write to his father as soon as the ship should dock, to refuse any part in the mercantile affairs of the business and to announce his engagement and imminent marriage to Miss Susannah Brokenshire.

Miss Brokenshire, however, had dissuaded him from this step. Although being as in love with him as he could wish, she deferred her agreement to be his wife until Philip should have returned home and sought his family's approval to the match. She had no wealth and no name to offer him, nothing at all that would be an inducement to the Mosley family to accept her as Philip's bride or to mitigate their disappointment in him. She ardently hoped that although Philip declined to take part in his family's business it would not necessarily mean that he had to break with them entirely. She urged him to speak to them with humility and respect but also with strength of purpose. She did not wish to be the cause of a family schism that would be painful, damaging and irreversible. At last Philip agreed. He was certain of himself and of her and was encouraged by her to believe his parents would ultimately relent if he approached them with due diffidence, honour and love.

All the company on board the ship knew of the young people's attachment and, once they disembarked and established themselves in Falmouth society, it was well known there too that the couple were as promised to one another as possible without being positively engaged. They had 'an understanding' that awaited only parental approval to be made official. This situation was common in the Indies, where many months were required to bring a letter from home. Society there assumed no impediment other than the vastness of the ocean and entertained the couple as an established pair.

Philip executed his father's business in the region but he did so with bad grace, his heart being distracted and his mind filled with abhorrence at its nature. Negotiations with the merchant he had gone there to meet went ill and then foundered altogether and when Philip parted from Susannah to set sail back to England it was without the contract, the deposit in gold coin or the assurances of future trade that he had been sent there expressly to get. This was his second crime. A blow, a setback and a disappointment—all these he knew it would be to his father. What he did not—could not—know was that his elder brother was at that moment travelling on the business' behalf in the East Indies, attempting to buy, on the surety of the money Philip was supposed to have secured, silks and spices to sell on the home market.

'And so,' Mr Mosley concluded as they made their way along High Street, 'you can imagine the rest. My father was confounded by my failure in the Indies—he had depended upon the success of the venture. The business teetered on a knife-edge and my brother was oceans away. My mother's condition worsened—with shock with disappointment ...'

'Or with the natural progress of her illness,' Jane put in quietly.

' ... and then she died. My father was inconsolable and violently angry. He blamed me for it all. He will not hear of my marrying Susannah, or any lady who cannot bring to the business what I have lost, or, preferably a great deal more. The company *must* have funds. He has a woman in mind—the widow of a man lately in the same line of trade— *she* will bring capital, contacts and a fleet of vessels. If I defy him he will cut me off entirely. So then where will I be? I could not afford even a steerage passage back to Jamaica and once I got there, what could I do? I am not ordained. I am fit for nothing.' He looked despairingly down at his hands. They were delicate and soft. 'I could not even cut sugar cane with these,' he lamented.

'And Susannah?' Jane prompted. The church clock showed only a moment or two before four o'clock, the Bates' dinner hour. She must go home.

'My failure to return and my family's refusal to endorse our engagement has been received very ill by polite society in Falmouth. They suspect some strong objection to her, something vicious they have yet to discover. She has given me up, of course. I am free and so is she. But she is ostracised and her family likewise. All the good they hoped to do … It has all come to nought. And I fear it has brought Susannah very low. The climate there, you know, is very unhealthy. I fear for her wellbeing.'

'As, I have no doubt, she fears for yours,' Jane said. 'To have loved, as you both have done, and, in acting honourably, to have been separated …'

' …is a terrible injustice, a waste and a needless sacrifice,' Mr Mosley said witheringly. 'We have both lost everything for the sake of others.'

'Not *everything,*' said Jane, very eager to find some glint of hope in the otherwise dark sea of Mr Mosley's situation, but unable, at that moment, to point it out.

'Susannah is lost to me. Of *that* there can be no doubt. Oh!' he threw Jane a look full of agony and desolation, 'that I had married her in Jamaica! *This* is the crime with which I most reproach myself Miss Fairfax. I should have followed my heart and married her. Then, regardless of what my father had said, she would have been respectable in society's eyes. We would still have been poor, separated, perhaps condemned never to have met again on earth, but I could have given her *that.*'

'No woman would wish to marry in defiance of family wishes,' Jane said, thinking about what Mr Weston had told her, 'it could only lead to unhappiness.'

Mr Mosley looked at her doubtfully, but took her hand. 'I cannot say how our conversation has eased me,' he said earnestly. 'There *is* no happy ending but to pour it out as I have done is a relief. And, I do begin to see that the blame is not *all* mine. My father's intractability has played a part. My mother's illness—perhaps it would have come upon her anyway. My business in Jamaica—the man I dealt with was objectionable and made quite as many difficulties as I.'

'I am glad you see things in a kinder light,' Jane said. She withdrew her hand. 'I hope I shall see you again Mr Mosley.'

'I hope so, too, Miss Fairfax,' he replied.

Chapter Twelve

It was Mr Knightley's annual custom to throw a summer dance for his tenants and neighbours and the day of it was now at hand. Mrs Winwood was by no wise persuaded that *she* would stand up with smiths and farriers and the lower orders. On the other hand, it would be an ideal opportunity to re-establish herself at the pinnacle of Highbury society; everybody in Highbury who was anybody would be present. This was the frame of mind in which she returned from London. It was unpleasant to learn, therefore, that there was some suggestion of error in her conduct towards the Mosleys. Hermia, indeed, was quite in high dudgeon over the matter, pointing out with a forcefulness Mrs Winwood had not known her capable of the very great injustice that had been done to Mr Mosley by her mother's wilful rumourmongering.

She chose to challenge her mother in her boudoir, when the maid had left Mrs Winwood defenceless in her night attire, her hair in curl papers and all her manifest authority laid aside, draped over clothes hangers or put away in the press.

'Mama, I must speak to you upon a subject which is uncomfortable,' Mrs Paling said, coming into the room with two cups of chocolate and seating herself on a low stool by the dressing room fire.

'My dear girl, you must feel no discomfort with *me*,' Mrs Winwood crooned, from her more comfortable chair on the other side of the hearth. 'I am your mama.'

'It is not *I* who will find our conversation painful. In your absence I have come at the truth about Mr Mosley.'

'Have you indeed? And what *is* the enormity of that young man's baseness?' said Mrs Winwood, sipping her chocolate. 'There is no evil I would not believe him capable of. Ah yes, indeed. Wickedness is always distressing to contemplate. I take no satisfaction in being right.'

Hermia removed a speck of something from the hearth and put it into the coal bucket. 'You are *not* right, in this instance. Mr Mosley's behaviour is so far from being reprehensible that I quite shudder at the ideas that have been broadcast in the town.'

'I am a very good judge of character,' Mrs Winwood said as archly as possible from beneath her nightcap. 'I am sure he is degenerate. You have been hoodwinked, Hermia. You are much too ready to believe well of people.'

Hermia got up to place her cup on the mantel and so that she could look down upon her mother who, in her shift and dressing gown, did appear very much reduced from her usual grandeur. 'You have not even been introduced to Mr Mosley and therefore you cannot possibly have formed an accurate opinion as to his character,' Hermia said sternly. 'The fact is that his character has been impugned. The vilest insinuations have been made. There is not a thread of truth in the wicked indictments that are abroad. People *now,* following the intervention of Mrs Bates and her daughter, and Mr Knightley, and others, are beginning to reverse their opinion of that poor, maligned young man but I must tell you, Mama, that by disseminating what was purely conjecture on your part you have made him even more unhappy than he was when he came here and he was sorely down-hearted *then*.'

Mrs Winwood quailed but said as stoutly as she could, '*I* bear no responsibility. If there *is* misapprehension—and I am by no means convinced of it—the fault lies with Miss Mosley. If she had owned the whole truth about her brother there would have been no need for conjecture. Where there is equivocation and unnecessary reticence, however, what *are* people to do but make assumptions?'

'Miss Mosley has a right to keep her own counsel, Mama, as you should have kept yours. What are the simple folk hereabouts to think? If *you* voice a suspicion of course they are going to adopt it and because they *are* simple people, they will exaggerate it. From being a young rascal—not that he ever *was* a rascal—Mr Mosley has become a vicious fiend. He has been reviled. One farmer threatened him with a pitchfork.'

Mrs Winwood did look a little ashamed. 'And you are quite sure that there is no substance to …'

Hermia shook her head. 'None whatsoever.' She sat down again and spoke more gently. 'People look to you for guidance, for an example.'

'Of course they do,' Mrs Winwood agreed readily.

'At the dance I look to you to lead the way in welcoming the Mosleys.'

Her mother gave an involuntary shudder. 'I will do no such thing. I shall not attend the dance, if they are to be there.'

Hermia sighed. 'Mama, there is nothing against them, no reason in the world to shun them and every reason in Christian charity to befriend them.'

'They are nothing to me!' Mrs Winwood declared. 'Miss Mosley did not return my call. Mr Mosley, so far as I know, has declined to be acquainted with Paling.'

'Since you went to London, all that has changed. We are now most cordially acquainted with the Mosleys.'

'What?' Mrs Winwood was aghast. It was her turn to rise and tower over her daughter. 'What have you done? What about my granddaughters? Are they to be polluted?'

Hermia faced her mama and although her heart beat very quickly and she felt her face flush very red she did not back down. 'You know nothing of Mr Mosley's history or situation. What do you imagine? That he foams at the mouth and grows talons? You are ridiculous! Do you think that I would welcome such a being into the vicarage, with my own daughters asleep upstairs? There is no question of pollution, Mama. It is only your prejudice and lurid imagination that believes it. You must shake it off. Mr Mosley is a gentleman.'

'He is a villain!' cried Mrs Winwood, but with less conviction.

'No, he is not. He is a perfectly affable, if rather shy and disillusioned young man.'

Mrs Winwood made no reply. She faced Hermia for a few moments. Then she turned and stirred the coals in the grate. 'I believe the dance will be a very rustic, inelegant affair,' she said, 'and I am tired after my journey.'

Hermia allowed herself a wry smile. She had won a small victory.

Mrs Winwood sat down and took up her chocolate. 'I must instruct your girl how to make this properly,' she said. 'She has no notion of how it ought to be done.'

'She will be happy to be taught. She is an upright, Christian girl. If she has been wrong, she will wish to make amends.'

'Humph,' said Mrs Winwood.

The question of Mrs Winwood's attendance at the dance was held in abeyance all the following day whilst half the town and most of Donwell busied itself in preparations for the festivities. Girls from all Mr Knightley's tenant farms brought rushes for the floor and flowers for the tables. Matrons came to help the cook in Donwell's cavernous kitchens. Farmhands chopped wood for the braziers and to feed the flames beneath the hogs slowly rotating on spits above a pit. Maids swept the cobbles and men hoisted garlands into the rafters of the barn.

All was in readiness by mid-afternoon and people went home to dine and dress. At last, the sun slipped behind the horizon and a purple gloaming descended. The lights were lit, fires kindled and violins could be heard tuning up.

Emma was all excitement and anticipation. She had liked Mr Mosley exceedingly. In her search for a protégé she had not considered that a young, inexperienced gentleman might be just as good as a naive young girl, but why should it not be so? And Mr Mosely had about him an air of romance and enigma that was extremely enticing. She hoped he would be present. She hoped to dance with him. She liked the notion that he might fall deeply in love with her. She imagined he would write passionate love letters and leave tokens of his affection around the

Hartfield gardens for her to find. A secret love affair would certainly enliven her days, which were often dull. She would be in no danger. His reputation—however underserved—would absolve *her* of all blame. Accordingly, Miss Woodhouse dressed with extreme care and had the maid take more than usual time over her hair. She had sent for new dancing shoes. Energy and elegance in the set was one superiority she could claim over Miss Fairfax; she was determined that, between the two of them, Mr Mosley would choose her.

Miss Taylor also dressed with care. Emma observed it, and smiled to herself. She had made so much of her governess' desire to dance that poor Mr Weston had been all but forced into engaging her for the first two dances. It was pleasing to see the blush that caressed Miss Taylor's face when Emma mentioned his name. Her matchmaking was going splendidly well.

Mr Knightley sent his carriage for Miss Bates, Miss Fairfax and Mr and Mrs Paling. Mrs Winwood, at the last possible moment, bundled herself in beside them, her eagerness to hold sway over the gathering at Donwell outweighing her reluctance to meet the Mosleys, who, after all, may not have the effrontery to turn up. Mr Weston walked to Donwell along with Mr and Mrs Ford and the Coxes. The Coles brought the Perrys. Hopley the miller and his wife walked the short distance from Abbey Mill, the Cropleys came in the little cart Mrs Cropley used to take her eggs to market. Mrs Goddard and three of her oldest girls— Miss Bickerton[ix], Miss Piggott and Miss Smith—came in the school trap. Mrs Martin, from Abbey Mill Farm, brought her oldest boy[x] and girl on foot. Ploughmen and farriers, carpenters and smiths loped across the meadows, their hair slicked back with water from the trough and their Sunday shirts fresh washed. Dairymaids scampered down lanes, their muslin dresses bright and white against the twilight. William Larkins called upon Miss Tremble, his hat and a little posy of flowers he had gathered from the hedgerow much mashed in his restless hands, his face scrubbed and his chin shaved raw, that he might escort her the half mile or so to the Abbey. She emerged from the little cottage she shared with her mother and a posse of younger siblings looking as fresh and pure as a new daisy, and William thought he would die if she did not consent to be his wife.

Mr Knightley came through the kitchens of Donwell, to see that the food was ready and to say a word of thanks to the cook and the kitchen staff. He put his dogs in the gunroom and then strode out into the yard to greet his guests.

At first all was greeting and exclamation, a great flood of arrival all at once, for no one wanted to be behindhand, to miss a moment of the great occasion. Carts and gigs and phaetons came up the gravel of the drive and into the yard, deposited their passengers and were driven off to a paddock beyond the orchard where the horses could be tethered until they were wanted again. Everyone desired to shake Mr Knightley's hand, to declare themselves amazed by the spectacle, to greet their friends and to reserve themselves a place at table. Mugs of cider and glasses of punch were handed round. All was noise and laughter and gaiety.

The Hartfield coach arrived a little after the rest. Miss Woodhouse had bidden the coachman wait at the top of the drive, 'For,' she had explained, 'look at the line of conveyances that are before us. We do not wish to arrive with farm carts and donkey drays, do we Miss Taylor? We will wait a few moments, until everyone is settled, and then surprise certain gentlemen with the splendour of our arrival.'

Miss Taylor blushed to the roots of her hair.

As Miss Woodhouse had designed, the Hartfield carriage arrived in the yard when all but a very few of the guests were already gathered. There was a hush and a little ripple of pleasure and approval as the occupants descended, which was very pleasing. Mr Knightley stepped forward to bid them welcome, Mr Weston only a step or two behind him. A way opened up as they were led to their seats at a reserved table on a raised platform. The rest of the company bowed and curtseyed as they passed. It was entirely satisfactory, Emma thought. But they had hardly gained their designated places, hardly had chance to admire the room or to be admired by the sea of onlookers when more wheels on the gravel and the whinny of a horse denoted another arrival. As one, the crowd turned its back, there was some craning and jostling then, 'The Mosleys,' was to be heard disseminating around the crowd.

'How rude to be so late,' Mrs Winwood said in a voice designed to carry. Like Emma, she was marooned on the raised dais but, unlike Emma, she found her separation from the new arrivals very agreeable. She resolutely refused to show an iota of interest in them, arranging her shawl with great care over the back of her chair, assiduously removing a wisp of straw from her seat and wiping her glass with her handkerchief.

The hush that had greeted the Mosleys was quite palpable, at first a blend of lurid interest and delicious disgust. The farmer who had shaken a pitchfork at Mr Mosley pushed his daughter behind him. Mrs Martin and Mrs Goddard, who had found themselves together near the wide-flung door of the barn, exchanged anxious looks. Highbury and Donwell held their collective breath. But as Mr Knightley received the Mosleys so cordially, and as Miss Bates hurried forward to greet them in her turn, and brought Jane Fairfax forward too without a shade of hesitation or reluctance, and as Mrs Paling and her husband shook their hands, they began to wonder. Perhaps they had been wrong? Who was this mild, diffident young man? Where was the monster they had been told to expect?

Mr Mosley stood uncertainly next to his sister, his face pale even in the light from the braziers, his eyes very large with apprehension. And then Jane Fairfax took his arm—*their* Jane Fairfax, dear Jane, known to them from her infancy, the girl they had been taught to know as a paragon of all that was modest and upright and laudable and good, their own Mrs Bates' particular darling. If *she* saw no evil in the young fellow then, certainly, there could be none.

The little party progressed into the body of the barn, the people parting again to let them through.

Miss Woodhouse, debarred from this theatre, looked on helplessly and with great annoyance as Miss Fairfax made herself the focal point of interest and attention. Upstart! Interloper! She was insufferable!

Mrs Paling was heard to say, clearly and deliberately, so that anyone in the near vicinity could hear, 'I would very much like to introduce you to my mama, Mr Mosley.'

Mr Mosley smiled, but with the air of a man girded to undergo an ordeal. The other guests looked on. *This* they would like to see.

Mrs Winwood had no alternative but to be introduced to Mr Mosley, although what it cost her was clear and rather satisfactory to the onlookers. 'How do you do?' she said coldly.

Now came Miss Woodhouse's chance. She stepped forward and gave Mr Mosley the benefit of her warmest, most inviting smile. 'Good evening, Mr Mosley,' she said. 'I am most happy to see you again. Mr Knightley's summer dances are very informal affairs but *some* customs are observed.' She gave him a coquettish smile. 'Ladies are as eager here, I think, as they are in any ballroom in England, to be engaged to dance.'

Mr Mosley bowed. 'I should be delighted to stand up with you for a later dance,' he said, 'but I am engaged to Miss Fairfax for the first two.'

A few moments more and Mr Knightley led Miss Mosley to the dance, her brother forming up behind with Miss Fairfax. Miss Taylor, Mrs Paling, even pert Miss Coxe were ready on the old flagstones of the barn floor, waiting for the music to begin. Emma was as angry as possible. She fumed and railed, but not far behind her anger were tears of mortification. What monstrous mismanagement had led to *this?* It was inconceivable! Was she to be thus slighted? Surely, she would not be without a partner? Then a stir of murmured conversation, significant looks cast her way and Mr Paling made his approach. The vicar? It was unthinkable! But if she did not stand up with him, no one else would ask her. She forced her face into a smile of acceptance, took his hand and allowed him to lead her to the floor. It was demeaning! She thought she would die of shame. But the violin struck up the tune and the dance begun.

Later, after supper had been eaten and cleared away, Mr Mosley and Miss Fairfax strolled in the cool of Donwell's garden. The moon had risen; the lawns and flowerbeds were as bright as day.

'And so, Mr Mosley,' said Jane, 'you have survived your ordeal.'

'Yes I have, thanks to you,' he said.

They strolled in silence for a while. Then Mr Mosley said, 'We had word from my father today.'

'Oh?' said Jane.

Mr Mosley sighed deeply. 'An ultimatum. My brother has returned from his travels and he is as angry as Father. From him, I hoped for some compassion, but it is not to be. I am to be thrown off, shall inherit nothing and my allowance will cease *unless* ...'

'Unless?' Jane breathed, and then, recalling, 'oh, the widow.'

'Yes, the widow. I *must* agree to marry her—or to woo her, at least. Perhaps she may object ... But I cannot think my father would have proposed such a thing without preparing the ground first.'

'Are you acquainted with her? Are there very great objections to the lady?'

Mr Mosley shrugged. 'Apart from the fact that I do not love her? I suppose she is pleasant enough. Our families have been acquainted for some years. She is of a respectable but not especially well-to-do family by the name of Clegg. An aunt of hers married *very* well but other than that they have not particularly distinguished themselves. In marrying Billinge she did creditably. She was much younger than her husband but they had no children, so there are no complications of that sort. I like

163

her well enough. To be married to her would be no great hardship except that I have given my heart to Susannah and I find, regardless of the insuperable impediments between us, I cannot recall it. When *you* have fallen in love, Miss Fairfax, you will understand what I mean.'

They came to a little arbour that stood in the centre of Mr Knightley's rose garden. The scent of the blooms was very sweet, almost cloying on the still night air.

'It sounds as though you are making your mind up to acquiesce to your family's wishes,' Jane said. She tried to sound no note of condemnation or of approval. Indeed, she could not tell which she felt. To be sure, a person ought to do their duty to their family, to be obedient as far as honour and moral judgement allowed; the heart could not be allowed to run away with the head if it meant dishonour or disgrace. But then, she suspected, the heart was not so easily governed. She could not imagine being so helplessly in love that her rational mind could not overrule her heart, but she believed it was possible. Was it not cruel of the older Mr Mosley to impose such a requirement upon his son? To present him with such a dilemma: to go so decidedly against his inclinations or to be cast off forever! It was unfathomable to Jane. She could not conceive of being forced against her will by the Campbells, or of losing their love and regard; they would not cast her into oblivion … but then, she realised, that is what they *would* do, when the time came. She would be set adrift to sink or float as she may.

'The business?' Jane prevaricated, 'Your brother met with no success? There is no other remedy?'

'It seems not.' Mr Mosley sat down heavily upon the little stone seat that nestled in the arbour. He put his head in his hands. 'Oh Susannah, Susannah,' he moaned.

Oh, thought Jane, the danger of loving the wrong person! The tribulations of being wholly dependent on others.

'I am very sorry,' was all she said.

'Save your sorrow for Susannah,' Mr Mosley said brokenly. 'I shall go on, a participant in a trade of which I do not approve, a partner in a marriage that is little more than a business arrangement. To all the world it will seem that I am happy and successful. More! With Mrs Billinge's money and ships our company will rise to undreamed of heights! But for Susannah there will be no comfort, no forgiveness, no respite. She will sink into oblivion.'

'I shall pray for you both,' said Jane, 'and hope to hear of happier times.'

Volume Two

Chapter Thirteen

'My dear,' said Mr Churchill to his wife, 'your relations the Branthwaites[xi] are in town. Shall we call on them this morning?'

Three more years had passed. Frank's life with the Churchills had become an interminable progress from country estate to town house, from watering place to seaside resort. Nowhere pleased Mrs Churchill for long; she professed to find the air noxious, the landscape disagreeable or the company tedious and urged their removal as soon as she discerned in Frank any preference for company other than hers. At this juncture they were in Weymouth. It was May, a time at which the air of the resort was reputed to be particularly healthful, the sea bathing especially beneficial and the society more than usually select. The Churchills had come to spend as many of the summer months as could contribute to the pleasure and entertainment of Frank before the ill humour and multitudinous indispositions of his aunt were exacerbated to such a degree that it must be at an end.

'Here in Weymouth?' Mrs Churchill cried, throwing up her hands. 'I can scarcely credit it! I was led to believe Weymouth accommodated only the most superior families. The Branthwaites! What presumption! I would not put it past them to have come here on purpose to waylay us. They *will* claim connection. People with no status themselves are always ready to attach themselves to those of higher estate. My sister Clegg was just the same while she lived and now her off-spring will do the same. You know I detest the Branthwaites. They are the worst kind of people—utterly without breeding—I decline to be related to them.'

They were sitting in the sunny breakfast parlour of their lodgings house in Chesterfield Place, a modern and well-appointed house ideally placed between the harbour and the sea front. Mr Churchill put down the town circular he had been reading. 'Your niece Matilda married Oswald Branthwaite—*there* is undeniable connection. We must acknowledge at least that much, even if we do not court the society of the wider Branthwaite family. For your late sister's sake, we ought to call on Tilly at the earliest opportunity. To neglect such a courtesy will be taken as a slight.'

Mrs Churchill sighed. 'Tilly was thrown away on Oswald Branthwaite. Her sister Ariadne did better—*she* married a merchant with a fleet of ships. I don't know why it should be so but a *merchant* is a more respectable kind of person than one who is merely in trade, don't you think? She has been widowed and re-married since—she is Mrs Mosley, now. With *her* I would not be ashamed to own kinship, but the Branthwaites are mere rabble, without air or education. If we call upon them we shall be forced to renew our invitation for them to visit us at Enscombe. You know how shamelessly they wheedle, hint and insinuate until we name a date. It was only the very great good fortune of my stumble and sprain last summer that allowed us to put them off the last time they squeezed an invitation from us. We cannot hope to be so lucky again.'

'I would not call any hurt or injury you may suffer as 'lucky' my dear, regardless of what it saved us from,' her husband observed mildly. 'The Branthwaites *do* wish to see Enscombe and they make little secret of it. I must confess I rather admire them for it. Enscombe is not known for its comfort, you know. The sport is not especially good and the weather is notoriously poor. I would not object to having them come to stay. A little company from time to time would be diverting. The Branthwaites are not in the top tier of society but they are agreeable enough. There are two young ladies I recall. Frank might enjoy *their* company.'

Mrs Churchill gave a little shriek. 'I would not have Frank within half a mile of the Branthwaite girls! Who knows what ideas they may get into their brazen heads? Once they gained access to Enscombe there would be no shifting them—they would be with us for the duration and would need only the smallest encouragement to begin rifling through the linen cupboards and making inventories of the silver against their coming there one day as mistress. The idea is abhorrent, Charles. Frank must look *much* higher. Where *is* Frank, by the way? His breakfast will be cold if he delays much longer. I do not like it when he goes out without us. He is too genial, too high spirited. He is likely to pick up undesirable acquaintance. Weymouth is full of mothers on the lookout for marriageable young men for their daughters. It would be just like Frank to fall into their clutches. He is not to be trusted. He has not the steadiness, the discernment or the foresight to withstand their blandishments. He must leave all that to me. I will find him a suitable wife. He will not have to lift a finger in the business.'

'Frank went sea-bathing this morning. He will be in no danger—the ladies' bathing is at the far end of the beach, you know.' Mr Churchill got up from the table and went to stand in the bay window. The promenade was already busy with families taking the air. Gentlemen on horseback and ladies in open carriages trotted along the wide, pleasant thoroughfare. The sea was dotted with gaily coloured sails as flotillas of yachts tacked to and fro across the bay. He longed to be out amongst them with a fishing rod in his hand, to walk along Chesil beach with the sea breeze in his face, to be free of the constant complaints of his wife. But it was impossible. To liberate himself would be to shackle Frank more tightly. If he went out Frank would be required to stay at home and Mr Churchill would by no means curtail the enjoyment of his nephew. 'I know you have high expectations for Frank - you mean him to make a very superior match,' he said quietly. 'But Eustacia, my dear, he is in the fortunate position of being able to choose a wife regardless of her circumstances. Elegant manners and good taste of course she must have, and a respectable family, but as to wealth—there is no necessity for it. I would have Frank marry for love. I wish him to be happy. I would not wish him to rush into an engagement or to enter one at all without a thorough understanding of the lady's character. Young people should know each other before they commit themselves. But,' with a significant pause, 'I would have him choose for himself.'

'Choose what, Uncle?' said Frank, coming just then into the breakfast room. His hair was still damp from the sea, his complexion energised, his eyes very bright.

'Whether your eggs shall be scrambled or fried,' said Mr Churchill, crossing to the fireplace and pulling the bell-rope. 'You will need fresh tea and toast also. You must be hungry.'

'Thank you, Uncle, you are very kind,' said Frank, rubbing his hands together. He approached his aunt at the far end of the table and kissed her cheek. 'Good morning to you, Aunt. I hope you slept well. I hope you were not much troubled with pain in the night?'

'I was very much troubled,' she grizzled, 'but what I suffer is of no consequence. *You* are all I care about. Did the Ball amuse you? Did you play cards? I surmise that you found it pleasant enough for I did not hear you return home until the small hours.'

'I am sorry to think I may have disturbed you Aunt. I crept in as quietly as a mouse. Yes, the Ball was vastly amusing. I danced all evening for there was a plethora of delightful young ladies.' He scooped kedgeree from a covered salver on the sideboard, added bacon and sundry other items before taking a seat at the table. 'And I made acquaintance with a fellow called Dixon. Dixon is Irish, just come into his father's estate in Wicklow. He is the second son—the oldest is recently married and on his honeymoon tour—but will be the de facto squire since his brother's wife inherits some hundreds of acres in Scotland. I liked him enormously. I beg leave to introduce him to you Uncle. He invites me to sail on his yacht later in the week. Shall I see if the boat can accommodate another passenger?'

'Your uncle has no intention of going sailing,' said Mrs Churchill. 'Dixon? I know no one of that name. Is he of good family?'

'*Very* good, Aunt. His grandfather is Lord Knox. And he is intimate with the Campbells. I am sure I have mentioned Colonel Campbell to you; I was introduced to him in town last year. What I did not know was that—the strangest coincidence in the world—the Campbells are guardians to another Highbury orphan; a Miss Fairfax.'

'*Another* Highbury orphan?' Mrs Churchill cried, 'is that how you look upon yourself, Frank? You quite wound me. I would have thought all association with that sorry little place to have quite disappeared from your consciousness. You have never been there, after all, and need never sink so low as to go.'

'My father lives there,' Frank said quietly.

'Fairfax,' his uncle put in quickly, 'that name is familiar to me.'

'Louisa was the intimate friend of Lady Cecily Fairfax,' Mrs Churchill reminded him. 'The Bates girl married Lady Cecily's brother-in-law. This girl must be their daughter. I presume she is a poor specimen of a thing. I heard she was left destitute.'

Frank chewed thoughtfully for a while. 'As much as it pains me to contradict you, Aunt, I must say that Miss Fairfax is far from being a poor specimen. I never saw such an elegant girl in all my life. She outshone every other lady in the place, including her friend Miss Campbell. I believe Dixon is in love with her. If she marries him she will want for nothing, for he will have the use and enjoyment of the whole of his father's estate in Wicklow.'

'A second son is nothing,' Mrs Churchill said, dismissing the topic. 'Frank, we must call upon the Branthwaites this morning. I depend upon you to accompany us and then to curtail the visit with the utmost alacrity. You will think of some reason why we must be elsewhere. On no account must you succumb to their fawning invitations to join them at their gimcrack picnics or tawdry at-homes.'

'Yes, Aunt,' said Frank.

Mrs Churchill rose from the table and went upstairs to collect her hat preparatory to going out. When the door had closed behind her Frank approached his uncle by the window.

'I shall be happy to make the acquaintance of your friend Mr Dixon,' said Mr Churchill genially, 'and also of Miss Fairfax. I remember her mother with great fondness—she was a bright, spirited girl. As to the sailing, with regret I fear I must decline. *You* should go, though. It will be an enjoyable excursion, I have no doubt.'

Frank placed his hand affectionately on his uncle's arm. 'Thank you, Uncle,' he said, 'but I am loath to leave my aunt to your sole supervision for an entire afternoon. Her spirits require much encouragement, do they not? I would not distress her but,' he pulled a letter from his pocket and handed it to his uncle, 'I fear that, between us, we must prepare her for my being absent in the autumn. My father is to be married in September. It is unthinkable that I should not attend. It would be considered a slight against the lady—who, I understand, is an exemplary woman of excellent character—as well as against my father. Whatever my aunt says, I have a great desire to visit Highbury. I *do* feel an affinity with it, an affection for it. It is meant as no ingratitude against you or Enscombe, I assure you.'

Mr Churchill looked down upon his nephew with a light of great warmth and approbation. 'I offer your father my heartiest congratulations,' he said. 'Do not concern yourself about the wedding. You shall certainly attend. Leave your aunt to me.'

Chapter Fourteen

The day was extraordinarily fine and the Churchills decided to walk the short distance through Weymouth to visit the Branthwaites. Weymouth was a town virtually cut in half by the tidal estuary of the river Wey. The eastern, landward side of the place housed the tenements of the local inhabitants, provided stabling for visitors' horses and had some of the less genteel lodgings houses used by lower orders of tourists. It was in this area that the Branthwaites' lodgings were located and the Churchills' perambulation took them across the bridge to a house in Bridge Street hard by the docks.

Mr Branthwaite was a draper who had, with diligence and some luck, expanded his father's business to encompass several stores and a sweatshop where cheap clothing was made by impecunious tailors and seamstresses with no more advantageous outlet for their skills. He had married Matilda Clegg on the strength of the great certainty that her *very* well-married aunt—Mrs Churchill—would, being childless herself, do something handsome for any off-spring. Mrs Churchill had disappointed Matilda, concentrating all her energies and her husband's fortune on her husband's nephew instead. Notwithstanding this disappointment, Mr Branthwaite had prospered to such a degree that he was able, each year, to take his wife and children to the seaside. Their choosing Weymouth this year had nothing whatever to do with the

Churchills being there but the coincidence, once discovered, certainly did excite hopes of a closer connection between the two families.

'She is my only aunt,' Mrs Branthwaite said, stirring her tea. They were breakfasting very late. Her hair was still in its curl papers and her person informally arrayed in a morning wrap, 'We must call on them in Chesterfield Place without delay.'

Also seated at breakfast were the Branthwaites' two daughters and their son. The girls were aged seventeen and nineteen. They were dressed, having that morning been sea-bathing, but their hair was in that state that the salt spray and lively surf will inflict upon a lady's coiffeur. Their manners, likewise, were untamed and their sundry appetites rather more voracious than is quite commensurate with a ladylike demeanour. One, the eldest, who had been named Eustacia to favour her great-aunt but who was known within the family as Stacie, made no reply to her mother but concentrated her attention on consuming bread thickly spread with butter and jam.

The other girl, Mary, said, 'Really, Mama they ought to call on *us*. We are the more recently-arrived party. No one is more eager than I to ingratiate myself with the Churchills. They are sure to have a barouche landau. There is no better way to see the countryside than from a barouche. However, if I am to hold my head up in their *barouche*, I cannot absolutely grovel to the Churchills beforehand.'

Mrs Branthwaite looked to where her husband perused the newspaper. He was partially dressed; his coat was slung over the back of his chair, his cravat hung loose around his neck, his shirt collar was unfastened. He had taken no part in their conversation, not so much as even looking up at her announcement that the Churchills had been discovered to be in town. That he had been listening, however, was evident from his next comment. 'Mary is right, Tilly. They ought to call on us first.'

'I hope they do not do so today,' said their son. Edgar was twin brother to Stacie, utterly unlike her in appearance but as fond of drink as she was of food. He had just been sent down from Oxford on account of a vulgar and reprehensible escapade involving a superfluity of wine and an inadequacy of clothing. He was a dissipated young man who had imbibed too freely the evening before and now felt bilious at the sight of his sister gobbling her breakfast. 'Stacie,' he went on, querulously, 'I wish you would close your mouth while you chew your food. And do not slurp your tea. With manners like yours you will certainly not be acknowledged by the Churchills.'

'I quite agree,' Mary said, sanctimoniously, taking the smallest bite of bread. 'Although,' she went on when she had swallowed, 'you look less than reputable, Edgar. You have not shaved, your hair is stuck up in tufts and you smell like a winery.'

It was at this juncture that the hired maid came in to announce, 'Mr and Mrs Churchill, and Mr Frank Churchill,' and the family from Enscombe was shown into the room.

The disruption attendant on their entrance was considerable. Mrs Branthwaite was on her feet immediately, one despairing hand to her curlers, the other clutching her wrap to her body. 'Upon my word,' she cried, 'you call on us unconscionably early. But I am very glad to see you.' She glanced around the room, where clothing, newspapers and sundry other articles littered every surface where the august company might be invited to sit.

Mr Branthwaite also rose to his feet and offered his hand to Mr Churchill and Frank. 'The girl should not have shown you in here,' he said by way of an apology for their disarray. 'We have a perfectly good parlour.'

'It is not so good as we would wish, however,' his wife put in. 'I wished for lodgings in Gloucester Row but Oswald said they were all spoken for.'

'I said they were too expensive,' her husband said under his breath.

Mr Churchill smiled benignly at the slatternly room. His wife gathered her skirts around her that they might not be sullied by the furnishings.

'This seems a most commodious house,' Frank said brightly. He walked to the window to look out. 'You have a fine view of the quays. I suppose you might view the fishermen bringing in their catch, if you were up early enough.'

'We hear and smell them, sir,' said Mary primly.

Stacie said nothing. She was struggling with a large wedge of bread that had become lodged in her throat because she had swallowed it too hastily. She went red, and then rather blue, before putting her hand to her mouth and rushing from the room.

'I hope my cousin is not unwell,' observed Frank.

'She is overcome with pleasure at seeing you,' Mrs Branthwaite said. 'We speak of you so often, and remember you with such regularity in our prayers, that to see you in the flesh is more than she is equal to. She is a sensitive, feeling child.'

Edgar and Mary exchanged a look that cast this assessment of their sister's character in some doubt.

'I must apologise for coming upon you so suddenly,' Mr Churchill said. 'I read but this morning that you were in Weymouth and Eustacia and I agreed we must waste no moment but call at the earliest opportunity. We should have sent a card. Madam, I pray you will continue your breakfast.'

'Oh,' Mrs Branthwaite waved an airy hand over the crumbs, smeary knives, congealed egg and tea stains that covered the table, 'we have long-finished. The maid is behind hand in clearing. I must have words with her.'

'You were at the Ball last evening?' Edgar hazarded. His own memory of the evening was dim but he partly recalled an argument over cards that would not, he feared, reflect well on him.

'I was,' Frank said cheerily. 'A most delightful evening, was it not? I danced every set, I believe. You?'

'I spent the evening in the card room,' Edgar mumbled.

'Indeed? You will have witnessed the dreadful fracas that broke out then. My friend Dixon said something about it. I believe two gentlemen almost came to blows. Quite shameful behaviour, do you not agree?'

Edgar blushed. 'I do not quite recall,' he said.

Frank flashed him a mischievous smile. 'I am certain, like me, you would have absented yourself the moment there was a whiff of impropriety,' he said.

'I hope your ankle is quite recovered, ma'am,' Mrs Branthwaite said, addressing Mrs Churchill. 'We were so distressed to hear of your accident last year. On your own account, naturally, we were concerned, but for ourselves also. We were devastated to be denied the opportunity to visit Yorkshire.'

'*I* was not devastated,' muttered Edgar. 'It sounds like a godforsaken place to me.'

'Yorkshire is well-known to be God's *own* county,' Mary reproved, 'therefore it is ridiculous to say He has forsaken it, Edgar.'

Frank smiled again, and winked at his cousin. 'God can own a place without inhabiting it,' he said dryly, 'I believe many Scottish land-owners follow His example. Enscombe is certainly very remote.'

'Oh, *I* should not care about that,' Mary gushed. 'A place cannot *be* too wild and out-of-the-way for me. When you have lived in industrial places—as we do—you cannot perhaps appreciate the appeal of open spaces and solitude. I long to see the moors and mountains. Your gardens,' she looked at Mr Churchill, 'are reputed to be quite splendid. I am wild about horticulture, am I not Mama? And wolves. I quite dote on wolves.'

'I do not think we have wolves in Yorkshire,' Mr Churchill said.

'Nevertheless, Yorkshire … at *Christmas*,' she narrowed a speculative eye, 'must be very beautiful.'

'We can be snowed in for weeks,' Frank said. 'It takes a very resilient kind of person to be able to withstand the winter at Enscombe. My aunt is one such. England has no more hardy woman than her, I believe, but,' (with a sad smile), 'not everyone is equal to it.'

'*I* am resilient,' Mary replied with a smile designed to be coquettish.

'I thought your health was very uncertain, ma'am' Mrs Branthwaite said, speaking to Mrs Churchill again. 'From what I hear you are the *last* person to be equal to a harsh winter in the north.'

'Ah!' cried Frank, 'that is what makes her all the more marvellous.'

'You will know that my sister Ariadne is also in Weymouth,' Mrs Branthwaite said, moving on. '*They* were so fortunate as to acquire lodgings in York Place.'

'We had not received that happy news,' Mr Churchill said. 'Of course, we will call. I shall be delighted to become acquainted with her husband Mr … Rosley?'

'Mosley,' Mr Branthwaite corrected. 'He is a much younger man than Billinge—her first husband, you know—but well connected in the import/export trade. With his contacts and her ships, they do very nicely, I am told.'

'Our fortunes have risen with theirs,' Mrs Branthwaite said complacently. 'We are the first to get silks from the Indies. The alliance with Mr Mosley has been most beneficial.'

'I find him rather sad and woebegone,' Edgar said. 'I can get no conversation out of him.'

'Weymouth will surely cheer him,' Frank said perkily. He consulted his pocket watch. 'Oh! I fear we must hurry away. That appointment of ours, Uncle? It wants but a quarter of an hour before we are due.' He turned to Mrs Churchill. 'I would not hurry *you* away, Aunt, if you wish to remain in comfortable chat with your relations for an hour. We can easily call back for you later.'

Mrs Churchill blanched. 'On no account,' she carped, speaking for the first time since entering the room. 'I shall walk with you, Frank.' She turned to the Branthwaite family. 'I hope you will do us the honour of calling upon us ... at some time. In the meantime, I wish you a very good day.'

The Churchills were all-but gone when Mary burst out, 'Oh, Uncle Churchill, do you have a barouche landau? Will you be going on any excursions around the countryside? Only, if you would be so kind, and if it would please my aunt to have the company of a lady, *I* would be only too pleased ... that is ... I do so long to ...'

'Mary!' her father barked.

But the Churchills must not have heard. They had left the building without acknowledging her question or giving the smallest clue as to their transportation arrangements. They hurried from the meaner streets of the old part of town and crossed the bridge back to the Narrows, the spit of land formed by the western, seaward bank of the river Wey. In this locale a large number of modern, fashionable lodgings, shops, coffee houses and the Assembly rooms had been built and naturally it housed their own accommodations. They made their way to the wide promenade that fronted the bay.

'I am to meet Dixon at Mrs Doolittle's coffee house,' said Frank, when they were well clear of Bridge Street. 'I entreat you to come and meet him. He is a capital fellow, I do assure you.'

'For myself, I would be delighted to make his acquaintance,' said Mr Churchill. He took his wife's arm. 'Eustacia? What say you? Are you equal to it?'

'The walk is very short, Aunt, and Mrs Doolittle's coffee house is quite genteel, you need have no fear,' urged Frank. 'Besides, I think the fresh air does you good. Your complexion is quite glowing.'

'I do not know why it is assumed that I am unequal to a walk, or too proud to enter a coffee house,' Mrs Churchill grumbled. 'As to my complexion, well, *anything,* after the miserable confines of that dreadful lodgings-house, is a boon.'

'We did not catch our relatives at their best,' Frank said gallantly. 'We should not have burst in upon them as we did.'

'I am ashamed to own them as relations,' Mrs Churchill said darkly. 'Ariadne was always infinitely the superior of my two nieces.'

'We will call upon Mr and Mrs Mosley tomorrow,' her husband said, 'but I will send a card today. I am not a man to make the same mistake twice.'

'Oh! I can assure you *she* would not be caught in her curl papers at gone midday.'

'Oh dear, yes,' Frank laughed, '*that* was unfortunate.'

'I was disgusted by them all,' Mrs Churchill lamented. 'The two girls looked as disreputable as possible—you would not know from their dress that their father is a highly reputed draper. The elder was too intent upon her breakfast to pay us the least attention and the younger all-but prostrated herself for a ride in our carriage and Christmas at Enscombe. As for the son—I thought him surly to the point of rudeness. My niece is clearly a slattern of the worst description. Her husband is all I feared - a contemptible kind of man, self-evidently a low order of tradesman who believes a little success in business—and *that* more due to the beneficial alliance of his sister-in-law than to his own industry—can make him the equal of long-established families and noblemen. It is a terrible presumption.'

'I can assure you that Dixon is a different kind of fellow altogether,' said Frank, 'and Miss Fairfax and Miss Campbell put the likes of the Branthwaite girls quite in the shade. Wait until you see them, Aunt. I wager that even you will be forced to acknowledge their charms.'

'Upon my word,' his aunt said sourly, '*you* are very taken with them. But *I* am the last person to judge.'

'They may well be charming,' Mr Churchill cautioned, 'but your aunt has a keen eye for character and substance. *She* will not be bamboozled—as *we* might, Frank—by a sweet smile or an alluring eye. A young lady would have to have very superior qualities of understanding and manner to impress your aunt.'

'I am fully conscious of it, sir,' said Frank as he guided them to the corner where the coffee house was located, 'and the more so do I … but here they are, coming along the road towards us. Well! I must say this is most happily arranged.'

Chapter Fifteen

Walking along the pavement towards them was a party of two gentlemen and three ladies. The older gentleman, from his proud and erect bearing, identified himself immediately as a military man. Colonel Campbell—for it was he—held his wife's arm, pointing out to her as they strolled various things of interest in shop windows. Mrs Campbell had grown rather stout in latter years; her face was round and dimpled, her chins perhaps one or two above the perfect quantity and she walked awkwardly, with the aid of her husband on one side and a cane on the other. Nevertheless, she had retained that strong, maternal sensibility that made her girls the very centre of her care. What did it matter if her legs ached or her shoes pinched so long as Rowena and Jane were happy?

The bright smile and evident pleasure of the girl on Colonel Campbell's other side gave ample satisfaction to Mrs Campbell's selflessness. *She* was extraordinarily beautiful, with chestnut hair tending to that shade of auburn that is always remarkably pleasing, a perfectly formed nose and finely shaped grey eyes. Jane Fairfax walked without air, without consciousness that anyone might be watching her. She contributed little to the chat of the party but looked around her and took in the scene— the brightly sparkling sea, the strolling couples, the jolly family groups on the sands—as though she would gather it up and store it away to lighten darker days ahead. For she had come—or imminently *would* come—to that time in her life when she had determined that the softness and luxury of the Campbells must be left behind. The velvet path, as she had always described it to herself, must end and the arduous trail begin. Their summer at Weymouth would be her swansong and in the autumn she would begin to look about her. So it was that everything, in these indulgent and delightful summer days by the sea, had added significance, added poignancy. No more could she say to herself, 'Next summer we will see if such another place is equal to this,' since there was no knowing where the next summer would find her. No more could she sigh, 'Ah, being away is very agreeable but *home* is always the most comfortable place to be,' since Bute Square must cease to be her home. 'Home' in the next six or twelvemonth might be anywhere; a dismal antechamber attached to a schoolroom, a mean garret or a dormitory shared with other teachers and pupils at a second- or third-rate school. These thoughts inhabited Jane's mind but she did not allow them to torment her; she had taught herself to accept her fate from her earliest years.

Behind Jane and the Campbells walked a gentleman of easy gait, tall and well-made about the shoulder, bicep and upper torso, with a crop of dark, glossy curls, an elegant coat and brilliantly polished boots. He was not a handsome man as regards regularity of feature; a sporting injury had left him with a nose not altogether straight and teeth in sympathy with the nose. His brows were heavy and his chin rather square. But he had a ready smile and kind, genial eyes that lingered often on Miss Fairfax as she walked beside her guardian. Mr Patrick Dixon had graduated from Trinity College Dublin and apprenticed himself to a number of landed families with the intention of becoming schooled in the practical management of arable land, livestock, forestry and moorland, all of which were comprised in his father's vast acreage in Wicklow. He had laboured hard amongst the tenant farmers and yeomanry, developing his natural tendency for what is sometimes called the 'common' touch so that he was accepted and liked by every degree of person. He had a particular affinity with sick or injured livestock, patiently coaxing many a weakly new-born lamb and calf to health. His father's decease the previous winter, and the marriage of his brother Hugh to a Scottish heiress had accelerated the time at which he must put to use all he had learned. The present time saw him more or less on his way to Baly-Craig to assume the mantle of responsibility for its tenant farmers and cottagers, its flocks and herds, plantations, watercourses and heaths. Only hearing that the Campbells were to spend the summer months in Weymouth had delayed his departure.

The Dixons had kept up acquaintance with the Campbells since the disastrous events at Knoxbury. The late Mr Dixon had esteemed Colonel Campbell very highly, their shared abhorrence of Lady Sowerby uniting them at first and other mutual interests and opinions strengthening the bond over the years. Since the death of his mother and then his father, Patrick Dixon had come to look upon Colonel and Mrs Campbell almost *in loco parentis;* with no sisters of his own he had become particularly fond of the Campbells' two girls—they were capital sports and, in short, he had decided he would not deny himself the pleasure of a few weeks in their company before taking ship home.

The young lady who walked beside him was small of stature, with brown hair and a face that, though it could never be called beautiful or even pretty, had about it at that moment such a glow of unrestrained happiness and pleasure that its inherent plainness was leavened *almost* to that distinction. Her complexion had a radiance of healthfulness, her eyes that quality of brightness that always serves to illuminate and improve the demeanour as a whole even if individual parts might be wanting in fineness or distinction. This was Miss Rowena Campbell. Now aged twenty-one, she had attained the fullness of what blessings of feature she was ever to receive and it seemed that here, in the warm sunshine and the energising breeze of Weymouth, and in the present company, they were bountiful enough.

This, then, was the party that walked towards Frank Churchill, his aunt and uncle that fine May afternoon. Introductions were made, curtseys and bows duly executed, hands shaken and agreement formed on the spot to eschew the coffee house in favour of the pleasure of a further promenade.

'Unless you are at all fatigued, ladies,' said Mr Dixon, looking first at Mrs Campbell and then at Mrs Churchill. 'If you are, I shall procure you Sedans without delay, or,' he looked up and down the street, 'we can seek rest and refreshment. There must be a respectable place where we could procure tea.'

'I am not tired,' Mrs Campbell asserted bravely, 'and I know Rowena and Jane will not want to end their walk so soon.'

'Do not give up your exercise on my account,' Mrs Churchill said—she could hardly say anything else without making herself out to be either an invalid or a kill-joy—'but if I *were* I should not need a third champion to summon a conveyance, young man.' She nodded to her husband and nephew, 'You see I am amply supplied with knights errant.'

'I offer you my humblest apology,' Mr Dixon said with an elegant bow, 'I meant no presumption.'

'Let us walk the length of the promenade,' Frank said, indicating the way. 'The sight of the water is so very fine, is it not Miss Fairfax?' He stepped forward and offered his arm. 'Would you do me the great honour?'

Jane hesitated a moment and glanced at her uncle. He loosed his grip on her, signalling his assent to the offer, and she transferred her hand to Mr Churchill's arm. Mr Dixon retained Miss Campbell, an arrangement very much to the lady's taste, the Campbells and the Churchills fell in abreast and the company moved off.

Jane and Frank walked in silence for a few moments before Jane said, 'Well, Mr Churchill, when I write to my grandmother and aunt in Highbury of *this* they will be dumb-founded. You can be sure the news will envelop the village like wildfire.'

'The news that you walked along Weymouth promenade?' offered Frank, being deliberately obtuse.

'The news that I walked with *you*,' she clarified. 'You must know that you are Highbury's most revered—if elusive—son. Everyone speaks of you, speculates about you and claims connection with you even if it be the most obscure or tangential in the world. Mrs Spriggs at the post office gets a frisson every time she handles your correspondence. Mr Weston's housekeeper was invited to tea every evening for a fortnight on the strength of the fact that one of your handkerchiefs had inadvertently found its way into Mr Weston's valise once. She laundered it as though it were a holy relic! I believe it had passed through every hand in the parish before she presented it to Mr Weston. It was monogrammed with an F and the Churchill seal.'

'Good gracious,' exclaimed Frank. 'Can it really be so? I own myself astonished! I have never been to Highbury although it holds a particular appeal to me. My father resides there—*that* in itself is a high claim. He writes to me of his involvement in local affairs—I know there was a fracas recently about the closure of a footpath and lately some gypsies have made a nuisance of themselves in the fields and woods thereabouts. He talks of his neighbours—he speaks with great respect of *your* relations—and I know the names Knightley and Paling and Woodworm … Or is it Woodlouse?'

Jane let out a peal of laughter. 'You mean Woodhouse!'

' … but I had no notion of my own notoriety. How odd, when I have never been there.'

'Perhaps it is *because* you have never been there?'

'Ah yes,' Frank considered, 'I am sure I shall be a disappointment when I do visit, which must be soon, you know. My father is to marry. I am sure I am not breaching any confidence. Such good friends of his as your grandmother and aunt are, they are sure to have been informed.'

'Indeed yes,' Jane said. 'It is not a secret. Mr Weston is to marry Miss Taylor in September.'

'Are you acquainted with Miss Taylor?'

'Yes, she is very highly regarded in Highbury. She was Miss Woodhouse's governess at first but it is many years since that arrangement ceased. She is now known as the intimate friend of Miss

Woodhouse and is considered a valued and respected member of the Hartfield family.'

'And she is … she is fond of my father?'

Jane turned to look at him. 'You suspect her of ulterior motives in agreeing to marry him?'

Frank shrugged. 'I do not know the lady. But recently my father's business has been very successful … and a *governess,* you know, although always respectable and usually better informed on a wide range of subjects than many a lady of noble birth, can, in the usual course of things, only rise so far.'

'Ah yes,' said Jane heavily, 'hers is a very delicate situation. Higher than the servants but never equal to the family, not *really* equal, no matter how fond of her they may be, and, once her work is done, dispensed with more often than not.' Frank Churchill could not know with what careful discipline and harsh honesty Jane had schooled herself in these realities so she might have no illusions about the life before her. He made no reply to her comments but he watched her closely, discerning more than disinterested observation in her remarks. 'But *that* is not Miss Taylor's fate,' Jane went on, after a few moments. '*She* would have remained at Hartfield into her dotage, living as comfortably as any unmarried sister or favourite aunt, had your father not proposed.'

'It reassures me greatly,' Frank said, 'to know that her agreeing to be his wife is an act of pure, impartial affection.'

Jane considered. 'I believe that his success has been more of a motivation to him to seek Miss Taylor's hand, than it has been to her to accept it,' she said at last. 'He has bought a property in the village—

Randalls—a house I think he has long desired to own. He wishes to settle and part of that desire is to have someone by him who will be a companion, a helpmate, an equal sharer in all the joys that may be before him, as well as any sorrows that may come. For Miss Taylor, she has a home at Hartfield for as long as she may wish; neither Miss Woodhouse nor her father would dream of parting with her for any inducement. She is loved and honoured by them. That all governesses were so fortunate as to find such a happy, respectable situation! No, there is no reason on earth that she would wish to change her situation other than that she has fallen in love.'

Frank sighed. 'It must be a great blessing when two people who know their own minds, who are independent and free, find their equals in temper and idea and situation,' he said, 'when there is no one else to please, no one whose opinion must be sought, whose sanction given, whose interests consulted; when all those nearly concerned are united in their approbation and good wishes for the couple, without the least thought for their own comfort.'

Jane looked at him narrowly. 'You speak from the heart,' she said.

'Yes,' he said soberly, 'I do. But also,' he glanced over his shoulder at Mr Dixon, who had just then led Miss Campbell to a low wall that she might sit on it and admire the view. Mr Dixon himself, however, did not look out across the sands and the waves. *His* eyes were fixed on Miss Fairfax. He snatched them away as soon as she turned to follow the direction of Frank's glance, but not quick enough to prevent her from seeing, just for a fleeting moment, the intensity and admiration in their gaze. ' …also,' Frank resumed, when he was sure that his companion had seen and understood, 'I speak as I find.'

The party stopped for a while and the ladies rested on the wall. Mrs Campbell was glad of the opportunity to ease her aching legs. Mrs Churchill looked with distaste on the rough stones until her husband spread his handkerchief on them for her. Jane was too full of the inference Frank had made to pay much heed to the conversation that ensued. Under guise of admiring the sea she separated herself a little to take stock. Could it be true? She liked Mr Dixon very much but she had no warmer feeling than that towards him; her feelings were more what she imagined they might be for a brother than for a lover. She doubted Frank—*he* was just such a one as to create mischief. The merriment in his eye and the readiness of his smile denoted a character that was not as steady as it should be. But a short consideration of evidences she *could* rely on—proofs she herself had seen and heard but not understood—soon convinced her that Frank had not sought to mislead but to appraise her. There *had* been a decided keenness in Mr Dixon to dance with her at the Assembly, to sit next to her when they dined, and he had been speaking with eloquence and in detail of Baly-Craig since his father's death the previous winter. Had he been preparing her for the idea that she might become its mistress? The prospect was certainly very agreeable—infinitely more agreeable than the course that Jane would otherwise be obliged to pursue. To be mistress of her own establishment, and that such a substantial and eminently desirable one as Baly-Craig! To abandon forever the necessity of making her own way in the world! What joy! She had never looked for such an opportunity— that she, the daughter of nobody, with no fortune, a mere ward, a dependent, a charity-case, should marry well and happily a man whom she could like and respect even if she did not, at first, love him. It was beyond her dreams! The wonder of it drew her eye from the far horizon

192

to the little group on the promenade, and to Mr Patrick Dixon. He, seeing her, smiled and held out his hand to bring her back into their midst.

'I have just been pointing out,' he said, 'the route I intend for our sailing party later his week. Miss Campbell has her reservations, but *you* have no horror of it I hope?'

'I do not know if I will be equal to it,' said Rowena, looking very white. 'I have never sailed, other than when Papa rows us across the Serpentine.'

'You will be perfectly safe, Miss Campbell,' Mr Dixon avowed. 'Do you think I would put you or Miss Fairfax in any danger? I would not have you suffer the least anxiety for what I intend to be a pleasurable day out for you both. Your father, you know, has agreed to accompany us, and Churchill will make one of the party also, and Barron, my skipper, is as capable as any man who ever handled a sail.'

'I have perfect confidence in you,' Jane said in a low voice.

Mr Dixon's pleasure at her words was all too apparent. 'We can sail to Lulworth Cove,' he said through an irrepressible smile, 'or to the island of Portland, whichever you prefer. I shall have my people meet us with refreshments. If the sea is calm and you are feeling brave, ladies, we will sail round the island and see Chesil Beach although we will not be able to land upon it. The surf is too dangerous for ladies.' He turned to the Churchills with a bow. 'I do most sincerely regret that on this occasion I cannot extend my invitation to include you sir, or you, ma'am.'

'*I* would not consider accepting if you did,' said Mrs Churchill, 'although I am an extremely good sailor.'

'On another occasion, perhaps,' Mr Churchill murmured, 'a spot of fishing would be agreeable, but only if it does not inconvenience Mrs Churchill.'

'Consider it arranged,' Mr Dixon cried.

The group reconfigured itself to walk on and this time Jane found herself walking alongside Mr Churchill. 'I am very glad of the opportunity to meet you, Miss Fairfax,' he said. 'I knew your mother slightly. I liked her very much indeed.'

'*Did* you sir? How extraordinary! Where did you encounter her?'

'In Brighton. To be exact: on the *way* to Brighton. She and your grandmother stopped off at an inn where we were also pausing to rest and change horses. My sister Louisa struck up an immediate friendship with her but I am afraid … that is, I am sorry to say, that in the course of events Louisa proved a poor friend. It is my conviction that she stole your mother's beau.'

Jane frowned. 'But your sister Miss Louisa Churchill married Mr Weston! You do not mean to say that …?' She recalled her conversation with Mr Weston some three years previously. Had he not hinted at something?

'They were never engaged, there was never anything absolutely declared between them, but afterwards, after Louisa's betrothal was announced, I witnessed a deterioration in your mother's health and general demeanour. Her friend Lady Cecily Fairfax—your father's sister-in-law—hinted to Mrs Churchill that there had been an attachment the previous Christmas. But!' he waved his hand, 'all turned out to be well. Your father was a fine fellow and he made your mother very happy. It is more than I can say for Louisa and Mr Weston. Theirs was not a happy match.'

This much Jane had gathered from Mr Weston. The Churchills' coldness towards *him* had been at the root of the unhappiness but she could not assert that now.

'I hear Weston is to remarry,' Mr Churchill said.

'Indeed, sir,' Jane replied, and provided as much information as she felt was judicious about Miss Taylor.

'I wish him extremely well,' Mr Churchill concluded, 'he deserves to be happy.'

Presently they reached the end of the promenade and looked back along the curve of the bay.

'A delightful prospect,' said Mrs Campbell, 'I confess I never tire of it. Do you walk this way often Mrs Churchill?'

'I have never *walked*—the carriage comes this way often enough. The view is very nice.'

Mrs Campbell looked along the facades of the white, elegant buildings that faced the sea, the bright splashes of colourful awnings that shaded the shops, the feathered plumes of the horses that trotted along the thoroughfare, the azure sea and cloudless sky. Nice? The woman has not an iota of taste, she decided, no eye for beauty. Nevertheless she said, 'I do hope you will do us the great honour of dining with us one day soon. The young people would like it particularly, I think.'

'The young people?' Mrs Churchill repeated. 'You arrange your social calendar for *their* benefit, do you?' The idea was a novelty to Mrs

Churchill, who had never set anyone's pleasure above her own. She concluded that Mrs Campbell had designs upon Frank for one of her girls. She looked across the sands to where they were searching for shells and interesting pebbles. 'Your ward, Miss Fairfax, you provide for her, do you? A marriage settlement, I mean.'

'Lamentably, that is beyond our power,' Mrs Campbell replied.

'She will bring nothing to any alliance she might make?'

Mrs Campbell bridled. 'Beyond her own faultless self, you mean?' she said sharply. She began to enumerate on her fingers, 'Her many accomplishments and excellent sense; her eminently respectable family; her gentle, kindly character; her superior education and undeniable beauty? No. *If* she marries,' she concluded dryly, 'she will bring nothing at all.'

'I see. And your daughter?'

'All of the aforementioned, plus a dowry of some twelve thousand pounds.'

Mrs Churchill sniffed. 'Frank will marry an heiress from some noble family or other. That is to say, I do not absolutely stipulate for the money—*that* is of less consequence. Churchill will provide as handsome a fortune as anyone could require—but the superior birth I unequivocally insist upon. You will do well to mention the fact to the young ladies. I would not have them labour under any misapprehension concerning my nephew.'

Mrs Campbell felt as though her girls and their prospects had been fingered like flawed fabric at a market stall and rejected with as little ceremony. 'They have only just made Mr Churchill's acquaintance,' she said stiffly. 'Neither of them is so precipitate in their thoughts or their feelings to have made such a leap in so short a time.'

'I am glad of it,' Mrs Churchill replied, 'but it is better to have these things clear at the outset. I thank you for your kind invitation. You have a tolerable dining room in your lodgings? It is the one deficiency at Chesterfield Place. Nevertheless, we will be obliged to entertain, cramped as we will be. I have relatives in town—distant, and not what one would wish—but the courtesies must be observed.'

'I understand,' said Mrs Campbell, although she did not; she thought Mrs Churchill's remarks showed appalling hubris and pitied the poor relations who must be invited and entertained with such evident reluctance. 'When you have fixed a date with *them* I hope to hear when you will be at liberty to come to *us*. We reside in Augusta Place - the dining room is quite large enough to seat a dozen or more.'

They sat for a while and watched the young people on the beach. The tide was out, revealing an expanse of clean, smooth sand dotted with shells. Mr Dixon used his cane to write their names. Rowena collected shells to add decoration to his artwork.

'The tide will come in and obliterate your calligraphy,' Jane said when they were done. She stood with her face to the sea breeze. Tendrils of her hair had loosed themselves and blew becomingly round the rim of her bonnet. Her gown frisked and fluttered around her ankles. The sun and air had brightened her complexion to even greater bloom and her smile was so unstudied, so full of genuine, unaffected pleasure that it bathed them all in its glory.

'But it will not obliterate *us*,' Patrick Dixon said, looking at her with a flushed countenance. 'The tide will come and go, come and go, but *I*, for one, will remain constant.' He gave her such a speaking look as it was impossible to misinterpret. Jane's mouth flapped uselessly for a few seconds before she could collect herself. She felt overwhelmed with self-consciousness, suddenly very hot despite the breeze, close to tears although she had nothing whatever to cry about. She had never suffered this confusion before. Was she in love? Or simply grateful, as a drowning man is grateful to the rescuing hand? Mr Dixon's gaze remained, unwavering. Did he expect some answer? Jane glanced to where Frank Churchill was busy trying to light a cheroot—*he* seemed oblivious to the little crisis that Jane felt raged like a tempest all around them. Then she looked at Rowena, who stood a little to one side, purporting to admire the writing in the sand. But something about her demeanour alarmed Jane. Her head was down, her shoulders rounded. Her arms were clasped about her body. Her expression, when at last she lifted her head, was anguished to the point of pain.

'Rowena, dear, you are unwell,' Jane said, rushing to her side. 'Let us see if a Sedan can be found, or a carriage of some sort. You need to go home.'

'Yes,' said Rowena through lips that almost chattered. 'I think I have walked too far, or taken too much sun. *Something*—I do not know what—suddenly came over me and, I do apologise,' she looked at the two gentlemen, 'for spoiling your walk.'

They denied it, even as they took one arm each and escorted her back to the promenade, and promised to see her home safe. They declared themselves confident that some refreshment and a rest would put the roses back in her cheeks. She drooped between them, and said nothing more.

Chapter Sixteen

Although they had made tentative arrangements to meet Frank Churchill and Patrick Dixon at the theatre that evening, Jane and Rowena found, after their long walk and prolonged exposure to sun and air, that they were equal to nothing after dinner than a quiet hour reading in the peace of the drawing room. The prospect of tea and an early night was more tempting than the play. They sent a note with their apologies.

Rowena rallied somewhat once she returned home but she did not regain her high spirits of earlier in the day. She spoke—but falteringly—of her pleasure in the walk, of her regret of being unequal to the theatre. After that she lapsed into pensive silence. Conversation over dinner was desultory in any case - all the family had something private to preoccupy them. Mrs Campbell rehearsed in her mind the multiple evidences of insufferable pride and sickening hauteur of Mrs Churchill. Her behaviour and declarations had been nothing less than disgusting, her warning the girls off her nephew had been presumptuous in the extreme. But Mrs Campbell would not lower herself to relate any of it other than to hint that, 'Mrs Churchill certainly has great matrimonial expectations for her nephew.'

Colonel Campbell found himself very taken up with memories of Jane's parents—his friend Angus Fairfax and his spirited wife. He recalled now what Mr Churchill had alluded to earlier to Jane—the attachment that was suspected to have existed between Jane's mother and Frank Churchill's father before both had married elsewhere. There would be a certain serendipity, he considered, a pleasing closing of the circle in their children achieving what *they* had miscarried. For certainly, if Jane Bates had married James Weston she might not have been *happier,* but she would not have travelled as she had and would not have encountered the conditions aboard ship and in foreign climes that no doubt contributed to her consumption and early demise. Frank Churchill and his dear Jane might have been brother and sister but as it was, why should they not be husband and wife?

He looked across the table to where Jane sat toying with her dinner. 'Indeed, dear?' he said, in reply to his wife's observation, 'and who can blame her? A fine young man like that will naturally be looking for exceptional qualities in his wife.' In the colonel's opinion no lady, be she titled or as wealthy as the Queen of Sheba, could surpass Jane in any respect.

In spite of the exercise and fresh air Jane found she had little appetite. Her mind revolved around the revelations of the day. The unlooked for opening that Mr Dixon seemed to be ushering her towards was the outlook that claimed most of her attention; it was by no means a displeasing prospect. Many, many women, she knew, settled for matches, which, while they might be without love, had sufficient mutual respect and regard to make them perfectly satisfactory. From Mr Dixon she hoped for more—she was almost conscious that more already existed: the warm friendship and affection of a longstanding relationship, the alignment of ideas and tempers that were complementary. Jane had taught herself to be self-deprecating but she was not naturally modest; in her true self she was self-assured, confident. She knew she was clever, accomplished and nice to look at. She felt comfortable in company and had plenty of personal resources to keep her busy and entertained when alone. She did not lack for conversation and had opinions on a wide variety of topics. She had reined all these propensities in, however, in deference to her more timid friend, and in respect of her situation. It did not do for a governess to state her views too decidedly or to outshine her employers in looks, ability or understanding. Patrick Dixon really was as Jane pretended to be—self-effacing and quiet, likely to let others take his share of the conversation, preferring the company of a book or, more recently, a Dexter heifer, to people. In a marriage, the reticence of the one would be balanced by the true out-going nature of the other. *That,* Jane considered, augured well for the match. On balance, she thought that if he proposed—something she had never expected from *anyone,* let alone him—she could do much, *much* worse than accept.

But—and here the skein of her thoughts became mashed and tangled—something about Rowena's behaviour at the end of their walk did not sit comfortably. The two girls were as close as possible; they shared every waking thought and sleeping dream. Jane did not think it conceivable that Rowena had feelings to which she—Jane—was not privy. But clearly something troubled Rowena very much and that it was connected to Mr Patrick Dixon was equally apparent. It could be, Jane speculated, that realising Mr Dixon's attachment to Jane at the same moment as Jane herself had become aware of it, Rowena's immediate response had not been the wondrous potential of it for Jane but the woeful prospect of separation it would necessarily entail for herself.

This, she felt, she could counter easily enough. There could be no objection to Rowena coming to Baly-Craig for very extended visits. Colonel Campbell was at the point in his service at the War Office when retirement might be granted; they could remove themselves lock, stock and barrel to Wicklow and *would* do, Jane was sure, if Rowena would be the happier by it. On the other hand, there might be quite a different cause to Rowena's discomposure and one that could not be so readily smoothed away. Either way, Jane determined to find it out.

When the girls retired to their room, they said nothing while the maid helped them with their things, brushed their hair and sorted their linen for the laundry. At last she was done and they were alone.

'If you are not too tired, dear,' Jane said, 'come and sit with me by the fire for a spell. It is pleasant, is it not, to *have* a small fire? These May evenings are not *so* warm that they make the room oppressive.'

Rowena took a chair by the fire and Jane sat on the hearthrug and leant against her friend's legs. Jane opened their talk with, 'It was very agreeable today to walk the length of the promenade with Mr Dixon and the Churchills. Mr Frank Churchill is a lively character! Quite the mischief-maker, I think. What is your impression of him?'

'He seems very agreeable,' Rowena replied dully, staring into the flames. 'He speaks very quickly. Sometimes I cannot quite follow him.'

'You confirm my opinion,' Jane said. 'A lively tongue is evidence of a lively mind, I think. Mr Dixon has a slower, more considered mode of address. You walked with him for a long period of time today. What did you discuss?'

'Oh, all kinds of things. He has plans to renovate several of the farms at Baly-Craig, and to build new cottages for the labourers. He told me about that at some length. And he told me something of the natural history of Dorset. I am afraid I did not follow all that he said.'

'He makes a study of such things. Do you recall him showing us the beehives at Knoxbury? He was a fount of information on Apiology even then! Who would have thought, after that agonising start, that we should have become such good friends with the Dixons? He *is* a very dear friend, isn't he?'

Rowena did not reply for a moment. Jane listened carefully for any little sounds that might indicate that she was close to tears, but heard none. At last Rowena said, 'He *is* a valued friend. Apart from you, Jane, he is the person I esteem more highly than anyone in the world. I *thought* we had a particular affinity. Since you mention it I will tell you that I date it from that stay with Lord and Lady Knox. He was so kind, so very considerate …'

'*All* the Dixon boys were. They were our allies against the horrendous Lady Sowerby.'

'Yes, yes, they were all kind. But, of them all, I felt Patrick Dixon was the most considerate. Since that time there have been many occasions when my sense of his particular consideration has been reinforced. You recall two or three Christmases ago, when we were at the Dewhursts' and I was unwell? He brought me ginger tea and read to me for three hours without a pause. And again, at Lady Sowerby's funeral, he made a point of standing by me as the cortège passed by. I think he knew the turbulence of my feelings; my horror of Lady Sowerby herself, and the added dreadfulness of the idea of her being dead and cold in her coffin, and my sadness for Lady Knox and her sister, for she was *their* mother, and of course they loved her. He seemed to understand it all and he took my elbow and squeezed it. And then today when he seemed to wish so particularly to walk with me, Jane, it made me feel so happy. But now,' with a heavy sigh, 'I perceive that I have been mistaken. His regard for me is no more than—well, indeed, it is a good deal less than—it is for you.'

Jane scrambled to her knees so that she might turn and look at Rowena. 'My dear,' she cried, 'you are in love with Patrick Dixon! I had no notion of it! How … why have you kept this a secret from me?'

A secret, between these two, who had known only openness and complete confidence since their earliest days, was a new and not at all welcome intrusion. Jane was almost angry that it should come between them, as it inevitably must. It changed everything, for now *she* would have to keep a secret too.

Rowena smiled, but the tears now began to flow down her sallow cheeks. 'I have kept it a secret from myself. I have not dared own it. I knew he would not think of me … would not consider me. Who would, when *you* are near? But since he arrived here in Weymouth, my joy has been all but insuperable. When he danced with me at the Ball last night, I felt sure you would see … I thought *everyone* would see. I thought my heart would burst with happiness.'

'Dear Rowena,' Jane murmured, her mind working very fast to assimilate her new situation and produce some plan that would address it, 'I am so happy for you …'

'Happy for *me?*' Rowena replied. 'Why so? When I have absolutely no hope *now* of my feelings being returned? While I discerned no decided inclination for any other person, I taught myself to hope. I thought the idea might one day occur to him that, in the absence of anyone else, *I* might do quite well. But now—today on the beach … do not deny it for I know you perceived it as I did—he as good as declared himself to *you*. And so, my hopes are ended as I think I always knew, in my heart, that they would be.'

Jane resisted the impulse to gather her friend into her arms. Instead, she got up from the rug and went across to the window where the light from the candle did not penetrate. She could not allow Rowena to see her face. 'Declared himself to me? Of course not! I think you misunderstood,' she said lightly—but feeling very heavy in her heart. 'I heard nothing extraordinary in Mr Dixon's words beyond the fact that he compared his own constancy to the tide. And he *is* a constant friend—to *all* of us. He goes to Baly-Craig very soon. He takes up the mantle he has studied and prepared for, without the oversight of his beloved father or the support of his brother. His world shifts beneath his feet—like the sands beneath the tide. Naturally he invites the support of friends and does so by offering his in return.'

Rowena stood slowly and turned to face Jane. She stood close to the candle and the fire and her face was plainly visible to Jane, who had the advantage of gloom and better practice at masking her own feelings. In the past Jane had cajoled and encouraged, she had explained away and soothed over, but she had never lied. But *this,* Rowena instinctively understood, was something close to a lie. It was a prevarication. The way Jane twitched at the curtains and avoided her eye was so unlike her.

'So, you had no consciousness of … any particular meaning in Patrick's words?'

'None whatsoever,' Jane asserted, drawing down the bedsheet and climbing in. 'I think I will go to sleep now. Will you blow out the candle dear?'

'Yes,' said Rowena, and did so. But she did not get into bed immediately. She stood in the dark and allowed the tears to roll down her face. She did not know for sure that Jane had lied but she did know that she had not been offered the tender comfort and fulsome assurance she would normally receive when doubt or vexation overcame her. Some shutter had come down between the two girls that had never—in all the years of their friendship—been there before. It left her doubly bereft. She could not garner back to herself the comfort of the hope that she had nursed in the past about Patrick Dixon; she held it still, but in a grasp that was tenuous, filled with doubt. Neither could she gain her usual comfort from Jane.

She went to bed very miserable indeed, cried silently into her pillow and then slept at last. Jane lay wakeful much longer. She did not weep—she was not the kind of girl to give way to tears—but she agonised. The slim gleam of light that had seemed to shine during the day must be doused. How could she marry Patrick Dixon—even if he asked her—when it would make Rowena so miserable? It went against everything she had schooled herself to do. No, she must discipline herself once more; inure herself to her fate. Perhaps she ought not to delay even until the end of their holiday her search for a suitable situation. Next, she must convince Rowena that Mr Dixon felt nothing for her by discouraging his advances. She must not walk with him. She must on no account be alone with him. She must show, with as many cold shoulders and withering looks, that she would not welcome a proposal. Indeed, she must do more. She must transfer his affections to her friend.

'It will be my final act of service to the family,' she thought to herself, as the clock down the hall struck one. 'I have been Rowena's rock and mainstay. Now I must give her another before I set myself adrift.'

Chapter Seventeen

The following day the Churchills called upon Ariadne Mosley—formerly Billinge—and her husband Philip in York Buildings. Mr Mosley had improved only slightly in looks and demeanour since his marriage—he was still a somewhat drooping figure, sombre, with a dull light of unhappiness in his eye. Ariadne was not an unpleasant wife; she neither harangued nor sulked, she was not shrill or gloomy. She had a better temperament than her sister Matilda, having learned from the irascible rages of her late husband that some opinions are better left unexpressed. The two got along tolerably well for a couple who had been matched largely for the convenience of others, and yet there was, between them, something fundamental lacking.

Ariadne greeted her aunt Eustacia Churchill with cordiality and brought her husband forward, from where he loitered in a bay window, a book in his hand, to be introduced.

'My aunt Eustacia Churchill and her husband, Mr Charles Churchill of Enscombe,' she murmured, 'and their nephew Mr Frank Churchill.'

With evident reluctance, Mr Mosley placed his book upon a side table and shook hands. 'Honoured to make your acquaintance,' he said stiffly.

'And I yours, sir,' Frank replied, with as much heartiness as he hoped would make up for Mr Mosley's reticence. He looked about him at the high-ceilinged room, the well-appointed furnishings and tasteful décor.

'We called upon your sister Mrs Branthwaite yesterday. *She* is not so well accommodated as you. This is a pleasant situation indeed. It is quite as good as ours, in Chesterfield Place. Indeed, I think your rooms are larger.'

'And you have sight of the sea,' Mrs Churchill remarked sourly, with a cutting glance at her husband.

'*We* have sight of the sea, dear,' Mr Churchill replied mildly.

'Only if you stand on a chair and lean out of the window,' came the withering reply, 'not, of course, that I would debase myself by doing any such thing.'

'You probably have more rooms than us,' Mrs Mosley said. 'We have just this parlour and a dining room on this floor, and a chamber above. The house is divided into several similar apartments. I would not have you think we occupy the whole place.'

'I see,' said Mrs Churchill, mollified. The idea that her sister Clegg's girl should equal or even surpass her in anything was not to be borne. 'Yes, we have the whole of the property in Chesterfield Place. Several sleeping chambers. I am not sure how many. I have not inspected them all.'

'I need at least two,' Frank said gaily. 'I carry all my belongings around with me—some dozen or so trunks. One never knows how long one may be staying in any one place, or what one may need. Yorkshire is the devil of a long way to send for a tennis racquet or a favourite shooting stick, you know.'

Mr Mosley managed a half smile at this attempt at levity. 'I carry a large quantity of books for the same reason,' he offered.

'And so, Mr Mosley, you are a mercantile man,' Mr Churchill said, 'supervising the provision of goods from across the globe, I understand.'

Mr Mosley gave a self-deprecating shrug. 'My father and brother manage the business between them. I am really just a glorified clerk.'

'My dear,' said his wife, placing her small hand on his arm, 'you are *much* more than that.' She turned to their visitors. 'Philip supervises the customs arrangements, import and export taxes and bills of lading. It is *very* complex work. And then there is our contract to convey provisions to His Majesty's forces billeted abroad—*that* was won quite on the strength of Philip's diligence. Lately he spends a great deal of time at the War Office. Lord Knox depends upon him.'

'Lord Knox?' Frank cried. 'I was just yesterday in company with his grandson - Patrick Dixon. Are you acquainted with him?'

Mr Mosley muttered something about having often heard the name from Lord Knox.

'I shall be delighted to introduce you,' Frank said. 'He is a capital fellow. I am to sail with him tomorrow and I think they are all to dine with us.' He turned to his aunt. 'Is that not so?'

Mrs Churchill said, 'The Campbells are to host the dinner, but of course, we will have to have them back and when we do I suppose Mr and Mrs Mosley might join us.'

'We make a splendid party,' Frank said. 'Dixon is fast friends with a fine family by the name of Campbell. But, of course, you must know him too, if you are a regular at the War Office. I have a strange kind of connection with them in that their ward, a Miss Jane Fairfax, is a native of Highbury in Surrey, where my father abides. Is that not an extraordinary coincidence?'

Mr Mosley went pale, paler even than his normal insipid hue. 'Miss Fairfax?' he mouthed, 'I *know* the lady. I met her—let me see—three years ago. My sister and I took a house for a short time in Highbury. It was called Roundells.'

'Randalls?' Frank almost shouted. 'Astonishing! My father has just bought the place. He is James Weston. Perhaps you met him also?'

'I certainly did,' Mr Mosley said, with more animation than he had yet evinced. 'He was kindness itself to me.'

'Ah, my good fellow,' said Frank, his eye almost teary. He grasped Mr Mosley's hand and shook it once again. 'Any friend of my father's is a friend of mine.' The two walked by unspoken accord to the other end of the room.

Meanwhile Mrs Mosley sent for refreshments and bade her visitors be seated. 'I knew you were in Weymouth of course,' she said to Mrs Churchill. 'I would not have ventured to call on you. As gratified as we Cleggs are to be connected to you, I would not have presumed upon it to that degree. Matilda was not of my opinion, her daughter Mary less so.'

'Your discrimination does you credit,' Mrs Churchill said. 'Mary is avid to be seen in our barouche. Indeed, I believe *any* barouche would suffice, she is not very particular as to who owns it.'

'Poor Mary,' sighed Mrs Mosley, 'she has all my sister's ambition but not the sense to see that, if she did climb so high, she would soon expose herself. It is my opinion that one should know one's natural sphere, and remain within it.'

'I am quite of your mind,' Mrs Churchill said. 'But Matilda expects to be invited to dine at the very least, and I suppose we must oblige.'

'Philip and I neither seek nor expect such an honour,' Mrs Mosley said. 'Indeed, between you and me, my husband is somewhat taciturn. His spirits are easily depressed. He works diligently for his father but gets neither pleasure nor satisfaction from the work, or any word of thanks or praise. There is a schism between them. You see, he sought ordination but was refused it.'

'By the church?'

'Oh no. By his father. He took me in exchange for his vocation.' Mrs Mosley looked sadly at her hands. 'I believe he thinks he got the worst of the bargain.'

Mrs Churchill sipped suspiciously at her tea. 'The church is all very well for the younger sons of the nobility,' she pronounced at last. 'Very ancient and respectable families—even if they are not titled—can comfortably place their superfluous sons there. But for a family dependant on commerce, it seems to me to be the waste of a resource. You will recall that your grandparents—my parents—the Fishwicks— were so positioned; in a *very* superior, very *respectable* trade. Had they been blessed with sons there would have been no question of them being spared for any profession that did not materially contribute to the family good. I have not the honour of knowing your father-in-law but in my opinion he did quite right to deny Mr Mosley an occupation that could have been of no use to the dynastic cause. It is a child's duty to obey his parents. I am only sorry to hear that Mr Mosley does so with such a small amount of gratitude. And to take his disappointment out on *you* is unconscionable.'

'He does not reproach me,' Ariadne faltered. 'But I know he is not happy.'

Mrs Churchill could have said a word of comfort; she could have laid a compassionate hand on her niece's shoulder. But she was so devoid of natural sympathy that these things did not occur to her. In fact, Mrs Mosley's confidence embarrassed and unsettled her.

'I should very much like to meet Miss Fairfax again,' Mr Mosley confided to Frank Churchill in another part of the room. 'I found her to be an extraordinary young woman—wise beyond her years, with an innate sympathy one rarely encounters.'

'I have had little opportunity to acquaint myself with her,' Frank admitted. 'One doesn't, does one, in seaside places such as these? A ball is no place to converse—the music is so loud and conversation can only be very general during the set. A dinner is better, but I have not dined with the Campbells yet. I walked with Miss Fairfax yesterday—we walked the entire length of the promenade. I agree with you that she is an unusually deep thinker and a keen observer of human nature. I found her ...' he hesitated for a moment, his head on one side, only just coming to the realisation of what he had found Miss Fairfax to be. He gave a little laugh that was all self-consciousness, 'I found her to be a kind of kindred spirit. It must be the Highbury connection. I find I do most earnestly wish to speak with her again.'

'A long sea voyage is an ideal situation in which to become intimately acquainted with a person,' Mr Mosley observed cryptically.

'Indeed? Yes, I suppose so. Perhaps I had better bundle her aboard a barque and sail her off to the Indies! In point of fact, I *shall* sail with Miss Fairfax tomorrow, but only as far as Portland.'

Mr Mosley paled again, but only said, 'I pray you will remember me most kindly to Miss Fairfax and say that I would be honoured to renew our acquaintance.'

Chapter Eighteen

The following day dawned bright and clear—perfect in every respect for an excursion in the bay—and messages were quickly exchanged between Augusta and Chesterfield Places and the hotel whereat Mr Dixon lodged, assuring all parties that the sailing jaunt was certain to take place. Accordingly, at a little before midday the adventurers met at the quayside where Mr Dixon's little sloop *The Pride of Wicklow* was moored. Rowena Campbell was pale from the outset, and clung to her papa with both hands. Jane had more spirit about her. She looked forward very much to the outing although dreaded Mr Dixon making any comments that Rowena might interpret as evidence of peculiar regard. But she held her own feelings back, as usual, making Rowena's comfort and pleasure all of her concern.

Colonel Campbell looked upon the excursion as a mere nothing; *he* had sailed so many thousands of miles in vessels ten or twenty times the size of this small rig, but he encouraged his daughter with many a reassuring pat and with words that were calculated to assuage her anxiety. Mr Dixon and Frank Churchill were the most enthusiastic of the party. Mr Dixon was keen to show his guests around the sloop—which was soon accomplished, the vessel being not much more than twenty foot from bow to stern. He showed them the seat at the stern by the tiller, where he would steer them on their way, the benches either side of the cockpit where he hoped the ladies would be comfortable but, if they were not, the cabin below decks awaited where he had provided rugs and blankets and—with a blush—a bucket. The gentlemen might accommodate themselves on the deck; fishing tackle was to be had in the locker if they fancied their luck. Barron, the skipper, greeted all with a curt nod and busied himself about the boat, checking ropes and squinting at the high clouds with a knowing eye.

At last Rowena was got with difficulty along the narrow gangplank and aboard *The Pride of Wicklow*. Mr Dixon held out his hand to Miss Fairfax to guide her but she ignored it, to his evident confusion, and made her own sure-footed way to a place on the gunwales where she perched and looked out into the harbour. Frank Churchill followed, carrying sundry shawls, supernumerary bonnets and baskets of provisions that Mrs Campbell had provided at the last moment.

'Won't you sit closer to me, Miss Fairfax?' Mr Dixon tried again to engage Jane, patting the bench at the stern. 'There is plenty of room, and I can show you the tiller, and explain what Barron is about as he looses the topsail.'

Jane glanced at Rowena. In spite of her anxiety about the excursion her friend watched and listened with great attentiveness, was alert to any suggestion that there was something more between Mr Dixon and Jane Fairfax than common courtesy.

'Oh no, thank you,' Jane threw off. 'I have no interest in the mechanics of sailing. Rowena will be more interested and a good deal better at understanding, I am sure.'

The sloop began to move away from the quay, towed by a small rowing boat manned by two oarsmen.

'Very well,' replied Mr Dixon, nonplussed. But he turned to Miss Campbell and, nodding at the straining rowers, said, 'Once we are out of harbour and can catch the wind, they will let go the towline and return to the harbour. Then we will skim over the water like a bird. You need only watch the boom.' He pointed out a horizontal timber that swung over the cockpit. 'When we go about it swings right out. You will have to duck your head and scuttle to the other side.'

'I hope we shall not go *very* fast,' Miss Campbell said.

'The wind is very light, my dear,' her father said, patting her hand, 'have no fear.'

'And you see I have a little wherry in tow,' Mr Dixon said, indicating a small craft that was tied to the back of the sloop and followed behind it like a foal behind its dam. '*That* is to save you swimming to shore when we arrive at Portland.'

The first part of the voyage was indeed most pleasurable. A breeze—favourable in direction and benign in strength—sent them out of the harbour and across the bay towards Portland. Jane amused Rowena and distracted her from the considerable distance between them and land, the dark profundity of the sea beneath them and the alarming angle at which the boat sometimes listed as the wind filled her sails, by pointing out the shops and coffee houses they had frequented, which now seemed as small as dolls' houses in a child's nursery.

'Mama said she would stand on the promenade and wave to us,' Rowena said, scanning the length of the thoroughfare. 'She said she would wear her red shawl, so we could be sure to make her out. Oh! I cannot see her at all. You do not suppose she has lost her way?'

'It is early,' Mr Dixon said. 'She may not have realised with what alacrity we would get underway. Miss Fairfax, would you like to go forward? The deck is not slippery. Barron will take the tiller and I will help you. I am sure you will get a better view of Portland from the bow.'

'Oh no, thank you,' said Jane as coldly as possible. 'I am quite comfortable.' She turned to the vista around them. 'Look how the sun makes the sea glister, Rowena,' she said brightly. 'Is it not beautiful? What seabirds are those overhead? Are they terns? You are always better at identifying birds than I am.'

Frank Churchill, who had been standing forward, interesting himself in the various cleats and stanchions and getting rather in Barron's way as he coiled rope and trimmed the sails, now came back to the cockpit to sit near Miss Fairfax. She gave him a warm smile—much warmer than any she had thus far favoured Mr Dixon with—and invited him with all her powers of attentiveness to conversation.

'I met an old acquaintance of yours yesterday,' he began, much inclined to accept her tacit invitation. 'A Mr Mosley. He wished to be remembered to you.'

'Mr Mosley?' repeated Jane.

'Indeed. He resided in Highbury for a short time with his sister. They stayed at Randalls.'

'Oh yes,' said Jane, recalling the sad, badly treated young man. 'And how is Mr Mosley?'

'He is married to my aunt's niece, a Mrs Billinge as was. I suppose that makes me a sort of cousin by marriage to Mosley.'

'And is he happy?' asked Jane.

'Happy?'

'Yes. When I met Mr Mosley he was only just in contemplation of his marriage.'

Frank pondered the question. 'He appeared … well now, let me think. No, I think I would not be going too far to say that he does not seem to be a man of altogether sanguine humour.'

'I am sorry to hear it,' remarked Jane with a sad shake of her head. 'Tell me about Mrs Mosley. Is she a personable lady? Do they seem well-matched?'

Frank considered. 'She brought him a flotilla of merchant vessels from her first marriage. His family is in trade—a global concern. I suppose he provides the cargo for her ships; it seems to me to be a happy arrangement.'

'But,' Jane said with a little impatience—he had not understood her— 'are they alike in temper? Is there equality of intellect? Did you see evidence of affection? Mr Mosley is a gentleman of considerable sensibility. Does Mrs Mosley understand him?'

'Ah,' said Frank, understanding at last, 'you mean, is theirs a marriage of love? *That* is something rarely achieved, I think. Not many can aspire to it. It is as we discussed the other day; so often there are other considerations that impede the union of,' he searched for a suitable term and recollected his words of the previous day, 'kindred spirits.'

'Then I pity him,' Jane said in a low voice.

Frank threw her an ironical look, 'It was ever thus,' he said.

It was impossible, in such a confined space, to have conversation that was private and Miss Campbell was in no mind to allow Jane to say or do anything that she herself could not witness and weigh.

'I think,' she put in timorously, 'that where there is *friendship*—longstanding, intimate acquaintance—there can be happiness in marriage.' She allowed her eyes to glance fleetingly at Mr Dixon, where he sat and plied the tiller. It was difficult to say whether he noticed her glance, or took in the gist of her meaning. As they were nearing their destination he began to concern himself with matters aboard the ship, calling out the occasional question or instruction to Barron; he did not *seem* to be attending. Colonel Campbell was just then very intent upon a fishing line that he had dangled over the side of the boat and, being rather hard of hearing, took in nothing of the discussion.

'Undoubtedly there *can* be,' Jane agreed. 'Married love of that sort is very comfortable and much to be desired *if* there are no other claims to a person's affection *or* if one did not have an *alternative*, very *fixed* course of life to pursue.' She spoke of Mr Mosley, of course; his heart already given away to Miss Brokenshire and his fixed desire for ordination. But she spoke of herself also. Rowena had first claim on *her* affections and it suited her that the others should think her determination to be a governess absolutely unalterable. 'I *hoped* with all my heart that Mr Mosley might find that kind of accord with his wife. But—when one has known *another* kind of love—I will say nothing more specific for I would not for all the world betray a confidence—the passionate ardency of heart that Romeo and Juliet shared, for example—then the security of friendship, be it ever so genuine and warmly felt, must seem a pale imitation.'

'Juliet loved Romeo on a very slight acquaintance,' Mr Dixon said, showing that he *had* been attending their discourse, 'and it did not end happily for either.'

'Because there was enmity between their families,' Frank remarked heavily, comprehending in part the thrust of Miss Fairfax's argument but applying it with woe to his own situation. His aunt was sure to object to the family of any young lady he might prefer, unless they were ennobled, and even *then* she might well scruple. A girl with neither family nor wealth, however deeply he might love her, would be out of the question.

'But,' Rowena persisted, 'where there is no enmity—very decidedly no enmity, indeed, on the contrary, where there is established connection—*and* there is mutual regard and liking,' with a blush, and lowering her voice, 'the passion you mentioned, Jane, surely *that* will follow?' Boldly, with more courage that she had ever summoned in her life, she threw Mr Dixon a look, speaking and full of significance.

'Oh yes indeed,' he said warmly.

'One hopes so,' Jane said, very quietly indeed, 'and that is why I questioned Mr Churchill about Mr Mosley. We are speaking of *him*, of course. Let us not misunderstand each other. He … he … but no. I cannot say more. I have said too much already.'

'We are nearing our destination,' Mr Dixon said.

The sloop neared the place on Portland Island where Mr Dixon had arranged to be met by his retainers with a buffet of cold collations for their refreshment. Barron dropped the anchor close to a rock formation known as Durdle Door, which made a natural archway over the sea.

The young ladies admired it very much and lamented that they had not brought their sketching materials. Barron pulled the wherry alongside, dropped aboard the smaller vessel and tied it as closely as possible that the ladies might find it easier to transfer from the one to the other. But the sea being a little more choppy just here, and the wind freshening, Rowena tried and failed to take the step, clinging to her father, declining to do so much as to reach out and take hold of the skipper's strong supportive hand.

'Jane,' she said at last, 'do you go first and show me how it might be done. The distance seems too far for me, the drop too precipitate.'

Inwardly Jane fumed. *This* was no way for Rowena to behave if she wished to gain the admiration of Mr Dixon, a committed and enthusiastic sailor. She could see, by the slight roll in his eye, that he despaired of the party ever getting ashore and consuming the victuals he had ordered.

Rather than showing Rowena up, Jane decided to be as timid and reluctant in her turn. 'I do not know,' she said, feigning hesitancy. 'Could not the wherry be sent ashore and the food brought out to us? I had no notion, when I agreed to the voyage, that we would be asked to walk the gangplank.'

Both girls attached themselves to Colonel Campbell and looked with dismay at the small, vulnerable rowboat.

'Look,' said Mr Dixon, 'it is quite safe and very steady.' He demonstrated the security and stability by stepping deftly from one boat to the other a few times. He stood in the wherry and held his arms out to Miss Fairfax. 'Entrust yourself to my care,' he said with a blush that had nothing to do with the lively breeze or the bright sun.

'Oh no,' Jane demurred, shrinking away. 'Show me one more time.'

Mr Dixon stepped from the smaller boat to the larger and Jane showed, by a slight lessening of her resistance, that she was ready to do as she was asked.

'Come, Jane,' said Colonel Campbell. He took a strong grip on her and all-but hoisted her over the gunwales to the waiting arms of Barron. In her absence, Jane was pleased to see, Mr Dixon took a proprietary hold of Miss Campbell's waist. Mr Churchill skipped from one boat to the other and, two being its maximum capacity with a dedicated oarsman, the wherry rowed the few hundred yards to a pleasant sandy beach where attendants were waiting.

'*That* was an interesting exhibition,' said Frank, raising a knowing eyebrow. 'You seem determined to snub my friend Dixon today.'

'I do not know what you mean,' said Jane.

'Do you not?' Frank enquired. He thought the change in Miss Fairfax's demeanour towards Dixon was quite striking. It looked like the poor fellow would be refused *if* he got himself to the point of a proposal. On today's reckoning it didn't look as though there would be much point. For Dixon's sake, Frank felt sorry, but on his own he looked upon the development with cheer. What harm was there, if it encroached on no one's feelings, in a little seaside flirtation? Jane Fairfax was certainly the most beautiful girl in Weymouth; what young man would *not* like to squire her around town, dance with her at the Assembly and generally make every other chap green at the gills? She was amusing company and an interesting conversationalist. And then there was that sense he had of being in some odd way allied to her—the Highbury connection—that answered some deep and almost unsuspected longing in him for a friend.

The little boat beached itself on the sand and there were many willing arms ready to lift Jane on to dry land. Rowena and Colonel Campbell soon joined them and at last Mr Dixon was ferried by Barron to enjoy the bounty of his own generosity and foresight.

They spent some two hours enjoying the seclusion of the cove, the view of Durdle Door and Swyre Head that raised its chalky face to the sea at the end of the beach.

After they had eaten, Colonel Campbell declared his intention of walking to the top. 'It will be good to stretch the legs,' he said. 'Will anyone accompany me?'

Jane and Rowena regretted their inadequate footwear.

'I have a hankering to try a line off that outcrop of rocks,' said Frank.

The colonel walked off alone. Frank and Mr Dixon gathered some tackle together that had been brought from the sloop and scrambled over the rocks at one end of the bay, leaving the girls to their own devices.

Since their discussion two evenings before there had been a reserve between the two young women that had taken both by surprise, had unnerved and distressed them both. Both were conscious of Jane's dissimulation on the subject of Mr Dixon. Rowena did not believe in his indifference to Jane. Had he not expressly offered *her* the seat beside him at the tiller, invited *her* to accompany him to the bow and held out his arms to *her* in the wherry? Had not his invitation to 'entrust herself to his care' been as good as a declaration? And why would Mr Dixon *not* be in love with Jane? Any man with eyes and a modicum of discernment would single her out. This much had Miss Campbell the perspicacity to make out but beyond that she was all at sea. From being dismissive of Mr Dixon Jane now seemed positively cold. Her talk in the sloop of two kinds of love—the comfortable and the passionate—had intrigued. Could it be … could it *possibly* be that Jane was in love? Rowena cast around her for some young man, a London acquaintance perhaps, who could have won Jane's heart, but could think of none. She had noted no preference for a dance partner or a dinner companion amongst their wide circle. Then, Rowena reasoned, it must be some person who she met at Highbury, the only place Jane ever went where she was away from Rowena's own observation. Jane had mentioned meeting this Mr Mosley at Highbury. Could *he* be the object of her passion? In some ways this—entirely erroneous—deduction comforted Miss Campbell. If Jane loved another she could not be a rival for Mr Dixon's affections. It would explain her seeming unaware of his attentions. She had as good as said that, once one had known the ache of romantic love, one would not settle for the other, more measured and reasonable kind. But—and here Miss Campbell quailed very much in her reasoning—Mr Mosley was a married gentleman. Surely Jane would not allow whatever ardent feelings she had harboured for him to trespass on her own innate sense of propriety and moral rectitude?

'You have been very cold towards Mr Dixon,' Rowena said, when they girls had sat for a long time watching the sea and the servants had cleared away the remains of the meal.

'Yes, dear, I have,' Jane admitted. 'I mean him no unkindness. I like and esteem him very much. But if *you* have misconstrued my purely platonic regard for Mr Dixon it occurs to me that *he* may have done too. This would be a cruelty I would by no means inflict upon him. Therefore, I have moderated my behaviour. Do you think I have taken the correct course?'

'Do you think, then, that he *might?*'

'No, as I told you,' Jane dissembled, 'I discern no partiality in his conduct. It is my own behaviour that I call in to question.'

'Your behaviour is always exemplary,' Rowena replied. 'But *if* he has feelings for you, it would be hard on him—on you *both*—to force him to a declaration only so that you can tell him that they are not reciprocated.'

'Exactly my reasoning,' said Jane. How could she tell Rowena that she had been on the cusp of making whatever little gesture, saying whatever small word would have brought Mr Dixon to exactly that point, with the view of *accepting* him? She *would* have settled for that comfortable, easy marriage of one friend to another. How gladly would she have reconciled herself to it, as an alternative to what must otherwise be! But it could not be, not if Rowena's tender little heart should be broken in the process.

Presently Frank and Mr Dixon returned. They had caught no fish, but had thoroughly enjoyed exploring the rocks. Both men seemed a little flushed. It *could* have been the sea air and exercise but it was more likely due to Frank's hipflask, to which they had had recourse some half dozen times.

'My father is not yet returned from his walk,' said Rowena, looking anxiously in the direction he had gone.

'Barron says the weather has turned,' Mr Dixon said. He gazed at the sky in a way he hoped would indicate that he understood every nuance of the dark clouds that scudded, now, across the hazy blue. 'No matter, *The Pride of Wicklow* is a sturdy craft in a squall.'

'A squall?' Rowena almost shrieked. 'Oh, had Jane and I better not return with the servants in the pony cart?'

'There will not be room, Miss Campbell, and if it does come on to rain you will be better sheltered in the cabin,' Mr Dixon said. 'However, I see no possibility of rain for some hours yet. I will have the servants brew some tea and by the time we have drunk it your father is sure to be returned.'

The tea was brewed, and served and drunk, and still there was no sign of Colonel Campbell coming towards them across the sands. The wind had strengthened and the ladies were glad of the extra wraps that Mrs Campbell had insisted that they bring with them. Frank Churchill suggested sending one of the menservants to look for the colonel, or even going himself, 'For there can be but one path along the cliff there. I am sure to encounter him.'

Miss Campbell became more and more agitated with every minute that her father did not appear. Jane, who would normally have done her utmost to comfort and reassure her little friend, walked away a little distance, to abandon her to the kindness of Mr Dixon's sanguinity. She hoped Mr Churchill would follow her, leaving the others alone. But in fact both Mr Churchill and Mr Dixon stepped away from Rowena, leaving her solitary and very unhappy on the part of the beach that had been their camp, in order to share a whispered conference. If Jane had overheard it she would not have acquiesced so readily to what followed.

'I think your time would be better spent ferrying the ladies back to *The Pride,'* Mr Dixon said, 'than pursuing the colonel.' He did not like the prospect of having two faint-hearted ladies to deal with, bucketed and thrown about, as they would be now the tide and the weather had turned, with only the bluff Barron to assist him. 'If necessary, we will send one of the servants after the colonel if there is no sign of him once that is achieved. The colonel is a strong and resourceful fellow. He can take care of himself. My responsibility is to see the ladies safely home to their mama.'

'Very well Dixon,' said Frank, happy enough not to be faced with the stiff climb up Swyre Head.

'Only let me travel with Miss Fairfax,' Mr Dixon added in a hiss. 'I will send Barron back to bring you and Miss Campbell.'

So Jane was helped into the little rowing boat, Barron pushed it off from the beach into the high-rolling surf and at the last possible minute Mr Dixon leapt in after her. He sat close to her as Barron rowed manfully against the incoming tide and the boisterous waves. Naturally nothing could be said while the skipper was present, but as soon as he had deposited them aboard the sloop and set off back to the beach, Mr Dixon said, 'Miss Fairfax, I am glad of this opportunity to speak to you alone for a few moments. I wonder if I have done or said anything to offend you?'

'Not at all,' said Jane, with as much levity in her voice as she could muster. The boat was very unstable, rocking decidedly from one side to the other and also bucking from front to back. Considerable quantities of water threw themselves from the surface of the sea, wetting her face, hair and dress. In addition, a light rain had begun to fall.

'Shall we go below?' Mr Dixon asked, indicating the companionway that led down to the cabin. 'We would be drier.' But the thought of being confined there with him, out of sight, and of what Rowena might construe from such a compromising situation, filled Jane with horror.

'I would rather stay out here,' she said. She wrapped her shawl tightly around her and took a seat in the cockpit. 'Rowena should be our first consideration. She will not like these conditions. If we have anything to discuss—I cannot think what—but *if* we have, let us delay our conversation until a time when we are less likely to be drowned.'

'Miss Campbell need have no fear,' Mr Dixon said, distractedly, 'she will be safe enough. She might be a little queasy, but that will be all. Barron has reached the beach again. Oh Miss Fairfax,' Mr Dixon threw himself—or was thrown, by a sudden surge of the sea—onto the seat next to Jane. He took her hand. 'For many long months I have harboured a hope … a desire …'

The sea was quite rough, now. The anchor rope strained and creaked under the pressure being exerted on the boat to run before the vigorous wind and powerful current. Mr Dixon couldn't help but be pressed closely to Jane's side, a situation that pleased, rather than incommoded him.

'I beg you, sir,' said Jane, into the teeth of the tempest, 'say nothing that will force me to disappoint you.' She leaned back, away from his face, which was very close to hers. Behind her she could hear the sharp slap of the waves as they hit the boat, the spray of rain on water and above her the angry howl of the wind through the boat's rigging.

The boat lurched again. Mr Dixon was pulled away from her. She was lifted from her seat but a strong grip on a nearby stanchion prevented her from being thrown into his arms.

'*Would* you disappoint me, then?' His expression was stricken. Water coursed over his hair and face and soaked his clothing. He had never looked so ... handsome was not the right word, he would never be that, but so full of masculinity and ardour. 'Forgive me, but I know your situation. I know what 'alternative' course you believe is so very 'fixed'—yes, I heard and understood every word—but believe me when I say that it does not have to be so. I can offer you so much more.'

The movement of the sloop catapulted him forward once more. He was next to her, almost on top of her. The frisson this produced in Jane was startling and delicious—she had never imagined, much less experienced such a sensation before. He put his face forward as though to kiss her. She released her handhold and fastened herself to the lapel of his coat. Whether it was to fend him off or to pull him to her, she did not know. He reached for her other hand where it held the ties of her shawl at her throat.

'I cannot,' she cried in anguish, 'there is another ...' She bethought herself of poor Rowena, the duty she owed her as friend, the course she had adopted from an early age of always putting Rowena first, promoting *her* happiness and encouraging *her* spirits above and before her own.

'Another?' Mr Dixon gasped, misunderstanding, his eyes tormented.

The boat listed violently. Both Jane and Mr Dixon were thrown almost on to their feet. Mr Dixon had better sea-legs and took up a sturdy stance and Jane found herself, momentarily, in his arms. They exchanged an anguished look, such a look as would have broken Jane's heart if she had loved him. *His,* she knew, was cracked from top to bottom. Then the side of the boat fell away beneath them. Jane was thrown from Mr Dixon's embrace. The boom broke free of its restraint and swung across the cockpit. Instinctively, Dixon ducked. She took a glancing blow from the sturdy timber across her shoulders. She was flung back to her seat, which seemed to fall away from her as the boat rolled into a trough between the waves. She grappled for some purchase but found none. There was nothing at her back but the swell of the sea. She felt herself tip, her feet lost their contact with the floor of the cockpit, the chill of the sea was on her back and her hair was caught up in the current. Water filled her ears. Then she was grabbed, her habit, shawl, person—anywhere Mr Dixon could get a purchase—and she was hauled back into the boat. She huddled, drenched and gasping, on the floor of the cockpit.

Then Barron was alongside. Rowena, Frank Churchill and Colonel Campbell had all squashed into the wherry to save him the trouble and fatigue of a further journey. Jane found herself below in the cramped cabin with Rowena, wet and trembling, both of them very frightened, as, above them, the men weighed anchor and began the buffeting journey back to Weymouth.

Chapter Nineteen

Jane and Rowena stayed at home for a few days after their outing. The fine weather had deserted Weymouth for a spell in any case, making walking and riding unpleasant. They stayed indoors during the day and collated the sketches they had made in the foregoing weeks, while a fine rain beaded the windows. Rowena's confidence was bruised, her spirits enervated; she had no appetite for the Assembly or the play so they did not venture out in the evenings either. Jane was not seriously hurt apart from a little bruising around the shoulders. She did not catch cold, much less the pneumonia that would have pleased many a romance writer, but she was anxious to avoid Mr Dixon until they both should have recovered from their ordeal and their exchange. He called daily, and Jane made sure that Rowena greeted and entertained him, claiming an indisposition she did not feel. Rowena did not question this subterfuge but entered into it; next to Jane and her parents, Mr Dixon was the person she felt most comforted by.

Gradually, the distresses experienced by both young ladies ceased to have power over them. They both accustomed themselves to disappointed hopes. Jane's hopes had known such a brief life—only a day or so—and she soon regained that control of them which she had exercised since childhood, reminding herself again and again that it was Rowena who had first claim to all her care, whose happiness must be promoted. Rowena's hopes of Mr Dixon had been closeted secretly within her breast for a number of years, unsuspected at first, then acknowledged with wonder and tentatively nurtured, only to be dashed as Mr Dixon's preference for Jane had become more and more marked. Although now she had no real hope of him, she did not cease to love and revere him, but gathered those feelings back to languish in the crucible of her heart.

The weather cleared and there was no reason why the Campbells should not resume their programme of outings. Weymouth was such a seaside town as invited one out, enticed one with splendid vistas and interesting shops and where agreeable families, spectacles and entertainments were to be met everywhere. Inevitably Mr Dixon accompanied them as they promenaded along the esplanade and rode out to Maiden Castle and Chesil Beach. He behaved as naturally as he always had, but there was that degree of deference towards Miss Fairfax that marked an alteration in their acquaintance. It helped them all that Frank Churchill was often of their party when he could be spared by Mrs Churchill, making himself congenial, happy to be away from his aunt, suggesting such schemes of recreation that were novel and amusing to all. In her discreet efforts to ensure that Rowena enjoyed the lion's share of Mr Dixon's attention and conversation it was invariably the case that Jane should find herself often on Frank's arm, riding in his gig and partnering him at the Assembly. She saw, sometimes, a light of hurt and confusion in Mr Dixon's eyes but she refused to let the import of it penetrate her soul; *she* had not courted his attention or set out to win his affection. She hoped that by throwing Rowena in his way as often as possible he would soon see a better alternative.

For Frank's part, nothing could be more delightful than the company of Miss Fairfax. The harmless flirtation he had initially contemplated enjoying in her company soon advanced into something more profound. He found himself daily more anxious to be sure of securing an *exeat* from his aunt so that he could be at Jane's side. Thoughts of Jane cheered the interminable hours he was required to sit in the cloistered confines of Chesterfield Place. Full knowledge of Mrs Churchill's disapproval, had she known of his increasing preoccupation with Miss Fairfax, only increased his eagerness; Jane's conversation and smiles grew ever more pleasurable to him. They had sung together some once or twice; their voices were an excellent match. She danced very well indeed. But far above the usual intercourse permitted between young men and women at the Assembly or at private dinners, he felt, with her, a sense of kinship. They had both been orphaned and sent from home. To her he could speak without reserve of his father, of Highbury—the place he instinctively thought of as 'home'—and of the people there of whom he had heard so much but never seen. She described them all with kindness, humour and affection, painting for him a vivid picture of the narrow streets, the little shops, the church and principal houses.

'I feel,' he said to her one evening as they took a moonlit stroll along the beach, 'as though I know them all, now. You have made them real to me.' The beach had been lit with flaming torches, their light reflected in the glassy sheen of the water on the sand. Musicians were stationed along the promenade; the sound of their instruments melded with the rush and pull of the distant tide. Frank Churchill lifted a corner of Jane's shawl that had slipped from its anchorage and in the action of tucking it back, drew her arm through his. 'I see Mrs Goddard's quiet strength and pride,' he went on, moved, by the dulcet scenery and by the picture she had painted of the quaint little town, to a sort of rapture. 'To have started that school as a young widow, and to have made of it such a success as she has done is really admirable. And the little girls all in smocks and pigtails as they play on the lawns along the riverbank are as real to me as those minstrels there. I feel I would recognise Mr Cole if he were to ride by—his upright bearing and famous green coat! And Miss Woodlouse,' laughing, 'I know, I know, but so I will always think of her now—what a creature she is! The epitome of beauty, charm, wit and complacence!'

'I am sure she is very amiable,' Jane demurred, 'but the two of us have never found that level of friendship which, perhaps, might have benefitted us both. For some reason she does not like me.'

'I cannot conceive it,' Frank replied, gallantly, 'or, at least, if she does not *like* she must *respect* you. Who would not? Is she without understanding? There is a saying, is there not—*there but for the grace of God*. Surely, she sees that you have endured what she was spared. In the beginning your circumstances were comparable—come to that, I must count myself in the equation also. We *all* lost our mothers, but you lost both parents. You and I were sent from home but Miss Woodhouse was able to stay amongst familiar people. She was raised by a fond father while we have had to make do with strangers.'

'I have not a word to say against the Campbells,' Jane interrupted. 'If you think me in any sense lacking in regard and gratitude to them you are mistaken. No daughter could have been loved more than I have been or the recipient of more disinterested care.'

'There you have been luckier than I,' Frank murmured, 'but,' resuming his former bantering tone, 'you see the thrust of my argument? Miss Woodhouse must be blind if she does not see how magnificent you are notwithstanding all that you have been through.'

'I fear,' said Jane slowly, 'and it is awkward to have to say it out loud, but I fear that Miss Woodhouse sees it all too clearly. She sees that she has had all the advantages; the hearth of her own loving father, her situation in Highbury—the Woodhouses are of first consequence there—but she has not made of them what I have of those that have fallen to me. But I do not censure her. She has not the need that I have. What is the mastery of a piano concerto more or less to her? What does it matter if she has not read Milton or does not know her *Midsummer Night's Dream* from her *Tempest?* It does not matter if *she* cannot do algebra.'

'Which of us can?' Frank quipped.

But Jane turned a serious eye towards him. '*I* can,' she said. 'It is essential that I can. You must know, Mr Churchill, that in due course I will be required to seek a position as a governess.'

Frank looked astonished. 'A *governess?*'

'Oh yes,' Jane said, walking on across the sand. 'It has always been understood that someday I must earn my bread and I have always told myself that my twenty first year will be the time at which I will begin to look about. That year is upon me now, and so …'

'Miss Fairfax!' Frank spluttered, genuinely astounded, 'I am so surprised I can hardly speak! I had no idea, no notion …'

'But it is so, sir,' Jane said with a slight smile. 'Do not be sorry, do not be embarrassed. *I* am not.'

'But then …' Frank began, looking behind them to where Mr Dixon and Miss Campbell strolled. 'But then, *surely,* the prospect of …'

'Ah,' said Jane, following his gaze and his train of thought, 'but *that* could never have been.'

'Dixon's people would have raised no objection I am sure,' Frank argued. 'He is only a second son but the first is admirably married and, to be frank, they are so wealthy that the question of,' he gave an embarrassed little cough, 'a *settlement* would not have been any impediment.'

'None of those matters carried any weight with me,' Jane observed. She looked fondly at her friend who walked beside Mr Dixon, her face turned up to his, her eyes alight, her ear tuned to every word he uttered.

It was Frank's turn to follow her look. 'Ah,' he breathed, understanding. 'You gave him up for her.'

Her sacrifice amazed and enamoured him. She seemed to him like a kind of saint. In looking back at where Dixon walked with Miss Campbell Frank had released Miss Fairfax's arm and he felt hesitant, now, to repossess it. He had never known such selflessness, such generosity in anyone, much less his aunt, who was, on every score, the complete opposite. The contrast stirred his feelings. If he had been asked to describe his ideal of womanhood it would have been the possessor of every contrary attribute evinced by Mrs Churchill. And here she was!

'I confess,' he said presently, 'I am quite speechless.' Speechless indeed, and, for a moment, rather confused. Frank was not a young man of deep sensibility, but *now* he felt his feelings move powerfully.

Jane said, 'It is easy to think that a girl with no family and no fortune must snatch any opportunity for matrimony that might present itself—that she has no choice. But I have a choice that the goodness of the Campbells and my own resolve, settled from an early age, has secured for me. Of course, I *can* marry if I wish, but I do not *need* to. I do not have to settle for the kind of needy dependence with which some wives burden their husbands and sour their marriage. I will not saddle myself with that perpetual sense of gratitude and unworthiness that assail poor wives of rich husbands. Neither would I burden a good, poor man to perpetual poverty with me when he might find a fine lady who would make him happy and rich. I have taught myself that small, earned independence is my destiny and I am content with it.'

It was getting late. The tide had turned and brought with it a chill breeze that made the torches gutter. Along the esplanade carriages were waiting to take ladies and gentlemen for the final sets at the Assembly or home to warm fires and sleepy servants. The musicians began to pack up their instruments. By unspoken accord the pair bent their path towards a flight of steps that would take them off the beach.

'I envy you,' said Frank simply. He had been denied any opportunity of a profession by which he might attain independence. His education at the hands of Tunnock had been thorough but he had neither degree nor vocation. *He* was doomed to a life of idleness. The pointlessness of it oppressed him now more than it ever had done before. And on the subject of marriage … he would be forced to marry a girl of his aunt's choice. If she had her way it would be a girl of high estate. The prospect was more depressing than ever when he considered Miss Fairfax's picture of what such a union would be. Would *he* be doomed to that sense of perpetual gratitude and unworthiness to which she had referred? Or, if his aunt's choice were noble but impecunious, would his wife be a constantly draining dependent? His aunt herself, in all conscience, was enough of a burden on him; he was sick of being indispensable, always required to raise her spirits, hand her medicine, sit by her on interminable carriage rides, and endure hours of carking complaint. He would not wish to exchange a needy relative for a needy wife. The notion was intolerable.

Jane turned by the steps and understood his expression. 'In a few years, when you are master of Enscombe, your sacrifice will seem worthwhile,' she said. 'My case is quite different. I have had my reward beforehand. Now, I must pay the price.'

Their time of private converse was coming to an end. Miss Campbell and Mr Dixon were approaching from the beach. On the promenade above Mrs Campbell was hurrying forward with extra shawls.

'But, to have a choice,' Frank blurted out, 'to be free, is a splendid thing!'

Jane lifted her eyes to where Mr Dixon lingered with Rowena. He was speaking most enthusiastically to her about something—his words did not carry, so Jane could not hear what—which animated his features. The two stood in easy proximity to each other, there was a degree of naturalness and simple trust that spoke more, perhaps, to an onlooker than it did to them. 'We cannot choose to love,' she said, 'but sometimes we find that we *do* love, perhaps without knowing it.' She narrowed an inviting eye. 'Look at them. Look at *him*. He is so fond of Rowena that it is as close as makes no difference to being in love. He just needs to be made to realise it.'

Frank had his father's mildness, which did not allow him to be troubled by anything for periods of long duration. Now he laughed, the intensity of only a moment before forgotten and his mischievous bent excited by Jane's suggestion. 'I see your meaning,' he said, nodding roguishly, 'and I will aid you in your endeavour if I can.'

Of all things, Frank enjoyed a subterfuge; the idea of nudging his friend Dixon toward Miss Campbell was highly appealing in itself but the opportunity to edge him *away* from Miss Fairfax was also viscerally alluring. With Mr Dixon affianced to Miss Campbell there would be nothing to prevent him—Frank—from taking the path he had been daily more persuaded towards and that *now* seemed more appealing than ever. Miss Fairfax was without doubt the most extraordinary young lady of his acquaintance, the most honourable and selfless. She was utterly unlike the other young ladies he knew, who flocked around him and simpered because he was Frank Churchill and would inherit the Churchill fortune and Enscombe. *She* had no interest in these things; she had a spirit of independence that he found powerfully attractive and was so wholly juxtaposed to his aunt as made him almost wild with desire.

Mrs Campbell arrived, breathless and wincing a little from the pain in her legs, 'Girls, girls,' she said, shaking out coverings and wrapping them up, 'the moon has gone down and it has turned quite chilly. You will catch your deaths if you stay out a moment longer. The Colonel has gone to fetch the carriage though it is but a five-minute walk back to Augusta Place. Mr Dixon, Mr Churchill, we must bid you goodnight.'

Chapter Twenty

Mr Dixon and Mr Churchill were left alone on the promenade.

'Shall we take a nightcap, Churchill?' Mr Dixon offered, 'I know a capital little place with the best brandy and cigars in Weymouth.'

'By all means,' said Frank, falling into step beside him, awed and excited by the revelations of the past few moments. 'I have had a delightful evening and am not ready for it to end yet. I must say the Campbell girls are splendid company, are they not? You have known them since you were a boy. They must feel like sisters to you.'

'Sure, I used to think so,' said Patrick Dixon, thoughtfully, 'but now I do not know.'

'Oh?' queried Frank.

Mr Dixon hesitated. They crossed the thoroughfare and ducked down a narrow side street towards the harbour. 'I will be truthful with you, Churchill,' Mr Dixon said at last. 'These last few weeks I have been harbouring very unbrotherly feelings towards one of those girls, if you get my meaning.'

'Oh yes?' said Frank, feigning a frown, 'I wonder which it could be?'

'Do you? I would have thought it obvious.'

'Obvious? Oh no. Why would it be, when *both* are so charming, albeit in rather different ways.'

'You are right, they are both extremely nice girls and it would be disrespectful to compare them. My grandmother, Lady Knox, would tell me that comparisons are odious.'

'But she is not here.'

Mr Dixon laughed. 'No, mercifully she is not! She would not approve of the drinking den I am taking you to.'

'I am all anticipation! But, since Lady Knox is not here, and since I am most interested to hear your opinion on the matter, let *me* suggest very tentatively that Miss Campbell has not quite the brilliancy of feature of her friend Miss Fairfax.'

'No, she has not the *brilliancy*,' Mr Dixon concurred, 'but she has a certain prettiness about her. I will not hear anyone say that Miss Campbell is not pretty.'

'I will not venture to do so, then. Yes, you are correct. Miss Campbell's eyes in particular are very pretty. Her hair is not as lustrous as Miss Fairfax's though. I believe that is incontrovertible.'

They crossed the bridge towards the quays, and a row of low, dilapidated buildings. 'I will allow you that,' Mr Dixon agreed, 'but it is a very nice shade of brown. It reminds me of a wren's wing.'

'Ah yes,' sighed Frank, 'and it is as soft as one too, I expect.'

'I do not know,' Mr Dixon said, and the note of regret in his voice was quite affecting, 'I have never touched it.'

'Would you like to?' asked Frank in a low voice.

'Yes, now you mention it. I thought ... I have been used to thinking I would rather ... Miss Fairfax's ringlets, you know, and the colour ... but now I think of it, a soft, natural curl is very appealing.' Mr Dixon had drifted into a sort of reverie—as Frank had intended—but he shook himself out of it to say, 'Here is the place, Churchill. It looks somewhat seedy, I grant you, but I think we will be warmly welcomed.'

They entered the low doorway, went down a narrow and rather smelly passageway and emerged into a small parlour furnished with a makeshift bar and a few scarred and wonky tables and chairs. Gentlemen of various degrees played cards, spun yarns and drank hot porter, punch and brandy.

'The brandy comes across from France by night, if you get my meaning,' Mr Dixon whispered to Frank as they took their seats in a secluded corner close to the embers of a fire. 'With the war, more legitimate deliveries aren't possible. This fellow circumvents the war ships and the customs men to serve his clientele. I hope it won't trouble your conscience to take a flagon with me?'

'My conscience shall be as clear as my head tomorrow,' said Frank. 'Set them up.'

When the liquor had been delivered to them and they had exchanged some playful banter with the dimpled serving girl, Frank returned their conversation to Miss Campbell and Miss Fairfax. 'As to character, I think there the two young ladies we were discussing differ quite markedly. There is no gainsaying that Miss F—I will not name her, for fear of being overheard and misconstrued, although I do not *believe* she has a belligerent brother who might take offense and call me out?'

'She has nobody, so far as I know, except an elderly grandmother and a talkative aunt.'

'It would be just my luck to be challenged to a duel by knitting needles,' said Frank, draining his glass, 'but I will take that chance. Miss F has the readier wit, does she not?'

'She is altogether the livelier of the two young ladies, but the *other* has a quiet, thoughtful mind. She thinks deeply about things. Speaking for myself, I love to converse with her.'

Frank allowed his eye to be distracted by the buxom serving girl as she cleared dishes from another table. When she had disappeared into the scullery he said, 'I have not had the opportunity to talk to her beyond the usual pleasantries. She seems rather shy.'

'She *is* shy. But I do not think that a fault in itself. Come to that, I am rather shy myself. At least,' with a sly glance at Frank, 'I know *she* harbours no secrets.'

'Secrets?'

'Yes,' said Mr Dixon, finishing his drink. 'From something Miss F said to me on our disastrous outing to Portland, I suspect her to be involved in a secret liaison. I would not have thought her capable of such duplicity. The Campbells would be mortified if they knew. It explains her recent coldness.' Mr Dixon replenished both their glasses from an earthenware jug whose homeliness belied the fineness of its contents. 'I will be candid with you, Churchill; I have suspected *you* of being her secret lover. From the way you extoll her sundry virtues, I am becoming more convinced of it.'

'Me?' Frank said with a shout of laughter. 'Well! I will not deceive you: I have had secret lovers in the past, but I am not currently entangled. It's possible you misunderstood,' he extemporised, knowing the real reason for Jane's aloof air towards his friend. 'That day was all confusion. But you are right; the *other* young lady is all openness, warmth and softness. I never met a sweeter natured girl in my life.'

'Nor I.' Mr Dixon stared thoughtfully into the bottom of his glass for a while before gulping it down.

'She has not Miss F's accomplishments, though,' Frank said with a jocular tone. 'She cannot play a note! Oh my, did you hear her attempts at the pianoforte the other evening, poor thing?'

'I confess that I would rather hear Miss F play, but the other plays quite nicely enough,' said Mr Dixon, 'with a touch that is natural and artless.'

'And as to singing! Oh my!' Frank said with a burst of laughter, 'what a cacophony!'

'She sings in her own key,' Dixon retorted. 'I will not have you abuse her, Churchill.'

'Oh no,' said Frank, thinking what excellent progress he was making. He poured more brandy. The maid had reappeared behind the bar and was polishing glasses with a suggestive hand. When he caught her eye, she pouted her lips and waggled her eyebrows. 'But,' he went on, with a cough, 'I believe women set more store by these things than men do. In any case, a farmer's wife—for that, I take it, is what you are considering making one or other of these girls—would have little time for such things. From what you tell me Baly-Craig does not offer a numerous or very superior society. There are not regular dinners and balls.'

Mr Dixon shook his head. 'No, neither. A bit of a shindy[xii] in the barn at Christmas when the locals like to drink themselves into a stupor with poteen—the lady of the house makes a brief appearance and then leaves the men to it. As far as society goes, I can name perhaps four or five families within reach and two of those are too barbaric to be invited to any occasion that does not require the wholesale destruction of china or the disembowelling of every piece of upholstered furniture in the house. My mother detested the place and remained there under sufferance only as long as the harvest was gathered in, before crossing back to England for a season that was as long as she could possibly stretch it out to be. I believe she loved my father, but *she* was no farmer's wife.'

Mr Dixon swirled the brandy round his glass, thinking of his mother and on the verge, perhaps, of becoming rather maudlin.

'Perhaps, then,' mused Frank, to bring his friend back to the point, 'you need a lady for whom society is not her most comfortable milieu? A shyer, more retiring young lady? Upon my word, Dixon, I believe I am beginning to solve your conundrum!'

'My conundrum?' asked Dixon blearily.

'Yes indeed! I am to guess which of the two ladies of whom we are speaking is the one who has provoked your less than brotherly attentions, am I not?'

'Oh yes,' said Mr Dixon, who had forgotten how their conversation had commenced. He knew he had set out to sing the praises of one lady but had been diverted into defending the virtues of another. Was he really so fickle? He had thought of nothing but Jane Fairfax for months. Could he be so easily convinced that another would make a better wife?

But now he thought of it—and he felt the brandy had clarified his thoughts to no small degree—while he was excited by Jane Fairfax's company, she did rather over-awe him; her beauty and wit were almost overpowering. But with Rowena Campbell he felt comfortable. More, she made him feel manly, always looking up to him as she did, asking his opinion and being guided by it, standing half a pace behind him as though he could protect her. *She* needed the shelter of a man. Miss Fairfax needed no one. She was independent and reserved and—as he *still* half suspected—duplicitous. Churchill was right; even if he persuaded Miss Fairfax to become his wife she would be wasted and miserable at Baly-Craig.

Frank swallowed down his brandy and recharged his glass. He felt his work was as good as done. 'This flagon is empty,' he remarked, 'I will stand us another, and what say you that we enquire of that young serving wench if she has a friend to keep us company?'

Chapter Twenty-One

The following day—not early, for he had retired so late that the dawn had been blushing the sky above his lodgings house as he returned to it—Patrick Dixon awoke with a thick head and a dry mouth but a rather pleasurable sense of having achieved something most satisfactory the night before. He rang the bell for his valet, ordered coffee, a veal and ham pie and a hot bath and lay back in bed waiting for one of those things to arrive, his hands folded behind his head. At length the valet returned with the coffee and the pie and a letter on a silver salver.

'This arrived for you this morning, sir, and Colonel Campbell waits below. He begs an interview, sir, if convenient.'

Dixon leapt out of bed. 'Did I arrange to meet the colonel today, Burke? Am I late for some excursion or other?' He began to hurry into his clothes.

'Not that I am aware, sir. Perhaps it has to do with the note you had me deliver before you retired?' The manservant began to tidy the room.

'A note?'

'Yes, sir. You had it in your pocket when you got in and I delivered it, on your instructions, to Augusta Place. It was early, sir. It took me a while to rouse the house.'

Mr Dixon went, first, very white and then very red. 'To whom was the note addressed, Burke?' he asked through thin lips.

'To the young lady, sir.' He proffered his salver again. 'Perhaps you should read the reply.'

Mr Dixon snatched the envelope and glanced at the handwriting—very neat and small, a lady's hand—before tearing the seal. But he had not been able to unfold the paper or read its contents before a perfunctory knock at the door brought Colonel Campbell into the room.

'Patrick, my boy,' he boomed, striding forward and taking Mr Dixon's hand. 'I could wait no longer below once your fellow told me you were awake. Out revelling into the small hours, were you? And no wonder! It is a glorious thing. If I had known, I would have joined you. I am not beyond a gentlemanly glass or two, you know! You have turned Augusta Place on its head and no mistake! Never was there such a scene of joy and excitement as I have had to endure since your letter woke us at dawn. The ladies have exhausted every lawn handkerchief in their possession with their tears. Tears of happiness, of course. You should have come to me first, of course, before addressing her, but what does it matter? *She* is happy. Indeed, she is undone. She swooned quite away at first. But if I can entrust her to any man, it would be to you. You have my permission, you have my blessing indeed. God bless you, my boy. God bless you both,' and it was the colonel's turn to find that he needed a handkerchief.

Patrick stood, bewildered and astounded, while the colonel faced the fireplace to compose his features. 'Sir,' he began, 'Colonel Campbell, I fear …' but it was no good. Whatever had been done could not, by a gentleman, be undone. Whichever girl he had addressed in his note he could not now avoid taking to wife. Damn Frank Churchill! What had he been about, getting him so drunk? Had Frank suggested writing a

251

note? Had Frank *written* it? He could not remember. The only thing he could call to mind was a fleeting recollection of a dirty attic room, two tumbled beds, squeaking springs and ardent moans from one, a shy giggle from another. He recalled a stockinged leg, a soft pillow of thigh above and, higher still, a dark, warm … he swallowed a tide of rising vomit and looked down at the letter in his hand.

Dear Sir

I thank you for your note. My father begs the honour of an interview later today, but if you are so fortunate as to gain his agreement, I grant you mine with all my heart.

Yours,

Rowena Campbell

So, it was done, and he would honour it. He could no more disappoint that poor bird of a girl than he could undo his sordid fumble with the barmaid the night before. Both acts were irrevocable. One would live in his conscience, the other in wedlock.

'I ask your forgiveness, sir,' he said now, his voice wavering. 'I … I should have observed the formalities. Not to do so displays a lack of duty which, I assure you, I by no means feel towards you—you, who have been like a father to me since mine passed away. I ask you now, humbly, with all deference, if you will do me the great honour of allowing me to take your beau … your special daughter to wife. I promise to love and take care of her. She shall be first in all my doings. She will lack for nothing that I can supply. I will treasure and protect her.'

As he spoke, it crashed upon him just *what* care and protection little Rowena Campbell would require, as timid and unworldly as she was. Even the crossing to Dublin might be an ordeal she would find herself hardly equal to, if her behaviour aboard *The Pride of Wicklow* was anything to go by. How she would cling to him! What a deal of guidance and reassurance she would need. But what was the point in questioning, *now,* a situation that was beyond reversal?

Colonel Campbell was speaking to him, holding out his hand again, his eyes awash with tears, as he reiterated his assent. 'Come to Augusta Place with me, Patrick, and see her yourself. She is full of doubt and dismay, hope and happiness. You must console her, reassure her. You are all she needs, now.'

'You go ahead,' Mr Dixon said. 'I will bathe quickly and follow. Give her … give her my love.'

An hour later he presented himself at Augusta place and was shown into a small drawing room where Rowena waited alone. She trembled so violently that she could hardly keep her feet. She kept her face so resolutely down that he had difficulty seeing it. Her hands toyed restlessly with a ball of handkerchief. When she spoke it was falteringly. He had to stoop to make out her words.

'I thought, when I saw it, that the letter was for Jane,' he made out at last.

'For Miss Fairfax?' he blustered. 'Not at all. I am sorry if I have not been clear enough. I would not have you suffer the agony of doubt, my dear. Dispense with it now.' He was already standing very close to her. He took her hand and prised the moist handkerchief from it. 'Believe me, dear Miss Campbell—dear *Rowena,* for so I have been so bold as to think of you these last weeks, in the privacy of my heart—to be as wholeheartedly yours as you declare yourself to be mine. From now on we will be together in all things, indivisible in heart and mind. Should you like that?'

She nodded. A tear dropped from her eye and landed with a splash on their clasped hands.

'And you will not be afraid? Afraid, I mean, of all that being married will entail?'

She shook her head, but in a way that suggested she was very afraid of all that he implied. 'We will go and live in Ireland,' she whispered at last. 'Just you and I. Not Mama or Papa or Jane.'

'Not at first, but they will soon come for a visit, which shall be as long as you like,' he said softly.

'And I will be your wife,' she went on, even more quietly, 'and you will know all …' The words caught in her throat and she struggled to get them to her lips. When she did, they were all breath and susurration, 'All the secret things,' she got out.

His heart melted and tears sprang to his eyes so that when he lifted her chin with his finger, their moist eyes reflected each other. 'We will discover them together, dear, as slowly and gently as we like. Have no fear, Rowena. I promise you, I *promise* you I will never hurt you.'

He kissed her then, very gently, and put a tentative hand in the feather softness of her hair. 'My little bird,' he murmured.

Chapter Twenty-Two

Mr Dixon and the Campbells had much to discuss over the next few days; plans to make, letters to write and receive, pecuniary matters to set in train. He was at Augusta Place for such extended periods of time that it was laughingly suggested that he had in fact clandestinely moved from his lodgings and into the house! The date for the wedding exercised them all. For the young couple it seemed that it could not come too quickly. It now being early June, August or even July was urged by them as allowing plenty of time for all the arrangements to be made. Mr Dixon was adamant that he must be back at Baly-Craig by early September; the harvest could not be got in without his supervision. On the other hand, he acknowledged that this scarcely provided time for other considerations. The manor house at Baly-Craig, he feared, would be hardly suitable to receive a bride. It had been empty of all but an elderly housekeeper and the steward since January; it could not be supposed that everything would be in such perfect order as he would wish for Rowena. Then there was the matter of his brothers. The eldest, Hugh, could be got from Scotland at a week's notice but Andrew and Connor were both serving in the Peninsular War and might not be granted leave. Even his grandfather, Lord Knox, from his elevated position in the War office, might not be able to manage their extraction.

Colonel Campbell proposed returning to town for a fortnight or so—as long as it would take him to put his affairs in such order that Rowena's dowry could be liberated from his other capital and paid over. Of course, Mr Dixon made a scruple as to *that;* it was not necessary, could be put off or even disregarded altogether. He would not have the colonel think for one moment that Rowena's twelve thousand pounds would make an iota of difference in the short to medium term.

'As to financial comfort, sir,' he said, as they sat over their claret one evening, 'I can say that Rowena will have everything her heart desires that can be got to Baly-Craig. The conveyancing of it will be more of a sticking point than the acquisition. I will not deceive you, sir. The roads around about the place are rough; an experienced carter and a steady team can navigate the way but it is something of an undertaking. Notwithstanding, I shall move heaven and earth to see that she lacks nothing. My brother Hugh, you know, inherits my father's fortune, but he provides handsomely—*very* handsomely—for Baly-Craig, (by which I mean me), and my younger brothers are not left in want either. I would not wish to denigrate the munificence of your provision, but it is not necessary. Perhaps, this being the case, you might reconsider your ability to do something for Miss Fairfax?'

'I have considered it, and even broached the subject with her,' the colonel replied with a rueful sigh, 'but she will not hear of it. She is determined on an independent course. In fact, she tells me that when Rowena is married, she will begin to look about her. She is quite fixed on the scheme and I cannot move her from it.'

Jane had managed matters so as to be missing from Augusta Place when the wedding was under discussion. She had made various acquaintances in Weymouth who insisted upon including her in their excursions and having her to dine. She had congratulated Mr Dixon with warmth and openness, and participated in Rowena's happiness as fully as the happy bride-to-be could wish, but seemed reluctant to involve herself in the more intimate plans for the wedding. Naturally, she would be bridesmaid but no, she would not accompany the Dixons on their wedding tour nor commit herself to living with them as a permanent guest afterwards.

'You will not need me,' she said gently when Rowena, with many tears and supplications, pressed her suit. 'You will have Mr Dixon to be your guide and support. *He* will be your all-in-all and I should only be in the way. It is right, so, my dear.'

'Oh, but Jane,' wailed Rowena, 'how shall I manage?'

Jane took Rowena's hand. 'I will grant you this. I will write to my grandmother and ask to be excused my visit this year. You know I usually spend June in Highbury and that time is already upon us. They must be expecting a letter from me any day announcing my arrival. But I will write and say I cannot come. This year, your need is greater. How will that be?'[xiii]

Rowena smiled though her tears, and was content.

The letter was written and replied to—at length—the summary of the four or five crossed sheets being that of course Jane's grandmother and aunt would forgo the very great pleasure of dear Jane's company for June. The whole of Highbury, being itself just then in the delightful throes of wedding preparations for good Mr Weston and the amiable Miss Taylor, Mrs Bates and Miss Bates entered most cordially, and, they liked to think, with some understanding, into the great excitement of the Campbell household. Of course, they had never met Mr Dixon—

nor, for that matter, Miss Campbell—but they imagined both to be as charming as possible. They earnestly wished to send a gift—not that it was within their power to send much—but if Jane could indicate some small household item that would be useful and—underlined—affordable, they would be grateful. Naturally, dear Jane would be sorely missed by everyone in Highbury. Mrs Cole in particular had said … and Mr Perry had been so good as to declare … Miss Woodhouse expressed her congratulations to Miss Campbell and Mr Dixon but lamented that she would not have the pleasure &c. &c. The bed socks her grandmother had been labouring over since Easter—when Jane had mentioned, in a letter, that her feet had been a little cold—could be posted. And speaking of socks, Mrs Cropley's daughter—now in possession of the poultry business, her mother being very elderly and almost crippled with arthritis—had just got a new pony for her gig that had three very pretty white socks …

At last it was decided that Mr Dixon would return to Ireland alone in August, to supervise the harvest and get things in readiness for his new bride. He would return in late September and the wedding would be in October.

'The sea will not be too bad at that time, for the crossing,' he said. 'October weather can be mild and pleasant. There will be opportunity for us to see the countryside a little. We can stop in Dublin for a few weeks, if you please.'

Rowena was distressed at the idea of being parted from him. What if the ship were to sink? What if storms kept him from her for the wedding day? What if some other reason—and her mind conjured illness, assault and the press-gang as well as pirates and malevolent pixies—prevented his return? It took all of Mr Dixon's powers—and some of Jane's—to soothe her fears, but at last she agreed and the arrangements were put in motion for a wedding on 5th October at St John's, the little church at the corner of Bute Square where Rowena had been worshiping since she was a child.

'Papa and I will walk across the park to it, as we have done every Sunday,' she said. 'I shall tell myself it is just the same, except that I am dressed a little finer, and hold flowers as well as my prayer book. And it will not be until I get there, and see you waiting, that I shall feel any apprehension at all.'

'I hope you will feel no apprehension *then*,' Mr Dixon said patiently, bending close to her. 'I hope you will feel only joy and confidence.'

Chapter Twenty-Three

Jane's circle of acquaintance included a family she had met at another seaside resort in a previous year: the Quills. As well as two older girls the family boasted three high spirited young ones who often needed firm management. Jane soon discovered she had an excellent way of staving off their excesses of behaviour by interesting them in the world around them and promising—and withholding—treats dependent on their conduct. They, in their turn, liked and respected her and would take instruction from her when their own mama and elder sisters cajoled and scolded in vain. So it was that Jane found herself increasingly invited to make one of their party and she was happy to oblige. They were not perhaps the noblest connections she could have made in Weymouth but they were excellent company. As much as Jane loved Rowena the burden of having constantly to encourage and buoy her had, in recent months, become more onerous. Now that Rowena had Mr Dixon to lean upon Jane found a certain sense of liberation in being able to go out and about on her own account. To be invited *alone,* rather than as a permanent adjunct to Miss Campbell, was refreshing. *This* was the foretaste of the independence for which she had been disciplining herself for many years and while, of course, as a governess she would have none of the freedoms she now enjoyed, learning to be without Rowena was an important step. There was a further reason why Jane allowed herself a closer intercourse with the Quill family. Mrs Quill had a large circle of acquaintance with children in the nursery or schoolroom. Once she discovered that Jane was destined to be a governess, she declared herself certain to be able to find an eminently suitable position. Jane was not proud—she would take any respectable position so long as the family was well thought of and the children governable—but the prospect of being placed with a family of the Quills' standing did not thrill her. Their circle encompassed thoroughly reputable but not especially genteel proprietors of tanneries and dye-works, middling merchants, apothecaries, chief-clerks and wholesalers. Nevertheless, she told herself that this was the level she had been born to inhabit. Her people—her *real* people—were undeniably poor, and children in the middle tiers of society were as much—or more—in need of education and guidance as those in higher ones.

Mr Quill was an older man, widowed but now re-married and raising a new gaggle of girls, who had been successful enough in his trade to be able to sell it as a going concern and retire on the profits. His aim now, having laboured honourably for thirty years in his professional milieu, was to distance himself from it as thoroughly as possible. In this his young wife was all encouragement, his former trade being such as garnered to it no degree of élan, and yet *some* associations from his previous life proved impossible to shake off, and one of these was the determined acquaintance of the Branthwaite family. The Branthwaites had followed the Quills to Weymouth, and while it had been beyond their power to secure lodgings on the fashionable side of the river Wey they made it their business to call at the Quills' on an almost daily basis. Only the fact of their aunt Mrs Churchill also being in the town eclipsed the importance of their acquaintance with the Quills. So it was that Jane was introduced to Miss Stacie Branthwaite, Miss Mary and Mr Edgar before she was apprised of their connection with Frank Churchill and it was through the Branthwaites, rather than through Frank, that she encountered Mr Mosley once more.

This transpired at a dinner in a private suite at the Assembly, hosted by Mr Quill. The Branthwaites were present as well as some dozen others. Frank Churchill had been invited and had been expected until a hasty note was received that expressed his last-minute regret; his aunt was ill and could not be left. Jane spied Mr Mosley across the reception room, at last caught his eye and was delighted to see him make his way over to where she stood. It pleased her greatly to see him, and for his part he appeared happy to re-establish their association. In looks he was little altered; somewhat thinner perhaps but better dressed and his hair neatly cut; he was altogether the gentleman. The good looks that had been marred by unhappiness the last time she had seen him were now fully come into their own; he was decidedly handsome. He spoke animatedly of their time together in Highbury; the walks he had enjoyed in the surrounding countryside, the friendliness of the village inhabitants. She enquired after and was promised sight of his most recent sketches—all landscapes and architecture, he told her, his bent for likenesses had been allowed to lapse. Presently he introduced his wife. She was quiet, elegant and pretty, but somewhat watchful. She greeted Jane with reserved coolness and said little beyond the usual pleasantries. Jane observed the two of them carefully, anxious to know whether Mr Mosley's former disappointment, and his reluctance to marry against his inclination, had melted away in genuine attachment to his wife. He was doggedly dutiful to Mrs Mosley but there seemed no spark of affection between them that she could discern. As the reception progressed, she noted that he was apt to linger at the back of the company, to stare fixedly at some point in a far corner rather than to engage in conversation. She heard others speak of him behind their hands as morose and taciturn, a calumny she was powerless to contradict without betraying his secret.

'I am very happy,' he said to her when it had fallen to his lot to escort her into the dining chamber, 'to have made your acquaintance again, Miss Fairfax. I have thought of you often.'

'And I of you,' she admitted, although feeling that it might be unwise to say as much. 'You left Highbury so suddenly and my aunt ... that is, I did not hear anything more of you or your sister.'

'Hester corresponded with Mrs Paling for a time,' Mr Mosley said. 'But then she married and the communication ceased. She married very well,' he observed with a rueful smile. 'My father was able to offer *her* a sizeable dowry because I had ...'

'Because of Mrs Mosley's contribution?' Jane finished for him, in a low voice.

Mr Mosley nodded and Jane thought it politic to change the topic of the conversation. 'Mr and Mrs Paling have left Highbury,' she said. 'They were very much loved by the congregation but Mrs Paling's mother suffered a seizure that left her incapacitated, and Mrs Paling has gone to nurse her. Mr Paling now holds a pastoral position on the bishop's staff. A new man ministers at Highbury - a Mr Elton.'

'Your acquaintance with the Branthwaites,' Mr Mosley said hesitantly, 'it is recent?'

'Yes,' Jane said. 'I met them through Mr and Mrs Quill. Mrs Quill hopes to find me a situation as a governess when she returns to Clapham.'

'Mrs Quill does?' Mr Mosley could not mask his astonishment. 'My dear Miss Fairfax, if you must take up such a position, I hope it shall be in a more superior sphere than that.'

'Mr Quill is our host,' Jane admonished quietly, 'and perhaps I shall not have the luxury of choice.'

Then the soup came, and Jane turned to her other neighbour. She was glad to do so. From the cold looks that came at Jane across the table it was clear Mrs Mosley viewed her with a degree of suspicion—as perhaps, any wife *will* do when confronted with a lady whose connection with her husband predates her own—and Jane was hard pressed to show that degree of interest and warm friendliness that would enliven Mr Mosley without exacerbating the natural distrust of his wife.

When the ladies had left the gentlemen to their claret Jane made it a point to sit next to Mrs Mosley in the little sitting room that adjoined the dining parlour.

'You knew my husband before we were married, I think Miss Fairfax?' Mrs Mosley asked, opening the topic that was uppermost in her mind.

'*Just* before, I believe,' Jane conceded. 'But that was three or four years ago. I was hardly more than a child. I visit Highbury annually, as a rule, to see my grandmother and aunt. It just so happened that Mr Mosley and his sister's time there coincided with mine for a week or so.'

'As a place, he seems to have conflicted memories of it,' Mrs Mosley observed.

There was no reply Jane could make to this so she made none.

'Do you find him much changed?' Mrs Mosley pressed on.

'I hardly knew him well enough then to form any opinion as to his character,' Jane hedged.

'He hoped at that time to be ordained,' Mrs Mosley offered.

'I recall that much. I have very little understanding of these things but it seemed to me at the time that it was a vocation that would have suited him,' Jane replied.

'I believe he labours still under the disappointment of being denied his metier,' Mrs Mosley mused. 'He gets little satisfaction from his current work.'

'Oh?' Jane mumbled. It was obvious that Mrs Mosley knew nothing of Susannah Brokenshire.

'Yes. Tell me, Miss Fairfax, does he seem to you to be … unhappy?' Mrs Mosley asked.

'I cannot say,' Jane said awkwardly. On the whole she felt rather sorry for Mrs Mosley, who had plainly not plumbed the secret of her husband's low spirits. Her instinct was to urge Mr Mosley to tell his wife about his failed romance. He was not alone in having loved and lost. Had not Mrs Mosley likewise loved and lost her first husband?

Happily, the Miss Quills came to her then, and begged her to play. 'And then, when the gentlemen come, we will go upstairs and dance,' enthused Miss Sally Quill. 'What a pity it is that Mr Frank Churchill is not with us.'

'His aunt is indisposed,' her sister said.

'We were promised a dinner at Chesterfield Place,' Miss Mary Branthwaite wailed as Jane arranged her music, 'and now it seems we will be denied it.'

Sally and Amy Quill, who had no hope whatsoever of entering Mrs Churchill's portals, much less of sitting at her dining table, were scarcely less dismayed. 'Mr Frank Churchill is quite a favourite of ours,' they declared. 'He is such fun! Do you not think so, Miss Fairfax? And handsome to boot.'

'And *rich*,' sighed Miss Mary, 'but you two girls have no hope of him,' she added spitefully. 'He would not lower himself to marry a girl with connections such as yours, no matter how well-off their father may be.'

'I am sure *my* papa's business is no lower than yours,' Miss Quill retorted, 'and he has quit it.'

'It *was* infinitely lower. But I am family, a cousin just distant enough to make a match highly desirable,' simpered Mary. 'Do you not think Mr Frank Churchill an eligible young man in every way, Miss Fairfax?'

'I have not considered it,' said Jane, not quite truthfully. 'I am very sorry to hear that Mrs Churchill is indisposed and wish her a speedy recovery.'

'If she *is* indisposed,' Miss Branthwaite added, darkly. 'Mama says she is always inventing disorders. When you question her closely you never can get to the bottom of what actually ails her. We have called ever so many times but we are always sent away; 'Mrs Churchill's compliments, but she is too ill to receive callers' is our invariable reply.'

'I suspect she does it just to prevent her nephew from enjoying himself. She is a kill-joy,' Miss Mary agreed. 'I am sure that *he* would not scruple to invite us to Enscombe.'

'I have heard that Yorkshire is very disagreeable,' opined Miss Quill. 'I should not go there if I were invited.'

'You shall *not* be, so that will suit,' retorted Mary. 'Miss Fairfax, will you accompany us to the promenade tomorrow afternoon?'

'I am afraid not,' said Jane, beginning to play. 'I am to join the Campbells and Mr Dixon for some shopping.'

The rest of the evening passed off in diversion and pleasure. Mr Frank Churchill may have been absent but there were plenty of other young men willing to engage Jane and her friends for dances, and she enjoyed herself very much. She stood up once with Mr Mosley, but the dance was a lively one and private conversation was not possible.

'I hope I shall see you out and about in Weymouth,' he said, as he escorted her back to her seat and, leaning closer, 'there are things to be said that cannot be said *here*. I walk most afternoons on the sands. Ariadne likes to rest between two and four, and so I find myself at liberty.'

Jane smiled, and he was gone. She chose not to understand the import of his final remark. *She* would not walk out alone in the hope of meeting him; it would be extremely injudicious. But she would welcome the opportunity of some private intercourse if it meant she could ease the burden of his unhappiness.

Chapter Twenty-Four

The following day presented Jane with an opportunity to meet Mr Mosley without any lack of propriety whatsoever. She awoke with something of a headache.

'Too much dancing,' Mrs Campbell opined, placing a cool, scented cloth across Jane's temples, 'and too much society. Those Quill girls are very high-spirited and Miss Mary Branthwaite talks enough nonsense for a dozen young ladies. And then they *will* leave the management of the little ones to you. No wonder you are indisposed. You should walk out this afternoon for some fresh air and solitary contemplation before we meet at the draper's shop. Then, if they call here for you, I can tell them you are from home. Certainly, there is no rest to be had here for we are up to our necks in wedding preparations; the seamstress comes at one o'clock to fit Rowena for her wedding gown.'

Accordingly, after a morning spent resting, and a light luncheon, Jane collected her shawl and bonnet and set out towards the beach with Mrs Campbell's full approbation. The tide was out, revealing a broad expanse of smooth, hard sand. The sky was somewhat overcast but no rain threatened and Jane strode energetically across the beach, enjoying the fresh air and freedom Mrs Campbell's prescription had provided. She made no particular effort to espy Mr Mosley but if she encountered him by accident there could be no impropriety in their conversing. The town clock tolled two as she made her way towards the far end of the beach where sand gave way to shingle and the higher part of the shore provided smooth rocks where she could rest and enjoy the view. She knew by some instinct that this—the least frequented part of Weymouth sands—would be Mr Mosley's most probable destination. It was no surprise, therefore, as she approached the place, to see him already in situ, his sketch pad upon his knee.

'Ah,' he said, seeing her approach and putting away his pencils. 'You have come. I had little hope of it.'

'I walk at Mrs Campbell's desire, to clear a slight headache,' Jane said formally. 'How do you do, Mr Mosley? I hope Mrs Mosley is quite well.'

'Oh yes,' Mr Mosley said with a sigh, 'she is very well. Will you sit down?' he indicated a dry rock adjacent to the one he had occupied, 'or will you walk on?'

'Let us sit for a while,' Jane said. 'You can continue with your sketch. It will be as it was that time in Highbury.' She lowered herself onto the stone and arranged her skirts.

Mr Mosley resumed his seat and opened his sketch book. 'I recall it most vividly,' he said. 'In the weeks of tumult I had spent since leaving Susannah in Jamaica, my conversation with you was an oasis of calm.'

'I did nothing but listen,' Jane said.

'You did much more,' Mr Mosley maintained. 'You made me think that I was not altogether to blame for what had occurred. When I met my father again I was able to hold my head up to that extent. And even though I did acquiesce with his scheme I was able to stipulate that I would have no personal involvement with buying or selling … of certain cargo. He and my brother arrange all that; I have not the stomach for it.'

'A victory, then,' said Jane

'But a pyrrhic one,' Mr Mosley grumbled. 'The trade goes on. But we will not speak of that now. You are here with the Campbells. They are a very respectable family.'

'Indeed they are. My particular friend Miss Campbell is engaged to be married. A gentleman by the name of Dixon. Perhaps you are acquainted?'

'Lord Knox has spoken of him. I wish them much happiness in their marriage.'

Mr Mosley plied his pencil for a while. Jane hesitated to bring up the topic that was uppermost in her mind. At last she said, 'And have you found happiness in your marriage, sir? I hope you do not think me impertinent for asking, but after our conversation in Highbury …'

' … It is natural that you should wonder.' Mr Mosley considered. 'Ariadne is gentle and obliging. Although she brought all the wealth and property to the match, she never refers to it. She defers to me in all matters of the business—it is as though the ships were never hers at all! At home she is all consideration for my well-being and happiness. So, I have nothing to complain of! And yet there is, between us, a reserve. We never speak of what went before. I know nothing of her life with Billinge and she does not enquire about my bachelor life. I think we both fear the past is a Pandora's Box; we do not know what might emerge if we lift the lid.'

Jane nodded thoughtfully. In the sky the clouds parted sufficiently to allow a thin sunshine to warm her skin. Mr Mosley added shading to his sketch to reflect the altered light.

'From what she said to me last evening I believe she feels you labour under the disappointment of being denied ordination,' Jane offered. 'She did not go quite so far as to admit it, but I gather she feels that you blame her.'

'Blame her?' Mr Mosley turned towards her. 'Not at all! I blame my father.'

Jane smiled, '*That* may emerge from Pandora's Box, if you were to open it. How it would comfort her.'

'I suppose so,' Mr Mosley allowed. 'I would not have Ariadne labour under that misunderstanding.'

'Do you not think it misguided to have secrets between husband and wife?' Jane pressed gently. 'Who knows what Mrs Mosley's former marriage was like? Mr Billinge may have been a brute! Or he may have been kindness personified. Either way, what a relief it would be to her to speak of it to you. In the same way, would it not ease your soul to tell her about Miss Brokenshire? The blame was not yours; you acted in truth and good faith. Your heart is not fully healed but Mrs Mosley could assist you if she only knew …'

'I do not know,' Mr Mosley said brokenly. 'I only know this, Miss Fairfax, and I offer it to you so that you may not suffer as I have done; when you find love, hold it fast. Do not, for any consideration, let it go. When your heart speaks, listen.'

Behind them the town clock struck three.

'I must go,' Jane said, rising to her feet. 'I am to meet the Campbells and Mr Dixon at the draper's.' She held out her hand. 'I have enjoyed seeing you again, Mr Mosley. I urge you to consider my advice.'

He rose and took her hand, and then, impulsively, pressed it to his lips. 'I will,' he replied hoarsely. 'And I implore you to remember mine.'

Jane's appointment with the other members of her party was to choose a wedding gift for her grandmamma. Mr Dixon and Miss Campbell, on hearing of the old lady's determination to buy *them* something, had been unanimous in their determination to turn the compliment the other way.

'We will not hear of it,' Mr Dixon had said. 'That good old soul shall not deplete her resources on our account, shall she, dear?'

Rowena had beamed and suggested, 'A nice new shawl, very warm,' would be the ideal offering.

Accordingly, the whole party was to meet at a certain draper's to choose something suitable.

Jane arrived some few moments after the rest to find them much engrossed at the counter, a large number of shawls already brought out for their consideration.

Mrs Campbell said that a woollen shawl would be quite the best. Mr Dixon thought silk might be preferred. Rowena liked both but said that it should be fringed. Colonel Campbell picked out an olive-coloured shawl and said he thought it would do very well but Mr Dixon thought the colour too drab and had the assistant bring forth a rich blue one he had spied on a high shelf. It was so large it could easily double as a knee-blanket, was finely wrought and had about it an air of opulence as well as comfort. It was quite the most expensive shawl they had considered but that, he declared, was of no consequence. It meeting with the approbation of all, it was duly bought, carefully wrapped in tissue paper and was to be delivered to Augusta Place before the day was out.

They quit the shop to encounter Mr Frank Churchill. He seemed, from the outset, animated to an unusual degree, somewhat flushed about the face and not dressed with his usual care.

'Ah,' he said, sweeping off his hat, 'I set out on purpose to see you. I dashed out without a moment of preparation. I would not be surprised to find I have on odd shoes or my uncle's coat! But I was so anxious to see you all. How do you do? How do you all do? I called at your lodgings, Dixon, and at Augusta Place. I wandered about the town and had almost given up hope. No man was ever more disappointed than I! But here you are! Miss Fairfax, I am *very* pleased to see you.' They had not seen each other for many days, since their moonlit walk on the beach. 'Miss Campbell,' he went on, anxious not to betray, by too earnest an interest in Miss Fairfax, how comprehensively she had occupied his thoughts, 'let me congratulate you. It is the first opportunity I have had since hearing the happy news!' He embraced Miss Campbell, rather to her confusion, and shook Mr Dixon warmly by the hand, giving his friend a sly wink. The Campbells received their share of felicitations and the party loitered on the pavement while their immediate plans were discussed and agreed.

'My aunt has been unwell,' Frank burst out. 'I have been nowhere and seen no one for days and days. If it does not inconvenience you, let us walk, as we did that first day, along the promenade. I need air and exercise!'

The scheme meeting with everyone's approval they set out. Mrs Campbell, as usual, took her husband's arm. They walked slowly and chose the side of the roadway that allowed them to look into all the shop windows. Miss Campbell was claimed by her fiancé, who soon led her down the steps to the sands. Jane fell into step beside Frank. He walked quickly and they were soon well ahead of the Campbells and separated by some distance from Rowena and Mr Dixon.

'I am sorry your aunt has been ill,' she began. 'I knew of it, in fact, from some acquaintance I believe we have in common. I have lately been introduced to the Branthwaites.'

'Oh, have you?' Frank replied with a slightly embarrassed air. 'In my defence I must assert they are but distant cousins.'

'They claim closer connection,' Jane said with a smile. 'They consider themselves quite on visiting terms. Miss Mary hopes to go to Enscombe.'

'Oh yes,' Frank laughed, 'she makes no secret of *that*.'

'I rather think she views everything connected to your family with a romantic eye,' Jane observed lightly.

'Ladies enjoy romance,' Frank said cryptically. 'Machinations of a romantic nature occupy their thoughts a great deal, I think.'

'They do not occupy mine,' Jane asserted.

'Do they not?' Frank almost shouted. 'I disagree. Look how you manipulated me into arranging things between Dixon and Miss

Campbell. It seems to me that you are quite Machiavellian in your amorous manoeuvrings.' He gave Jane no opportunity to defend herself, forging on with, 'So, are you happy with the outcome of your plotting? Do you not think I acted my part admirably?'

'I hardly recognise the slight hint I gave you in your rendition of it,' Jane said with a frown, 'but you have made two people happy. There is great satisfaction in that, I think. A little boost was wanting, which you supplied. I take it that not *much* persuasion was needed?'

'A flagon of brandy, pen, paper and it was done,' Frank said. 'How did you come to be acquainted with the Branthwaites?'

Jane told her story, describing the Quills and also her encounter with Mr and Mrs Mosley. 'He is in low spirits, I find,' she confided. 'His wife seems a sympathetic, amiable lady. She cares for him a great deal, I think; enough to be jealous, anyway. I take that as a good sign, although it is uncomfortable to be suspected. If I could give you another commission it would be to bring *him* out. Do you think you are equal to it?'

'You interest yourself very keenly in Mr Mosley,' Frank cried. 'Is it a knight errant you require, or a go-between?'

Jane opened her mouth to speak, taken aback by the import of his remark, but he went on with specious gaiety, 'But whichever it is, very well, I will undertake the quest.'

The utter ennui of the past days at Chesterfield Place, his pleasure in finding himself once more tête-à-tête with Miss Fairfax and something else that he only half-understood energised his spirits to an almost dangerous degree. He had kept his hat in his hand. The breeze from the sea ruffled his curls and further brightened his complexion. 'Ah!' he cried, 'this is what I needed. Hours and hours at my aunt's bedside have almost worn me away. She would not have the curtains opened, much less the windows. It has been so stiflingly hot I have almost sickened myself. And I am heartily bored of Fordyce! His sermons are interminable!'

'And what is the nature of your aunt's indisposition, if it is not indelicate to enquire?'

'It is a conundrum the greatest medical minds have failed to solve,' Frank said cynically. 'She has palpitations, dizziness, is cold, and then hot. She trembles, then stiffens, then faints away altogether. She complains of tingles, throbbing, aches and itches. Every day brings a new symptom. Personally, I am convinced … but no, there are some secrets better kept within the family.'

'I truly hope she sees better days,' Jane said, sincerely.

They walked briskly for a while. It seemed to Jane that more than once Mr Churchill was on the cusp of speaking, of confiding in her his conviction about his aunt.

Presently, with Frank Churchill's troubles in mind as well as Mr Mosley's, Jane said, 'It is burdensome, is it not, to have a secret, especially when one feels that in *sharing* it one could bring relief.'

'A secret?' he pounced on her word. 'Yes. To have a secret, or to be the subject of one, as you suggested that *you* are, is a weighty burden,' Frank agreed waspishly. 'So,' with a mischievous, almost malevolent, twinkle, 'Mrs Mosley suspects you of dishonourable involvement with her husband? Oh Miss Fairfax, I fear I must tell you that she is not alone in her suspicions.'

This was not at all the direction Jane had expected the conversation to take. She did not like it; she did not wish to hear that she was doubted. Frank's almost manic demeanour was of a nature to confuse her; was he in earnest? Or did he jest? 'Do others question my honesty?'

'Dixon is convinced you are head over heels in love with someone; he thinks it is me! Can you imagine anything more ridiculous?' Frank cried.

'No,' Jane said.

'But now my interest is piqued,' Frank went on, wounded by the decided nature of her unequivocal response and further goaded to a mood that became more volatile with each passing moment. 'I am asking myself: why should it not be Mr Mosley? You know, Miss Fairfax, there is nothing I like better than an intrigue. It is because my life in general is so dull; a monotonous plodding from breakfast to tea to dinner to bed; reading to my aunt, listening to my aunt, squiring her from one tedious place to another, hearing the litany of her complaints and disappointments. So any suspicion of trickery is sure to excite my interest. I am never happier than when winkling out secrets and I give you fair warning that I am rather accomplished at it. You may as well tell me at once that you were Mr Mosley's lover in Highbury, that you have been secretly corresponding ever since and that you brought the Campbells to Weymouth on purpose to engineer assignations of the most sordid and clandestine kinds. Oh! You must not deny it! For I have seen you with my own eyes! If you do not confess to me I may decide to spread the report in any case.' He jumped onto the low wall that separated the esplanade from the beach and shouted, 'I declare to all of Weymouth that Miss Fairfax is in love with …'

'Mr Churchill!' Jane shrieked, aghast. Thankfully the pathway just there, and the area of sand beyond, was deserted, but the atrocious slander he had been on the point of declaring made Jane feel sick and faint. She grabbed his hand and pulled him down from the wall. 'You would not be so specious,' Jane hissed. 'That would be a baseless calumny. The merest whisper of anything so monstrous would destroy the Campbells and ruin any chance I ever had of finding employment.' She dropped his hand and stepped away from him as though in horror from a monster.

'A calumny? I do not think so! Do you deny that you were with him just now at the far end of the sands?'

'I deny nothing,' gasped Jane. 'I walked out and encountered him. I spoke to him for a while. Anyone may have seen us. Anyone may know it. I am not ashamed.'

'And what did you speak of that moved him to such heights of emotion? I saw him kiss your hand.'

Jane gathered herself to her fullest height. '*That* is none of your business. If Mrs Campbell requires me to, I shall confide in her, and no one else. I will say only this; that I made Mr Mosley's acquaintance in Highbury three years ago and my conversation with him today was pursuant on a matter we discussed then. I have neither seen him, nor corresponded with him, nor had any dealings with him since that time up until I met him at the Assembly yesterday.' In spite of her great desire to appear mistress of herself and of the situation she had found herself in, Jane could not prevent her voice from faltering nor tears from filling her eyes.

Frank, seeing the stricken expression on Jane's face and believing her to be telling him the truth, immediately tamed his madness. 'My dear Miss Fairfax,' he said sincerely, appalled by his own rashness and by her reaction, 'I spoke thoughtlessly and—I will confess it to you—jealously.'

His pallor, such a contrast to the wind-tanned colour of his face only moments before, showed his contrition and softened to some extent Jane's anger.

'I know that a lady's reputation is, above all things, no subject for banter. I upbraid myself most severely for being so thoughtless,' he said. 'And,' (bitterly), 'after all, what business is it of mine whom you speak to? Can you forgive me?'

'I do not know,' Jane faltered. The feeling that she might, perhaps, share something of Mr Mosley's secret with Mr Churchill had utterly evaporated; the man could not be trusted. She had presumed too far on their shared Highbury connection. Some sense of common belonging to that place, and of the mutual bereavement that had caused them both to leave it, had deceived her into thinking him like her. He was not like her. He was wild and unpredictable, careless in a way she could never be. And yet, when she looked into his eyes, she saw there an unhappiness she understood. He had spoken of jealousy. What could he have meant?

Suddenly, Frank Churchill sank down onto the wall and put his head in his hands. 'I hate myself,' he said brokenly, 'I abhor my situation and detest myself for abhorring it. Miss Fairfax, you can have no notion of what I suffer. Not that it is any excuse for what just occurred, but my aunt …' He dragged his hands through his hair like a man in agony, 'My *aunt* …' he said again, his voice most anguished. 'What kind of ingrate would rail at my situation? I have wealth and consequence beyond most men's dreams. But she … *she* is just impossible. She hems me in. She prevents me from doing what I know is my duty. I may as well be incarcerated, for all the liberty I have to do what I want, and what I know to be right.'

A few strollers walked by, casting curious glances at Frank as he sat, drooped and distressed, on the little wall. Jane, her misgivings overcome by compassion, came closer to him and gently took his arm.

'Come, let us walk,' she murmured. 'People are looking at us. The colonel and Mrs Campbell will be upon us any moment. Let us continue on our walk. The exercise will calm you.'

He allowed her to lift him and thread her arm through his. When opportunity presented itself they descended a little flight of steps and went out onto the empty expanse of the sands.

'It is more private here,' Jane said. 'You can give vent to your feelings if you wish. Would you rather I left you alone? I see Miss Campbell and Mr Dixon at the shoreline. I can easily join them.'

'Oh no,' Frank replied, turning eyes upon her that were quite wild. He covered her hand with his. 'Do not leave me, Miss Fairfax. I feel, in spite of my dreadful behaviour a moment ago, that you are a friend. In fact,' he went on, his face gaunt and earnest, 'I feel that just now you are my *only* friend.'

'Very well,' said Jane, and they went on together.

Confinement with his aunt had frustrated and annoyed Frank almost beyond bearing. He had left the house in Chesterfield Place feeling restless and reckless, full of unspent energy that demanded release and very angry at what had, within the hour, occurred. Failing to find any of his friends at home he had wandered the town almost in despair. It was thus that he had seen Jane and Mr Mosley in private conversation in a secluded part of the beach and the wave of jealousy that had assailed him had been almost too much to bear. Thoughts of her had been his only comfort through the endless days of his incarceration. He had replayed in his mind's eye images of her dancing at the Assembly, riding in his gig, walking in the torchlight. If not for the idea of her strength and determination he did not know how he could have endured the tedium of the sickroom or his aunt's histrionics. The idea of Jane taking a post as a governess had exercised him very much. On more than one occasion he had almost broached the subject with his uncle. Could not something be done? One thing, he knew, could be done to spare her ever having to debase herself to such servitude, and he had all but convinced himself to do it. Then he had spied her with Mr Mosley—an accidental encounter and an innocent conversation as he now believed them to be—and the conviction that she had been snatched from him had made him almost violent with jealousy. Now, with her arm in his and after the relief of brisk exercise, he felt calmer.

Presently he said, 'Miss Fairfax, I wonder if you will allow me to share with you the secret I alluded to before? It will do no dishonour to my family to tell *you* for my suspicion is that an hour spent in my aunt's company would lay it plain before you. And, to tell the truth, it will ease my mind to speak it aloud. And although it cannot excuse, it may explain to some degree my outburst a few moments ago.'

'I will respect your confidence,' said Jane.

'Ah yes,' said Frank with a rueful smile, 'I am beginning to see that you are rather good at keeping other people's secrets. Well, here is mine. A week or ten days ago I received my invitation to my father's wedding. The day is named and all the preparations are in train. My father is all generosity, as always, and very anxious for me to be acquainted with Miss Taylor. So, of course, I wish to go. It is not unreasonable, is it? Any man of sense and honour would consider it his duty. I consider it a pleasure, as well as a duty, to attend my father on his day of joy, and to give that recognition to my stepmother that will assure her of my respect and my affection. So, I announced my intention of leaving my aunt and uncle here in Weymouth, or wherever they may be at that time, to attend my father in Highbury for a week or so before the wedding day and for as much time again afterwards as will not trespass on their felicity. I screwed my courage to the sticking point before I broached the subject, I do assure you. I chose my moment with care. Some reluctance on my aunt's part I anticipated. It is always so, when I wish to go somewhere that she cannot go also. My uncle is an ally. *He* is sometimes able to bring her round. But this time, no amount of persuasion could convince her and she had an attack of the most violent kind. Spasms and hysterics I have seen often. She can conjure fevers at will. Headaches are her friend. But now she added apoplexy, periods of panting and gasping, eye-rolling and even foaming at the mouth. I have never witnessed such a display! My uncle was so distressed he summoned the doctor. She took to her bed and lay alternately so listless that it seemed she was hardly conscious at all, and then gripped by paroxysms of violent thrashing and hysterical outbursts that almost threw her from the bed on more than one occasion. From that day to this she has been—or has *seemed* to be—so ill that at times I really feared for her life. And so today, this morning, it fell to my lot to sit with her, and in true contrition and agony of remorse I whispered to her that I would give up my scheme of attending my father's wedding. And lo! Two hours later she is recovered, sitting in her chair, drinking soup and discussing a drive to Chesil beach.'

'I am astonished,' said Jane, and meant it. She had never heard of such a display of wilfulness and temper in even the most determined child, let alone in an adult.

Mr Churchill stood before her, his hands held out in supplication, his face a picture of aggrieved despair, hopelessness, anger and misery. 'The truth is,' he said, 'and it is a shameful truth I would rather not admit to, but if you *did* have a secret lover or some private matter that was yours and yours alone, I would envy you. I have nothing that is only mine. Oh! I have wealth and horses and carriages and clothes! But none of those things are what I long for. I desire a love that is mine alone, that my aunt cannot take from me, or spoil or deny me and that I know that the touch of *her* caprice will not wither. If you have such a thing, Miss Fairfax, hold on to it. I will not expose you.'

'I have not,' Jane said. She had held, for a precious few hours, something like it; the half promise that Mr Dixon had almost offered. It was gone now as *he* was gone, dancing on the edge of the surf with her friend Rowena Campbell, and it assailed her at that moment how she missed it. For all her bravado she would not choose the lonely, lowly life of a governess if there was a truly egalitarian, honourable alternative. It struck her also that she had now received, in one day, the same advice from two gentlemen. Mr Mosley had also told her to hold on to love when she found it.

She roused herself from these thoughts to find Mr Churchill looking at her with an earnestness of expression she could not ignore. 'I do understand you,' she said. 'Indeed, I pity you. I can offer no solace other that in time, her malign influence will fade and you will step out from beneath it. But the interim is hard for you. I do pity you with all my heart.'

They had come to part of the beach where sand became shingle, almost the same place that Jane had sat earlier with Mr Mosley. Behind them by some distance, Mr Dixon and Miss Campbell bent together over something of interest they had discovered in the sand. Of the colonel and Mrs Campbell there was no sign at all. Frank and Jane were entirely alone. The sun shone pleasantly, and a cooling breeze teased the hair from beneath Jane's bonnet so that tendrils played around her face. The light in her eye was all sympathy and concern. Frank thought he might weep at her beauty and her compassion and her complete disinterest to all he possessed and would possess in years to come in favour of what he suffered at this exact moment.

'I never met anyone like you,' he faltered, all his usual animation as well as his recent torment now discharged. Jane continued to look up at him, her eye unwavering. 'And look how you receive even *that* remark!' Frank said in astonishment. 'There is no false humility in you, Miss Fairfax, no simpering looks, no pretence at modesty. How many young ladies would have continued to meet my eyes as you do? I do not think there is one! Who but *you* would not have thought to themselves 'and now he is vulnerable, weak and unhappy, so now is my opportunity to ensnare him.'

Jane shook her head. 'Many, I suppose, would have done. I could not, for example, answer for Miss Mary Branthwaite. But I do not wish to ensnare you, Mr Churchill. I would not, by loving him, make any man less. I would make him more, if I could.'

'And you, Jane,' whispered Frank, stepping nearer to her, 'although I do now believe that you are not embroiled in a clandestine affair, do you not need to be loved? Do you not need the security that love and marriage could bring you?'

He had used the wrong word. If he had asked her if she *wished* to be loved, he would have got a different answer. She was almost disappointed. His earlier outburst had frightened her but she understood it now, she understood him. Apart from Rowena's she did not think she had ever comprehended anyone's heart as thoroughly as she comprehended his. As it was, Jane shrugged. 'I have told you, I do not need anything. I am sufficient to myself.'

'Ah,' breathed Frank, 'and that is the most wonderful thing of all.'

Chapter Twenty-Five

❦

June melded into July. The weather continued glorious and Weymouth became ever busier with families seeking respite from the heat and dirt of the town. The Assembly held balls every other evening, the theatre rotated its repertoire so that it was not unusual to see two or even three different plays in a fortnight. Troubadours of every kind flocked to the promenade to sell their wares and perform feats of daring and trickery. In the evenings torches flickered the length of the beach, musicians played and visitors strolled about in the coolness of the twilight air.

Mrs Churchill, her point over Frank's attendance at his father's nuptials gained, enjoyed as robustly good health as she would ever admit to. She deigned to accept an invitation to dine with the Campbells and participated in outings to Chesil Beach, Maiden Castle and the village of Upwey to sample the clear spring waters. Often Frank was able to manage matters so that Miss Fairfax was included in the party and, in order not to seem to distinguish her, the company of the Branthwaite girls and Mr and Mrs Mosley was often sought also. To her unutterable delight, Mary Branthwaite got her ride in the Churchill barouche and perhaps, with hindsight, Frank paid her more attention than was judicious in an effort to divert his aunt's attention from his real object. He watched Jane as closely as was wise, however, and he was almost persuaded that her demeanour towards him had undergone a change. They exchanged smiles that were full of their shared recollection of their walk on Weymouth sands. He fancied her gaze was more lustrous when he was its object. She seemed to him to dance, sing and play with more vitality when he was near. She did not flirt, as so many girls did; there was none of that coquettishness about *her* with which other young ladies liked to confuse a fellow. He had no sense at all that she aspired to become mistress of Enscombe; if she liked him, it was for himself alone. It gratified the rebellious nature that was all Frank had to counter Mrs Churchill's overbearing influence to prefer a young lady who would decidedly not meet with his aunt's approval. Last of all, Frank felt sure that if he so much as hinted to his father that Miss Fairfax was the lady who had won his heart he would be slapped on the back and told that he could scarcely do better. Only Miss Woodhouse stood higher in Mr Weston's opinion than Miss Fairfax but, from what little Frank knew of her, he did not think he would warm to the mistress of Hartfield.

For Jane's part she had to admit that her time on the beach with Mr Churchill had changed her view of him. Their conversation had o'er-leapt that boundary of decorum and manner that usually characterises relations between ladies and gentlemen in fashionable watering places. They understood each other as two people rarely did, having established, in those two or so hours, a meeting of minds that was natural and honest, unfettered by empty etiquette. Mouths spoke all the time at social gatherings but lowered eyes, a titled head or a raised eyebrow often communicated more than words. But heart rarely, if ever, spoke to heart as Jane's and Frank's had done. She found him increasingly in her mind. She wondered, as she dressed for an engagement, if Mr Frank Churchill would be present. She pondered what manoeuvrings the Churchill men might have to undergo to ensure the aunt made no difficulty that would prevent Frank stepping out of the door. She pictured, too, with amusement but also with pity, the sudden onslaught of spasms, the swoons, the febrile assaults Mrs Churchill might manufacture to keep her nephew at home. Jane might enter the Assembly room and discover she was searching the faces gathered there for his. She would climb into a carriage and be alert for any hint that would let her know that Frank Churchill would—or would not—be one of the party. It was not—yet—that she loved him. In some ways she rather distrusted him; he was unpredictable, rascally and imprudent. But something he had said to her on the beach had struck a chord; the idea of having something that was hers alone. Could he be it? She did not owe her acquaintance with him to the Campbells. Her connection with Frank had Highbury as its origin; they both felt it to be their natural home although Frank had never been there. They both concerned themselves with Highbury's daily doings and both were thought of by Highbury residents as particularly belonging there. *That,* for two people who had been fostered by strangers and who had lived to some degree as grateful guests, counted for much. He had not, since their conversation, hounded her or imposed upon her with a litany of his woes; indeed, he had kept a watchful distance and favoured Miss Mary Branthwaite with more of his attention than her. He was troubled but he was not needy. Jane could not save him from his aunt and he did not expect her to; she was simply, as he had said, a disinterested person who understood. He had heard of her determination to be a governess with astonishment but he had not attempted to dissuade her from it. Indeed, he seemed to respect and admire her for it. He saw her independent spirit and it did not intimidate him, as it would many men.

An attachment to Mr Frank Churchill would be all complication and trouble. The aunt, no doubt, would be against it. Frank himself was of such a character as made her doubt. But understanding, as she now did, the difficulties of the life he led explained to some degree the strange moods and excess of spirits that sometimes assailed him. If, without these, he was half the man his father was, he would be an easy and worthy husband to any woman lucky enough to engage him.

She liked him. This was her summing up of her feelings toward Frank. She liked him very much. He was handsome and witty, very charming. Life in Weymouth was improved by his being there. Her life was improved by knowing him.

Chapter Twenty-Six

Rowena Campbell's engagement to Mr Patrick Dixon of Baly-Craig, County Wicklow was formally announced. The business of wedding clothes was thoroughly gone into; seamstresses called in, extra girls hired to stitch linen, 'For,' said Mrs Campbell happily, 'we cannot be sure of the quantity or the condition of napkins at Baly-Craig. The pillowcases may be moth-eaten, the sheets threadbare. I have written to Lady Knox, but I fear the state of her granddaughter-in-law's linen is the last thing to interest her. Her broodmare has contracted some illness and that is all she can think about.'

Cards were left at Augusta Place daily, invitations sent and letters of congratulation received. In every salon and coffee house the engagement was discussed and dissected. Girls of little personal charm, shy girls, girls of small accomplishment and smaller wit took comfort from Rowena's coup. If timid, mousey Miss Campbell could land a man who was as close to an heir as made no difference, then surely, there was hope for them? Mamas directed their daughters to think differently of the gawky, gaggle-toothed or gross little boys they had known in the nursery, now gawky, gaggle-toothed or gross young men with fortunes in need of wives. The importance of Miss Campbell's twelve thousand pounds was much debated. Some said it had been Mr Dixon's main inducement, others that it had been of no consequence; though only a second son he was as well provided for as a first. Rowena herself, and

Mr Dixon also, were fêted and congratulated wherever they went. The distinction rather astounded Rowena, of course, but it pleased her too. She basked in her success. For the first time in her life, she did not instinctively hold back, shrink into the shadows or eschew notice. This was her moment. She glowed, she gloried; she was almost beautiful. Whereas Jane had habitually had to encourage and promote her friend, now she could simply observe as Rowena nodded and smiled, surrounded by sighing maidens and men who were asking themselves what they had failed to see in her.

Mr Dixon was to return to County Wicklow in August. He had petitioned for and received his brother's permission to marry Miss Campbell. Hugh promised to be present at the wedding although his wife would be unable to travel so far as she was with child. Lord Knox was working to ensure Andrew and Connor could be given furlough. Lady Knox promised Rowena a Spaniel puppy.

'Although there are dogs in superfluity at Baly-Craig,' Mr Dixon confided to his fiancée. 'If it is dogs you want, you shall have plenty, probably too many, for they are adept at escaping from the barn where they are supposed to sleep and finding their way into the house. It is not unusual to wake up and find three or four of them on the bed.'

Rowena blushed, the idea of anyone other than Jane or their maid in her bedchamber still causing her some anxiety. 'But do not fret, my little bird,' Mr Dixon added, seeing her confusion. 'You shall have one of grandmamma's puppies for your own, if you wish. It shall sleep by your side, and not be allowed to run wild like the others, or wallow in the manure pit, so long as,' leaning closer, 'you allow *me* the same privilege.'

Rowena coloured more, but her eyes twinkled as she replied, 'And do you *often* feel called to wallow in the manure pit?'

'No, little bird,' he replied, slipping his arm around her waist, 'not *very* often.'

'My father returns to Bute Square this afternoon,' Rowena said after a while, smoothing her skirt and tucking a loose lock of hair back into place, 'and Jane is to accompany him. Mrs Quill has found a family in need of a governess and Jane is to go and see if it will suit.'

'I hope it will *not*,' Mr Dixon replied bluntly, 'unless Mrs Quill's acquaintance is a noble lady of aristocratic lineage, which I doubt.'

'The lady of the family is with the angels,' Rowena replied, 'but her husband is left on earth with three children to manage.'

'Is he an earl or a duke? For nothing less is good enough for Miss Fairfax in my opinion.'

'I believe he is a tanner.'

'Good God,' Mr Dixon ejaculated, 'I wonder that your father and mother even consider it. Something must be done.'

'They have tried. Jane will not be swayed. She will only compromise on the date. She will not take up her position until after we are married, and she stipulates for a month with her grandmamma and aunt. That will bring her to November. If this gentleman—his name is Goole—is prepared to wait until then, and if all else is acceptable, she will go to Battersea then.'

'Battersea? Worse and worse! Tell me, does Mr Churchill know of this?'

Rowena shook her head. 'I do not think so. Why should he? It is no business of his. Mrs Quill's note only came last evening. We have been all at sixes and sevens getting Jane's trunk packed so that she may accompany Papa.'

Suddenly Mr Dixon was on his feet and searching for his hat. 'You must excuse me, my dear. I must find Churchill. I do not know why it is, but if anyone can persuade a person from one course to another, it is him. We simply cannot allow Miss Fairfax to throw herself away in this manner.'

Mr Dixon hurried off to Chesterfield Place but found the whole family to be from home, with no indication of when they might return. The manservant thought that perhaps they might have gone to Portland, but wasn't certain. Even with this thin sliver of hope, Mr Dixon returned to his lodgings to have his horse saddled, rode towards the island with all despatch and at last did locate the Churchills picnicking on the sands that overlooked Durdle Door, in company with the Branthwaites and the Mosleys.

He communicated his tidings as quickly as possible. 'You must come back with me, Churchill,' he urged. 'The colonel is due to leave Weymouth this afternoon, taking Miss Fairfax with him. She is to consider taking up employment with a tanner in Battersea. Can you imagine anything less suitable?'

'No,' said Frank, 'but I don't know what I can do or say to prevent it.'

'Do you not?' asked Mr Dixon, giving his friend a direct look. 'Do you think I have not fathomed your design? I do not upbraid you; I am happy. You saw more clearly than I did, but you were not entirely disinterested when you steered me as you did. Stir yourself, man, or you will lose your prize.'

'What prize is that,' enquired Mary Branthwaite, walking with apparent casualness toward where the two young men had withdrawn for private discourse, but in reality quite burning to know what had brought Mr Dixon to Portland in such haste. She had been luxuriating in Mr Frank Churchill's undivided attention—the absence of Miss Fairfax from their party having added to its enjoyment most materially—and did not wish him to be distracted now.

'Oh, Miss Mary,' Frank faltered, 'an acquaintance of mine … there is a matter I must attend to …'

'Concerning whom?' Miss Mary pressed, most intrigued.

'I have just come from Augusta Place—the Campbells reside there, you know, and Miss Fairfax …' panted Mr Dixon.

'There is nothing to concern yourself about,' Frank cut in, anxious that Mr Dixon should not reveal too much.

'Is Miss Fairfax unwell? And why should *you* be required, Mr Churchill?' Miss Mary enquired. She fluttered what little eyelashes she had, although this merely gave the impression that she had something in her eye. 'This is really most perplexing.'

'Frank! Frank!' called Mrs Churchill. She sat on a folding chair amply padded with cushions. The chair had been placed on a thick carpet so that the roughness of the stones might not bruise her feet and she was protected from the breeze and the gaze of onlookers by a number of screens. 'Come back to me. I have need of you. The wind has tangled my embroidery threads and I cannot unpick them.'

'Perhaps Miss Branthwaite can assist you, Aunt,' Frank replied, exasperated, 'or, Miss Mary, would *you* be so kind?' He gave her what he hoped was a winning smile.

'By no means,' Mary simpered. 'I have no skill with such things. Stacie will aid Mrs Churchill far better. In any case, I am too anxious about dear Miss Fairfax. Are you certain there is nothing seriously amiss? And I still cannot fathom why *you* should be needed.'

'Nor I,' Frank threw off, mustering an air of levity he did not feel, 'but there it is. I have been summoned and must answer; no gentleman can do less. I pray you will excuse me, Miss Mary, and convey my apologies to the remainder of the party.' He began to walk towards where his horse was tethered.

'But wait, Mr Churchill,' cried Miss Mary, very loathe indeed to be parted from her beau, and sensing also, without quite understanding, a serious threat to her claim. 'You will surely bid adieu to your aunt? Look how she beckons you. She really is most anxious for your assistance.'

Mrs Churchill was indeed signalling most imperiously to Frank, and had upon her face a look of thunderous displeasure that almost made him quail. 'Frank! Frank!' she almost bawled.

'Aunt Churchill,' Frank shouted across the shingle, 'you must forgive me. Something has occurred, or *may* occur, and I must ride back to Weymouth immediately. There is no time for explanations.' He turned and half ran towards his horse. Dixon was already mounted and they scaled the bank to the pathway with the sound of Mrs Churchill's rage and Miss Mary's falsetto dismay in their ears.

They rode hard, but when they got back to Augusta Place it was to find the colonel's coach and Miss Fairfax with it, gone this past hour.

'I am minded to ride after them,' Frank said, slapping his crop against his boot.

'I think you should,' Mr Dixon urged. 'Your horse has wind enough, I think.'

'She does but I … I do not know …' Frank prevaricated. 'I had not thought … But that is not true. I have thought of nothing else for weeks. But my aunt; she must be managed. The whole affair must be carefully handled. If I ride off now, and offer my hand, the colonel will be witness and all must be out in the open. My aunt will quash the match as easily as she would drown a puppy. And where will that leave any of us? No,' with a grimace, 'if I had known, and secured an interview with her this morning, all might have been arranged. But as it is I must hope the tanner is a disagreeable fellow and his children are all uneducable brats. Now I shall have to return to Portland and make some excuse to my aunt and uncle.'

'I am sorry,' Mr Dixon said. 'Blame me. Tell them I made a mistake, that it was all my misunderstanding. You will think of something.'

Frank turned his horse back towards Portland but soon met with his uncle's equipage on the road. The party had been broken up, the picnic abandoned, all was disappointment and concern. Mrs Churchill had suffered a serious relapse of her recent illness. She lolled insensible in the corner of the barouche, her eyes closed, a thin stream of saliva oozing from the corner of her mouth.

Chapter Twenty-Seven

The colonel and Jane returned to Bute Square the following day. The colonel directed the coach to take Jane to her appointment in Low Street, Battersea on the day after, dropping him in the city on the way that he might initiate the arrangement of Rowena's dowry.

The coach took Jane across the river and through a number of streets that were increasingly dark and narrow and slick with ordure. More than once did the coachman have to stop and enquire for direction. Warehouses and places of manufacture made for plentiful traffic; great wagons came and went, smaller carts choked up the thoroughfares, horses stamped and whinnied while men unloaded bales and crates. The noise from within the buildings—cries of instruction and complaint, the grinding of machinery, hammering and sawing—was loud and alarming but this was nothing to the rank and rancid smell that pervaded the air. The going was difficult indeed and Jane was sure that they had mistook the way until a sharp turn past a dye works brought them into Low Street. Here, houses interspersed places of commerce where tailors, cobblers and laundry women plied their trades. Jane saw shabby, mean-looking places with thin grey washing strung on lines and no vestige of green—no tree, shrub or flower—to brighten the overwhelming gloom.

At the far end of Low Street, a house stood a little apart from the rest, considerably bigger and somewhat better appointed than its neighbours, with a railing in front enclosing a tiny area of private pavement and a heavy door with self-important brass furniture. Jane dismissed the coachman, telling him to return in an hour, and went up the few, slick steps to knock on the door.

She was admitted by a careworn woman wearing a dress that was drab and not very clean.

'You'll be the new gov'ness,' the woman said. 'Mr Goole isn't back from the works yet. You can wait in the parlour.'

Jane was shown into a room that was small and rather dark. No sunlight could have penetrated the grimy windows even if it had managed to gain access between the closely packed buildings outside. The fireplace was unswept. A small table was littered with newspapers and other documents of a mercantile nature. There was no pianoforte or any other accoutrement that suggested an iota of elegant living.

Jane sat gingerly on the edge of a chair and waited. Above her head the thunderous echo of scurrying feet resounded through the ceiling, along with the cries of children seemingly running amok. The occasional shout of remonstrance from some harried nursery maid went utterly unheeded. No one came to offer tea or even to properly open the curtain that had been but half drawn back, or to remove the dirty cup that sat on the mantelpiece.

Presently, the clock on the mantel telling her that a quarter of her hour had already elapsed, Jane emboldened herself to step back into the hall to enquire if she might see the children. A scullery maid gave her a doubtful look before wiping a sooty hand across her face and saying, 'All right Miss, if you're sure.'

She led Jane up a flight of dusty stairs, along a landing with a threadbare carpet and through another door to a second floor. This area was not carpeted but it was brighter, the windows being higher than their neighbours' and, although no cleaner, having some view over the crowded roofs to the river beyond. She was shown into what she presumed to be the schoolroom. Two ramshackle tables and three or four wobble-legged chairs occupied the centre of the room. A cupboard showed a few ragged books and some crumpled sheets of paper. Three boys ran in manic circles round and round the room, engaged in some game. Theirs had been the footsteps Jane had heard from two floors down, but there was no sign of the maid who had briefly protested at their noise.

'Do you do no schoolwork today, gentlemen,' said Jane.

The boys stopped their game and looked curiously at her.

'We're waiting for the new governess,' the oldest boy, who might have been ten years of age, said. 'We can do no learning till then.'

'You might teach your brothers what you know,' Jane said, pulling one of the chairs to the table and sitting upon it. 'Why do you not begin by showing me your letters? Then the others can copy.'

The boys looked sceptical but drew round as the oldest boy began to oblige Jane by writing his alphabet, which he did without difficulty and in fact with some calligraphic flair.

'What is your name?' Jane murmured as he worked.

'I'm Cedric,' the boy said. 'I'm eleven. This is Wally, he's nine, and Bobby is eight.'

'We can all do our letters,' Bobby asserted, losing interest in Cedric's writing. 'I like stories. Do you tell stories?'

'I know a few,' Jane said, 'but being able to read yourself will open the way to all the stories in the world.' She pulled one of the books from the cupboard. 'Can you read this, Bobby?'

'Oh yes,' he said. 'I've read it a hundred times. Papa promises us more books, when the new governess comes.'

'And what became of your old governess?' Jane enquired.

The middle boy, Wally, who had not yet spoken, said quietly, 'She died. Our mama taught us, but she got ill and …' his face began to crease.

'Now Wally,' said Cedric, kindly enough, 'you have managed nearly all morning without crying at all. Here,' he pulled another piece of paper towards his brother, 'why don't you do some equations? You know that always cheers you.'

Just then the maid returned to say that Mr Goole was home and waiting for Jane in the dining room. 'He hopes you will not mind,' the girl said as she preceded Jane down the stairs. 'He has his luncheon to eat and then must return to the tannery in half an hour. He must eat while you talk.'

'No,' said Jane, 'I do not mind.'

The dining room was the mirror image of the parlour in point of untidiness, dreariness, dilapidation and want of taste. Mr Goole sat at one end of an oval table eating a mutton chop, his napkin tucked into this waistcoat. He half rose to greet Jane, wiping his hand with his napkin before extending it to her. Then he resumed his meal, waving her towards a seat at the other end of the table. He was a man of about thirty or thirty-five years of age, florid of complexion and broad of girth, with a high expanse of brow beneath a thin covering of hair.

'You will take no refreshment, I suppose?' he asked, and then, before she could decline—which she decidedly would have done—went on, 'You have seen the boys?'

'Yes, sir. I find them well advanced with their education. They have been well taught.'

'My wife saw to it,' Mr Goole said. 'Take no account of the state of the schoolroom. I shall put things right there. Did you see your accommodations? No? Oh well. I think they will serve. Mrs Bees, the housekeeper, has the adjacent rooms and *she* makes no complaint. You shall have a fire of course, if you wish it, and wax candles. I can't say fairer than that. I understand there is a difficulty about your starting straight away.'

'Yes, sir. *If* I take up the post, I cannot do so until November.'

'November?' Mr Goole almost shouted, spraying gravy across the cloth. 'I do not see how that can be countenanced. The boys need management. They are growing quite feral. I caught them at Miss Fidget's Sweet Emporium yesterday and that is four streets away.'

'They are bored, sir. They need supervision and occupation,' Jane suggested.

'Of course they do! Why do you think I have asked you to come? Upon my word I think Mrs Quill has misrepresented you, ma'am. She told me you were quick-witted.'

Jane took a deep breath. 'I hope Mrs Quill made clear that I have come today only to take a look at your situation, to meet the boys and to speak with you *preparatory* to us *both* deciding whether the arrangement would agree.'

Mr Goole shook his head and wiped his mouth. 'By no means. She described you as inexperienced, eager to begin and desirous merely of a respectable situation. She implied—forgive me ma'am, I mean no offense—that having no particular family connections yourself, and no other prospect of, shall we say, advancement, and being, as I say, without prior experience of the role, you would offer easy terms.'

Jane rose to her feet. 'I beg your forgiveness then, Mr Goole. We have *both* been misled. My visit here has wasted both our mornings. I must bid you good day.' She had taken a few steps towards the door when the image of the three boys above came powerfully to her mind. 'If you will allow me to be so presumptuous though,' she said, turning back to where Mr Goole sat, open mouthed, at the table, 'I will just suggest that your boys are beyond a governess on any terms, easy or otherwise. They are ready for school, sir. The late Mrs Goole was evidently an excellent teacher and the boys are bright. Send them to school, Mr Goole, that is my counsel, for what it is worth. Good day.'

She left the house in Low Street and began to walk along the road in the hopes of meeting the coach, which she did at the corner by the dye works.

'Take me home,' she said to the coachman, before sinking into the corner of the coach overcome by misery.

The next few days saw Jane very low in spirits. The colonel was away from home, busy in the city and sorting through the accrual of correspondence at the War office, and Jane spent the days alone. Even a letter from her aunt Hetty, forwarded from Weymouth, did little to cheer her up, full as it was of preparations at Randalls for its new mistress and the niceties of wedding arrangements in train at Hartfield. It reminded her all too cruelly of the imminence of Rowena's nuptials. A gift of strawberries from the Donwell gardens and a nasty carbuncle that Mr Perry had been called in to lance for Patty gave her more comfort; whatever uncertainties *she* faced, life in Highbury went on as usual.

As fixed as Jane's resolution had always been about becoming a governess she had never, until that day at Low Street, seen with her own eyes what it might entail. Miss Blossom—her own and Rowena's governess—had been a respected and fondly appreciated member of the colonel's household, living elegantly alongside the family. Miss Taylor had been more sister than teacher to the Misses Woodhouse. But now, Jane realised, not all governesses were so lucky. For each one as happily situated as Miss Blossom and Miss Taylor there must be twenty or thirty others living in cramped houses with too many children to manage. They were considered as little more than servants and paid a pittance, their fine learning and well-honed accomplishments gone utterly to waste. Was *that* to be her fate? Mr Goole had spoken truly; she had neither family connection nor previous employer to recommend her, she really had no superior claim by which she might stipulate a more than ordinarily respectable position in a middling class of home. She ought not to be too proud to take work with a tanner.

Who were her own family, after all, but an impecunious widow and a busy-body spinster aunt? And yet the idea of taking up residence in Low Street or somewhere like it was intolerable. The grime and meanness alone would make her ill. She did not think she could live without a glimmer of green, a sliver of garden or the smallest stand of trees even if she found she could forgo her music. Life with the Campbells had been too kind, too soft. She had become, after all, nothing more than a pleasing ornament. Her diligence with her studies, her hours of music practice, her extensive reading all counted for nought. They had not prepared her for what real life would bring.

Colonel Campbell was successful in arranging his business affairs and was able to announce to Jane that they would be able to return to Weymouth a few days earlier than planned.

'I have expedited matters,' he told her, 'for I have not liked to see how a return to the town has affected your health. You are pale, my dear. You miss the healthful air and sun of the coast.'

'I miss Rowena too,' Jane had admitted to him, 'and dear Mrs Campbell. I shall be happy to return to them if you are sure your business is done.'

She had told the colonel only that the children at Low Street were too advanced for a governess, saying nothing of the dreariness of the situation or of Mr Goole's insulting insinuations. 'I shall sever my connections with the Quills, however,' she added. 'I fear Mrs Quill's idea of a respectable situation and mine are at variance.'

'Quite right, my dear Jane,' said the colonel, patting her hand. 'Emily and I had my doubts about them. You can remove the man from the glue works but he must travel a long way before he is rid of the whiff of boiled down hooves. So, my dear, have the maid pack your trunk and we will be in Weymouth by dinner time the day after tomorrow.'

'Mrs Campbell will be pleased,' Jane remarked. 'That is the day the Churchills are due to dine. She will not like to have them there without you.'

'Or you,' the colonel added.

So, thought Jane, as she retired for the night in the room she had shared with Rowena since coming to Bute Square as a girl, I shall see Frank Churchill again. Her heart made a little leap, and as she brushed her hair before the mirror, she found she was smiling again.

Chapter Twenty-Eight

Jane and Colonel Campbell arrived back in Augusta Place in good time for the dinner, and Mrs Campbell was indeed very happy to see them.

'The Churchills *are* coming,' she told them before her husband had removed his hat or put his walking stick in its accustomed place. 'We had a note this morning. I doubted for some days that the dinner would go ahead at all, for she has been ill again. You will not know; we got word of it after you had left for town. Rowena and I fully expected to hear that Mrs Churchill was still indisposed. But it seems she is well again. And now we expect the Branthwaites and Mosleys to dine also. I did not mean to, but Miss Mary was so importunate. She implied so strongly that Mrs Churchill goes nowhere without them, and suggested that there is that level of relationship between herself and Mr Frank Churchill that would make it discourteous to exclude them. She made it so difficult for me to do anything other than ask them too that the words were out of my mouth before I knew it. And having invited the Branthwaites it seemed ill-mannered not to include the Mosleys; *they* are as much family to Mrs Churchill as the Branthwaites, and a good deal more agreeable, I must say. But now Rowena tells me that Mrs Churchill abhors her relatives, and that Miss Mary Branthwaite is a notorious toady who attaches herself to her betters like a leech. Mrs Churchill will in all likelihood be appalled to find them here. But what am I to do?'

'Do not worry, my dear,' said Colonel Campbell, embracing his wife. 'We have mutton enough to stretch, I suppose, and sufficient chairs to accommodate them? Mrs Churchill will be our guest and must make herself agreeable to whomever she meets here. In five hours—or perhaps six—we will be rid of them and you will see that your concerns have been over nothing.'

'I hope you are right,' said Mrs Campbell doubtfully.

'Are Mr Churchill and Miss Mary Branthwaite engaged, then?' Jane asked Rowena with as casual an air as she could muster, as they dressed.

'Oh no. That is, not to my knowledge. I do not think the aunt would allow it, do you? Perhaps they are engaged in secret? I would put nothing past Mary Branthwaite but depend upon it, if the aunt cuts him off because of it Mary will not take Frank Churchill without Enscombe. Oh! But if they are engaged, secretly or not, I wish them happiness,' sighed Rowena. 'Being engaged is such bliss. Do you think Patrick will like this ribbon in my hair? I shall ask Annette to weave it into my chignon, I think.'

'Yes, dear, it is very pretty. I am sure he will like it,' Jane replied distractedly. Rowena was full of her wedding plans, her ideas for Baly-Craig, what Patrick had said about this, his opinion on that. She had asked nothing about Jane's visit to town or the situation at Mr Goole's.

She really is able to do without me, Jane thought, as she found her gloves and a clean handkerchief in a drawer.

The preparations at Augusta Place were nothing in comparison to the furore in Bridge Street, where the Branthwaites had been readying themselves for their dinner engagement since a little after noon. Even so the time for their departure came and went without the ladies being ready. Mr Branthwaite and Edgar loitered in the cramped hallway while, above, the shrieks and apostrophic cries of the women went on unabated.

'Lucy has done my hair wrong, mama,' cried Mary, 'I cannot go to Augusta Place like this. Augusta Place is not Chesterfield Place—I doubt the Campbells entertain in such style as the Churchills—but in the absence of an invitation *there, this* is the next best thing.'

'Mary borrowed my best gloves last week and has lost one,' this from Stacie. 'I have only my second-best pair and there is a hole in the thumb. How many courses do you suppose there will be? Will we have syllabub? I do adore it so.'

'I cannot decide whether to wear my pearl pendant or my sapphire brooch,' Mrs Branthwaite wailed. '*Both* would seem excessive but then Eustacia Churchill will no doubt be smothered in gems and my sister Billinge—that is, Mosley (I keep forgetting she is remarried. That new husband of hers is so vapid and dreary)—will be just as bad. Did you see her new bracelet? If there is one ruby in it I swear there must be a dozen. Your father is very backward when it comes to jewels. My trinket box is a disgrace.'

'I have your brooch, Mama, so you cannot wear *that*,' called Mary from her chamber. 'The colour is exactly right for my gown and I need it to hide a little rent in the yoke that I have not had time to sew up. Papa should have bought you a corsage. Corsages are all the rage. I suppose it is too late for him to get one for you now. I asked Frank Churchill to buy me one, but he just laughed off my suggestion.'

And so it was that the Mosleys arrived at Augusta Place first. Jane was placed in readiness to receive the guests, Mrs Campbell having hurried to the kitchen to make some final amendments to the menu and Rowena being ensconced in the small parlour with Mr Dixon for the waist-clasping and sweet murmurings that seemed essential to both after a few hours' separation. The colonel was on parade, naturally, but his slight deafness made him little use for the exchange of pleasantries and observations about the weather that generally characterise the first few moments of any social occasion. He barked his welcome and bowed to Mrs Mosley before taking up a sentinel stance on the hearth rug.

Jane immediately discerned a difference in the atmosphere between Mr Mosley and his wife. They were warmer, easier together than when she had seen them before. He was fuller of smiles and carried himself with greater pride and dignity; she almost glowed as he helped her with her wraps and handed her to a chair.

'Mr Mosley,' said Jane, shaking hands, 'I am delighted to see you. This is a boon I had not anticipated this afternoon. I returned from town only an hour or so ago to discover that we were to have the pleasure of your company.'

She turned to Mrs Mosley to receive a smile whose benediction could not be misinterpreted. 'Dear Miss Fairfax,' said Mrs Mosley, 'I cannot express, I can hardly articulate … I have much to thank you for.'

Jane did not pretend to misunderstand her, but could say no more as the Branthwaites were announced.

Mary, having spent the whole day since breakfast in the preparation of her toilette, was most magnificently made up; her hair dressed very high, her costume richly ornamented with trimmings and flounces, ribbons and ruches of every description including her mother's sapphire brooch. She gazed around her at the high ceilings and elegant staircase of the Campbells' residence and almost clapped her hands with glee. Her sister Stacie was less interested in the décor than she was in the dinner. She tried to peep into the dining room to see what gastronomic delights might await her once she had got through the tedium of polite conversation in the drawing room above. Edgar came under extreme sufferance—he had been engaged to accompany a party of young rakes to the races that day but his mother had insisted the jape be given up in favour of the Campbells' dinner.

'It is almost as good as being invited to Chesterfield Place,' she had told him, 'and if we comport ourselves properly an invitation *there* is sure to follow. What, then, can prevent our being asked to Enscombe?'

His parents held themselves with as much stiffness and decorum as they could muster, very sensible of the great honour of the occasion but at the same time prepared to be affronted by any condescension that the Churchills might betray, 'For,' Mrs Branthwaite had said as they travelled in the hired carriage, 'I am heartily sick of hearing how magnificently Aunt Eustacia has married and what a poor match my own mother made in comparison. It is all of a piece with Ariadne's good fortune and our comparative ignominy. The disparity is pushed down our throats at every opportunity but when it comes to the point we are all equally descended from our grandfather Fishwick; his blood runs in all our veins and for one branch of the family to claim superiority over another is humbug.'

'The disparity, my dear,' demurred Mr Branthwaite as he tried to ease the tightness of his collar, 'is not in the Fishwick women but in the men they married. Your aunt Eustacia married Mr Churchill, a wealthy, landed gentleman of ancient family. Your mother chose Clegg, an ironmonger. Likewise, your sister's good fortune is all down to the mercantile success of old Billinge. If she had married my brother, as we all expected she would, you and she would have been equally placed. But I regret to hear, my dear, that you consider my own enterprise so contemptible. Drapery is not perhaps a very elegant profession but it is lucrative. I think I have provided well enough for you.'

'I do not complain,' said Mrs Branthwaite, ironically—for she was given to complaint and lamentation on the smallest pretext—'only I would not have the Churchills or the Mosleys think they can lord it over us. Indeed, it is my intention to wrest something from the Churchills. They *ought* to do something for our children, having none of their own. I do not see why Mr Churchill's nephew should get so much and Eustacia's nothing at all. It is not fair.'

'Oh,' said Mary, inspecting her nails, 'if I have my way it will be all one, in the end.'

'You deceive yourself if you think Frank Churchill is going to propose,' said her sister darkly. 'Anyone with eyes can see he is smitten by Miss Fairfax.'

'Stacie, I hate you,' spat Mary. 'Who is *she?* She has nothing and she is nothing. She will soon be buried in Low Street with that odious Mr Goole and all her clothes will stink of boiled cows.'

Considering the venom of this remark nothing could have been more ingratiating than Mary's demeanour on greeting Jane. 'I had so little hope of your being back in Weymouth,' she crooned. 'What an utter delight that you are. We have missed you excessively. Sally and Amy Quill are almost ill for the lack of you; their sisters are utterly ungovernable, only *you* can manage them. Your metier for dealing with small children is beyond doubt. I hope Mr Goole snapped you up?'

Jane smiled but did not rise to the bait. 'We await only the Churchills,' she remarked as the two progressed up the staircase arm in arm, 'and then our party will be complete.'

'I have corresponded with Mr Frank Churchill daily, on the subject of Mrs Churchill's health,' Mary simpered. 'Lor'! Anyone might misconstrue the constant passing of notes we have engaged in these past days.'

'I have no doubt that Mrs Churchill has been moved beyond words by your concern,' Jane said. 'Happily, she is recovered enough to join us today. There will be no need for further communication between Chesterfield Place and Bridge Street.'

'Oh,' Mary threw off with an arch smile, 'I do not know, we *may* find a pretext. There are Mr Dixon and Miss Campbell. Everyone is astounded at her coup. Has she not surpassed everyone's expectations? I think Weymouth boasts no greater catch than Mr Dixon—unless it be Mr Frank Churchill. Mr Dixon's fortune is *nothing* to Frank's. Now *there* will be a happy and fortunate lady, to secure the hand of Mr Frank Churchill. It will put Rowena's marriage quite in the shade. Ah, but until such time, do not Miss Campbell and Mr Dixon make a … I will not say a handsome couple, but a happy one!'

'Handsome *and* happy,' Jane said through clenched teeth. 'Perhaps you will take a glass of Madeira? Excuse me, I hear the Churchills arriving below.'

Mrs Churchill had hesitated even up to ten minutes before their carriage came round, as to whether she should attend the Campbells' dinner. Really, it was too demeaning, she considered, being associated with the Campbells; they were inherently low. Only the colonel's connection with Lord Knox saved them from utter ignominy. She wished Frank were not so set on his acquaintance with Mr Dixon. When one got past his commonplace acreage and so many thousands of pounds, he was nothing more than an Irish farmer. She considered conjuring a spasm, a swelling, even a pustular outbreak—anything that could excuse them from setting out. But she had a brooding suspicion that even if *she* did not attend the dinner, Frank would. He was becoming, every day, more likely to challenge her authority or circumvent her commands. She did not know what she would do if he outright defied her. *Would* she disown him? Could she bear, even in the face of his treachery, to let him go? His uncle, of course, would argue Frank's case, but he was weak and always had been. If he had had his way the Westons would have been welcomed to Enscombe on their return from honeymoon. Louisa might not have sickened and died and what chance would there have been then, of getting Frank to themselves?

No, Mrs Churchill sighed as she rose from her dressing table and picked up her wrap. As always, it would be left to her to manage things.

So Mr and Mrs Churchill and Frank were the last to arrive in Augusta Place but this suited Mrs Churchill's sense of her own importance. They progressed through the hallway and up the stairs with much ceremony, flanked by footmen. The ladies in the drawing room made elaborate curtseys and the men bowed before Mr Churchill handed his wife to a stately chair, placed at an exact angle between the fireplace and the window, which no one else had dared sit upon. He stood to her right, slightly behind her, and Frank took up a position to her left. In unison, almost as though choreographed, the footmen brought other—harder, more upright and infinitely less comfortable—chairs forward to form a semi-circle around her and the ladies sat in them in helpless acquiescence. Even Mrs Campbell, as hostess, could do nothing other than follow suit. The gentlemen remained standing, sipping their sherry, themselves arranged in a sort of guard of honour of which Mrs Churchill was the undoubted centre. The servants arrayed themselves in a peripheral tier, their gazes fixed at some point above the fireplace, their gloved hands folded before them. Stacie stifled a nervous giggle, Mary almost groaned in exquisite pleasure. Edgar drank off his sherry at a gulp and held out his glass for more.

Mrs Churchill surveyed the company in haughty silence. 'I am delighted to see you all here,' she finally announced, without any discernible evidence of delight at all. 'I hope I find you all well. Matilda, Ariadne, I did not know you were acquainted with the Campbells.'

'Oh yes, ma'am, we had the honour of being introduced by a mutual acquaintance of the girls'. A family by the name of Quill,' Mrs Branthwaite said, 'one of the most superior families in our circle in Clapham, before they removed to Chelsea.'

'Indeed,' Mrs Churchill replied with a shrivelled lip. She subjected the young ladies to minute scrutiny. 'Remind me of the name of that tall young lady with the chestnut hair,' she said, leaning backwards and speaking to Frank.

Frank bent over his aunt's ear. 'That is Miss Fairfax, Aunt. You have seen her before, I think. She is acquainted with my father. She has relatives in Highbury.'

'Oh yes, the young orphan girl,' Mrs Churchill said, adding in a tone that was not a decibel lower, 'I believe you think her a beauty.'

'Aunt,' Frank remonstrated, blushing but daring to lift his eyes to where Jane sat amongst the others. She sat very stiffly, beautifully proud. He did not think she had ever looked more beautiful. 'Yes indeed,' he said, emboldened, 'if I am asked for an opinion, I will state that I think her very beautiful.'

Mary Branthwaite gave a little cry of dismay before blurting out, 'But Miss Fairfax will not be amongst us for long. She is to take up a post as governess with a family in Battersea.'

'That is not decided,' Mrs Campbell said quickly.

'I hope it is not,' Frank spluttered.

But Mrs Churchill broke in, 'A most suitable course for a woman in her circumstances. I applaud your common sense, Miss Fairfax. I think it most lamentable when people try to rise from their own sphere. It leads to confusion in the natural order of things.'

Jane bit her tongue so hard that she could taste blood in her mouth. She knew that if she opened her mouth to speak she would disgrace herself.

Beside her, Mrs Mosley said, 'Miss Fairfax, it appears to me that your windows here command an exceptionally fine view of the bay. Would you be so good as to show me?'

Jane nodded and the two rose from their seats and made their way towards the far window.

'I cannot sufficiently apologise for the unspeakable hubris of my aunt,' Mrs Mosley said when they were quite out of earshot. 'For her to speak in such terms is beyond hypocrisy. Did not *she* rise from her natural sphere? I am ashamed to admit kinship with her. I hope you do not mind my being so forthright with you, Miss Fairfax. Although we have only spoken twice, I feel that I can be unreserved. '

'No indeed,' Jane said, 'I welcome your honesty Mrs Mosley. But Mrs Churchill is quite right. I have no claim to anything. My family is very poor.'

'My dear,' said Mrs Mosley kindly, 'you do yourself an injustice. Philip cannot speak highly enough of your cleverness and accomplishments, and as to your wisdom, *that* is far beyond your years. I understand that it was at *your* urging that he told me about his … about Miss Brokenshire.'

'Ah,' breathed Jane, 'so he has opened his heart to you?'

'He has. And I must say his story almost broke mine. The poor, poor girl! Poor Philip! What a terrible tragedy the whole thing was. But it explains so much. I had taught myself to believe that he resented me, because he had been forced to abandon his vocation. But no! This old wound has been the barrier between us and we have determined to break it down, stone by stone and to build something new that encompasses and secures us both. We have sent letters to enquire after

316

the Brokenshire family in Jamaica, and we will do what we can for them. The girl died, we have ascertained that much. We intend to found a hospital or some such, in her name, that her reputation might be restored and good might be done.'

'That is an excellent and generous idea,' Jane said.

'And in return,' Mrs Mosley went on, 'I have been able to tell Philip something of my life with Mr Billinge. It was not happy, and I must say that for my part I have been guilty of some reserve towards Philip in case he should … in case he was of a similar cast.'

'He is not, if Mr Billinge was unkind.' Jane averred.

Mrs Mosley nodded. 'He *was* unkind. But Philip is nothing like him.' She toyed with a heavy ruby bracelet that adorned her wrist. She lifted it, now, in evidence. 'He is generous,' she said, shiny eyed. 'He is gentle. And I have told him, if he wishes, he shall give up the business and take orders and I shall be a happy vicar's wife.'

'Oh Mrs Mosley,' said Jane, visibly moved by all she had heard, 'what delight it is when two people overcome the impediments that keep them asunder to meet each other as they are, to defy the expectations and decrees of others to take their own happiness.'

Mary Branthwaite patted the seat next to her, which had been vacated by Mrs Mosley. 'You might sit here next to me, Mr Churchill,' she said to Frank as winningly as she could, 'since Mrs Mosley has no further need of this seat for the present.'

Frank could do no other than take the proffered place. He perched there uncomfortably but showed by his constant glances towards the window that he would rather be in that part of the room than this.

Presently Mrs Branthwaite said, 'You are very well accommodated here, Mrs Campbell. What splendid rooms! I cannot imagine what the rent might be on such a fine house.'

'Oh,' said Mrs Campbell awkwardly, 'I ...'

'I am sure Mrs Campbell does not concern herself with such matters,' Mrs Churchill interrupted, 'but, whatever it is, it is too high. Of all charlatans and usurers, landlords are the worst for extorting money from honest people. However, in general the cost of things is something that is beneath my notice. Money is so sordid.'

'Sordid, but necessary,' Mrs Branthwaite murmured.

'Oh, quite,' Mrs Churchill agreed sourly. 'Someone somewhere must concern themselves with it. Someone *does*, I assume, at Enscombe. There must be a clerk or a steward who busies himself with our pecuniary affairs, but *I* know nothing of them.'

'Naturally not, my dear,' said Mr Churchill uneasily.

'If you needed a trustworthy clerk, or some such reliable person to oversee things, Edgar has a very quick head for figures,' Mrs Branthwaite said.

'I thought he was at Oxford?' Mrs Churchill mused.

'Oh, he *was*,' the young rake's mother replied, 'but he found the academic life too stultifying. Branthwaite thinks to take him into the business, but if he can be of use to you, Aunt, Branthwaite will sacrifice all claim.'

'No, thank you,' Mrs Churchill returned stiffly.

Mr Churchill turned to Edgar Branthwaite. 'Have you fished much, since you arrived in Weymouth?' he asked, to divert the conversation. 'I hear there is good sport to be had from the beach or along the banks of the Wey.'

The gentlemen pursued a desultory conversation amongst themselves about the sporting opportunities in the vicinity but it was short-lived since neither Mr Branthwaite nor Mr Mosley shot, hunted or fished. Mr Dixon issued a vague invitation for them to go out aboard *The Pride of Wicklow,* 'But only if there is time before I must take ship to Ireland,' he said. Edgar had the most to say, concerning horse racing. 'I hoped to attend the races today,' he concluded glumly, 'but Mama said I must come here instead.'

'Perhaps you and I may make the journey another day,' said Frank, using the topic to abandon Mary Branthwaite and join the gentlemen. 'I like to think I have an eye for horse-flesh and,' in a lowered voice, 'I have a contact in the trade. He is most reliable.'

'*Do* you?' said Edgar, suddenly alert. 'I say, is there any more of this sherry?'

Conversation amongst the ladies faltered until Stacie spied a tray of canapes that had not been handed round. At last she piped up, 'Mrs Campbell, at what time do you generally dine? We dine early at home, because it suits Papa, but I believe the fashion nowadays is to dine rather late. Here in Weymouth, it seems to be the general habit to dine *very* late. Last week, at the Assembly, most carriages did not begin to arrive until nine or ten.'

'We dine at the civilised hour of four,' Mrs Churchill said, as though she and not Mrs Campbell had been addressed. 'We have no truck with modern trends. I do not attend the Assembly—with my poor health, my dancing days were over before they had begun. I am a perfect invalid, you know—but if I did, I should want a proper amount of time to elapse between dinner and dancing. To dance on a full stomach is a recipe for dyspepsia. I would caution against it.'

Stacie glanced at the ornate clock that graced the marble mantel. It wanted a quarter of an hour to four.

'I will ring the bell presently,' Mrs Campbell said.

'Stacie does everything on a full stomach,' Mary trilled, 'for she never stops eating from morning till night. Mama says that she eats as much as the rest of us put together. I have better manners, I hope,' she concluded with a simper.

'But not a better disposition,' Stacie retorted in a hiss. 'You are the nastiest person I know.'

'Girls!' shrilled Mrs Branthwaite, throwing them a look black with menace. She turned to her aunt. 'I do not know, ma'am, if you have ever considered it, but a female companion at Enscombe might be a benefit to you. Either of my girls would be honoured to attend you. Mary is a lively conversationalist, with quick wits and a fund of resources. She reads aloud very nicely. Stacie is quieter; she knows how to hold her tongue if you require peace and quiet. She is a neat needlewoman ...'

'I need no companion,' Mrs Churchill interrupted. 'Frank is the only attendant I require. He knows my ways and understands my indispositions. He is indispensable to me.'

'Forgive me, Aunt,' Mrs Branthwaite replied with an ingratiating smile, 'but young men such as Mr Frank Churchill seek the companionship of *young* ladies. He is certain to marry and when he does …'

' …he will choose a young lady who understands that *my* needs are of the first consideration to him,' Mrs Churchill finished. 'Now, I am sure it is time we went in to dinner.'

Poor Mrs Campbell could do nothing other than ring the bell. Frank took the opportunity to step across to the window where Jane and Mrs Mosley were in deep discussion. 'I hope you will allow me to hand you in to dinner,' he said, holding out his arm to Jane. 'Look, the colonel escorts my aunt, so I am not needed there, and I would rather hand in your butler than escort Miss Mary Branthwaite, or suffer her conversation at dinner.'

Jane looked across at where Mrs Campbell was attempting to organise an odd number of people into couples without a remainder.

'If you take me as well, Mr Churchill,' Mrs Mosley said with a smile, 'Philip will take one of the Branthwaite girls and Edgar can take the other.'

'Honoured, ma'am,' said Frank, holding out his other arm, and thus they went down to dine.

Chapter Twenty-Nine

Frank was unlucky, however. Finding himself placed between Miss Fairfax and Miss Mary Branthwaite, he was required to suffer Mary's conversation for at least half of the courses.

The dinner progressed with due decorum, the Campbells trying and sometimes managing to assert themselves as host and hostess before an imperious command from Mrs Churchill—a complaint about the dishes or a perceived draught—tottered them once more from their rightful place. The dishes came too slowly and in insufficient quantity for Miss Stacie Branthwaite, who addressed all her attention to her plate and none at all to her brother, who sat beside her. Mary, on Edgar's other side, compounded Stacie's reticence by likewise ignoring him and he comforted himself by drinking glass after glass of wine. Mary monopolised Frank through the soup, cheese and dessert concerning the size and luxury of the accommodations at Enscombe, the number of drawing rooms, principal chambers and linen closets, the quantity and value of Enscombe's solid silver, Turkey rugs, medieval tapestries and ancient familial artefacts. She asked about the scope of the gardens, the acreage of moorland and the extent of the forestry. She enquired about the likely opportunities for balls and card parties amongst the local families, requiring an exact census of the premier families, their sons and—more precisely—their marriageable daughters.

'Oh,' she sighed as the last course was placed before her, 'what an idyllic picture you paint. How I long to visit Enscombe. I think it the most ideal, the most perfect place on earth. How proud you must be of it, Mr Churchill. How you must glory in it and look forward to the day when it will be your own dominion.'

'No,' said Frank flatly. 'I hate the place with a vengeance and spend as little time there as possible. I dread the day when it becomes mine, for it will mean the demise of my dear uncle. I would rather have him alive and well than possess any number of Enscombes.'

'Oh,' Mary said haughtily, 'you do surprise me, Mr Churchill. Perhaps you do not know how fortunate you are. Edgar would give his eye teeth to be in your shoes.'

'There are many times when he would be welcome to them,' said Frank, turning from her at last. A dinner table was no place to converse privately and Frank had to content himself with saying, as earnestly as possible, 'I was dismayed to find you had left Weymouth, Miss Fairfax, and on such an errand, without giving me … that is, without allowing me to say farewell.'

'I had little notice of it myself,' Jane said. 'But since the colonel had business in town it seemed sensible to go with him. Mrs Quill had secured me an opening with a widower of her acquaintance.'

'Yes, I gathered as much. Of course, I know nothing of it—that, is *next* to nothing—but, forgive me if I say what small detail I do know makes me think that the situation would not be suitable.'

'You are right,' Jane said with a sigh, 'it was not suitable, or, more truly, I came to see that I was not suitable for it.'

'Oh?' Frank offered her a dish of nuts and dried fruit. 'How so? Perhaps the children were unpleasant?'

'No,' Jane shook her head, 'the boys were amiable, but too old for a governess, in my opinion. It was not that, though, it was … have you ever been to Battersea?'

'I cannot say that I have. Is it very dreadful?'

Jane nodded. The remembrance of it made her shudder. 'Very. I had no notion … and the smell was beyond anything. But,' (gathering herself), 'I must accustom myself to being there, or somewhere like it.' Her hands toyed with her napkin on her lap. Under the cover of the tablecloth, Frank placed his own over them.

'No,' he said, quietly, 'you shall have a choice.'

'Frank!' Mrs Churchill shrilled from her place towards the top of the table, 'what do you discuss so secretly? I will not be excluded from the conversation.'

'No, of course, Aunt,' Frank said, withdrawing his hand. 'Miss Fairfax and I were discussing the delights of Battersea.'

'Battersea is not so genteel as Clapham,' Mrs Branthwaite said. She had drunk more than her usual allowance of wine during dinner to embolden her to broach the topic uppermost on her mind 'There is a superfluity of dye works and other commercial enterprises there that makes it unpleasant, especially in the heat of summer. *We* are better placed in Clapham, I do assure you; we are quite rural in comparison, except that we overlook the weaving sheds. But I wonder, ma'am,' she rushed on, 'have you ever visited Billinge Gate, my sister's residence? It is as far out as Tooting.'

'No, I have not,' said Mrs Churchill.

'Neither have I. And yet I believe it behoves us, as family, to strengthen the bonds with which our grandfather Fishwick endowed us. Had *I* room to entertain in Pickling Street as *you* do at Enscombe, or that Ariadne has at Billinge Gate, nothing would prevent me from inviting you for extended visits. Branthwaite and I are blessed with a wide circle of acquaintance. I believe we need not dine at home five days in seven if we do not wish it. Branthwaite is *very* highly thought of amongst the businessmen of the area, and I like to think that I have established for myself amongst the ladies of the town a reputation that is second to none. But,' with a bleary smile, 'all our friends and acquaintances together cannot substitute for *family* connection. I am sure you feel the same. My mother, your *only* sister, when she lived, looked upon you quite as her most cherished confidante, and came to you with any little troubles she had. But alas,' dabbing her eye with her napkin—noting the thickness of its linen and the superiority of its stitching and wondering if she might accidently spirit it into her reticule—'Mama has been taken from us. How she must have been comforted, as she lay on her death bed, to think that she left *you* to succour her daughters.'

'In general, she concerned herself with extorting money from me whenever she could,' Mrs Churchill said, 'I cannot say what thoughts were in her mind at the end.'

'She had none,' Mrs Mosley said quietly, 'she was quite insensible with laudanum. However, sister, I fear I cannot ask you to come to Billinge Gate because Philip and I have decided to sell it and move elsewhere. When we are settled in our new house, of course you will be welcome.'

'What kind of place is Billinge Gate?' Mr Churchill enquired. 'Have you much garden?'

'The grounds are not extensive,' Mr Mosley replied. 'An insignificant paddock, a shrubbery that hardly warrants the name—just a bed of bushes, really—and an orchard that consists of a gnarled old apple tree and a pear tree with the blight. That is one of the reasons Ariadne and I have decided to remove. We would both prefer a larger plot of land and the house has unhappy associations for Ariadne that there is no need to perpetuate by our continuing to live there.'

'When you fix on your new abode, I would be most happy to give my opinion on the gardens,' said Mr Churchill.

'I have no interest in gardens,' Mrs Churchill remarked in a bored tone.

'But *your* grounds are *very* extensive, are they not Mr Churchill?' Mary gushed, to bring the conversation back to the point. 'How I *long* to see them, for I am passionately fond of flowers.'

'You will find few at Enscombe,' Mrs Churchill sneered. 'The air is too cold, the wind too keen and they do not flourish. Mr Churchill cultivates only the hardiest evergreen shrubs.'

Mary sighed, 'We have no garden at all, just a yard with a high brick wall around it. One feels so enclosed, almost suffocated, especially in the warm weather. I expect even Yorkshire is beautiful in September and October, Aunt Churchill, and it will be a convenient time for Papa to be away from the business.'

'It will not,' Mr Branthwaite said.

'We are rarely at home during the autumn,' Mrs Churchill said. 'Frank requires more entertainment than Yorkshire can supply. Our society is very limited.'

'Oh well,' Mary smiled, 'perhaps, after all, Christmas will be better then.'

'I think,' Mrs Campbell said, rising, 'we ladies should leave the gentlemen to their claret.'

Chapter Thirty

The gentlemen were not long over their wine, Edgar Branthwaite having already taken so much that he was lolling and half asleep at the table. Neither Mr Churchill nor Colonel Campbell was able to establish much of a conversational rapport with Mr Branthwaite; they had no acquaintance in common and insufficient understanding of drapery to be able to make any but the most general enquiries. Mr Churchill was sorry not to be alone with the colonel; *he* seemed just the kind of sensible, well-informed, well-travelled gentleman of whom he could make a friend. Mr Dixon, Mr Mosley and Mr Frank Churchill were all eager to re-join the ladies and refused the decanter when it came round to them.

Conversation in the parlour had also been stilted. Mrs Churchill, most affronted that the Branthwaites now considered their visit to Enscombe at Christmas a settled thing, seated herself apart in high dudgeon. Mrs Branthwaite, fuelled by an excess of wine, had turned giddy; she giggled at nothing, uttered half sentences and sang snatches of vaudeville while reclining on a chaise. Stacie had eaten too much and wished for nothing more than to be able to loosen her stays and take an hour's repose on a settee. She sat in a far corner with a book on her lap and hoped her flatulence would be attributed to someone else. Jane and Mrs Mosley had decided to try some duets at the piano, and were happily occupied.

Mrs Campbell, Rowena and Mary Branthwaite kept up a desultory conversation around the tea table.

'And how many bridesmaids shall you have, Miss Campbell?' Mary Branthwaite enquired.

'Oh, just Jane. I only want Jane,' Rowena replied.

'Only one!' cried Mary, 'I am scandalised. I shall have a half dozen at least. I suppose Lord Knox will host your wedding breakfast at his London house. It is not to be supposed you could accommodate them all at yours.'

'Oh, but we shall,' Mrs Campbell said. 'Rowena wishes a small, family wedding. Bute Square will be perfectly sufficient.'

'Oh,' said Mary, very disgusted. 'Nothing short of a very superior home will do for my wedding. But then, *that* will not be an impediment, since *those* will be available in abundance.'

'Miss Mary,' said Mrs Campbell, pouring tea, 'am I to understand that you are engaged?'

Mary gave a little smirk, 'Not *yet,* ma'am, but I will confide to you that the hour is very near.'

'And who is the fortunate gentleman?'

Mary threw a significant glance at where Mrs Churchill sat a little apart. Her eyes were closed but there was an air of deviousness about her face that suggested she was not asleep. 'I cannot name names just now,' Mary said, sotto voce, 'but the gentleman and I have such ties in common—which we have lately had occasion to strengthen—that I doubt not of the outcome. There may be a little family scruple on one side, but the gentleman is not such a person as to allow *that* to deter him.'

'I see,' said Mrs Campbell. 'My mama used to have a saying that I believe it might be pertinent to offer to you, Miss Mary: *do not count your chickens before they are hatched.'*

Mary gave an affected little laugh. 'Oh, but I have been nurturing this particular clutch of eggs so carefully that I do not fear the conclusion. For *his* part, well, he has shown by very particular attention to me that he is extremely attached to me. No, I have no qualm at all. '

Just then the gentlemen re-entered the room and, the evening outside being particularly benign, a walk on the esplanade was mooted.

'I think I must take my family home,' said Mr Branthwaite. 'I have called already for our conveyance. Edgar has over-imbibed and is asleep in the dining room.'

Stacie was immediately on her feet and asking for her wrap. 'I am quite ready,' she said.

Mrs Branthwaite made some objections to being taken home. 'I am having such a delightful evening,' she slurred, 'indeed,' (turning a bleary eye on Mrs Campbell), 'I do not think I have enjoyed myself so much for many years.'

'I am glad to hear it, ma'am,' replied Mrs Campbell.

'We shall return to Chesterfield Place,' said Mrs Churchill. 'Frank, you will give me your arm.'

'Oh, but Mrs Churchill,' Mary cried. 'Mr Frank Churchill has promised to take me to the pleasure ground. There are to be conjurors and jugglers and I do not know what else, this evening. He gave me his word most particularly, ma'am. You would not wish him to disappoint a lady.'

'If you *were* a lady,' Mrs Churchill said with an arch expression.

'I do not know that I absolutely gave you my word, Miss Mary,' Frank demurred. 'I mentioned that there were to be acrobats this evening, that is all.'

'But you implied,' Mary pouted, 'and I have set my heart upon it.'

'You shall join us, Miss Mary,' said Rowena. 'Mr Dixon and Jane and I will go, if you desire it, and Mr and Mrs Mosley are also intrigued to see the curiosities.'

'Yes, indeed,' Mrs Mosley said, 'you shall join us, Mary, and we will see you safely home to Bridge Street.'

'And Frank will do his duty,' Mrs Churchill said stiffly, holding out her arm to him. 'He will accompany me.'

'Eustacia, my dear,' said Mr Churchill, moving to be near to her, 'let us allow Frank to join the young people.'

'I must confess myself somewhat curious,' Frank admitted, 'if you *can* spare me, Aunt. I shall not be more than an hour, or two, at most. I shall bring you back a full account of the menagerie.'

'I cannot spare you,' Mrs Churchill carked, 'but what are *my* needs when your pleasure is at stake? I abdicate them entirely. There is no one, I think, more thoroughly selfless than I.'

Mr Churchill and Frank exchanged a look and soon the dinner party was broken up, the Branthwaites to return to Bridge Street, the

Churchills to Chesterfield Place and the young people to the esplanade. Mary possessed herself of Frank's arm and wore a decidedly triumphant smile.

Jane walked with Mr and Mrs Mosley, and received an invitation to visit them for an extended period once Rowena had departed to Ireland. 'For we shall be settled in our new home by then,' Mrs Mosley said, 'and you, who have done so much for us, will be our first and most important guest.'

They made their way to the part of the beach where a caravan of brightly painted wagons and a number of striped awnings had been erected. Men on stilts, jugglers of fire, sword-swallowers and contortionists performed for the crowds. A bear on a stout chain cried mournfully and birds with exotic plumage fluttered in a large cage. A dog walked on its hind legs while a monkey carried a little hat round the crowd in quest of pennies. There were a good number of onlookers and the party from Augusta Place soon encountered acquaintance. Frank managed to slip away from Mary Branthwaite as the sun began to set and Jane found him at her elbow.

'Come,' he said. 'Dixon knows I have you safe; you will not be missed.'

Jane followed him, her heart in her mouth but her hand in his. Without discussing their destination, they found themselves back up on the wide thoroughfare, which was almost deserted of pedestrians. The shopkeepers were closing their stalls, bringing in the goods that had been displayed on the pavements. Lamps were being lit.

'I have been trying to rid myself of Mary Branthwaite this past half hour,' Frank said with a rueful smile.

'She sets great store by your company and, from the way you have singled her out lately, I am not surprised,' Jane said.

'I *have* singled her out, but only to throw my aunt off the scent. I have no doubt, when I return, that I will receive a lecture about how utterly unsuitable she is; her family in trade, her poor manners, low wit, questionable beauty,' he counted off poor Mary's failings on his fingers.

'Then why have you paid her the attentions that you have?' Jane asked but knowing, in her heart, the answer.

'Oh, because it pleases me to be mischievous,' Frank threw off. 'Since my aunt delights in tormenting *me,* I find that a little reciprocal teasing helps me bear it.'

'And is that all?'

Frank turned to her, and caught her hands in his. 'Oh Miss Fairfax— Jane—you must know that it is not. It is to protect *you.* Mary is family, and however my aunt may regret the association it cannot be severed. No paroxysms, chills or cramps can achieve it and she would not waste her energy in manifesting them. And I can claim to be paying Mary no more than cousinly courtesy. But if Aunt Churchill knew how I felt about *you* I don't know what the outcome might be.'

Jane held his gaze. It bored into her with such heat and intensity that she felt she might melt, but she managed to croak, 'Surely, then, you had better master your feelings.'

'Master them?' Frank almost shouted. 'No! I shall not! I shall let *them* master *me*! I determined on this course the moment I heard about your opportunity in Battersea. Impossible! Unthinkable for you to be buried there amongst sweatshops and squalid manufactories. A tanner? How could *he* deserve you? No. It could not be. I resolved to prevent it. And Jane—*dear* Jane, for so you are to me—from that minute I have felt more master of myself than I have ever done before. I will *not* be her vassal; I will *not* bow to her will. I will be my own man in this, Jane, if you will only consent to be my wife. There. I have said it,' he finished, lifting his eyes from hers at last and looking up at the first stars that shone in the evening sky. The expression of delight and relief on his face was almost beatific. He laughed aloud. 'Oh Jane,' he burst out again, 'say you will marry me and I will go back to the menagerie and eat fire, swallow a dozen swords, fight the bear, whatever you desire. I could do it. I know I could, if you will tell me I have your heart.'

At that moment Jane almost believed him capable of it. But the consequences of his declaration quashed all her joy. 'You have so much to lose,' she said thinking of Mr Mosley and Miss Brokenshire. '*I* would not be the cause of your breaking with the Churchills.'

'And I will not permit them to stand between us,' Frank declared. 'That will be their choice. *You* are mine and I will not be turned from it. Now there is only you who must choose, Jane. I do not offer you Enscombe or the Churchill fortune, for that may not be mine to give. I offer you myself, only. You once told me that you did not *need* to marry but you could do so if you wished. Do you wish? Do you wish to marry me? There will not be, between us, that dependence we spoke of. We will be equals. I shall ask my father to teach me his business, if it comes to it.'

'It must not come to that,' Jane said, shaking her head. 'In time you will blame me for the loss of the Churchill wealth.'

'Never. I will bless you, for giving me my independence and my self-worth.'

They stood together in silence for a while, very close together, in the shadow of one of the plane trees that lined the promenade. Jane hesitated. Frank could see the confusion in her face.

'I shall be yours alone,' he whispered. 'You will not have to give *me* up to comfort your friend. You will not owe me to the Campbells' good will. If it is truly your desire to teach, you *shall* do. You shall tutor our own children, if we are fortunate enough to have them. If not, you shall establish your own school. You see, Jane, I do not seek to save you from anything you do not wish to be saved from. I respect your independence. Respect it? It is one of your chief merits, in my eyes. Not only do I wish to promote it, I desire to share it.'

Frank had loosed his hold on Jane's hand and slipped an arm around her waist. She leaned against him and rested her head on his shoulder. He could have spoken no words more calculated to appeal to her. She revelled in them. But the sensations his proximity provoked in her precluded all rational thought and she gave herself up to them for a few moments of pure, hedonistic indulgence. Her heart was his entirely—of that she was wholly certain. Then she untangled herself from his embrace and took a pace away. When she spoke, her voice was very low but quite steady.

'Will you allow me time to think? I cannot just say yes or no. This is so unexpected. I have not, as you have, had time to consider this step. Please, take me home, and we will speak again tomorrow.'

If Frank was deflated he did not show it. 'Of course,' he said, offering his arm. 'You must think, as I have done, and make your choice. But may I enquire, if it is not an immediate 'yes', dare I assume—can I hope—that it is not a definite 'no'?'

'Oh,' said Jane, as they began to walk towards Augusta Place, 'if it were only a matter of love ...'

Chapter Thirty-One

Jane returned to the Campbells' lodgings and went almost immediately to her room. It was too early to retire and she sent the maid away to have the quiet and space for solitary contemplation.

Her heart sang aloud at Frank's words. He loved her! And she knew that the feelings of attraction and affinity that had furtively stolen into her heart over the previous weeks were the answer of her own heart to his. She loved him! She had had her misgivings about his behaviour, even distrusted him on occasion. He had seemed to her to be wild and unreliable. But she had come to understand his unhappy situation, to see his helpless entrapment in the machinations of his aunt and that had explained his actions. It had been some weeks now since she had acknowledged that she preferred him to any other gentleman she knew, but she had not expected this—or any—outcome. Now, she *did* indulge the prospect and it swept upon her that her feelings for Frank were quite other than the brotherly affection for Mr Dixon she had briefly believed she could kindle into married love. She was head-over-heels in love. This, if she consented, would be a match in the most quixotic sense; no business arrangement, no judicious alliance. It would be a marriage of passionate, romantic love.

But there were impediments. He had much to lose. The Churchills would certainly object. If Mary Branthwaite was a nobody, how much more was she? What was her family, even compared to the

Branthwaites? She would be sneered at and denigrated, her frail old grandmother and chattering aunt brought out as evidence of the lamentable lowness of the connection. She feared that Frank did not sufficiently appreciate what he said he would sacrifice with such ease; not just the monetary value of the Churchill estate but also the goodwill of the people who had brought him up and adopted him as their heir. Honour and duty were undoubtedly due to them and it would reflect poorly on Frank if he turned from them. His aunt—and Jane had to confess she did fear Mrs Churchill although Mr Churchill seemed kind—would wreak a terrible revenge. Jane called to mind again and again the situation that had been thrust upon Mr Mosley by *his* family. Mrs Churchill would certainly break Frank as cruelly as Philip Mosley had been broken. Could she—Jane—be the cause of reducing him as he inevitably would be reduced if the Churchills threw him off? She feared exposing Frank to Mrs Churchill's outrage. That would destroy Frank and by association her own reputation would be tainted; she would always be the social climber who had ruined him.

And then there was her own situation. She had taught herself not to expect this. She was not Frank's equal by birth or fortune and while she had acquired education and manners to help her attain a station in life above her natural level, she had never hoped to win the affection of any gentleman of consequence. She had schooled herself not to expect it; she had even prided herself on being immune to the idea of it. Here was a reversal of all that; her plans and schemes and designs of martyrdom were laid waste. Would she be accused, after all she had said—would she accuse herself—of taking the easy path?

And lastly there was Rowena. It had been Jane's invariable practice to promote her friend's wellbeing above her own. It would go against every habit to eclipse her now. Marriage to Mr Dixon, with his score of thousands of pounds, was one thing, but marriage to Mr Frank Churchill, with his multiplicity of scores, was quite another. Rowena had just stepped into her renown. Jane's engagement to Frank Churchill would push her right back into the shadows again. It went against every grain of Jane's character to be so cruel. Whatever the outcome between herself and Mr Churchill, Rowena's happiness must not for one moment be put in the shade.

Rowena returned and the two girls exchanged their impressions of the day's events; the Branthwaites were much discussed. Rowena stated her opinion that perhaps there was more to the flirtation between Mary Branthwaite and Frank Churchill than she had thought, 'For she speaks of wedding arrangements with decided confidence,' Rowena said, 'as though the whole thing is all but arranged. I do not think Mrs Churchill knows of it, though. Perhaps they intend an elopement.'

Her words, quite casually uttered, gave Jane more food for thought as their hair was brushed and their night-time preparations concluded. At last, the candle was blown out and Jane returned to the private consideration of her dilemma.

Mr Mosley had regretted not marrying Miss Brokenshire, of not presenting his father with a *fait accompli*. It would have saved her reputation and made his father powerless to keep the two asunder. But Jane did not think she could do so ignominious, so reckless a thing. To elope! To absolutely run away under cover of darkness! It would be too shameful to bear, and the consequences for the Campbells would be incalculable; it would hurt them beyond words.

Oh, it was all too much! She ought to refuse him. There were too many obstacles, too many difficulties between them. This is what she told herself, as midnight sounded and then one o'clock. It was impossible, unlooked for, too complicated and beset with trouble. But as two o'clock rang out she admitted that she did not think she could give him up, not now she knew her own heart. And she knew to a certainty that he would not renounce her; he would do something reckless, she feared to think what he might do if she refused him. He had spoken to her of having something that was his alone, and the idea had sounded an answering note in her own heart that once acknowledged could not be argued away again. He was only and wholly hers! She did not think she could say the same of anything or anyone else that had come within her orbit. It was precious, too exquisite to be let go of.

Long into the night and as dawn blushed in the sky did Jane debate these matters, and by the morning she was no closer to a resolution of them than she had been at first. Only one voice sounded clear to her, in her fatigue and confusion. It was Mr Mosley. 'When you find love, hold it fast. Do not, for any consideration, let it go. When your heart speaks, listen.'

Chapter Thirty-Two

Six months later, on a cold but bright January day, Jane sat alone in the Campbells' coach. She was on her way to Highbury. The coachman did not drive fast, but Jane did not mind. She brought no maid with her, for there was no space to accommodate one in the confines of the Bates's apartments even if the expense of feeding one would not have stretched resources already distended to extremity. To have a few hours of perfect solitude was a joy. For once she could give herself up to thought and expression, to sighs and tears, to the full manifestation of all the accumulation of emotions that had wracked and uplifted her, troubled and thrilled her since the previous July.

She spent the first hour or so looking out of the window but seeing nothing of the passing countryside, going over in her mind the time that had gone by since that sleepless night. Others had followed, of course, many, many of them, but it was *that* night from which she dated all her wretchedness and misgiving as well as those few moments of unutterable joy that had leavened the rest.

The only determination she had been able to fix on was that, whatever she decided about Frank's proposal in the end, she would do nothing until Rowena's nuptials were done. Rowena must have the sole glory of the wedding preparations, the attention and fuss attendant on them as well as the reassurance and care. Nothing would eclipse them, not even the suspicion of a greater triumph beneath the same roof.

Frank had accepted her decision and her rationale. 'It will give me time to work on my aunt,' he had said.

August had been both kind and cruel to the couple. It saw the departure of Mr Dixon for Ireland but it brought the arrival of the dowager Lady Scolding and her sister the Honourable Miss Brine to Weymouth. These were just the type and quality of ladies that Mrs Churchill preferred and she soon established acquaintance with them. Joining *them* for dinners and excursions, being encompassed in *their* entourage to receive her own share of obsequious notice miraculously cured all Mrs Churchill's ailments and Frank was at more liberty to pursue his own enjoyment than ever before. Thankfully there was no niece or daughter in Lady Scolding's court to whom Frank was required to make love, and he and Jane managed to see a good deal of each other; *this* was the kindness of it. The cruelty was that they could not escape their predicament; every joyous encounter had been marred by the endless reiteration of the possible outcomes of a declared engagement and the sheer misery of acknowledging it to be impossible. There had been joy, of course; their mutual confidence in one another; the shared love they treasured in the privacy of their hearts; that they each had, at last, something that was wholly and only theirs. Joy, yes, but never unadulterated. As often and as fiercely as Jane felt herself drawn to Frank, she was assailed by the conviction that she acted wrongly, and pushed him away. She battled in and against her own soul. Frank's character was more reckless than hers—he was prepared to risk suspicion, even discovery, for the bliss of pressing her hand to his lips, the joy of encircling her waist. Jane was more circumspect but felt that in governing his impulses she also but barely ruled her own. Being thus at war with herself was exquisite agony.

They must be careful. They danced together, but also with others. Frank might sometimes contrive to hand her in to dine but he would as often squire another lady to the table. They exchanged as many looks as would be reasonable for a handsome young man and a beautiful lady, but not so many as would attract untoward notice. Jane was very strict on this score. Until she accepted him—*if* she accepted him—there must be no hint of anything more than common acquaintance. Mary Branthwaite continued her campaign to engage Frank and was at times a useful foil, but Frank addressed her with a jocular tone, more of a brother than a lover, that she might not deceive herself as to his intentions.

In addition to speaking looks, Frank and Jane exchanged letters. It was perhaps peculiar to be corresponding with a person whom they might encounter, in the normal run of things, every day, but they could not say *then* what they could say in writing, and gradually, through the medium of the written word, Frank and Jane became deeply acquainted with each other's innermost thoughts and feelings, more deeply, perhaps, than couples who courted in the ordinary way. Jane's daily visit to the post office was almost a pilgrimage. She went purportedly to collect Mr Dixon's letters to Rowena, or to see if her aunt had sent word, but it was Frank Churchill's handwriting she longed to see. He wrote entertainingly; long, lively letters. He spoke of his childhood, his tutor, his various escapades, his hopes and his regrets.

Jane pulled the letters from her reticule as the coach passed through Richmond, a thick bundle tied with ribbon. She perused them again with avid attention. Here, she believed, lay the true root and anchor of her love for Frank Churchill for here lay the true heart of Frank himself. Here, in these pages, he had been honest and tender. His deep unhappiness as well as evidences of his great courage and resilience had been poured out for her. He had held back nothing, embroidered nothing, excused, evaded, affected nothing.

About September time Frank's tone had become somewhat morose. The delay, in spite of Jane's confessed love, had made him wretched. He wanted her promise; he was ready to brave his aunt, to forswear the Churchills if it came to it. But this was a course she had argued against with all her power. Then the time of his father's nuptials had drawn near. He tried once more to secure an *exeat* from his aunt, with the usual consequence; an onslaught of blinding headaches assailed her. In spite of engagements with Lady Scolding and the Honourable Lady Brine Mrs Churchill took to her bed and could not be moved from it for a fortnight, until the day of the wedding had passed. Frank had to content himself with writing a letter to his father and stepmother. 'I doubt not,' Jane read in a note written about that time, 'my letter will be passed from hand to hand in Highbury, pored over and criticised, my handwriting subjected to scrutiny and my style called to account. Some will say it is a handsome letter, and perhaps it is. But anyone of sense and judgement will see that it is a poor excuse for what is due to my father and Mrs Weston which is, in the stead of any letter, myself.'[xiv]

At the end of September, the Campbells had quit Weymouth and returned to Bute Square. Mr Dixon was expected any day and the wedding was set to take place in the first week of October. Frank was able to prevail on Mrs Churchill to remove to their London house in

Manchester Street for a few weeks at least. He urged her to consult London doctors; his genuine concern for her health vying with his sense that her illness was all histrionic theatrical put on to curb him.

The day of Rowena's wedding had arrived; a calm day of bright October sunshine. The trees in the little park at the centre of Bute Square were glorious in their autumn foliage. Rowena and her father had walked across the little patch of green together, as she had said they would, and on entering the church and seeing Mr Dixon waiting for her she had almost skipped down the aisle and into his arms. Jane, walking behind, had wished with all her heart to do the same, for there beside Mr Dixon was Frank Churchill. He had eyes only for Jane, and could scarcely attend to his duties for looking at her.

The wedding breakfast had been a quiet affair, as both bride and groom had preferred. As momentous a day as it had been for Rowena, it proved to have equal consequence to Jane for it was on this day that she had at last agreed to be engaged to Frank Churchill. She did it in a maelstrom of doubt but so deluged in the excitement of her passion for him and her desire to secure him absolutely and irrevocably to herself that the warning voice in her mind was drowned out. It must, for the time being, be a secret engagement. It had been *her* suggestion, a fact which, now, in the carriage, tortured and recriminated her, but which had seemed in the all too limited time available to them to be a viable compromise, a temporary alleviation to their difficulties. It assuaged the agony of frustrated affection. It placed, as it were, on deposit, their whole-hearted commitment to one another without bringing down the immediate violence and ensuing schism upon the house of Churchill. Frank and Jane had found themselves, for some quarter of an hour, alone in a small sitting room that had been used by the milliners and flower women for the last-minute addendums to Rowena's dress. It had been left in some disarray and the door closed on it for the duration of the breakfast. Frank watched Jane go into the room to find something for Rowena, and followed her inside, leaning heavily of the door and opening his arms. The first few moments were occupied by the bliss of private reunion, ardent assurances of unaltered affection from him, shy but unequivocal confessions of love from her. But these were followed by a rehearsal of all that stood between them; *his* promise that he would, in time, persuade his aunt, *her* conviction of the impossibility of it. *She* urged him to think of what he would give up by standing against Mrs Churchill. *He* declared it nothing to the great prize of winning Jane's hand. At last, motivated by her great love for him, her overwhelming and reason-defying love, she had suggested this foolhardy compromise; a secret, she amended the word, a *private* engagement. No one, she had emphasised, absolutely no soul in the whole world, must know if it. This was her outright and unchangeable condition. It would give him time to bring his aunt around, if she *could* be brought round, and in the meantime, it would be a vestige, a mere thread of hope that would buoy them both up against the separation and trials that would come. He had been all readiness and approbation for the scheme, delighted in her ingenuity of thinking of it and thrilled with the mischief and espionage it would entail. She had doubted his steadiness again, and almost retracted, but Rowena coming herself to look for the pearl-headed hat pin, had cut short their discussion and they both left the room with the understanding that they were engaged. A few days later he had contrived to drive her to Hampstead Heath alone, and there, with the expanse of London below them and the birds wheeling above, he had plighted his troth so solemnly, and with tears shining in his eyes, and kissed her so ardently, that she had been convinced of his love and constancy once more. He would be true. He would tell no one.

'I will bring my aunt round,' he had promised. 'A very few weeks should do it. But, if she is intractable I will forswear all the Churchill fortune for you'.

'I will never ask it,' she had sobbed, 'I will give you up, if it comes to that.'

'I will not be given up,' he had declared, with equal seriousness, 'for *that* at least. If you have other complaint, naturally, you will be free.'

'A few weeks, then,' she had agreed, 'and, in the meantime ...'

'I understand. It is utterly secret.'

Rowena had gone away, with many tears and much doubt once the time for separation came, leaving Jane with the Campbells. All things being equal, *now* would have been the time for Jane to begin in earnest to find a governess' post. Letters of enquiry should have been sent out, an advertisement perhaps posted in the newspaper. But she made no move in the matter and the Campbells did not question her delay. As far as they were concerned Jane need never seek employment while they lived; their home would be hers for as long as they had breath. They missed Rowena and were all the more reliant on Jane. The days passed slowly. Jane's letters from Frank were all of Mrs Churchill's consultations with doctors; eminent men, but all as perplexed by Mrs Churchill's symptoms as their fellows in Yorkshire had been. 'I am sceptical,' Frank wrote. 'I see a direct correlation between the most violent of her attacks and the incidences of her being thwarted. By way of experiment, I wrote to my father and promised a visit before Christmas, which I showed her. Oh Jane! One moment my aunt was contentedly reclined on a chaise, the next she was gripped by a tantrum that threw her bodily onto the hearth rug and had her rolling on the floor, thrashing her limbs like one possessed by a fiend. I almost wonder if an exorcist might be more use to us than a physician. The letter was torn to smithereens and thrown in the fire. It took the whole of the rest of the day for her to recover herself and I felt sure she would not be fit for her evening engagement. But lo! At eight she descended in full regalia and went out to a dinner given in honour of the Marquis de Montfort, an *émigré* recently arrived in London. I had cancelled my engagements, sure to be required at her bedside, so spent the evening alone and very angry.'

London was quiet, the season finished and most families returned to their country houses until after Christmas. November was the month set for the Churchills' return to Enscombe. 'I set myself absolutely to the task of bringing Aunt Churchill round by then,' he had written. 'There is little else to distract her other than the queue of physicians who wait to examine the medical conundrum she presents. I shall do all I can to avoid returning to Yorkshire with them. I cannot stomach the idea of the place after the balmy months we have spent in beautiful Weymouth. I cannot sufficiently describe to you the cold and dreariness of Enscombe at any time of year, but in winter it is insupportable. Heat from the fires hardly penetrates the rooms—everything tends to huddle round the hearths, even the furniture, leaving the remainder of the room as chill and inhospitable as a vast empty church. The wind howls in the chimneys at night. For a long time, as a boy, I was convinced that there were ghosts in the flues. Food arrives cold from the kitchens.

Often there is ice on my washing water by the time my man gets it to my rooms. So much for the interior of Enscombe. Outside, the weather is likely to be dreadful; we are often snowed up for days together. I cannot depend upon being able to get to the post office. I have allies in two gamekeepers there, but I am mindful of my promise to you and will not trust our secret even to them. The thought of being denied your letters is intolerable. Oh Jane, if we are married, we will not live at Enscombe. We will live anywhere you choose, but not there.'

But the date in November set for the Churchills' departure for Yorkshire drew inexorably nearer and, with it, the time by which he had vowed to settle things with his aunt. Just beforehand Jane snatched a private half hour with Frank, both finding themselves at a dinner hosted by a mutual connection. One of the party being taken ill, there was enough confusion and distraction to allow the couple to retire into a recess while an apothecary was sent for, servants chastised and the hostess revived from a swoon.

'Frank,' Jane said, pulling back from his passionate kisses, 'I fear cannot continue in the deception much longer; it feels daily more wrong to hide our engagement from the Campbells. Tell me you make some progress. Tell me that the time is near. I thought I was equal to it, but the agony of conscience is too much.'

'I know it,' Frank said. 'I see how it troubles you. But my aunt, oh Jane …' he turned from her and put his head in his hands, 'she is impossible. I *know* that she playacts but on the other hand, just recently, there have been signs that make me doubt. Perhaps she *is* ill.'

'What signs?' Jane narrowed a sceptical eye.

Frank frowned. 'A want of appetite. A slight loss of flesh. I do not know that they add to up anything serious but if she really is unwell and I exacerbate things by announcing our engagement … how would I feel?'

'Terrible, as she desires,' Jane replied, but mindful, even as she spoke, of Mr Mosley's mother. 'But do not risk it, if you really think her ill.'

'Do not doubt me, Jane. But a little more time is needed; just a month or two, until I can be sure that there is no danger. Will you trust me that far?'

'You will return to Enscombe, then?' Jane asked dully.

'I see no alternative. It is the last place on earth I wish to go. To be so far from you. To be incarcerated with my aunt. But I can do no other. The Branthwaites come to us after Christmas. I will use their visit as leverage to escape. My aunt will not wish me to be exposed to Mary Branthwaite's charms for such an extended period. We might meet in January, perhaps.'

'Perhaps,' Jane said, but in a tone that left him in no doubt of her disappointment. 'I am invited to the Mosleys in January. They have moved to Henley.'

'Perfect,' Frank said. 'I will visit you there.'

They had not time for more discourse, but Jane came away from the dinner most anxious about her situation, full of distrust and doubt. She had not expected to remain in her anomalous and distasteful position beyond a few weeks, and here was Frank speaking in terms of months. Perhaps his love for her would wane. Perhaps it *had* waned, and this was his way of extracting himself from the summer romance. Or perhaps, in

Yorkshire, Mrs Churchill would exert the full force of her influence over him, and bend him to her will. She would be given up. Her reputation would be intact, supposing Frank kept his word, but her heart would be broken and her self-respect would never recover. How could she have been so rash? What had possessed her? The answer to that was simple: Frank Churchill had possessed her, heart and soul.

Jane's predicament began to take its toll on her health.[xv] She fell prey to a virulent cold that stayed with her over Christmas and into the New Year. What agonies of mind and spirit her physical symptoms reflected can only be imagined. She was very, very unhappy, upbraiding herself again and again with having got into such a parlous predicament. It was her own doing, all her own fault. All rational thought and practical sense had argued against the course she had taken but the rebellious heart would not be gainsaid. She sank under self-accusation and misery. Her cold—and all the anxieties that caused it—laid her low to such a degree that her visit to the Mosleys had to be given up. She was as close as possible to telling Frank their engagement must end; *that,* she was convinced, was at the seat of her malady and until she rooted out the cause the symptoms would persist. At the very least she would present Frank with an ultimatum: he *must* tell his aunt the truth. Postponing the writing of that awful letter she wrote to inform the Mosleys that she would not be able to visit. As she did so Mr Mosley's story came again forcefully to her mind. *He* had owned the truth and his mother's death had been the result. Not just that; the irreparable divide of his family. What agonies of guilt he had been made to suffer! To be thus ostracised! She would not expose Frank to such torture. She would not threaten, she would not force him to a point that would be the cause of him breaking with the Churchills. If it came to *that*, she resolved, she would give him up. Instead of writing as she had intended, she told Frank only that she would allow him a further six months. In doing so much she did more than her reason and dictated and far more, she feared, than her health could bear. But it was apparent that Mrs Churchill would be a tougher nut to crack than Frank had anticipated. A slow melting of resistance resulting at last in acquiescence would be better than the sudden shock of schism; better for Mrs Churchill, better for Frank and better for Jane herself.

By June a year would have passed since his first declaration. She would prolong the deceit no longer than that.

The coach had come to Kingston and Jane began to fold away the letters that were strewn across the seats. Many of these she had received since Frank's return to the country. They were full of loving words and fond endearments. He loved her still. He loved her, if possible, *more*. But they brought to her no hope beyond that. Mrs Churchill remained unwell in non-specific but variously debilitating ways. As far as Jane could tell the subject of a prospective engagement had not even been broached. Frank's scheme for an escape after Christmas had been mooted, however. Surprisingly it was not the Branthwaites' presence but their absence that had been Mrs Churchill's condition of Frank's departure. If they could be put off, she would allow him furlough.[xvi] Not to visit Highbury of course, he did not mention that part of his plan. Mrs Churchill believed he had been invited to Walcot, the Oxfordshire home of Earl Withering, where a noble collection of marriageable young ladies would be on display. He was also, being so close, to call on his relations at Blenheim. Frank had written to his father and he was expected in Highbury in January.[xvii] 'I will come to you in London,' Frank wrote to Jane. 'I will make some excuse or other. It is only sixteen miles. Perhaps I might find a pressing need for a haircut!'

But in the event the Branthwaites' determination to visit Enscombe could not by any means be doused by ever so many descriptions of the frugal fayre, a vermin infestation in the kitchens or an outbreak of scarlet fever in the village. They had arrived at Enscombe for their visit equipped for a stay of some duration and were deaf to every hint that their visit should be curtailed. Consequently, Frank had had to give back word to his father. Highbury—and Jane—were disappointed again.

Then a letter from Rowena announced that she was to supply an addition to the household at Baly-Craig in June. She was happy, but unwell, and begged that her mother, father and Jane would go to her there without delay to support her through the indisposition and the anxieties naturally attendant on such a circumstance and also to share in the joy of its conclusion. Jane's mind was thrown into confusion. Of course, she wished very much to see Rowena, to share again that intimate friendship they had enjoyed since girlhood, to see for herself the house and countryside around Baly-Craig and to witness how Mrs Dixon differed from Miss Campbell. But to enjoy again that openness and perfect unreserve would make keeping her secret impossible. And then again, to leave England—and Frank—for a period of so many months as would certainly be four or five would be torture. How could she support him when—or if—the moment of crisis with Mrs Churchill came? Would her being so far away in person make her commensurately distant in his mind and heart?

Jane's health continued to give cause for concern. She spoke seriously of doubting her ability to make the voyage to Ireland and Mrs Campbell suggested that the Highbury air—her own, native air—would provide a better restorative even than seeing Rowena.

Jane wrote to Frank. 'From next week you should direct your letters to Highbury post office,' she told him. 'I will write to my grandmamma and propose a visit of at least three months.'

Frank's reply had been by return. 'The Branthwaites have at last vacated Enscombe. Their vulgarity and presumption were to be borne no longer and my aunt all-but packed their valises for them. Their absence relieves us all, but I have more encouraging news still; our stars align at last. My aunt and uncle have been invited to stay with the Dowager Lady Scolding in February. I will be at liberty for the fortnight or so of their time there. We will meet at Highbury, in our own home village where we are loved. It seems to me to be no more than fate. We will be where we *should* have been from children, growing up side by side. Oh, the perfect pleasure of being in Highbury at last! You cannot conceive how I long for it. In my mind there is no more peaceful, bucolic or beautiful place in England. I shall go to Ford's. I shall attend church and see the Perrys and the Coxes and—yes, I will admit to a curiosity—Mr and Miss Woodhouse. And *we* shall be thrown together! What more natural than but two returning orphans such as we should find much to discuss and compare? No one will remark us choosing to spend time in each other's company, especially when we let it be known that there was that degree of acquaintance between us in Weymouth that would make our continuance of it as unremarkable as snowdrops in February. But do not fear. I will contrive to throw everyone off the scent. We know what busy-bodies there are in Highbury. No one can sneeze but Mrs Cole will know of it and half an hour later the news will be disseminated from Ford's to every corner of the parish. My father speaks so highly of Miss W; I am certain he expects me to fall in love with her. Mrs Weston thinks her a paragon of every virtue, one of these being her avid curiosity to see me. It will be expected as well as natural for me to seem to single her out.'

And so it was arranged. Jane wrote to her grandmamma announcing a visit to commence the following week. [xviii] Frank forbore to announce *his* visit, partly in case his aunt's caprice intervened at the last minute to thwart it and partly to prevent any possible coincidence between his arrival and Jane's to arise in any more than usually perspicacious mind.

Volume Three

Chapter Thirty Three

It seemed to Jane that Frank's information concerning Miss Woodhouse was correct; she was *avidly* interested in Frank Churchill. Jane found herself, from their first encounter, subjected to an interrogation of Mr Churchill's looks, manner and character. She got through it as best she could by a plethora of generalities and by claiming a much slighter acquaintance with him than any report from Weymouth would ever have justified, knowing that when Frank *did* arrive in Highbury, she would have to be rather cooler towards him than she would wish, at least at first. The necessity for concealment sickened her again. Why could she not smile and admit an intimate understanding of everything pertaining to Mr Churchill? Why could she not claim him as her own love? She wished to open her mouth and speak of him without ceasing but instead she must pretend nonchalant unconcern in the subject most near to her heart. She came away from Hartfield with nerves quite shattered.

No sooner had she got over *that* but she must go again. A hind quarter of pork had been sent by Miss Woodhouse and, more pressingly still, a note from Mrs Cole brought news of an engagement between the

Highbury vicar and some lady from Bath. This dual impetus propelled her aunt into her bonnet and spencer and Jane was hurried along the lane to offer rapturous thanks for the one and to share the happy news about the other. She could not help but observe the exasperation in Miss Woodhouse's eye as Aunt Hetty went on and on about the pork and speculated about the Miss Hawkins who was so fortunate to have secured the heart of the vicar. Jane, who had no knowledge—and really no interest—in either, had to ask asinine questions about the couple for fear of seeming aloof; she despised herself even as she spoke. The courtship was compared to that between Mr Dixon and Rowena; old news to Jane. Her own engagement was more recent and more interesting, but of course she could breathe no word of that.[xx]

A week or so passed by and Jane was spared further intercourse with the family at Hartfield other than the chance daily encounters that are inevitable in a small town. Everyone in Highbury visited the main street at least once a day and her aunt had an open invitation to almost everyone to step up and pay a call whenever they passed. Miss Woodhouse, however, always seemed on the point of being expected elsewhere and was rarely at liberty to spend ten minutes in the Bates's parlour, which was a relief to Jane even if it was a disappointment to her grandmamma. She met the vicar, Mr Elton, who returned briefly to receive those congratulations that were due to him—he was a small, rather vapid young man with sweaty palms and shifty eyes—and also Miss Woodhouse's little protégé Miss Smith, for whom Jane felt rather sorry. Harriet Smith was utterly in the thrall of the mistress of Hartfield; spoke of her and looked at her as a mouse will at a particularly predacious cat.

There was much that Jane missed. As loved as she was by her aunt and grandmother, and as pleasant as it was to be away from the noise and bustle of town, Jane could not help but lament the absence of Rowena and the Campbells. She missed the easy comfort of Bute Square and the diversion of daily outings but most of all she missed her pianoforte. Music had ever been a solace to her, a distraction and a pleasurable challenge. Now, with feelings over-charged to breaking point she felt more than ever the need of the emotional relief that playing would bring. Unexpectedly, there came a promise of alleviation to *this* if not to other woes. Mrs Cole had recently taken delivery of a new instrument— very superior, with excellent tone—and Jane was invited in a general way to play it. In return Mrs Cole hinted that Jane might in due course instruct her two little girls in the rudiments and that, more immediately, she might prepare a recital that would entertain guests at a forthcoming dinner. Mrs Cole had two sons, neither of whom were so much younger than Jane to make an alliance out of the question. She had always regarded Jane Fairfax in the light of that potential. Having Jane in the house under any pretext was sure to expedite matters. How glad she was that she had persuaded Mr Cole to buy the pianoforte!

Now the Coles were not habitual givers of dinners. Mr Cole entertained gentlemen to cards regularly but they had not until recently thought of extending their hospitality beyond that. But some relatives had recently risen in fortune and brought themselves to live at a distance from Highbury not inconsistent with the possibility of their being invited to dine and get themselves home again afterwards. Mrs Cole had long wished to elevate herself to the first circle of Highbury. The Woodhouses and Westons gave dinners; why should not she? Her house had been extended to incorporate a capacious dining room and now she had a pianoforte to entertain her guests if only she could find someone who could do it justice. Jane's arrival in Highbury seemed serendipitous to Mrs Cole and the invitations had been sent out.

Miss Woodhouse, however, posed a difficulty and many hours did Mrs Cole spend discussing it with Miss Bates. It might well be considered a presumption on the part of the Coles to invite so very elevated a personage as Miss Woodhouse to dine, although why it should be so was hard to fathom. Mr Knightley had expressed himself most willing and the Westons had accepted also. If *they* saw no difficulty, why would Miss Woodhouse? And yet there was something so very superior about the mistress of Hartfield. She was considered—and considered herself—to be so very far above the rest. She might be insulted by their impertinence. That would be a thing most awkward to endure. On the other hand, she might condescend to accept; this was perhaps worse, and caused Mrs Cole a most pressing anxiety. Miss Woodhouse would have to be made much of, much more than any other guest, and this would detract altogether from the attention that was due to the newly rich relatives. More evil still, Miss Woodhouse would have to be given precedence at the pianoforte, even though her playing and singing were not to be compared with Miss Fairfax's.

Round and round the Bates's parlour did the discussion go, Mrs Cole now in favour of inviting Miss Woodhouse, now against, and Miss Bates quite as undecided as her friend. Jane bore as much as she could and then made her excuses; she must take her morning walk, she was in need of exercise.

The habit of long, solitary walks had been established by Jane during previous sojourns in Highbury. She needed to escape the confines of the small parlour over the grocer's shop and the endless whimsical litany of her aunt. Now she had also the claim of benefit to her health; her native air was sure to do her good. Her walk generally took her past the post office where she enquired for her letters. Rowena and Mrs Campbell were both faithful correspondents and now, of course, she had Frank Churchill's letters to treasure also. It was thus that she knew before anyone else, just as February was a week old, of Frank's imminent arrival. 'I post this to you today, and shall be in Highbury tomorrow morning, but will tell my father not to expect me until the day after,' he wrote. 'He thinks I intend to rest at Oxford but I shall ride straight to Kingston and put up at an inn there. Thus, I shall have the pleasure of a few hours spent with you before my being in the vicinity is suspected. Where shall we meet? Let it be a romantic trysting spot away from prying eyes for I have business with you that had better not be observed. Write to me at The White Hart. My dear Jane I cannot contain my eagerness to see you once more.'

Jane could think of no better or more discreet spot than the place where she had taken Mr Mosley, and she wrote by return to describe the place to Frank. 'I shall take the green lane from Highbury,' she said. 'You will be able to ride over the hill from Kingston. There is a gate to a field that has a copse beyond. I shall wait for you there.'

Jane hardly slept for fear, trepidation and longing—fear that Frank might, despite his assurances, be ready to let her go, trepidation of being seen in his company by some eagle-eyed Highbury gossip, longing to see him and be in his arms once more—but this was now her habitual state. The daily war between her head and her heart was utter agony. How she maintained an outward demeanour of calm was a mystery. She talked of ordinary things to her aunt and grandmother, received and offered the usual compliments and enquiries when Mrs Cole and Mrs Perry called, but all the time her soul was in turmoil. Her heart beat with unnatural speed. Sometimes her mouth was so dry she could hardly swallow, making food almost impossible to eat. She pushed it round her plate and was glad when Patty cleared the dishes even though she would be chastised by her well-meaning relatives and she knew they could not afford the waste.

The morning of her rendezvous with Frank dawned overcast. Rain seemed likely. Nothing—not even a storm—would keep her from meeting him but she knew her aunt and grandmother would not sanction her going out in inclement weather. The hours dragged by. She hemmed some linen for her aunt and read a little to her grandmother while her eye was drawn again and again to the sky over Highbury. At last, at a little before the time when she would really need to set forth, the slightest possible parting of the clouds and a glimmer of blue was sufficient promise for her to be able to fetch her bonnet and shawl and set out.

'I do not like the look of the weather, Jane,' Aunt Hetty warned. 'I hope you will not walk far for …' a litany of possible consequences— incidences of sudden floods and accounts of people washed away— followed but Jane was through the parlour door and down the stairs before they were half expounded.

She called at the post office as she passed it, not because she expected a letter but because it had become her invariable habit and to break it might cause notice. But in fact there was a letter—postmarked Kingston, very short, indeed but four words, 'I shall be there,'—and she read it with glee as her feet carried her along the street and out of the village. Her way took her past the gates of Hartfield. She feared being seen, especially by Mr Woodhouse, whose exercise was confined wholly to the precincts of his own shrubbery but who might see her from there and summon her indoors for fear of the rain which, again, pressed down the clouds above. But she was safe; Hartfield's grounds were empty. She took the lane at a half run, entered the green lane and, after half a mile or so, saw Frank's horse tethered to the gate.

He sat astride the gate—as Mr Mosley had done—as nonchalant and at ease as she was fretful, surveying the view and holding a little posy of celandine, primroses and wild daffodils.

'Ah, there you are,' he said upon seeing her approach. Without further words he hurried her through the gate, leading his horse behind them, into the seclusion of the copse at the top corner of the field.

A little while passed during which the horse made what he could of the greenery along the hedgerow and the little posy became somewhat crushed. Frank availed himself of the great comfort to be had from Jane's warm embrace. Such softness and affection! How he craved it! He had been starved of love and had a lifetime's deficit to make good.

'My darling girl,' he said at last, looking at her with concern, 'how ill you look. You are so much thinner than you were in the autumn. Where has the bloom gone from your cheek?'

'You know I have been unwell,' Jane said, looking down in some confusion. 'Our situation is such that must cause every kind of turmoil and unhappiness. I feel like a rabbit in a snare!'

'That is the last thing I want, Jane,' Frank re-joined. 'I wish, if anything, to set you free! I do not mean free from me, but from the future that you have disciplined yourself to expect.'

'That carries no weight with me, Frank,' Jane said, her eyes glassy. 'I have not entered onto this course to save myself. It is only love of you that pinions me. But oh! Because of your aunt, and your dependence on her goodwill, the shackle is a cruel one. That I must deceive those who trust me, that I must dissemble, *these* are the barbs that add to the torture.'

'I know, Jane,' Frank said, gathering her to him again. 'We are both at her mercy. You can have no conception how I have longed for you these weary weeks in Enscombe.'

'I have every understanding of them,' Jane said, drawing her handkerchief from her pocket. 'Do you think I suffer less than you? But where will this end, Frank? Do you make no progress at all with your aunt?'

'Oh,' Frank groaned, releasing her and bending to pick up his hat from where it had fallen on the ground, 'do not sully the moment with talk of her. She is impossible. I have approached the subject from every direction; fellows I know who have engaged themselves against their parents' wishes; exceptional girls who, from no fault of their own, live outside their natural sphere; her own rise from comparative obscurity … I have tried to cast them all in a light of reason and liberal-mindedness. I have debated—with myself, for the most-part; *she* sits shrivel-lipped and disapproving—that equality of birth, of understanding and of education are more important than any inequality of fortune. She does not soften by one iota.'

'I am glad, at least,' said Jane quietly, 'that you have tried.'

'Of course I have tried, and in doing so, I have tried her patience, Jane. Oh, but let us not mar these two precious weeks we have by thinking of her. We can be together. We will meet daily. And if our meeting must seem of less interest than it really is, it is a small price to pay. Only I do not know how I will prevent myself from smiling too much when you are near. My happiness is irrepressible. I can only be master of it by giving myself another preoccupation and I am determined that Miss Woodhouse will be my object. You will not be jealous, will you Jane, if I seem to make love to her? It will only be to protect you.'

'I do not know,' Jane said thoughtfully. 'She and I are not friends but I have no wish to see her injured. You must put her in no danger, Frank. But she will be an easy foil. I will own that she *is* very curious about you, ready to like you before she has even met you. But then, so is everyone in Highbury. No prodigal son was ever more eagerly anticipated than you.'

'I am no prodigal,' Frank said, a little sourly. 'I did not go away of my own volition and there has been no want of effort on my part to effect my return. However,' brightening, 'it is flattering to be the object of interest. For my part I am very eager to be introduced to Highbury society. I wish to be acquainted with my stepmother. I am disposed to become very attached to her indeed. In fact, I am *so* eager to know her that I have resolved to arrive a day early. They do not expect me until tomorrow but I shall ride back to the inn and order my things to be sent directly to Randalls. The pleasure of coming in upon one's friends before the look-out begins is worth a great deal. There are not many houses where I would presume to do it but in going home, I feel I might do anything.'

Jane turned and looked across the fields to where the church clock could be seen in the distance. 'I must go home too,' she said. 'But you will call tomorrow?'

'Oh yes,' Frank said gleefully. He gathered up his horse's reins and they began to walk back to the gate. 'I shall mention an acquaintance made in Weymouth—that degree of acquaintance that requires a visit. Now then,' he said, putting his head on one side and pretending to recall, 'what is the family name? Barnes?'

'Oh Frank!' Jane gave him a friendly push. 'Really, you are so consummately the actor that I second-guess everything you say and do. Perhaps your love is all simulation, a charade to entertain your leisure hours.'

'Oh no,' he said, suddenly serious again. He pulled her into his embrace. 'There is nothing sham about my love for you,' he said, with a catch in his throat.

Chapter Thirty-Four

Frank was as good as his word and called the following day. He called alone, his father having gone to the Crown to order hay and also to avoid, if possible, a protracted interview with Miss Bates. 'She is a worthy and estimable woman,' Mr Weston told Frank as they walked from Hartfield where Frank had been introduced to the Woodhouse family[xxi], 'but somewhat verbose.'

'Miss Woodhouse was so good as to hint as much,' Frank said with a laugh. 'She said she cannot hold her tongue.'

'Well,' Mr Weston frowned, 'that was perhaps not very polite. Amongst ourselves—a certain circle in Highbury—there is an unspoken understanding of Miss Bates' eccentricities, but to admit *you* into it was precipitate.'

'Oh Father, do not think ill of Miss Woodhouse, when I am so inclined towards her. She meant it only as a friendly hint, that is all.'

'You liked her then, did you Frank?' Mr Weston recovered his good humour to ask.

'I liked her immediately. I knew I would. *Your* approbation has guided mine, you see. Now, where do this family live?'

The visit was duly made. Ten minutes would have been sufficient, in the ordinary way of things, but Frank was so delighted to be sitting with Jane, to be seeing with his own eyes the little parlour and all its furnishings that she had described to him so often, to glance down from the casement and have pointed out to him the Highbury personalities he had so long pictured, that three quarters of an hour passed by.

Miss Bates was as delighted as possible to be so honoured. 'And you have really called nowhere else before us, Mr Churchill? Excepting Hartfield, of course, which must be the first object to everyone, I would certainly not presume to be before *them*. I would not presume to *any* notice whatsoever. Mother and I are very retired, you know,' (turning to Mrs Bates and raising her voice), 'VERY RETIRED, are we not, Mama. I am just telling Mr Churchill here.' The old lady nodded and raised an arthritic hand. 'But on dear Jane's account, I really am most gratified,' Miss Bates went on. 'Wait until I tell Mrs Cole and Mrs Perry. To be so honoured! And so, you met in Weymouth? Well, that is most interesting. You had mutual acquaintance I surmise.'

Frank murmured something about being slightly acquainted with Colonel Campbell, but Miss Bates hardly paused for breath before going on, 'But what a curious coincidence, having Highbury in common. And yet not so, for I understand that the world meets at these watering places nowadays. I have a friend in Kingston a Mrs Baxter. You do not know her, Jane, although I am sure I have mentioned her in my letters from time to time—who went all the way to Buxton only to meet with her near neighbour there. Yes indeed! A lady who lives not more than two streets away! And Mrs Coxe speaks of encountering a distant cousin in Bristol. She went there—well, I do not recall now quite the purpose of her visit, and it is of no consequence, not germane in the least—but she met a cousin, a distant relation at any rate, quite by chance in a cobbler's shop. She had broken the heel of her shoe and gone in to … But I am getting away from the point. Jane has travelled about a vast deal, I am sure she has told you that. Worthing, Bath, Lyme, Cheltenham. Oh! She has been to ever so many places and she writes so delightfully of them all. Mother and I have never been anywhere. Mother went to Brighton once, with Jane's mama. *She* was also a Jane. She travelled extensively—to the furthest continents! I do not believe Mrs Goddard's globe was ever more applied to than when our Jane was abroad, for some of the places, I do not mind owning to you Mr Churchill, were *so* odd and foreign-sounding that I did not know where in the world they could be! So, I used to walk down to Mrs Goddard and she would show me. Now I pray you will honour us by taking a slice of this apple pie. Patty's pastry improves enough for me to feel quite comfortable in offering you a slice. I would not risk it with Mr Woodhouse. *His* constitution is so very delicate and I believe the only way he will tolerate a cooked apple is baked. But this pie is really quite …'

Frank could only sit and nod and supply what half sentences and semi-interjections he could as Miss Bates talked on and on, and Jane sat beside him, half in shame, half in gladness. He cast unobtrusive glances around the room. Jane had described it to him many times but he had not understood with the clarity that now assailed him how very cramped her grandmamma's rooms were, nor how intrusive the sounds from the grocer's below. The furnishings were elderly, the carpet almost bald and everywhere so crowded with nick-nacks and mementoes that he wondered a woman such as Jane, so orderly and elegant, could survive amongst it. He saw books, but a glance at their titles revealed that they were such scholarly volumes as a clergyman might use. There was no pianoforte.

'You have no instrument,' he murmured to Jane while her aunt was busy looking for something or other she wished to show him.

'Alas no,' Miss Bates replied, showing her own hearing to be very acute. 'But Mrs Cole recently took delivery of a grand pianoforte and she is so good as to invite Jane to play upon it. Mrs Cole is to host a dinner party and Jane shall play. Jane is a *very* accomplished player, you know, and sings delightfully too. We shall go in the evening. Jane *was* to have dined and Mr Knightley promised his carriage—imagine that! To be so doubly singled out! It is not by any means a common occurrence; we are generally invited to tea only. But Jane was invited to dine. But *that* is not to be, now, for Miss Woodhouse has agreed to attend—most unexpectedly, it is a great condescension on her part—Mrs Cole is so very … She has endured sleepless nights over the whole affair I do assure you. For now Miss Woodhouse is to be present, how can Jane be asked to be the first to play and sing, even if her performance is superior? Not but what Miss Woodhouse does play and sing very nicely indeed. But Miss Woodhouse requires—indeed, she deserves—everyone's consideration. She is first amongst us, you know Mr Churchill. And it is the greatest honour … So, Mrs Cole came and begged that Jane might … and of course we are only too glad. Mrs Cole is *such* a friend. So Jane will dine here with us as usual and we will go to the Coles' for tea. Jane does not mind. She is the last to expect … and, in short, Miss Woodhouse will be asked to take the first seat at the pianoforte and no one will suspect … oh no, not at all, and I shall certainly breathe no word of the matter.'

At that moment Mr Weston was announced. Having looked for his son along the High Street and even returned to Randalls in the expectation of finding him there, he had at last surmised that Frank remained trapped at the Bates's and had come to rescue him. The two swiftly made their adieus leaving the ladies delighted with the length and the civility of Mr Frank Churchill's visit, and Frank with much to ponder. That Jane had been demoted to tea at the Coles' rankled very much. *She* was not the kind of surplus female who generally appeared in the second tier of invitation; the spinster aunts and superannuated nannies and impoverished widows who came to grovel and be grateful and gather the crumbs that fell from greater plates! It was an insult! It should not be tolerated! Whatever was due to Miss Woodhouse was certainly due to Miss Fairfax, and more! And she had no piano of her own!

Chapter Thirty-Five

To have Frank in Highbury was a delight to Jane, but not an unmitigated one. She might not have the power of meeting with him as openly or as frequently as she wished but she woke each morning with a frisson of pleasure that, as she lay in her bed, not a mile away he lay in his. On the other hand, it was hard to contemplate the hours he spent with others with equanimity and she often found her time went by in restlessness and anger.

The day after his call she had to content herself with merely watching Frank as he walked up and down the High Street in company with Miss Woodhouse and Mrs Weston.[xxii] Again and again he passed by, craning to look into the windows of The Crown, visiting Ford's, walking towards the vicarage one moment and back along the Hartfield road the next. Jane sat in the casement of the rooms above the grocer's and observed him with a mixture of pride and jealousy but of these two she was surprised to find that jealousy was uppermost. As much as Frank might parade himself for Jane's particular notice, she could almost feel that Miss Woodhouse did the same. Miss Woodhouse's air was so very self-satisfied, her pleasure in Frank's company so evident. Could she possibly know what pain and envy she provoked? Perhaps Frank's intention in passing again and again the little door of the Bates's apartments was that Jane should put on her bonnet and go down to join them, but she could not oblige him. Her acquaintance with Miss

Woodhouse and Mrs Weston was not of that nature that would have allowed her to join them so unceremoniously, and she could not quite trust herself not to reveal, by some cutting remark or cold, bold look, the true strength of her resentment towards the mistress of Hartfield.

This is what I must content myself with, she said to herself. At least I see him. I can almost hear his voice. How the sun shines on his curls and makes them glister! How splendidly his coat is cut. If I cannot be by his side, *this* is the next best alternative. But oh! How my heart beats. How will I endure it when I meet him in company? Will I betray myself? It was one thing, yesterday, to see him here, with grandmamma whose sight is not keen enough to discern the blush I am sure I wore, and Aunt Hetty, who has not the penetration to suspect double dealing of any sort. How I wish to go down to them! It is about my time for walking out. But no, I have not the courage for it.

Nobody at all saw Frank Churchill the following day. He was reported to have gone to London for a haircut.[xxiii] Highbury thought it a curious notion, but then Highbury was not used to London ways or fashionable ideas. The oddity was soon forgotten in a fluster of surprise that occupied Highbury's gossips to the exclusion of all else. The Bateses were disturbed at their breakfast the next morning by a carrier from London—a man and a lad with a sturdy covered cart and a pair of strong horses—to deliver a wooden crate containing a small square piano. Much doubt there was at first. Certainly, the Bateses had ordered no such commodity. Was it paid for? Yes, the carrier assured them, the goods and carriage both were fully paid up, and all they needed to do was to allow him and the lad to carry the thing in. Its best situation was the next question to be addressed. Certainly, it would have to go somewhere in the parlour; where else was there? Miss Bates threw herself into a flurry of speculation, considered and rejected the idea of removing the dresser, relocating the dining table, even knocking out the window seat that the instrument might take its place.

Meanwhile quite a crowd of Highbury shoppers and morning walkers had gathered in the High Street outside the Bates's sequestered doorway to observe the carter and make themselves masters and mistresses of the contents of the mysterious crate. Mrs Ford came out of her shop to see what the to-do was. Mr Abdy, pot-man and ostler at the Crown likewise emerged, blinking and bleary from a busy evening the night before. Mrs Cole, hurrying down the street to share with Miss Bates the very final alarms and addendums for the dinner—for the very day of it had arrived—almost forgot the pressing anxiety of whether three canapes would suffice, how much broth might be required and if her girls should or should not be brought down to see the company before they went to bed. She stood slack-jawed with the rest of the onlookers while the carrier and his aide awaited a resolution of the difficulty their arrival had occasioned and drank the tea that Patty had brought out to them.

In the end, at a murmured suggestion from Jane and a nod of agreement from Mrs Bates, the box was carried up the narrow stair, negotiated round the turn at the top and placed in a space between the dresser and a bureau, where it fitted perfectly.

Last of all was the curious question of who might have commissioned the gift, and this exercised the on-lookers quite as much as it did the residents above the grocer's shop. It was known that Mrs and Miss Bates could certainly not afford such a luxury. Mrs Bates had played very nicely when younger but her arthritic fingers had precluded that for many years. Miss Bates did not play at all, so far as any of them knew, and had no ear for music; her singing voice in church had been likened to a vixen in a trap. Therefore the extravagance of the gift for a young lady who was to be with them for only three months rather shocked than delighted the Bates's neighbours. Miss Bates was at a perfect loss to explain it, and said so volubly and repeatedly to anyone who would listen. Mrs Bates, as usual, said nothing, and in this case her silence really did reflect the absence of any cogent idea upon the matter in question. Jane, naturally, knew at once that Frank was her benefactor. Who else? And had he not specifically remarked on her lack of an instrument at the Bates's? Thankfully her aunt did not recall, or, if she did recall, she did not connect his observation with this provision. Jane was able to suggest that the Campbells were the only people she knew who had both the thoughtfulness and the means to supply such an extraordinarily generous gift, and this seemed to satisfy.

The pianoforte was unpacked and must be left to stand for a few hours before its touch and tone could be tried, but Jane did caress its keys most lovingly, and expressed herself more gratified and blessed than she could say.

By the time the piano had been unpacked and Miss Bates' surprise and consternation had subsided it was almost time for Jane to tackle the matter of her hair, which she would have to manage as best she could on her own. Mrs Bates was conveyed to Hartfield to keep Mr Woodhouse company; even a special kind of screen brought from London had been no inducement to *him* to attend the Coles' dinner.

'It is kind of Mr Woodhouse to invite your grandmamma, of course,' Aunt Hetty mumbled as she came back into the room from helping her mother into the Hartfield carriage, 'although how she is to be got back up the stairs and into bed without me here to assist her is beyond my ingenuity to fathom. Patty must do it, I suppose.'

Privately Jane wondered why a grown man could not entertain himself for an evening, but must be minded like a child. Naturally she did not voice this opinion but betook herself to her bedroom. She would see Frank. Perhaps they might spend a few moments in conversation together, although she knew she must prepare herself for seeing him pay court to other ladies and in particular to Miss Emma Woodhouse. But she would be able to sing and play and even if she did so second, *that* must always be a pleasure to her.

Jane and Miss Bates ate their dinner at the usual time although, as usual, Jane could manage but a few mouthfuls before she lay down her knife and fork.

'Jane, I declare you will fade away if you do not eat more,' said Miss Bates. 'The smallest slice of mutton and half a potato! Can you really not manage more? And Patty went to Mrs Martin's on purpose this morning to get these parsnips. I so hoped they would tempt you. Oh well, if you really cannot … I hope your grandmamma is able to eat a tolerable repast. Mr Woodhouse is kindness itself but he is likely to send the best dishes away and pare down the rest to crumbs and smidgens. I shall tell Patty to lay out supper for her, for when she gets home. There is nothing worse than trying to sleep with an empty stomach.'

After dinner they dressed, and watched carriages take the great and the good of Highbury to the Coles' villa to dine. In due course Mr Knightley's coachman knocked at their door and the ladies descended.[xxiv]

Chapter Thirty-Six

Jane awoke the next day from a troubled sleep. The Coles' party had been pleasant, the guests numerous enough to admit a good deal of circulation and private conversation. She had managed quite a long, if veiled, discussion with Frank, which would have been sufficient recompense for being relegated to the second tier of guests if what he had had to say to her had not troubled her very much.

The pianoforte, of course, was the first topic that must be raised. 'It was very wrong of you,' Jane chided, speaking from behind her napkin. 'How did you think I would explain it?'

'I supposed you would attribute it to the colonel.' He bent over her fan and pretended to examine it minutely. 'I did not much care. It is unsupportable that you should be deprived of music, and I will not have you under obligation to Mrs Cole, compelled from gratitude to tutor her girls.'

'It is what I will have to do, by and by.'

'*That* will never be.' He leant close to her ear on the pretext of reaching her teacup from a table behind the sofa on which they sat. 'Miss Woodhouse suspects you,' he murmured. 'She thinks you unnaturally reserved, for a start, and that has excited her suspicion—she believes you have something to hide. And what she has alighted on is this: she thinks there was something improper between you and our friend Patrick Dixon. I have not disabused her, naturally.'

'Have you not?' asked Jane, smiling inanely. 'I would hope my friends would quash any such scurrilous taints on my reputation.'

'Ordinarily, I would,' Frank said, laughing immoderately as though she had said something outrageously amusing. 'If she had been a man, I would have called her out on the spot. But it suits us if she is misdirected, does it not? And if she comes up with her own muddled notions, so much the better.'

Jane sipped her tea. 'I suppose she suspects *him* of being the donor of my piano?'

'Oh yes, she is convinced of it. Jane, you look very beautiful tonight.'

'Stop it, Frank. You will make me blush.'

Miss Woodhouse was then called to the piano, and all conversation must cease. Her recital was adequate, no more, but improved by Frank Churchill's adding his voice to hers. Afterwards he sang with Jane also, until Miss Bates put a stop to it.

'You will be hoarse, Jane,' she said. 'Mr Knightley was almost severe with me just now, and quite rightly. I should take better care of you.'

There had been dancing—just two sets—but Frank had danced them both with Miss Woodhouse; danced with energy and every sign of pleasure. The whole room saw it. Significant glances had been exchanged, knowing looks were on every face. Jane, dancing with one of the Otways, had hardly been able to contain her ire. The same irritation had kept her awake, her jealous demon once more shrivelling her stomach to gall. It still preoccupied her when Frank called the following day.

He came early, with Mrs Weston. 'To hear the instrument,' he declared, smiling broadly at the cleverness of his own invention. 'Mrs Weston promised you, you know, though *she* has no recollection of it. But I cannot allow her to renege on a promise and so here we are. Have you tried it yet, Miss Fairfax? How is its tone?'

'I …' Jane began.

But Miss Bates interjected with, 'Oh yes, she has tried a few pieces. But it is not quite level. See how it wobbles? Even so, it sounds very nice. My mother remarks particularly upon the quality of the lower notes— very mellow, she says. Her hearing is not quite acute, you know, in the higher registers, but the lower notes she hears very well. I hope you will take a seat Mrs Weston? Oh! But not there! I declare you almost sat upon my huswife!xxv Its contents are spread far and wide! To think you might have impaled yourself! Yes. The chair by the table will be much safer. My mother has broken her spectacles. The rivet is out and nothing I can contrive can get it to stay in again. See? That is why … I wondered if a darning needle might … But no. Without the aid of her spectacles I think she does not quite see who has been so kind as to call upon us.' (Turning to where Mrs Bates sat in a chair by the fire), 'It is good Mrs Weston, Mother, and Mr Churchill. They are come to hear Jane's pianoforte. Is that not kind of them?' The old lady nodded, squinting into the room, and raised her hand. Miss Bates resumed, 'We are greatly honoured, ma'am. I shall ring for tea. I hope you will take some refreshment?'

'We saw Miss Woodhouse and Miss Smith in the High Street,' Frank remarked with studied casualness. 'I am certain they are as eager as Mrs Weston to hear the pianoforte. We asked them to join us, but they held back. They did not wish to impose. They would not presume ...'

'Oh!' Miss Bates almost shrieked, 'but they are most welcome. Always welcome. Such friends should not stand on ceremony. Our door is always open—I speak in a figure, you understand. Our door is not *literally* open for that would cause an unconscionable draught, but metaphorically it is open to *all* our friends at all times. We delight in company. My mother, in particular, for she is not always able to get out these days. Last night, to be sure, she went to Hartfield, and had a most enjoyable time, but the exigencies of getting her back *in* ... I do not think Mr Woodhouse can quite appreciate ... However ... Let me just run down and beg Miss Woodhouse and Miss Smith to step up. I will not be a moment ...'

'If you really wish them to come, you could have no better advocate than Mrs Weston,' said Frank. 'If anyone can assist Miss Woodhouse to overcome her scruples it is Mrs Weston. In the meantime, let me see if I can repair Mrs Bates' spectacles. It is just the kind of job I like.'

'Indeed!' Miss Bates said, 'that would be most civil of you Mr Churchill. I wonder if you would be so good, Mrs Weston, as to just come with me ...'

Frank's object was gained. Miss Bates and Mrs Weston quit the little parlour leaving Frank and Jane under the sole supervision, rather deaf and almost blind, of Mrs Bates. *She,* obliging lady, settled herself for a snooze and was soon breathing deeply, her eyes closed, her hands folded across her lap.

'You are angry with me, Jane,' said Frank quietly, the moment the street door had closed behind the deputation, 'and I know why. I did not dance with you. I *would* have; I anticipated at least a dozen dances before the evening came to a close. But for some reason the party broke up *just* as it became enjoyable. It must be a country trait.'

'I am not angry,' Jane demurred, keeping her voice very low, 'but I will admit to being jealous. Why should Miss Woodhouse enjoy all that should be mine?'

'Why indeed? You injure me if you think I do not feel the injustice of it. But *she* thinks it her due and all of Highbury panders to her vanity.'

'And she believes me capable of improper feelings towards Mr Dixon?' Jane blurted out. She picked up her grandmamma's spectacles from the table. 'Here, Frank, you had better busy yourself with these, or people will wonder what we have been doing, up here alone.'

Frank nodded towards Mrs Bates. 'We are not alone. Did you not like my ploy? I did not bargain for the spectacles—*that* was a boon I had not anticipated—but I determined to have a few moments private conversation with you this morning if I had to introduce a rabid dog to your aunt's parlour. "I will save Miss Fairfax," I would have shouted, and run off with you in my arms to Donwell Abbey. I fantasised half the night about it, I assure you.'

'Miss Woodhouse has no sisterly feeling, no compassion, no proper reticence,' Jane said, still too angry to be amused by the picture Frank had conjured. 'To harbour such thoughts, and then to speak them to a man who is all-but a stranger. It is not honourable in her. But then she never did waste an opportunity to denigrate me.' Jane sat at the piano and ran her fingers over the keys. 'Do you see how the pianoforte wobbles?'

'She denigrated herself, last evening,' Frank said, kneeling down to assess the amount of packing he would need to stabilize the instrument. 'Her playing and singing are *nothing,* compared to yours. I like being at your feet, Jane. When we are married, we will sit so; you at your leisure, on a comfortable chaise, and me like this, on the floor, at your feet. Yes, there is some unevenness of the floorboard here. Some folded paper should suffice. I have some in my pocket, I believe.'

'Miss Woodhouse may not play or sing with any great skill, but she dances very well,' Jane said, sourly.

'I did not notice,' Frank replied judiciously. 'There, that is better, I think.'

'Nevertheless, Frank,' Jane murmured, 'I would have you tread carefully with Miss Woodhouse. She is not worldly, for all her airs. She is not used to the ways of young gentlemen. Most of the young men of Highbury avoid her. I know Mr Martin would rather take a detour along Broadway Lane than chance encountering her outside Hartfield. *She* may have no sisterly feeling, but *I* have. Do not put her in danger, Frank.'

He got up and stood behind Jane, his hands on her shoulders. He glanced over at Mrs Bates, who still slept soundly, and then leaned down to kiss Jane's neck. 'You are too nice,' he said. 'She is an excellent foil. But you need have no fear; I notice only you. And I promise you that I shall dance with you before my fortnight at Highbury is done. I am told they used to have balls at the Crown. I shall revive the custom. Will that please you?'

Jane lifted her hand and placed it over his where it lay on her shoulder. She squeezed it firmly. 'Yes, it will,' she said.

'I went the other day to look at the vicarage,' Frank observed presently. 'Your mother's old home, I think? A very pretty place. I found myself envying—what is his name? Eden? Evans?'

'Elton,' Jane supplied.

'Yes, Elton. He is to settle there on a modest income with the woman of his choice. The man must be a blockhead who wants more.'

Jane sighed, 'The man or the woman,' she agreed.

The banging of the street door, the thud of footsteps and, dominating all, the sound of Miss Bates as she led her visitors up the stairs made the couple spring apart. Frank snatched up the spectacles once more, Jane turned in confusion to the window, and when the party entered the room Frank began to speak quickly and loudly until she should have composed herself to face them.

Chapter Thirty-Seven

Frank's fortnight came and went. A further week's extension to it was granted by Mrs Churchill pending a ball at the Crown, which he had, through the gambit of suggesting impractical and impossible alternatives, occasioned to be thought possible and even desirable by the great and the good of Highbury. It was to be. Frank had brought it about for Jane (he said), only for her, for the pleasure of dancing with her, and this circumstance assuaged to some degree her mood of resentment and caprice. It was not like Jane to be bitter, and yet, as she reflected on her feelings, this was the sensation uppermost amongst them. Her umbrage against Miss Woodhouse added a hot, sour layer to the sense of discomfort, anxiety and shame that had assailed her hour by hour since November. Having Frank in Highbury, rather than bringing joy, had become almost a daily torture. The pain occasioned by the sight of him flirting—there really was no other word for it—with Miss Woodhouse had been surpassed only by that provoked by Emma's complacency and pride in thinking it very much her due.

That Miss Woodhouse's behaviour was reprehensible there could be no doubt. What kind of mind imagined the sort of duplicitous conduct of which Miss Woodhouse suspected her? A secret affair, and with her best friend's fiancé? It was unthinkable! And yet this was the low morality of which Miss Woodhouse thought her capable. Jane's blood almost boiled as she thought of it, and it took some miles of heavy trudging through the Highbury countryside before the truth assailed her. Miss Woodhouse was quite right! The object of Jane's illicit affection might be mistaken, but a furtive liaison there certainly was! No, Jane could not condemn Miss Woodhouse absolutely.

Of course, it was unconscionable that she had *shared* her squalid apprehensions, and that with a gentleman who was virtually unknown to her. Miss Woodhouse's instant intimacy with Frank Churchill had overleapt by bounds the gradual increase of civil intercourse dictated by good manners. They had gone from perfect strangers to the perfect unreserve of long-standing, confiding friends in a matter of just a few hours. It was not wise! It was barely rational! Miss Woodhouse had amply demonstrated her lack of judgement, her utter naivety to the world's ways. No young lady in Bath or Brighton could have behaved with such reckless impropriety without becoming the object of widespread censure. Jane contented herself with this thoroughgoing condemnation of Miss Woodhouse before, again, its hypocrisy brought her up short. Had not *she* committed precisely the same crime? Her outward conduct in Weymouth and since may have been eminently respectable but in the privacy of her heart and mind she had sunk to the lowest depths of improper behaviour. She had said and done things, thought, felt and indulged every wantonness conceivable with a man who, the previous May, had been a stranger to her. Did not the secrecy and deceit and all that had characterised her dealings since November signify a dearth of judgement that far outstripped Miss Woodhouse's innocent indiscretion?

Jane returned home much chastened and even more sickened at her own predicament. It would not do. No, no, it would not do at all. She would not attend the ball when the day of it arrived. If she did attend, she would certainly not dance with Frank Churchill. Indeed, she felt sure that the general indisposition that had troubled her all winter would render her unequal to going out at all.

She went to bed early, pleading a headache that was not entirely fabrication, very down-hearted indeed, troubled and full of bitter self-recrimination. She could not go on with the engagement; the spiritual anguish of it was too much, the shame, the deceit, the immorality; it tore her soul in two.

The following morning she woke and dressed with a heaviness of heart beyond anything she had experienced before. Her conscience accused her. She could barely look herself in the mirror.

Her aunt went out soon after breakfast to visit Mrs Goddard, taking Mrs Bates with her as far as the churchyard.

'There are graves she likes to visit, you know, and the weather is so mild today that I do not fear her being outdoors for half an hour or so, which is all the time my business with Mrs Goddard will require. If *you* feel equal to some air, however, Jane dear, you might walk in that direction. I never intend my visits to be long but somehow or other they do stretch out.'

'Certainly, Aunt Hetty,' said Jane, wrapping Mrs Bates' thick shawl around the old lady's shoulders. 'If you are not returned in half an hour or so, I will walk towards the church to meet you both.'

Mrs Bates gave Jane a speaking look.

'Half an hour *or so,*' Jane repeated with a slight nod at her grandmamma. Mrs Bates would be glad of an hour or more's solitude in the churchyard, she gathered, and Miss Bates' visits to anyone were rarely of shorter duration.

The two older ladies departed and Jane took the seat in the casement. She held neither book nor sewing, and although her eye was drawn again and again to the little pianoforte, she made no move to play it. Her thoughts pursued their usual course. The impossibility of being engaged to Frank—her moral sense revolted against it. But then the impossibility of parting with him—her heart clamoured within her in protest. She did not hear the knock at the door, Patty's voice as she answered or the soft tread of feet up the stairs. She lifted her eyes and there was Frank in the room before her, as though conjured by her thoughts and all of a piece with them; impossible that he should just *appear* and yet nothing was more desirable or necessary to her or impossible to deny.

'Frank,' she said dully, 'I did not hear you come up.'

'You were in a reverie,' he said quietly, taking the seat next to her and lifting her hands to his lips. 'I would give the moon and stars to know of what you were thinking.'

'Oh, you would not,' Jane said, with a sad smile.

'Of course I would,' he said stoutly. 'I wish to know every thought in your head, every desire of your heart; your every wish and dream and fear. I require you to have no secrets from me, dear Jane, for, being yours, they are also mine, as *you* are mine, and mine alone.'

'The wonder of it,' said Jane slowly, 'is that the thoughts that occupy me—that assail and torture me—are not already yours. Do you not lie awake at night, Frank, and anguish over our dissimulation? Does our treachery not impede your prayers? Oh, do you not suffer utter and unspeakable *misery* because of our base and wilful deceit? You do not seem to. You seem blithe and happy.' She paused for a moment to see the effect of her words on him, but he made no rejoinder and so she went on with a tone whose bitterness surprised even her. 'I see you, Frank, as you make love to Miss Woodhouse, as you offer little compliments to Miss Smith. Even Mrs Goddard was made to blush by some easy pleasantry you offered her. You are smooth and plausible; you delight in the role of perfectly unengaged man. The half of Mrs Goddard's pupils not in love with Mr Elton are convinced of your being on the point of a declaration to them! Did I not know otherwise I might almost believe it myself! How can you do it, Frank, for shame? No, I see no suffering in you. I see no misery. *That,* it seems, is all mine.'

For the first half of Jane's outburst the tears had merely swum in her eyes, but now they poured without check down her face. Frank lifted his hand to stem them, stroking her cheek with his thumb and looking upon her unhappiness with an expression that satisfied even her as to his wretchedness.

'Of course,' he said, but gently, without remonstrance. He pulled her towards him so that her head rested on his shoulder. 'I curse myself for the necessity of it, and every day think what a millstone of recrimination and blame will be mine when the truth is known. We balance on a knife-edge. As much as the Churchills may throw me over for going against their will, so may *these* good people, for misleading them in the way I do. I tell you, Jane, my fear of my father's displeasure—no, not that—his *disappointment* is far worse to me than any tantrum my aunt may bring forth. But what can we do? Jane, Jane,' he lifted her head so as to be able to look into her eyes. 'What *can* we do? You decree that it must not be, but I would rather lose my good name, my aunt and uncle, even my father and Mrs Weston—who, I will say, is becoming as dear to me as a mother—yes, I would give them *all* up, Jane, before I would forswear you.'

'And yet it must be done,' Jane cried out. 'It *must*. For this is agony. I am at war with myself. I told you once that I felt like an animal in a trap. I *am* in a trap, Frank, and it will slowly kill me—kill me spiritually, if not physically. If I free myself I will be maimed for life—I will never get over the pain of it—but my conscience will be clear. I will be shriven, perhaps, in time.'

'And what a waste that will be,' Frank returned, and his eyes now were full of tears. 'What a waste of your life, and of mine, and of all we have thus far endured, and all for just a little more time, Jane, just a little, until I can bring my aunt round.'

'You bargained for a little time in November, and again at Christmas. You will never bring her round.'

'I *will*. I promise you. I will redouble my efforts. I will grasp the nettle. But you are right.' He loosed her hands and rose to take a turn or two across the room. 'Yes, yes you are right,' he said at last. 'The deception is too much. It's possible that the innocent may be injured.'

'I think it highly possible, Frank. Miss Woodhouse has been injudicious but where her thoughtless head leads her heart may well follow. You must not ensnare her, Frank.'

'No,' he replied. 'Honesty is the best policy. I will … somehow … I will put things right. I wish there was someone in whom we might confide, someone to whom you could turn, in confidence, who might share your burden.'

'There is no one,' said Jane, 'not *here*, anyway. Not anywhere. It cannot be known anywhere but in our consciences and *that* is bad enough. If it were, well, it would be ruinous.'

Frank looked at her for a moment; her drooped demeanour and tear-washed eyes. 'But oh, Jane,' he cried, throwing himself at her feet, 'please do not break faith with me yet. Please, my darling girl, do not, for I must have love. I must have *your* love. All is coldness and complaint at Enscombe; it is a place of stone and ice.' It was Frank's turn to give way to emotion. He lowered his head so that it lay on Jane's lap and when he raised it again the place on her gown where it had lain was damp.

'I am come to say that I must go back there,' he said presently, when he could trust his voice to some steadiness. 'My aunt is worse, or believes herself so, and I am summoned at once. The ball is given up. I do not know when I may be spared to come back. If you think yourself unhappy, Jane, put yourself in my place. I must return to Enscombe.'

She looked down gravely at him. For all the weight of the terrible burden she must bear, the void he would leave behind him if she were to sever their tie would be worse. How could she give him up? Her one and only love?

'Of course,' said Jane, rising to her feet. 'And I must walk towards the church. I was to have met my grandmamma there a quarter of an hour ago.'

She reached for her shawl where it lay on a chair and he helped her to put it on.

'You will write to me?' he said.

She nodded, but could speak no words. She led him towards the door. Before they reached it he pulled her to him again. 'We are like Romeo and Juliet,' he said with an attempt at a smile. 'I would I had a vial of their poison about me, if it would free us both from this.'

'*That* would be a greater sin,' Jane said and, in spite of herself, she kissed him.[xxvi]

Chapter Thirty-Eight

Highbury

February 21st

Dear Frank

After you left me the other morning I was cast down with gloom. There never seems enough time to say what must be said. Must we always converse in half whispers and muttered asides? I think my grandmamma suspects something of my turmoil, though not its cause. After you went your way to Hartfield I met her in the church yard, by the tomb of old Mr Knightley. Neither of us said anything and yet I felt very much that our spirits were in accord; sadness and anguish for what cannot be. She watches me closely, but says nothing. How I wish I could confide in her! But even her great kindness and understanding would not forgive such sin as ours.

At least in our correspondence we can open our hearts fully and I sit down with my pen now to reveal mine to you as clearly as I can.

My friend Mr Mosley is often in my mind. Without betraying his confidence, I think I can say that he has known what it is to love against the wishes of family and friends. That he has suffered a great deal, even after subjugating himself to their will, is certain; I know he is filled with resentment against his father and the relationship between them is broken beyond repair. What other, or further, tortures he might have brought down upon himself had he gone against them is impossible to say. But this I wish you to understand most thoroughly, Frank. I will not marry you against your family's wishes. I will not burden either of us with the bitterness of family schism that will undoubtedly ensue if you marry without their consent. If you break with them for my sake, you will do so in vain. If you doubt the wisdom in my determination I suggest you speak to your father. He once confided in me that the division that his marriage to your mother wrought amongst the Churchills was a thorn in the side of it, a thorn I will not impale us with.

I ought to give you up, for I place you in an impossible position. But my heart and my own person rebel against my reason in this, and the addition of your assurances and entreaties means it is a battle I cannot win. I love you too dearly and while there remains the smallest glimmer of hope I will endure. I depend upon you bringing your aunt round and that is the task I set you. You once told me you would be my knight errant. So I now commission you.

As tired as I am, I know I promised to keep you abreast of all that transpires in Highbury and I must inform you that the departure of Mr Frank Churchill has been quite eclipsed by the arrival of Mrs Elton. She is come and of course the whole village flocks to her door to make their wedding calls. My aunt and I went yesterday. I had already formed a poor opinion of Mr Elton, who is simpering and shifty. I must say I did not warm to Mrs Elton either; she is high and mighty, very sure of herself, very full of herself indeed. She spoke at length of her brother-in-law, a Mr Suckling of Bristol, and seemed most put out when we had to admit that we had never heard of him and were quite unacquainted with Maple Grove, his mansion near Bristol. She is astonished and evidently disgusted at our parochialism. I foresee a great effort on her part to modernise us.

Mrs Perry called yesterday and told us that she is well on her way to persuading Mr Perry to acquire a carriage. He rides out on horseback, you know, in all weathers. No one can accuse him of not being a diligent and dedicated apothecary and he has been known to go out in blizzards and storm, and at any hour of the day or night, to attend his patients. Mrs Perry thinks the exertions too much for him now that he is gaining in years and as the practice thrives she is confident of gaining her point in respect of the carriage. She hints that, when it is not in use, it will be at her disposal. She spoke of possible outings to Kingston with my aunt, who was all enthusiasm for the scheme. In earlier years my aunt thought nothing of walking to Kingston but she has not done so recently. If she can get a ride in Miss Cropley's egg cart, she will do, but this is not often.

I shall call at the post office every day in the hope of a speedy reply.

Your very own—for so, in spite of myself, I am —

Jane

Dear Jane

I thank you for your letter although it caused me much heartache. To have your conditions laid out in plain script brought the imperative of my task very firmly home. Do not think for a moment that you and I are at odds over this matter. I understand your position perfectly because I share it. It is my absolute intention to bring my aunt round, my avowed intent on returning to Enscombe. Although she is capricious and volatile she is very fond of me and it is my belief that I can persuade her to anything, in time. In one detail only are we at variance, dear Jane; your decree that, in the end, if I am unsuccessful and if the worst comes to the worst, you will abandon me. I will not allow you to go so far. You must not oppose so rigidly the desire of your heart—and mine. It is needless self-sacrifice. That, I venture to say, is at the root of Mr Mosley's unhappiness; his greatest regret is what he lost, not the paucity of the remnant he managed to save.

I own to you that I am sometimes very angry at our situation. It is not we who are unreasonable. Any right-thinking person would see the equality of temper, mind, birth and education that exists between us. There is no impediment other than my aunt's caprice. I am not ashamed of loving you and would declare it from the rooftops if you would allow it. But I am ashamed at my aunt's prejudice and will do all in my power to bring it down. Have faith in me, dear Jane. Your knight will not fail.

My journey back—I will never call it 'home' again, since it has been made clear to me, at Randalls, what a real home can be—was as dreary as possible. We stopped at Northampton and again at Chesterfield, both inns dirty and cold and without the consolation of interesting fellow-travellers or local colour. We got to York in a blizzard and were held up two days there before a slight thaw allowed us to hurry the rest of the way.

Letters met me along the route from my uncle. My aunt was worse, then better, then worse again, so I knew not what to find when I eventually arrived. But she is tolerable enough, I think; I see no serious cause for concern now, whatever prompted her to write to me at Highbury as she did. She says I make her better; oh what a heavy responsibility she places on my unwilling shoulders.

The weather has turned wet. Sometimes the rain falls in such thick sheets it is as though grey blankets have been draped over the moors. Riding is out of the question; the horses can make no progress across the boggy ground. When I am at liberty— which is not frequently—I walk in the woodland, where the paths are drier and where I am made welcome at the cottage of my two excellent friends the gamekeepers. Neither of these gentlemen will see their fortieth year again, neither has succumbed to matrimony, they will likely live and die in their tumbledown cottage with whichever dozen or so dogs happen to be their companions at the time. But they are happy. Their mud-caked boots are thrown anyhow by the door. Their furniture is matted with dog hair. They have a pot of never-ending stew to which they simply add game or vegetables as they come to hand, stirring them in with a pint of ale before slopping it into bowls and going to. They know the value of friendly silence as well as the pleasure of conversation. I almost envy them, except in one respect; they have no wives; no tender smile to greet them each day, no kindred soul to share their woes. No, I do not think I am suited to the life of a bachelor. However, it is to their cottage that I repair when I can, and their fire thaws my blood as their company restores my faith in humanity.

March 2nd

The day of our ball has been and gone. I thought of you all. I almost caught the echo of disappointed hopes amongst the Miss Otways and the Master Coxes and all the young ladies at Miss Goddard's school. 'Now we would have been dressing,' 'Now we would have been setting forth,' 'Now we would have been dancing.' And so *I* thought, Jane. It pleased me to imagine you within the circle of my arm.

March 5th

Yesterday I spoke of you to my aunt. That is, I spoke about you. She had not enquired about my visit to Highbury beyond the coolest enquiries after my father, but I decided to regale her with a full account of it and, necessarily, 'Miss Fairfax said …' and 'Miss Fairfax suggested …' and 'Miss Fairfax looked …' punctuated every anecdote.

'You mention Miss Fairfax a great deal too often,' my aunt said to me at one juncture. 'You think highly of that young woman, I know, and she is pleasant enough, but it will not do to single her out. She is to be a governess—the kind of shadowy, silent person who everyone knows is there but no one notices, as necessary as a side table, but as unremarkable.'

'Miss Fairfax will never be unremarkable,' I said. 'she is inherently incapable of it and if her friends allow her to waste her accomplishments in the anonymity of a schoolroom they shall have me to answer to.'

My aunt gave me a most speaking, penetrating look but pursued the topic no further. She developed a blinding headache, however, and required me to close all the curtains and press a handkerchief scented with lavender to her temples for the rest of the day. And so I was punished. But so also I was rewarded. It was a small victory, I thought; she can be in no doubt of my regard for you.

March 7th

This evening my uncle bid me go to him in his counting room. It is a closet of a place between the kitchens and the gun room. My aunt has evicted him from every other habitable room where he can carry on the business of the estate and now he is reduced to this. But he called me to him and began to show me some of the deeds, accounts and maps that relate to the Churchill fortune. I cannot say what prompted him to do this. Perhaps he is unwell, but forebears to say so. Or perhaps my aunt has an inkling of my intentions and bids my uncle remind me of what I shall lose. It amounts to more than I had imagined; my uncle has been an excellent steward of what was left to him.

But I do not care, Jane. You are worth more.

I must post this now or the envelope will be too thick!

Your loving

Frank

Dear Frank

I collected your letter on the first fine day we have had since you went away, and took it with me to the little copse where we met when you first came to Highbury. Believe me I almost ran along the lane and up the slope, looking over my shoulder the while, ducking below the hedges for fear of being seen. I have more than my aunt's overweening concern to evade now for I have been taken under the wing of Mrs Elton. I do not quite know how it has come about. She was cool towards us at first; I suppose we did not occupy that standing in Highbury society that seemed to make it worth her while to make friends of us. But suddenly her manner changed and we were almost courted. I was, at any event; my aunt is suffered, my grandmother is patronised and petted as though she were a senile old spaniel. I suspect that Mrs Elton has taken me up in defiance of Miss Woodhouse, who has rebuffed her many advances and suggestions of musical evenings, 'conversazione', and 'soirees'. Miss Woodhouse has a protégé so of course Mrs Elton must have one also, and as Mrs Goddard's store of sufficiently pathetic, moderately pretty and adequately presentable pupils has run dry, I am to supply the lack. Hardly a day—an hour—goes by but I am summoned to walk with the Eltons, sit with the Eltons, ride and dine with the Eltons. I would not object if she had any elegance of manner or erudition of conversation but she is devoid of both. She is insufferable; vulgar, self-important and deaf to any suggestion that I am by no means as eager to receive her patronage as she is to bestow it. She speaks almost exclusively of her brother and his house at Maple Grove and I believe I am as intimately acquainted now with every cubbyhole and *pantry in that establishment as I would have been had I lived there for my entire life. My aunt is beside herself with gratitude and glee at my being the recipient of Mrs Elton's particular notice and offers me up on any pretext; 'Jane will be delighted,' 'Jane is quite at liberty,' 'Jane will benefit from the exercise.'*

Part of Mrs Elton's interest in me is her determination to find me a situation. She knows several families—unexceptionable, naturally, in the first tier of society, as close to or as similar to Maple Grove as makes no difference, which is sufficient recommendation for anyone—who may need a superior governess, and is as firm as possible in wishing to write to them on my behalf. So far I have held her off. I tell her that I will fix on nothing until June, or without consultation with the Campbells, but she hardly hears me. Do not be surprised if you hear that I am packed off to a schoolroom in Bristol to be petted, made much of, and illuminated by innumerable wax candles.

Your own

Jane

Dear Jane

I write to Highbury in the hope that you have not yet been carried off under the arm of the insufferable Mrs Elton. What presumption! How dare she commandeer your every hour and take the liberty of making enquiries on your behalf! Your letter made me want to take horse to Highbury and confront her. I shall do, when opportunity presents itself. Meddlesome woman!

On the other hand, I am glad of your being given some attention. I must say that although I did not dislike Miss Woodhouse as much as I had expected, her behaviour towards you did vex me. How ready she was to gossip about you! How she doted on that ninny Miss Smith when a young lady with real elegance of manners and refinement of mind was within her orbit. It showed a lack of judgement, I thought, which is not pleasing in any young lady but which served my purpose admirably. I do not think she is aware of the pointedness of my attentions to her. If she is, she is in no danger of being injured by them, you can be easy on that score.

I heard from Mrs Weston a day or so ago. She is a faithful and regular correspondent. Her letter, too, was full of Mrs Elton and the flurry of dinners and at-homes her arrival has occasioned. I pray that Mrs Weston will not overtax her strength; she has particular cause to take extreme care of herself.

I enjoyed the idea of you in our little copse, reading over my letter. I hope the spell of good weather you mentioned has endured. We have had rain and more rain. The ground across the moor is thigh-deep in mud. There are safe pathways for those who know them but even these are under water now. Enscombe is littered with pots to catch drips from the windows and roof—such desolation you cannot imagine! My aunt has not been outdoors this past month and I am certain it injures even further her indifferent health. It unquestionably makes her quarrelsome and dissatisfied. She reduced a new housemaid to tears for leaving a door slightly ajar and she has been very cutting even to my uncle, who is patience personified when it comes to her whims. As a consequence, I have set myself the task of persuading them to remove to the London house as soon as possible. London air is not healthful but it is drier and will permit some airings in the carriage that are impossible here. My uncle will be able to seek out acquaintance for respite. I speak of it as quite a settled thing, a matter of 'when' and not 'if'. Of course, I am not disinterested. Manchester Street is so much closer to you, Jane.

March 27th

A serious development. Yesterday my aunt suffered some kind of seizure. It was quite different to anything I have seen in her before, brought on by no annoyance or pique that I can fathom. I found her on her sitting room floor insensible, and when I brought her round with the sal volatile she always keeps to hand, she was at first unable to speak with any coherence, although that has since come right. The doctor was sent for again; bleeding and blistering prescribed. I think she was really frightened, for a time, but now seems calm and passes the incident off as a faint; she remembers standing up rather quickly, then nothing more. My uncle is as eager as I am to get her to London.

Write back to me here, however. I will ensure that all mail is sent on.

Your loving

Frank

Highbury

March 30th

Dear Frank

I received yours with concern. How is your aunt? I am of your mind; whatever advantage we may gain from the removal, she will be better served by coming to town. I hope you have prevailed. I remind you also of your other quest, although I would not have you take advantage of any weakness or infirmity in Mrs Churchill to press your suit.

March is over and so is the three months originally stipulated for my sojourn in Highbury. I cannot tell whether my stay here has materially benefitted my health. My troubles are of the spirit and the heart; wherever I go, they will travel with me. My grandmother sees my distress. From time to time she puts her hand over mine, and her eyes invite me to share my woes. But I cannot. How can I break the confidence we have both sworn to keep sacred? And I know what she would tell me to do. Where conscience leads, the heart and mind should follow, for it is through the conscience that God speaks to us. But I still have faith in you, Frank. I will hold on until all hope is gone.

Colonel and Mrs Campbell and Mrs Dixon all urge me to join them in County Wicklow. All difficulties of travel shall be got over, friends called upon, money paid out so that I may get there in safety and comfort. Mrs Dixon writes with most affecting prose; she misses me very much and has found no friend or acquaintance in the locality of Baly-Craig who can even begin to provide the perfect confidence we shared. It breaks my heart but I have declined. Where here I can pass off my enervated mood as a remnant of my indisposition, there I could not do it. I am too well known by the Campbells. They would soon understand what is only vaguely suspected here. They would press me until I owned the truth, while my aunt merely urges me to eat more pie.

My only escape from the fluttering care of my aunt is the mortification of being petted and patronised by Mrs Elton. It is a settled thing now that she does nothing without me. I am to sit alongside her while she plans her menus and instructs her housekeeper, for, she says, it may fall within my remit to manage household affairs as well as the schoolroom, in my new situation. She speaks leeringly of a governess she knew who went to manage the children of a widower and soon became his wife. The idea sickens me. I recall my interview with the tanner. We read and sew together if the weather is inclement, or we make calls in company with one another if it is fine. Thus I call upon those who have already called upon my aunt and hear all their news again.

When Mrs Elton and I are in private I am subjected to an almost endless litany of Miss Woodhouse's faults, and although the mistress of Hartfield has been no friend to me I am loathe to be implicated in her condemnation. Miss Woodhouse is as green as grass, has never travelled anywhere, has little musical appreciation, is not well-read, does not know what is due to her elders and betters, is proud, conceited, small-minded and jealous. This is Mrs Elton's opinion of her. Then there is something—I am not quite certain what—but she and Mr Elton often exchange winks and subtle, sneering remarks about Miss Smith and I infer that Miss Woodhouse was so indiscreet or incautious last Christmas as to virtually throw her little friend at Mr Elton's feet. Whatever it was, I decline to be associated with it. If there was an indiscretion it is better forgotten by everyone, for Miss Smith's sake if not for Miss Woodhouse's.

When I can I walk down to Donwell Abbey. There is a very pleasant walk through the woods along the river from there that brings one out at Mrs Goddard's school. But the little girls are not allowed to venture into the woods without supervision and so I can be sure of solitude and as much peace as I am ever able to enjoy. Even this respite is sometimes denied me. If Mrs Elton gets wind of my going out she will interfere, claiming dangers behind every hedgerow; I may fall and sprain my ankle, I may encounter gypsies, I may stray into old mine workings that do not exist, and my aunt takes her cue from Mrs Elton; she does not like to think she is less careful of me than the vicar's wife. So, from time to time my grandmother gives me a little commission; to carry a message to Mrs Martin, to deliver beef tea to Mr Cropley, to take a receipt to Mrs Larkins. I do not know why a young lady with a flask of beef tea in her hands is less liable to assault or stumble but it seems to be so. I am allowed to go out on my errand and am relieved beyond words at the opportunity to be alone.

But, as much as I desire the relief of solitude and exercise, I find more and more that I have no energy for it. I sit upon a fallen log or flat stone and spend my time in stillness. Frank, I begin to fear for my health. My aunt found me out yesterday altering a dress that fitted me perfectly when I arrived in January but is now too big. I have no appetite. My hair comes away in the comb. I lie wakeful at night. Mrs Elton importunes me at every opportunity; she is relentless. I do not know how much longer I can resist her.

Jane

Nottingham

5th April

Darling Jane

I am coming to you. Your letter found me here, forwarded from Enscombe, and I reply by return. I am more concerned than I can say.

I gained my point at last and the people in Manchester Street expect us the day after tomorrow. We travel slowly, for the comfort of Mrs Churchill, although she abhors staying in inns.

Be strong. Do not lose faith in me. I am determined, once Mrs Churchill has been pronounced fit by Sir Lester Garstang (the most eminent man to be found in England for complaints such as my aunt's), to grasp the nettle with her. A few weeks should see the matter settled. I will come to you at Highbury the instant I can be spared. I will write to my father by this same post.

Frank

Dear Frank

I collected your letter in a downpour. I cannot describe to you to what degree it lifted my spirits. You are the cure to all my ills, the antidote to the poison of guilt and self-disgust that courses through my veins. And yet you are also the poison. It is a conundrum I cannot solve although I weary myself in the attempt. And yet for just a few hours I felt better, buoyed, I believe I almost bloomed, which was as well, for I had been so honoured as to receive an invitation to dine at Hartfield.

Mr John Knightley is at Hartfield at present, delivering his two boys for a holiday. He saw me on my way to the post office as the shower began, and was so indiscreet as to mention the fact at dinner. Once Mrs Elton overheard it, nothing would do but she insists that from now on our letters will be collected with hers. I will lose the opportunity, the excuse, of my visit to the post office from now on. Believe me when I say that I argued most ardently against it, but even Mrs Weston overruled me. Do not write to me again until I can reverse their interference. Your handwriting may be recognised. God forbid but your letter may be opened by Mr or Mrs Elton in error. I am afraid of the risk and angry at the necessity for secrecy and lies.

Jane

Chapter Thirty-Nine

At Jane's command, Frank wrote no more and she had no news of him until he arrived at the Bates's doorstep some few days later. Both Miss Bates and Mrs Bates were at home; it would have been too providential for him to find Jane alone again.

He paid a short call, describing at length his aunt's symptoms and the range of palliatives that had been prescribed, a topic most interesting to Miss Bates, who enjoyed thoroughly good health herself but always entered fully into the indisposition of others.

'We are settled at Manchester Street for the time being,' he said, glancing at Jane to make her understand that it was to her that he chiefly spoke. 'I hope very much to be able to ride to Highbury frequently, but, *you understand* I may not be my own master in this; I must attend my aunt when she requires it.'

'Oh indeed, Mr Churchill, and we hope to see you as often as her health permits,' said Miss Bates. 'Jane, I know, looks forward to your visits. Mother and I are greatly honoured by them. The Westons, naturally, like to see as much as possible of you and Miss Woodhouse—your particular friend, I know—will be eager to see you. In short, all of Highbury adopts you as its own, Mr Churchill. I assume you have called at Hartfield?'

'No, not yet,' Frank said, looking again at Jane, 'nor even at Randalls. I did not wish to pass your door without calling in. Naturally, I shall go there directly.'

'Let us not delay you,' said Jane, standing up. 'It is time for my exercise. I will accompany you to the door, Mr Churchill.'

'I must call upon my father and Mrs Weston,' Frank said in an undertone as they hovered together outside the Bates's door. 'I *should* have gone there first, indeed. They will insist upon a call to Hartfield but I will stay the shortest amount of time permissible with the Woodhouses.' Frank fussed with his gloves. 'Let us meet in the copse in an hour, or, perhaps an hour and half. I shall think of some excuse. Perhaps I shall claim having seen other acquaintance in the village[xxvii]. I do not know. Something will come to me and I will get away as soon as I can.'

True to his word, Frank was in the copse some hour and a half later, but a long time after Jane, who had gone there directly after parting with him in the High Street.

'I stayed at Hartfield barely quarter of an hour,' he called, as he climbed the slope. 'And all the while I fidgeted and spoke in stops and starts. Miss Woodhouse must have remarked the oddity of my behaviour.[xxviii]

'I do not care what Miss Woodhouse thought,' said Jane, pressing herself to Frank's chest. 'Frank! Oh Frank! How I have missed you.'

'And I you, my darling girl,' he re-joined, enfolding her in his embrace. 'Oh! How thin you are.'

A few minutes passed as they stood thus in each other's arms. Then Frank led Jane to one of the flat boulders where they could sit together in relative comfort. 'I miss your letters, Jane. I want daily news of Highbury. If I cannot be here myself, your accounts of all its little comings and goings are the next best thing. And I want news of you. May we not write to each other again?'

'No,' Jane said fiercely. 'That is, I suppose I might write to you ... But I do not know. I feel as though I am being watched. Mrs Elton is everywhere, thrusting herself into my business. Someone is sure to report to her that I send letters and before I know it she will insist on her servant collecting those too. Oh Frank! How much longer must we endure this? It is beyond my ability to bear! Indeed, it is!'

'I want only a physician's confirmation that my aunt is quite well, then I shall go to it,' he told her, 'but these things cannot be instantaneous. Oh! They madden me with their tediousness! There are appointments to be made, questions to be asked, examinations to be undergone. These doctors are the slowest fellows at coming out with anything; their time is measured in guineas and sovereigns, you know. Believe me I am all impatience with them but they will not be rushed. Sir Lester Garstang is the worst—a most longwinded, rambling fellow—he took a full half hour to take off his coat and get through the preliminaries before a word of my aunt's symptoms could be broached. In the meantime, Jane dear, we must go on as we have begun.'

'You must continue to pay court to Miss Woodhouse?' said Jane with dismay. 'Oh, Frank I do not like it. She is not worldly. You will break her heart.'

'I do not think so. She greeted me with the kindness of a friend. I have seen girls in love and she is not so afflicted.'

'You will break mine, then,' Jane said bitterly, getting up and moving away from him. 'I hope I am not forced to witness you make love to her.'

'Oh, Jane,' Frank said with a half laugh that only just belied his frustration, 'do not be unreasonable.'

'Unreasonable?' she fired back. 'I think I am patient! I think I am long-suffering! How many other young ladies would have borne with you as I have done?'

'None in the world,' Frank admitted. 'You are a saint.'

'Do not patronise me, Frank. I get quite a sufficiency of that from Mrs Elton.'

'Ah,' said Frank, eager to change the subject. 'I have yet to meet her.'

'Oh she is most avid to make your acquaintance, although she gives fair warning that she will speak as she finds. If you are a puppy, she will say so.'

'A puppy? Well, I may be one, just to annoy her.'

Jane shook her head. 'This is just what vexes me, Frank; your ability to put on whatever appearance you choose. You are a master of disguise—so plausible that I wonder if the face you show me is just one of many.'

Frank stood up and drew on his gloves. 'I must ride back to London,' he said. 'You are capricious today. I will give you proof soon enough of my sincerity.'

'I hope so, Frank, for the waiting is excruciating.'

'I see it is. I will not fail you. And as proof of my honesty, I shall keep that promise I made to you in February. The idea of the ball shall be revived and I shall dance with you.'

'A ball?' Jane cried. 'You think *that* sufficient recompense? You think I am to be put off and placated with such frivolities?'

'No,' Frank said, keeping a tight rein on his temper, which was ebbing away, 'of course not. But it is *something*. At least it is one promise I can keep. I fear you doubt me.'

'I *do* doubt you.'

Frank sighed. 'That is cruel, Jane. All you have to do is wait. I must manage the thing. I think my task is infinitely harder.'

They walked together to the field gate where Frank's horse was tethered. Wild primroses grew along the hedgerow and the hawthorn was in bloom.

'Spring is here,' Jane remarked, but dully, as though it brought her no pleasure. 'Rowena's time is near. I should be with her.'

'When we are married, we will go to Ireland,' Frank said, mounting his horse.

'*If* we are married,' Jane corrected him, bitterly.

Frank clamped his lips closed, stifling the retort that was ready on his tongue.

Ten days went by and Frank did not return to Highbury. In accordance with their agreement, he did not write to Jane and so all the news she got of him was second and third hand. The sum of it was this: he was always hoping to come, but always prevented. Jane wondered very much what the outcome of Mrs Churchill's consultations might be. Each day she imagined that she had been proclaimed well, and that Frank might broach the subject of his marriage. If all went well, he would send a messenger straight to the Bates's door—there would be no need for secrecy. She found her ear tuned to the sound of hooves on the cobbles and such was her nervous state that as often as she heard a horse go by she would leap from her seat to look out of the window, hope and expectation lifting her spirit to a heady, almost intoxicated degree. But no messenger came and this threw her back into doubt and dismay, speculating that Mrs Churchill was really ill, there was no possibility of upsetting her by giving her news that would certainly make her worse; she and Frank were doomed.

Mrs Elton was as eager as ever to secure a situation for Jane. In direct contravention of Jane's request, she made enquiries of her friends in Bristol, 'For here is June almost upon us, just the very season that people begin to look about them, and if it is not known that you are available, the best situations will be snapped up.'

It took all of Jane's powers of patience and tenacity to rebuff Mrs Elton's onslaught of high-handed presumption. She smiled and nodded, and declared herself grateful for her friend's efforts, but could only reiterate that until June came, and with it, news of Mrs Dixon's successful confinement, and until she had corresponded specifically on the topic with Colonel and Mrs Campbell, and until she was quite settled in herself that her health was fully restored, she would make *no move* on the matter.

Mrs Elton was deaf to her stipulations however, as eager and determined as ever; she overruled Jane's objections at every turn.

Two things occurred to alleviate the anxiety of these weeks. It became known that the Churchills had removed to a house in Richmond. The air in London, the dirt, noise and bustle had all made Mrs Churchill feel worse. Even Manchester Street had been insupportable to her. But consultations with the medical men being as yet still in train, a return to Yorkshire had been unwise. Therefore, they had taken the lease of a house in Richmond; quieter, with better air, but still within the reach of Sir Lester Garstang. This first piece of news gave rise to the second. Richmond being only nine miles from Highbury, and it being presumed that Frank would find it more frequently within his power to travel thither, the idea of the ball had been taken up once more. Mrs Weston was in the throes of planning and preparing, closeted almost daily with old Mrs Stokes, who had brought herself out of retirement to oversee this important event.

The ball was certainly to take place; no impediment could occur this time, which had spoiled their plans before, and, in spite of herself, Jane delighted in the prospect; as he had said, it was *something*. She knew she would not be able to dance with Frank first—she must set her teeth to watch Miss Woodhouse claim that right—but it would be unthinkable that he would not stand up with her at all. And in the noise and bustle of a ballroom they might have that privacy to speak that was denied them now that their correspondence had perforce been terminated. Pleasure *then* would be no part of her design. She would require—she would demand—minute details of Mrs Churchill's condition, diagnosis and prognosis. And on this second point also Jane was quite determined; she would name a date by which Frank *must* have informed his aunt of their engagement. Midsummer's day would see their engagement either publicly acknowledged or over. If acknowledged, the relief would be immense. Questions of course there would be that would require answer. Confession and repentance would be requisite. Her shame would be overwhelming. *But,* if they were met with goodwill and forgiveness, beyond the censure would be happiness—a distant prospect Jane scarcely dared dream about and one she did not think she could ever persuade herself she deserved. If the alternative proved to be the case, if their engagement must end, well, there Jane could only grimly contemplate the course she must take. Mrs Elton's offer must be taken up, she supposed, or some other means by which she could find employment. It would be hard—bitterly hard—but at least she alone would bear the burden of what was lost. This was Jane's only consolation.

The day of the ball came and Frank arrived at Randalls from Richmond before dinner, no last moment interdiction of Mrs Churchill's having prevented his coming.

Jane dressed herself with much care, spending a great deal of time and trouble on the arrangement of her hair. She had not seen Frank since their tryst in the copse. She had been testy and disagreeable with him, then, she knew, and she wished to give him no cause to quarrel with her now. She would *look* as beautiful and elegant as she knew how and if she outshone Miss Woodhouse, all the better. On the other hand she had hard truths to impart; she must do so with all the charm she could muster.

She and her aunt were to be conveyed to the Crown in the Eltons' carriage, a needless provision since their house was directly across the street, the ground was dry and three or four steps would accomplish the distance from one door to the other. But Mrs Elton would hear of no other arrangement; she must be seen to take proper care of her friends, would expose herself to no want of attention and wished most particularly to enter the room with Miss Fairfax so that Miss Fairfax might, at last, be accorded the share of honour and acclaim she was so often denied.

'The ball is given to honour me,' she confided in Jane, 'although no one has been so crass as to say so. I make no claim for myself but I presume to think my being amongst you, a bride, has prompted this ball to be brought about, and if you are in *my* party the Miss Woodhouses of this world, who might suppose themselves the chief guest, shall have their noses put well and truly out of joint.'

So, at something after the time appointed—which was early, however, their having been bidden by Mr Weston ahead of time to give their opinion on arrangements that could not, at this stage, be altered, even if there was gross fault to be found with them—the Eltons' carriage drew up. Miss Bates and Jane alighted, the carriage turned and within two minutes deposited them outside the Crown. Frank was on hand immediately with umbrellas—an excuse, they were not needed—and after bowing deeply and with a stylized flourish to Mrs Elton, possessed himself of Miss Fairfax's arm to escort her into the ballroom. He pressed her hand very firmly, and his eyes spoke the words his lips could not—that he found her captivating and splendid. It took all Jane's powers to subdue the smile of happiness that his look inspired.

For all Jane's determination she had little stomach, during the course of the ball, to interrogate Frank Churchill as to the state of his aunt's health, the doctors' opinions and the prognosis that would have such a material impact on her own happiness and on his. He had about him such an air of resolute delight, a brightness of eye and a readiness of smile that showed his resolve to have a thoroughly splendid evening, and she found she could not readily bring herself to interfere with it. Indeed, it was quite infectious; everyone gathered there was disposed to pleasure and gave themselves up to it in respect of the uniqueness of the occasion, the particular efforts of Mrs Weston and in duty to Mrs Elton and Miss Woodhouse who both showed by their complacent smiles that they each thought themselves duty bound to be so honoured.

Jane danced with Mr Elton at first; something of a trial; his hands were sweaty and unpleasant, his breath redolent of an excess of Madeira wine and cigars. But afterwards she stood up with a number of unexceptionable partners and enjoyed herself very much. Then, for the last set before supper, Frank claimed her. It happened that at that juncture Miss Bates had slipped inconspicuously away to assist her mother to bed. At the same time the room's attention just then was diverted by the sight of Mr Knightley leading Harriet Smith to the set. No one had expected him to dance; he had declared with his own lips that he would not do so. Every eye was trained upon him in delight and approbation, with Miss Smith receiving her fair share of compliment and notice for having been so singled out. There was a good deal of whispered conversation amongst the matrons who had witnessed something just beforehand that had intrigued and, by their expression, shocked them very much. Mrs Gilbert was in deep conversation with Mrs Weston and Mrs Goddard. As a result of these two occurrences, nobody at all was taking any notice of Jane Fairfax or Mr Frank

Churchill and they slipped away down the corridor towards the supper room for a very few moments' brief conversation.

'Jane, you look so beautiful, I can hardly keep my eyes from you,' Frank said heatedly. 'Being parted from you is agony.'

'But surely, *by now*, you know how matters lie with your aunt,' Jane whispered. 'Sir Lester *must* have pronounced his diagnosis? I have been expecting a messenger every day, every hour.'

Frank shook his head. 'There is no certainty. We wait further investigations … we are told that only time can give us any degree of confidence …'

'Time?' Jane broke in, 'but that is just what we do not have. Every day that goes by, every hour that passes, mires us further in deceit and hypocrisy. I cannot go on with it, Frank.'

Frank paled but said, 'Of course not, not indefinitely.'

'Not indefinitely? Not at all!' Jane declared.

Frank went whiter still. He glanced up and down the passageway, anywhere but at Jane, whose expression made him quail.

In the ballroom the orchestra was bringing the dance to a close while in the supper room the servants were putting the last touches to the tables. 'Oh Frank, we cannot speak here,' said Jane, exasperated that he had not replied to her previous remark. 'We will be seen. We will be suspected. My aunt will be back at any moment and looking for me. Come tomorrow morning before you return to Richmond. Think of some excuse. Aunt Hetty is engaged to call on Mrs Goddard. We *must* agree on a way to proceed or I shall go mad.'

'Very well, Jane,' said Frank, 'but it must be early. I am to be back with my aunt by midday. Come now, let us return to the set. No one will have noticed our absence and if they do, we shall say that you were anxious about Miss Bates and we went to look for her. I shall contrive to escort you to supper. *That* will be a consolation, will it not? Nothing on earth will persuade me to hand Mrs Elton down. She is insufferable. My father must bear that burden.'[xxix]

'Perhaps you will be required to escort Miss Woodhouse,' said Jane, sourly.

Frank made no reply.

Chapter Forty

Frank was at the Bates' house early the following morning to return a pair of scissors he had borrowed from Miss Bates solely for that purpose the evening before. Miss Bates, as Jane had promised, was already from home and Mrs Bates was just then in consultation with Patty in the scullery and so Jane opened the door to him herself, her shawl in readiness.

'I have been looking out for you from the casement,' she said in a low voice, 'and when I saw you just now, I called down to my grandmamma that I was going to take my walk.'

'That is very good,' said Frank from the side of his mouth. 'See how our thoughts are one? I purposed as much and had my horse sent ahead to the Richmond road in anticipation of being able to walk with you that far.'

As they exchanged these words they went through a sort of pantomime; Mr Churchill exaggeratedly proffering the scissors and evincing much surprise to see Miss Fairfax open the door to him, Miss Fairfax pointing first to her shawl and then to the High Street, Mr Churchill stepping back with a bow and requesting the honour of accompanying her. The street was all-but deserted however, the hour being early, and Highbury enjoying a slow beginning to the day after the ball, so they had few witnesses to their performance. Notwithstanding, they set out on their walk as certain as they could be that they would satisfy any witness that it was an unpremeditated happenstance.

'There was no note from my aunt on my return to Randalls last night,' Frank said as they walked. 'I almost feared one, I confess to you. I would not have been surprised if a messenger had intruded upon the ball itself.'

'Because you fear your aunt is ill?'

Frank shook his head. 'Because it would please her to spoil my enjoyment and to trespass on my time with my father and Mrs Weston. She is jealous. She cannot abide the thought of me away from her.'

'Then you must oppose her, Frank,' Jane urged. 'She will ruin your life—and mine—if she continues to believe that these displays of histrionics succeed in gaining her end. Just once would be enough.'

'I know it,' Frank cried, 'I am sure of it, and then I catch a glimpse of her when she thinks no one is near, when there is no need to pretend what she does not really feel, and there is upon her face such a look of—I cannot adequately describe it; wretchedness and gall, as though she has eaten sour berries—that I mistrust myself. In the main I think she is the most narcissistic, calculating and conniving woman in God's creation. But then, when I see her private face, I wonder if she is not indeed long-suffering, if there *are* ailments that she keeps hidden.'

'If there were, Sir Lester would have found them out,' Jane stated.

'Sir Lester is cagey,' Frank replied, 'and there is much confidential chat between him and my aunt that my uncle and I are not party to.'

Their walk had taken them along the High Street, past Hartfield and to the place where Frank's road would take him away from the main thoroughfare. 'I told my man to wait a mile or so down the road,' Frank said. 'Can I prevail on you to accompany me that far?'

'Not so far that your man will see me,' Jane said. But it was an exceptionally fine morning; the hedgerows were alive with birdsong and blossom, the sky above a perfect arc of blue, the morning air warm and balmy. Frank, at her side, was an added incentive and one scarcely less compelling. 'But I will walk a little way further,' she concluded.

Frank pulled her arm through his and looked down upon her with pleasure. 'It was sheer joy to dance with you last night, Jane. I imagined to myself that the whole world knew of our engagement and that all the gentlemen were looking on in envy—as they surely *would* do, if they knew my great good fortune—and I felt as though I walked on air. At that moment I would not have cared if my aunt herself had walked in and seen my feelings plain upon my face.'

'Perhaps it would have suited you,' Jane said tartly, 'at least *then* you would not have had to grasp the nettle and broach the subject with her.'

Frank stopped in his tracks and turned to face her. 'You think I am afraid of her? You think I prevaricate unnecessarily? You wound me, Jane. *I* would have presented her with the facts and hang the consequences last July. It is *you* who have forced me to play this game of diplomacy.'

'Because I will not risk your breaking with her!' Jane said hotly.

'Perhaps you would not marry me if I were penniless,' Frank replied. 'Is *that* why you insist I get her approval?'

Jane stepped backward. 'That is unworthy of you,' she said, 'and wholly untrue. It is *you* I think of when I urge you to gain her sanction.'

'So you say,' Frank said mulishly, looking down at his feet, 'but if I do not care, why should you?'

'I will not bear the burden of it,' Jane said, her voice trembling. 'You say *now* that you do not care but in a year or two, when the shine has worn off our marriage and we are poor, you may think differently. I cannot bear the thought of your eyes upon me then, accusing, recriminating …'

'Never! I never shall.'

Their walk had taken them into a sunken section of road, shaded by high banks and over-canopied by tall elms. The sudden cool after the warmth of the morning was striking and, partly because of it and partly as an effect of the momentous declaration she had just made, Jane gave an involuntary shiver.

'For my own part,' Jane went on, summoning courage, 'I am worn thin and made ill by our situation. It has gone on much longer than I anticipated and my ability to keep up this wretched duplicity is almost gone. I give you until Midsummer Day, Frank. If you do not have your aunt's blessing for our marriage by then, I will dissolve our engagement.'

Frank's face was ashen, 'You stipulate an absolute date?' he said shakily.

'Yes,' said Jane, tears falling from her eyes. 'I am sorry, but I do.'

Just then the air around them was rent by a shrill scream. Up ahead, in the gloom of the road, a flash of white and a convergence of shadows indicated some disturbance, and shouts and more screams suggested some violent encounter was in progress. Out of the dim, running footsteps materialised into the form of Miss Bickerton, one of Mrs Goddard's parlour borders, with a wild expression on her face, her hair disordered and her dress very muddy. She ran towards them but, on seeing them, seemed to be more, rather than less, distressed. She screamed again, scrambled up the bank, leapt a hedge and was gone across the fields in the direction of Highbury before either Mr Churchill or Miss Fairfax could by any means detain, calm or question her. In the interim the furore further up the road continued; children's shouts and the voices of burly women joined by a barking cur could not drown out the pitiful pleas of another young lady.

'Go back, Jane,' Frank said grimly. 'Go home, as quickly as you can.' Then, flourishing his riding crop and shouting out in a manner most authoritative, he strode into the gloom of the road.

Jane did as she was bidden, arriving home very much shaken both by the idea of what might have been taking place along the Richmond Road to some poor girl and by the momentousness of what she had said to Frank. That she had hurt him very deeply was beyond doubt, and often, during the afternoon and evening that remained of that day, did she upbraid herself for it; she had been unkind, unreasonable. The poor man was now trapped between *two* capricious women. Her heart was sore for him; how they had wasted that half an hour of solitary communion in bickering and accusation when they could have been ... Jane blushed as she thought of the kisses and endearments they could have exchanged on the deserted road. But she did not regret her ultimatum; for her own sanity it was necessary. Now it was made she would do all in her power to soothe and encourage Frank, if he were so fortunate as to be allowed to come to Highbury again.

Jane had hardly taken off her bonnet before Highbury was astir with the news that Miss Bickerton and Miss Smith had been accosted by gypsies on the Richmond Road, that Miss Bickerton had run away leaving her friend in danger and that Miss Smith had been badly frightened and relieved of her small change but had come to no worse harm. Mr Frank Churchill was the hero of the hour; he had laid to with his crop and a few choice and unambiguous admonishments, scattering the rogues in an instant, before carrying the insensible Miss Smith to the sanctuary of Hartfield in his arms. Highbury sang his praises, while Mr Knightley, who went immediately to root out and arrest the miscreants, received barely a passing acknowledgement for *his* courage.

Chapter Forty-One

Highbury saw no more of Frank Churchill for a week but his heroics on the Richmond Road, and a conviction that *he* had been the instigator and facilitator of the delightful ball ensured that he was the topic of almost every conversation that took place in the meantime. Highbury matrons were proud to boast acquaintance with him. Those young ladies at Mrs Goddard's school who had persevered in their infatuation with Mr Elton in spite of his marriage now switched allegiance to Mr Churchill. *He* was without doubt the handsomest, bravest and most wondrous gentlemen any of them had ever beheld and it was certain that he featured in many a maidenly daydream. Miss Smith recovered from her ordeal and even attracted to herself a certain romantic prestige that rather elevated her status in Highbury than otherwise. Miss Bickerton was roundly criticised for abandoning her friend in her moment of need and for having neither the presence of mind nor the strength of character to stand up to what, after all, had been a few dirty children, some slatternly women and a toothless old dog.

Jane missed Frank and thought of him often. She called daily at the post office in defiance of Mrs Elton's edict but of course there was no word from him. News did come from Baly-Craig, however; Rowena had been delivered, some few weeks early, of a baby boy who was small but, so far, thriving. As a consequence of his premature arrival and the shock of the ordeal on Rowena the Campbells did not contemplate a return to

Bute Square until August at the very earliest. Jane's longing to be with her dearest friend and virtual parents was almost overwhelming and her pen hovered over her paper for many minutes as she fought the temptation to beg to be allowed to join them. She was convinced that it was all over with Frank. He would not stand for her ultimatum, and why should he? Already in the thrall of one demanding woman, why would he put himself under the power of another? Perhaps she had been unreasonable? She felt convicted that she *had*. This irascible facet of her character was new and unwelcome, wholly unlike her usual mild and rational self. She had schooled herself to be always in the shadows, the last to be considered, but now she was pushing, urging and demanding as though she was someone important. But then, if she did not, who would? In this situation she was her only advocate. When she looked at herself in the glass she felt very strongly that if she did not do *something* her health or her mind would break. She did not like to set herself against Frank; she did not think on the whole that she *was* in opposition to him. She wished to side with him against Mrs Churchill, to be his support and aid against that common adversary to their happiness. But she feared that, with her last gambit, she had gone too far. The stricken look on his face haunted her. Perhaps he would begin to think that, of the two women, Mrs Churchill was the lesser foe.

At last Jane defeated the temptation, writing instead of her great joy at the Dixons' news, sending fondest love and promising embroidered gowns and crocheted baby-shawls as fast as she could work them. She spoke of her great contentment in remaining in Highbury, the care and attention she received from her aunt and grandmamma and urged the

Campbells to give Rowena all their time and consideration for as long as it might be required.

Amidst these preoccupations, often interrupting and trampling on them, Mrs Elton continued her determined patronage of Miss Fairfax. *She* was in constant communion with the people at Maple Grove and its immediate environs, and expected to hear imminently that Mr and Mrs Suckling would be visiting Highbury for an extended period.

'For now the weather is so very conducive,' she said. 'I doubt not that the Sucklings will bring their barouche-landau and we shall have excursions. I do so enjoy exploring; I assure you Selina and I were quite wild for it in our younger days and although we had not the means *then* of travelling in such style and in such comfort as we do *now* it did not deter us from adventures that would quite shock you, Jane, if I were to relate them. Miss Smith's encounter with those gypsies,' with a curl of the lip, 'was nothing to the scrapes Selina and I got ourselves into. There was one occasion; a bull in a field, a gate inadvertently left open as we passed through, a farmer as irate as possible. Oh! How we laughed! You can be sure that *we* did not faint away. Oh no, we are made of sterner stuff.'

'A bull on the loose can be a very dangerous thing,' Jane suggested.

'Dangerous bulls should not be allowed, in my opinion. Mr Suckling is very adamant on *that* subject, I do assure you. He will not tolerate them at all.'

In direct contravention of Jane's clearly-stated request Mrs Elton had continued to make enquiries amongst her acquaintance, and to urge *them* to be on the lookout amongst *their* wider circle in an effort to find

Jane a situation. She was determined to have the satisfaction and the glory of it, 'For I have set myself the task and I never was one to shy away from something once I have determined to do it,' she declared, 'even though it will deprive me of your companionship. I am disinterested, you see Jane. *Your* well-being is my prime object.'

'I am gratified,' Jane said through pursed lips, 'but remind you *again,* ma'am, that I will do nothing until I can discuss matters with the Campbells. In the meantime, I am determined to enjoy my stay with my aunt and grandmother here in Highbury without a moment's thought as to what may follow.'

'Oh, but such short-sightedness cannot be allowed,' Mrs Elton declared. 'Your aunt and grandmother do not wish it, I am sure, and the Campbells will be very far from thinking it a wise choice. Perhaps I should write to them. A word from *me* will help them see the pressing necessity of action *now.* They need not concern themselves in the matter at all. I shall be your advocate, your patroness and your friend in this Jane. You may safely leave the whole matter in my hands.'

'But I do not choose to place it there, Mrs Elton,' said Jane firmly. 'You are kind, but please make no move, write no letter, initiate no enquiries on my behalf.'

'Oh, you are stubborn,' said Mrs Elton with an indulgent smile, 'but you have met your match in me.'

Mrs Elton had dined at all those houses in Highbury that offered such hospitality and was presently engaged on returning the compliment at her own home.

'It must be done before the family from Maple Grove arrives,' Mrs Elton declared, 'for, as respectable as the people of Highbury are, there is not that degree of éclat that the Sucklings expect. I make some exceptions, naturally,' she qualified, looking complacently at Jane, 'but in general ... well, the idea of Mr and Mrs Suckling sitting down with the likes of the Perrys or the Coxes ... Oh! The notion would be diverting if it were not so very abhorrent! In any case the dining room is not large enough. I cannot entertain here as Selina does in Maple Grove. But in one way it is propitious. If I invite the Westons and Mr Churchill, Mr Knightley and yourself I certainly cannot entertain the Woodhouses in addition, especially as Miss Woodhouse goes nowhere without Miss Smith and *that* young person, I assure you, I certainly will *not* have at my table. So I can leave them out with a clear conscience. You *will* come to dine, Jane, won't you?'

'Certainly,' Jane said, struggling to keep her composure, 'if I am at liberty on the day you fix. You hope to secure Mr Churchill? I do not know—I know nothing at all of him—but I am not aware, that is, I think I have not heard of him being expected in Highbury again?'

'He will come if I invite him, you can be sure of that,' said Mrs Elton airily. 'Now come and look at my summer gowns. I have had them re-trimmed. I despise excessive flouncing and no one can think less of such things in general than I do, but I must say I am rather pleased. Come and see. I do value your opinion.'

Invitations were duly sent out and Jane was surprised and inordinately pleased to hear a few days later that an invitation sent to Richmond had been accepted.

'Mr Frank Churchill is quite at liberty and declares himself delighted,' Mrs Elton told Jane. 'I told you there would be no difficulty there. Mrs Churchill is a harridan, no doubt, but I fancy I am equal to her hubris. I couched my invitation in such terms that she could not possibly refuse him permission.'

'Is that so?' Jane responded, not daring to enquire what lure Mrs Elton might have dangled. Frank was coming to Highbury! That is all that mattered. Jane was breathless with longing and anxiety. How would he greet her? Would he be cold and wounded? Would he be his usual gregarious self? Did he still love her? What progress had he made with his aunt? The pity was that in a small, select party such as the one Mrs Elton purposed there would be no opportunity for private discourse; the talk would be general, including the whole company. She would not be able to question him. There was danger too—in a smaller party everything was open to greater scrutiny. They must be careful.

The day of the dinner arrived and Jane watched anxiously from the casement to see Frank ride by. Would he look up? Would he smile? But there was no sign of him and at last Jane took herself off to dress. The Westons had promised to call in their carriage even though the day was very fine and warm and the vicarage an easy stroll both from Randalls and the Bates's lodgings. When the knock came Jane was ready and halfway down the stairs, anxious not to keep the Westons waiting, but when Patty opened the door it was not the Westons' coachman but Frank himself who stood on the step. He saw Jane on the stairs and smiled, before stepping back and sweeping off his hat in a low, courtly bow.

'I am not the conveyance you expected, I know,' he said loudly enough for anyone in the vicinity to hear, 'but the coachman mistook my direction. That is, to own the truth, I directed him wrongly for I did not know Mrs Weston had engaged to collect you. I sent him direct to the vicarage and so I have run back to escort you thither. You do not mind the walk? The roads are quite dry, I assure you, and,' (with a self-deprecating smile), 'I saw no gypsies as I came along.'

'I do not mind at all,' Jane replied. 'I enjoy the walk to the vicarage.' She took Frank's proffered arm and they set out. 'Which is a matter for celebration,' she went on dryly, when they were out of earshot of any eavesdroppers, 'for I seem to walk it a great deal these days. I am constantly required at the Eltons', too constantly for my liking, but she is not to be denied.'

'Indeed, she is not,' Frank said with a laugh. They passed the cottages on either side of the High Street and came to that stretch of lane where hedges and fields replaced the little gardens and humbler dwellings. 'I wish I had kept her invitation. A *summons* would be a better description. Her tone was imperious to a high degree. Oh,' turning towards Jane and wiping all sign of amusement from his face, 'how *are* you, Jane. I have been anxious for you. Are you well? Are you quite well?'

'And I have been concerned about *you,*' Jane replied, ignoring his enquiry. 'Have you been very angry with me? Have I lost your love?'

'Never in the world, my darling girl,' Frank said, pressing her hand most ardently before lifting it to his lips. 'But I have been thinking very hard about what you said. I am not fair to you, I know, and I *will* confront my aunt. Only, you know, it has to be done with care. You make a high stipulation. I could end up losing everything.'

'If it comes to that I will release you and you must retract. She will forgive you,' Jane said.

'But I will not forgive myself,' Frank murmured, 'and what will be the good of my aunt's good favour and all the Churchill wealth if I have not you to share it with?'

At the top of Vicarage Lane they paused in the shadow of a large, overhanging willow that grew just there. They spoke no words but stood closely together for a few moments, communing all the same with sighs on Frank's part and trembling on Jane's. As they emerged, they encountered Mr Knightley, who had just rounded the corner in his approach to the vicarage. He rarely used his carriage and certainly never for an occasion such as dinner with his neighbours. He walked. He liked to walk about the parish. A mile or more, at whatever time of day in almost any weather, was nothing to him and preferable to troubling his groom or his horse.

'Good afternoon,' he said, genially enough but with a look in his eye that betrayed that he wondered very much to find Frank and Jane in company with each other, and, as it seemed, lurking beneath a tree.

'Good day to you sir,' Frank said in his usual hearty and open tone. 'You are going to the Eltons'?'

'I am,' Mr Knightley admitted. 'And you?'

'Yes, we are on our way there. I misdirected the carriage which was to have collected Miss Fairfax, and as the originator of the error I undertook to set it straight by collecting her myself.'

'You might have done better to re-direct the carriage,' Mr Knightley observed. 'Miss Fairfax's slippers were not made for walking along the road, however dry.'

'I do not mind,' Miss Fairfax said as airily as possible. 'It is a very short walk.'

'And, naturally, the carriage will take her home again,' Frank said. 'Shall we continue together?'

The three of them walked the short distance down Vicarage Lane until the Eltons' house came into view.

'That willow tree …' began Mr Knightley, still unsettled and intrigued by what he had seen a few moments before.

But Frank interrupted with, 'And here we are at the Eltons'. Miss Fairfax, I apologise once more for my error, but I have delivered you in safety and only so very few minutes late as will not cause offense, I hope, with such kind and Christian people as the vicar and his lady. Ah! The maid opens the door. After you, Miss Fairfax, and after you, Mr Knightley sir.'

The occasion progressed with all that was usual for Highbury and with some additional touches of elegance and refinement that Mrs Elton fancied were *de rigueur*. Miss Woodhouse's absence from a gathering that ordinarily would include her gave the occasion a strangeness that affected everyone. As the principal lady she would naturally have taken precedence, her comfort and entertainment were usually the first priority. Other ladies deferred to her and the gentlemen were careful to give her the attention she believed herself due. Without her there was some doubt, something lacking, and the party was for some while rather disorientated despite Mrs Elton's vainglorious supervision.

The day being fine, the French doors in the drawing room were open to the garden and the party spent some time walking around the lawn. Mr Knightley's suspicions were piqued and he kept a careful watch on Frank Churchill. There was no question in his mind that the young man was a coxcomb. The squire had watched Frank delight Miss Woodhouse with his easy charm and mischievous humour and been quite shocked by the degree of dismay and resentment it had provoked in himself. The man was an upstart and an interloper, cavalier, unreliable, smooth and plausible. For the want of Miss Woodhouse to flirt with, had he simply turned his charisma to Miss Fairfax? She examined the roses that climbed over the stump of an old apple tree. Mr Churchill strolled towards her and spoke. Would she blush? Would she smile? Would his hand brush her arm? Maddeningly he could not see as Mrs Elton just then clapped her hands to cry, 'We are all informality here. My *caro sposo* will escort Mrs Weston. Mr Weston will take my arm, I hope? And Jane shall walk between Mr Churchill and Mr Knightley. There!' she sighed with satisfaction as they formed up as she had directed. 'At last, Jane, you receive what is due to you. *I* would never permit you to be relegated to tea, as some are wont to do. *I* see your worth if others do not.' She looked around to meet an assenting eye, but only her husband muttered, 'Quite so, my love.'

The company went through to the dining room in silence so she was forced to dispel it by continuing, 'There, now. No lack of *élan*, I think? I know some hostesses who would rather entertain no guests at all than have an odd number at her table, but I assure you I am not amongst them. Selina would not approve but then her soirees are so very popular that she is sometimes put in difficulty about keeping the numbers down to a manageable quantity. People are so very anxious to be invited! She need never struggle for an extra lady or gentleman. But, I tell her, things in the country are quite different. I would not presume to say so myself, but my friends have been known to state that when it comes to hospitality, I am equal to anything.'

There was nothing to do but for her guests to concur, which they did with politeness if not enthusiasm, and the soup was served.

Mr Knightley was unusually taciturn. Jane's attempts to engage him in conversation during dinner were met with monosyllabic replies and she wondered if he still pondered what he had seen at the top of the lane.

'I think you were going to say something about the willow tree,' she opened, to show him that she had nothing to fear from him.

'Oh?' He roused himself. 'Yes, only that it is proposed to fell it. It intrudes on the road too much. Carters tell me it interferes with their wagons. But there are some who speak against the proposition. It has a local reputation, Miss Fairfax.'

'Oh?'

'Yes,' he looked at her narrowly. 'Some courting couples use it as a trysting place.'

Jane felt herself blush but said as stoutly as she could, 'I have never heard it spoken of in such a way. I know it has sheltered my aunt on more than one occasion when she has been caught in a shower, and my grandmamma likes to cut off boughs of catkins to place on my grandfather's grave. For myself, I shall be sorry to see it cut down—it is a beautiful old tree—but not for any reason such as you imply.'

'Naturally not,' Mr Knightley replied.

It was time for Jane to address her other neighbour, Mr Churchill.

'You will be interested to know, I think Mr Churchill, that your friend Mr Dixon is a proud father,' she told him in such a way as the whole table might receive the intelligence.

'And *your* friend a delighted mama,' he replied when a chorus of congratulations had been made. 'I certainly am most happy to hear that news. Please offer them my good wishes when you write.'

'Your aunt enjoys better health at Richmond, I hope?' Jane enquired a little later, when the general conversation had lapsed for a moment and the servants cleared the dishes

'Thank you for asking, yes, she is a little improved,' Frank replied with studied politeness. 'I hope you will allow me to pour you a little more wine?'

'Thank you, sir,' was all that Jane could safely reply.

After dinner Jane was invited to play. 'With Miss Fairfax here we can be assured of a truly proficient performance,' Mrs Elton brayed to her guests as Jane looked through the music, 'such as one rarely hears in country places. Generally, one is subjected to indifferent renditions by young ladies whose talent is smaller than they have been led to believe.' She gave Jane a knowing look. No one could have doubted her reference to Miss Woodhouse. Mrs Weston bridled a little and Mr

Knightley actually humphed aloud. Jane covered her embarrassment by bending down to adjust the height of the stool.

'Let me assist you, Miss Fairfax,' Frank offered, hurrying to her side.

The situation of the pianoforte at the vicarage afforded a degree of isolation from the rest of the party and gave Frank enough privacy to whisper, 'I thought for a moment the squire's suspicions had been alerted. But I think he is reassured.'

'I do not,' Jane hissed. 'He is looking at us even now. Do not sing with me Frank. He will think it too familiar … he will discern … he will find us out.'

'Very well,' said Frank, getting up and resuming his natural voice. 'I think that is secure. Try it for height, Miss Fairfax, if you will.'

Jane played and sang and Frank sat and watched her as indifferently as he could. His indifference, however, was not so stoical as to prevent, from time to time, an expression of softness to brush his features.

Mr Knightley saw it all and nothing convinced him that his curiosity or his doubt was misplaced. His conscience urged him to question himself closely. What had he really seen in that fleeting second as Mr Churchill and Miss Fairfax emerged from beneath the shadow of the tree? Really nothing but that. There could be any number of innocent explanations for their being delayed there—a shoelace untied, a handkerchief dropped, a bird's nest spied—but they had offered none at all. In fairness it could be because there was truly nothing at all to explain, but he suspected that they simply had been unable to come up with a plausible excuse on the spur of the moment. Either way, they had seemed on very easy terms *then,* all stiff formality since. It was a conundrum he was determined to solve.

At the end of the evening the Randalls carriage returned to collect the Westons and Miss Fairfax but Frank Churchill and Mr Weston both elected to walk the half mile or so home. They parted with Mr Knightley halfway along their route, at the gates to Donwell Abbey.

'You have been quiet this evening, George,' Mr Weston said, placing his hand on the squire's shoulder. 'Is something amiss?'

'Nothing whatever,' was the reply, 'only I confess that I did not like the thinly-veiled insults that were offered to Miss Woodhouse in her absence.'

'Mrs Elton is less than charitable there, I grant you,' Mr Weston said. 'The ladies do not seem to have made friends.'

'I was surprised, sir,' said Mr Knightley, turning to Frank Churchill, 'that *you* were not moved to speak up for the lady, as you are her particular friend.'

Frank laughed awkwardly, 'Are we not *all* Miss Woodhouse's particular friends?'

'Lately I have discerned a partiality on your part for her. She has been your object in coming to Highbury, has she not? In addition, I mean, to your father and Mrs Weston? Forgive me if I speak out of turn, sir, but I say aloud only what my own observations, your father's hints and your stepmother's guarded silence have all led me to believe: that you are paying her your addresses.'

'Nothing has been said,' Mr Weston put in. 'I have not hinted, have I?'

'In every way but words you have indicated that you would approve the match,' Mr Knightley said. 'You do not deny it, Weston?'

'I certainly do not,' Mr Weston agreed. 'I *would* approve it with all my heart. But I think you are ahead of the game, George.' He turned to Frank. 'There is nothing agreed is there Frank, between you and Miss Woodhouse?'

'Nothing in the world,' Frank declared. 'Nothing ventured, nothing broached, nothing contemplated ...'

'Nothing contemplated? *That* I deny,' Mr Knightley stormed. 'You set out to make yourself agreeable to her and no one who has seen you in company with Miss Woodhouse can have the slightest doubt as to your decided partiality. You like her, do you not?'

'Of course I do,' said Frank, 'she is a delightful young lady. Anyone would be a blockhead who thought otherwise, but as to my intentions ... Well, sir, with respect, they are mine alone and I decline to reveal them.'

'You infer too much, George,' Mr Weston soothed. 'You imagine things have progressed far faster than they have.'

'I will not have Miss Woodhouse's affections toyed with,' Mr Knightley said sternly.

'No more would any of us here, sir,' Frank replied with equal gravity.

'No, indeed,' Mr Weston confirmed.

'Or any other young lady of my acquaintance,' said Mr Knightley, indicating with his arm the lane behind them and the willow at the corner of Vicarage Lane.

'Certainly not, on my honour.' Frank held out his hand to Mr Knightley. 'I bid you good night, sir. Will you shake my hand?'

Mr Knightley hesitated a moment, but then grasped Frank's hand. 'Good night,' he said, gruffly. He went his way home very dissatisfied with the whole evening and when he arrived, rather than going to bed, he let his dogs out of the gunroom and took them for a long, moonlit walk across his pastures.

Chapter Forty-Two

Frank had leave to remain in Highbury some three or four days after Mrs Elton's dinner party and on the second day, knowing that Jane and Miss Bates would be making their weekly visit to the grave of Jane's grandfather, he contrived to ensure that the Westons' after-dinner exercise took them in that direction. They met up as he had intended and the ladies readily agreed to accompany the Westons in further perambulations. The weather threatened rain later and they were all of the opinion that their exercise had better be taken before it came on.

'I had words with Knightley,' Frank managed to hiss as he pretended to show Miss Fairfax a thrushes' nest in the hedgerow.

She started backwards and would have stumbled over the hem of her dress if he had not caught her arm. 'Oh Frank! I cannot abide this deception. It is too dangerous,' she gasped.

'A thrush cannot harm you,' Frank laughed, sliding his eyes to where the rest of the company were in conversation with each other. Thankfully, no one seemed to have remarked the occurrence but after that Jane walked alongside her aunt and nothing Frank attempted could manoeuvre her back to him.

In due course they met the party from Hartfield; Miss Woodhouse, Miss Smith and Mr Knightley also intent on enjoying the air before the rain. Mr Churchill and Mr Knightley exchanged the usual pleasantries but there was a reserve in Mr Knightley's manner that told Frank that their previous exchange had not been forgotten. He thought he discerned a difference in Miss Woodhouse's address also; she was cooler, less eager to be engaged by him in their former banter. That Miss Fairfax found the situation awkward was obvious to him, if to no one else, and in order to smooth it over he began to speak generally about a subject that he hoped would interest everyone; Mr Perry's carriage. But within moments it was obvious to him that this was a matter known only in confidence to a very few. Mrs Weston declared she knew nothing of it and denied having written to him about it. Jane, then, must have been his source. It was a serious blunder. She had gone very white, her smile fixed and accusing. Miss Bates filled the awkwardness with a good deal of prattle, which revealed that *they* had known of the scheme, she and her mother and Jane, but had told no one of it. Worse and worse.

They came to the gates of Hartfield and Miss Woodhouse invited them all in to take tea; her father would be delighted to see them. *This* was just the kind of informal visiting he enjoyed the most. Frank could see that Jane would rather not go in but there was no denying Miss Bates an opportunity to eat someone else's cake and she was up the Hartfield drive and through the doors before any real attempt could be made to decline. As *she* was forced to go in, Frank could not abandon her, and so although Mrs Weston was rather tired and would have preferred to go home, he encouraged her not to disappoint Mr Woodhouse.

'I will run home and send the carriage to take you home, when you are ready,' he said as he helped his stepmother indoors. 'Do not allow any scruple on that score allow you to fail Mr Woodhouse. *He* would be very sorry to know you had been within earshot but not come in.'

It should have been a delightful evening. Good friends thrown together in pleasant surroundings for an impromptu entertainment, Miss Woodhouse's presence to ensure that everyone was amply served with things of which Mr Woodhouse most disapproved. The rain shower came and passed over, but while there was companionable chat, cards and a lexicon to entertain them it should have been no hardship to spend two hours at Hartfield. Frank threw himself into the occasion, eager to assuage Miss Fairfax's evident discomfort, to apologise for his error, to share at least a commiserating smile without it being detected. But the watchful stance of Mr Knightley and the stupidity of Miss Smith both contrived to make a bad situation worse.[xxx] Jane would not meet Frank's eye, would not respond to his jokes, would not allow him to help her with her shawl. She was angry with him, very angry, and when the time came to make their farewells, she refused absolutely any suggestion that she should ride in the Randalls coach, declined his arm and stalked off up the Hartfield drive before her aunt had even half completed her usual diatribe of adieus.

Chapter Forty-Three

The June weather continued very fine indeed, perfect for the kind of exploring that Mrs Elton yearned for, but the mortification was that the Sucklings did not come and *would not* come until at least September. She was forced instead to insinuate herself into a private expedition to Box Hill promised by Mr Weston to Miss Woodhouse. It was small beer indeed, not at all of the scale or scope of the excursions she had intended—and still *did* intend—to embark upon when Selina finally deigned to come to Highbury with her barouche-landau. But it was something for now, an opportunity to assuage her increasing sense of the apathy and provincialism that afflicted the small minds of Highbury. It seemed bizarre to Mrs Elton that Miss Woodhouse, a life-long resident of Surrey, should never have been to Box Hill which was, after all, only a very few miles away. That there had been a want of ambition in Miss Woodhouse's upbringing was only too evident. Mr Woodhouse's lethargy had infected the daughter and Mrs Weston, as governess, had done nothing to counter it. Clearly, *she*—Mrs Elton—was needed to show the way.

All these observations, criticisms and insults did Jane bear from Mrs Elton but she almost welcomed the distraction of them as, when Mrs Elton was decrying Miss Woodhouse's dearth of adventurous spirit, she was not forcing openings for would-be governesses and potential school mistresses on Jane.

Two weeks of June had passed without further news from Frank, and Midsummer's Day came inexorably nearer, coincidentally the very day planned for the Box Hill expedition. Jane was resigned but wretched; he would fail in his attempt to win his aunt's approval; in all likelihood he would not even broach the subject with her. Jane did not blame him. She did not know the exact nature of his relationship with Mrs Churchill, had not seen her conjure seizures and fits at will and was quite unacquainted with the kind of caprice and selfishness which defined her character. Having been brought up in an atmosphere of cordiality, affection and easiness it was difficult to imagine what life in a household of resentment and chagrin might be like. She had asked too much of him; their engagement had been doomed to fail from the first. *She* should have exercised better self-control; these were the accusations that plagued her conscience. She had known from the first that she had allowed her heart to rule her head but the sheer power of her love for Frank, her sense of kinship with him and their connection with Highbury, had all coalesced into an irresistible passion that had, for a time, overwhelmed her powers of reason. Perhaps she should have been more forceful, but a lifetime of putting the interests of others first had not conditioned her for self-promotion. What had worked for Rowena's confidence and happiness had merely allowed Frank Churchill to string her along. On reflection, her suggestion that they enter into a secret engagement had played to Frank's strengths and fed his only source of self-worth. *He* liked nothing better than the thrill of concealment and connivance; it had been his only weapon against his aunt, the only means by which he could feel that he was his own master.

The days passed in apparent pleasantness for Jane; nothing could be better than June in the English countryside, but each day of blue skies that dawned sounded a knell of doom in her ears as Midsummer drew closer and closer.

Frank was expected to join the Box Hill trip. She did not know how she would contrive it, but somehow she would use the occasion to tell him that their engagement was at an end. Her determination on this point made her heart-sore but she knew it was right; she would be able to look herself in the eye once more.

Events, however, provided Jane with an earlier opportunity, and a private one, of imparting her decision. The day before the Box Hill trip the principal members of Highbury's premier circle were invited to pick strawberries at Donwell. This occasion, too, Mrs Elton had attempted to commandeer by offering to have *carte blanche* with the invitations and catering, but Mr Knightley had firmly declined. Frank was expected, and although the day was rather hot for such exercise, and Jane suffered with a headache, she agreed to attend on the premise that, somewhere within the extensive grounds of the Abbey or in one of the sequestered rooms that offered themselves off the grand hall, there would be an opportunity for private conversation.

The hour came but Frank did not. Nevertheless Mrs Elton—for some reason best known to herself perched upon a donkey—and the rest made their way to Donwell and addressed themselves to picking strawberries. It should have been delightful; the strawberries were ripe and sweet and the soft fruit garden quite large enough to allow for some quiet industry. But the mood of the occasion was decidedly muted, Frank's continued absence made Mrs Weston anxious, the heat was found to be insupportable and the kneeling and stretching required to gather the fruit was far less entertaining than expected. After only half an hour the pickers abandoned their baskets and retreated to the comparative shade of a tree.

There, without hope of aid or escape, Jane was subjected to an offensive by Mrs Elton on the topic of her future. The lady was more strident and vulgar than ever, her hubris engorged by a letter she had that day received from her sister's friend's cousin, a Mrs Smallridge. This lady was simply wild to secure the services of Miss Fairfax for her children without delay. Mrs Elton was lyrical on the advantages of the situation; charming children, a well-equipped schoolroom, a salary that was above and beyond anything one could have imagined. The Smallridges were an unexceptionable family, in the first circle, of highest possible respectability, and—their strongest and most compelling recommendation—intimate with the Sucklings. What better endorsement could there be? What stronger inducement? She was all warmth and energy and triumph and insisted on being allowed to write an acquiescence immediately.

In vain did Jane decline, thank and decline again. Her repeated determination to do nothing until she could consult with the Campbells went unheard. She spoke as pointedly as she knew how but Mrs Elton was deaf to her and at last Jane rose to her feet while Mrs Elton was in mid flow and asked Mr Knightley to show her the gardens, all the gardens, she wished to see the whole extent.

Luncheon was served in the cool of the great hall and still Frank did not come. Mrs Weston expressed some anxiety about his horse. Miss Woodhouse suggested that Mrs Churchill had manifested some ailment.

Jane wondered very much about that too but naturally could not presume to know so much about it. Mr Weston declared himself quite easy about his son but his absence without a word of explanation cast a pall that the heat and Mrs Elton's insufferable conceit only exacerbated.

After luncheon it was proposed to walk some more, and Mrs Elton showed herself very ready to mount a further assault upon the fortification of Jane's reluctance by saying, 'Jane, you will walk with me and we will discuss,' (with a leering wink), 'that private matter.'

Jane absolutely baulked at the ordeal; she could not bear it and would not subject herself to it. She left her parasol in the great hall on purpose to shake Mrs Elton off in the guise of retrieving it, and with only the briefest word to Miss Woodhouse, who she unhappily met in the process, set off by a circuitous route to return to Highbury. She fled across the kitchen gardens and climbed over a locked gate to the rose garden. Hurrying past a little arbour there, she was reminded of Mr Knightley's summer dance three or four years ago. There she had sat with Mr Mosley, and what had he said to her? Something about the heart; that once given, it could not be easily recalled. How true! And yet it must, it *must,* or she did not know how she would go on. She passed through the rose garden and, skirting a shrubbery, she gained Donwell's drive well out of sight of the mansion itself. Only then did she slow her pace; surely, she would not be missed for some time and, if missed, Miss Woodhouse had undertaken to say she had gone home.

Alone, at last alone, Jane gave herself up to the misery that had besieged her for the past few weeks and which had only increased since her last encounter with Frank. She wept aloud, crying copious tears, her body wracked with unhappiness until she could barely stand. The heat was intense; the driveway had few trees and so offered little shade. She had eaten the smallest amount of luncheon and had barely sipped at the lemonade that Mrs Elton had been so presumptuous as to serve, disregarding the housekeeper and numerous servants that Mr Knightley had provided to attend them. The sum of these considerations was that she found herself half sitting, half lying on a patch of grass just inside Donwell's gates. She did not know how long she had lain there. The clatter of hooves brought her to her senses, she heard Frank's voice raised in alarm and within a moment he was raising her up.

'What do you here?' he demanded. 'You are alone, walking, in this heat? It is madness! Who has permitted it?'

He soaked his handkerchief from a flask of water he had attached to his saddle, and wiped her face and neck with it. Then he offered the flask to her lips and she found she was very thirsty.

'There,' he said, removing the bottle, 'not too much. Just a few sips for now, and by-and-by you shall have some more. Can you stand? Let us move into the shade of the hedge. It is not much, but it is something.'

The relative shade, the refreshment of the water and the relief of his aid soon revived Jane and she was restored to full lucidity.

'We must not be seen here together, Frank,' she said, 'it is too dangerous. People will conjecture.'

'You are too sensitive,' he replied. 'I came across you in a swoon; naturally I came to your aid, as I did to Miss Smith's. People would wonder if I did *not*. Why are you walking alone?'

'I came away to escape Mrs Elton,' she said. 'She has found a situation with a family called Smallridge—I must confess, it is very appealing. I never expected so much—but she will not hear my refusal and, to tell the truth, Frank, I am minded to accept the post.'

As she spoke, she moved herself to a respectable distance from him.

'Accept it?' Frank said, perplexed. 'Whatever for?'

'You know what for,' Jane said, as gently as she could. 'It must be at some time, so why not immediately?' She got to her feet and brushed a few loose blades of grass from her skirt, glancing all the while down the drive. 'I may have been followed,' she said. 'We should go our separate ways.'

'Not until I banish this ridiculous notion from your head,' Frank replied, getting to his feet also. 'It does not have to be, at *any* time,' In spite of the shade he looked very hot, the white material of his stock soaked in sweat, the hair on his forehead dark and damp.

'Have you spoken to your aunt, then?' Jane challenged.

Frank's eyes slid away from hers. 'Not yet,' he said.

'And tomorrow is Midsummer's Day.'

'I know it.' He thrashed at a patch of nettles with his crop. 'My aunt … her health … it has not been conducive …'

'And it never will be,' Jane concluded for him. 'If it has not been conducive these eleven months, it never will be.'

'It will! It *will!*' Frank insisted, but the expression in his eye belied his words. 'I cannot work to a day or time. I must wait and choose my moment …'

'I have waited long enough,' Jane said. The coldness of her tone surprised and chilled even her. 'I have waited *too* long. This entire scheme has been a mistake. We should never have entered upon it.' They looked at each other in shared despair until Jane burst out with an excess of emotion that was more awful than the sangfroid of a moment before. 'I have been on a rack, Frank,' she burst out, 'since the moment I agreed to it, my head pulling me one way, my heart another. My conscience is in tatters. I cannot pray. I cannot look my grandmother in the eye. In church I cannot sing the hymns. My mouth opens and closes but no words will come. I have sinned, Frank, in loving you.'

'You have *not*,' he cried, the tears in his eyes mirroring the ones in hers. 'It is impossible for you to sin. You are a saint. You are goodness itself, constitutionally unable to do wrong.' He reached for her hands but she snatched them away from him. 'Loving me is not wrong, Jane. Those who stand between us are the wrong-doers.'

'They should be shown the error of their ways, then.'

'They *should* ...'

'But you will not do it, Frank. You will not show them,' Jane's tone, and her words, were venomous. She had not realised how angry she had been with him. 'And there it is;' she went on, more evenly, 'the flaw, the impediment. It is *you*. I am disappointed in you, Frank. I have lost faith in you.' Speaking the words aloud was torture, but truth. Jane had never allowed herself to think it before, but Frank's weakness was the source of all her insecurity and doubt.

'Me?' Frank cried out, his voice almost breaking. '*You* are the one who is unreasonable. You make such provisions as no one could fulfil. I must tell my aunt, but I must not break with her! I wanted to confront her at once and thrust her inheritance down her throat but *you* would not allow it. You set me a task I was doomed to fail. But be patient, just a little while longer …'

'No,' Jane said. 'If you choose to place the blame on me, so be it. I accept it. I blame myself. You are right; I asked you to do something that could never be achieved. Except that you did tell me that it *could*.'

'And it *can* … in time.'

'I have no more time,' Jane said coldly. She tried to retie the ribbons of her bonnet but found she still had Frank's handkerchief balled in her palm. She held it out to him. Her hand was shaking. 'Thank you, Mr Churchill. I am quite recovered now. I can walk home without difficulty. I bid you good day.'

He took it from her with a shake of the head. 'You are unreasonable today,' he said in a low, wondering voice. 'The heat has unsettled you. It was madness to set out as you did. You are not rational, Jane.'

'I am perfectly rational,' she said, stepping away from him across the grass. 'You should continue to Donwell. You are looked for. Mrs Weston is anxious.'

'It is hardly worth going,' Frank said, nevertheless gathering his horse's reins from where he had thrown them over a fence. 'The party will be breaking up and I must ride back to Richmond.'

'That is for you to decide,' Jane said. 'Good day.'[xxxi]

Chapter Forty-Four

The following morning dawned bright and clear; there was no possibility of the outing to Box Hill being postponed. In due course the Eltons' carriage arrived to ferry Miss Bates and Jane Fairfax thither.

Jane had hardly expected to see Frank Churchill. His trouble the day before in getting away from his aunt, his argument with Jane herself, his heated mood and anger were all decidedly against it. If his heart was as badly wounded as hers, he would not have the stomach for it, surely. *She* had not the power to escape the ordeal—it would cause too many questions to be asked, her health would be scrutinised and even if she could persuade her aunt that she was not equal to it Mrs Elton would brook no denial—but *he* had the means to forgo the expedition if he wished. Jane was as certain as she could be that a messenger would come from Richmond with his excuses.

She was not prepared, therefore, to see him riding alongside Miss Woodhouse's carriage on his black mare. He raised his hat to Miss Fairfax and the others in the Eltons' carriage and said a word or two of apology for his lateness and dark mood the day before. His words were jumbled, however, without his usual erudition. If he directed his remarks to Jane, and tried to evince from her a kind response, he did so in vain. Jane pretended to look in her reticule for something and did not meet his eye.

As much as Mrs Elton might have imposed herself upon the outing it was well understood by all that the day was to be devoted to the entertainment of Miss Woodhouse. This was *her* treat, a real diversion from the usual habits and pursuits of her day. Even so there was a heaviness and want of spirits amongst the entire party. They tended to separate into smaller cohorts, which suited Jane because Mr Knightley, by some instinct, kept herself and her aunt with him, away from both the Eltons and Mr Churchill. Although everyone declared themselves happy, admired the views and had much to say on the generosity and thoughtfulness of Mr Weston's provision, their faces did not reflect their words. With Mr Knightley occupying himself with Jane and Miss Bates it was not surprising that Frank should offer himself as Miss Woodhouse's escort, helping her from the carriage, escorting her up the steeper paths and grassy inclines and sitting beside her on the blanket at the summit. Up to this point he seemed to fail in that level of banter and mischief that had so entertained Miss Woodhouse on previous occasions. He spoke little and it was plain from Miss Woodhouse's expression that she was bored to death. But once Mr Weston had succeeded in gathering the party together for the purpose of enjoying the picnic he had supplied, Frank seemed to rouse himself from his lethargy. Indeed, he was galvanised; from being dull and stupid he became animated, gay, and made Miss Woodhouse his first object. For a man engaged to another his behaviour would have been offensive, but for a man who believed himself free of encumbrance, as he surely now did, his attentions to Miss Woodhouse were unambiguous; he flirted. The lady was all readiness to receive and encourage his advances and it seemed clear to Jane that, overnight, Frank had determined to transfer his affections to a person who was eminently qualified to please his aunt. Miss Woodhouse was rich if she was not titled, she was beautiful enough to satisfy Frank and would be conceited enough to believe that she would be able to out-manoeuvre the interfering aunt before the full malevolence of that woman's character would prove otherwise.

The reckless badinage of Miss Woodhouse and Mr Churchill served to mask the sullenness of the others. Jane was glad to see she was not alone in feeling morose. Whilst Frank's manner and Miss Woodhouse's encouragement of it caused her considerable pain, it appalled Mrs Elton and made Mr Knightley rather angry. Harriet Smith smiled stupidly and Aunt Hetty did her best to talk everyone into a better humour. Only Mr Weston seemed pleased to see the renewal of Frank's attentions to Miss Woodhouse. Such was his delight in it that when an escalation of their thoughtless repartee resulted in a remark both cutting and cruel directed at Miss Bates, he persisted in emboldening them still further while the rest of the party squirmed with awkwardness and embarrassment. Jane herself was almost stung to retaliation. How could Miss Woodhouse be so callous? Her poor aunt faltered under the rebuke, heartily wounded. Jane seethed, but said nothing.

The Eltons stalked away. Frank looked after them, making a withering remark on the slim possibility of any attachment—such as the Eltons'—made after slight acquaintance at a public place resulting in a happy union. 'How many a man has committed himself on a short acquaintance,' he lamented, looking straight at Jane, 'and rued it all the rest of his life.'

Jane felt her throat close with tears; she *must* not cry. She gave a little cough and responded, 'Although such things do sometimes occur *to both men and women,* I cannot imagine them to be very frequent. A *hasty and imprudent* attachment may arise—but there is generally time to recover from it afterwards. I would be understood to mean that it is only *weak and irresolute characters,* whose happiness must always be at the mercy of,' she wished to say 'others' or even 'their relatives' but substituted 'chance' instead, 'who will suffer an unfortunate acquaintance to be an inconvenience, or an oppression forever.'

Surely, he would understand her. She rather wondered that everyone would not. She allowed her eyes to glance around the circle. Miss Smith smiled inanely, all uncomprehending. Miss Woodhouse had still not recovered her composure after insulting Miss Bates. Her aunt Hetty spoke in a low voice to Mr Knightley. Mr Weston seemed not to have heard at all; he was trying to attract the attention of one of the servants. Frank Churchill had understood her, though. He looked, and bowed in submission, and then, turning his back on her spoke some words that cut Jane to the quick. He engaged Miss Woodhouse to find him a wife.

'I shall go abroad for a couple of years,' he said loudly, 'and when I return, I shall come to you for my wife.'

There, Jane thought to herself. It is over.

'Now ma'am,' she said to her aunt in as steady a voice as she could muster, 'shall we join Mrs Elton?

The day that had offered every probability of pleasure and enjoyment ended in misery for more than one of its participants. On the journey homeward Mrs Elton was in high dudgeon.

'The day was ruined, absolutely spoiled by the appalling behaviour of that young woman and that insufferable puppy Frank Churchill,' she declared as their carriage pulled away. 'What a waste of a perfectly good day. I would have been better employed at home going through the linen cupboard. Wait until I tell Selina. She will be outraged. I would not be surprised if she refuses to meet Miss Woodhouse. Mr Weston let things get away from him. I do assure you, had *I* been given supervision of this outing I should not have let things go so far. That young woman needs a sound spanking although there is no hope of Mr Woodhouse laying to. Knightley looked as though he would undertake it, I thought. And if Mr Weston does not thrash his son I shall send you over, Philip, to do it for him. Atrocious! Unspeakable! Well, we must make what we can of the rest of the day. You are to come to us this evening and we shall have some cards and some tea and I shall make sure there is some of that raspberry turnover you like so much, Miss Bates. I shall prevail upon Knightley to join us although when I mentioned it, he said he would not. And dear Mrs Bates, I am sure, after a day spent at Hartfield, will be glad of the relief of *real* hospitality. I shall not invite the others, naturally, the Woodhouses and Westons have disgusted me, but you shall come and we will try to make amends.'

Accordingly, after dinner, the Bates household made their way to the vicarage. Jane's head ached very much. She would rather have stayed home. But now the die was set—or almost set; his words and hers, *between themselves,* could hardly be misconstrued—there was no reason why she should not know more about the situation Mrs Elton had procured. It made her heart heavy to contemplate the end of all her hopes, and the hopelessness of *his* future, to be always in the thrall of his aunt, also caused her pain. But what could she do?

Mrs Elton had recovered her spirits entirely and greeted them with smiles and cordiality. Nothing had been left undone that could give consequence to Mrs Bates, who was patronised and fawned over to a sickening degree; shown the rooms that once had been hers, guided round the garden that she had planted with her own hands and even allowed a peek into the study that her dear departed Frederick had occupied in years gone by. Mrs Bates exchanged a knowing look with Jane, full of irony and perspicacity. For all that she was old and frail she had more wit and penetration than the vicar and his wife put together, Jane thought. I shall miss her, when I go to Bristol—*if* I go to Bristol—I shall miss my grandmamma very much.

Mrs Elton's object in inviting Miss and Mrs Bates soon became clear. She began to regale them with the delights and privileges that would accrue to Jane if she were to accept Mrs Smallridge's offer; not another nursery establishment of such superiority to be found anywhere saving Maple Grove itself; a style of living almost equal to Maple Grove; elegant, sweet children; Jane would be treated with kindness and regard—her life would be one of unalloyed pleasure. Mrs Bates and Miss Bates listened in astonishment until Jane interrupted with her usual proviso; she was grateful, but she would settle nothing until she had spoken with the Campbells. She spoke, though, with less decidedness than formerly. She heard the doubt in her own voice and a fleeting glance exchanged between her aunt and grandmamma showed that they heard it too.

If Jane still hesitated on the cusp of indecision the next few moments ended it. A knock on the door as tea was served called Mr Elton from the room for a short time. Always eager to be party to her husband's business, especially if it related to the private affairs of his parishioners,

Mrs Elton made close enquiry of him when he came back into the room.

'Just John Abdy,' he reported, 'come to see about parish relief for his father.'

'Oh,' chimed Miss Bates, 'old John Abdy is an excellent man. He was my father's clerk, you know, for twenty-seven years, all the time that my father ministered here in Highbury. And when Papa died, he was instrumental in assisting us, was he not, Mama?'

Mrs Bates nodded. For an instant she looked like she might say a word or two on the subject, but she pursed her lips together and shook her head.

'Well, I must say it is not a very convenient time for Mr Abdy to be disturbing us,' Mrs Elton said with a sniff. 'Does he not know that respectable people take tea at this hour?'

'Papa used to say his door was always open, at any hour,' Miss Bates remarked, perhaps unwisely, 'and I believe Mr Paling had something of the same policy.'

'Well, *we* shall not,' Mrs Elton said sharply. 'We are not at the beck and call of our parishioners, are we Philip?'

'Well ...' Mr Elton prevaricated, 'in this case I make an exception. John's duties at the Crown prevented him coming earlier. There was word from Randalls. The chaise was sent for. Mr Churchill is to return to Richmond this evening, it seems. His horse was too fagged to take him back tonight, after the outing today, and so John had to put the horses to. It is late, to be sure ...'

'But that young man cares nothing for anyone else's inconvenience,' Mrs Elton concluded. 'I do not know why he could not wait until the morning. Had there been a message from the aunt?'

'From the uncle, yes,' Mr Elton said. 'A message assuring him that all was well, his aunt's health tolerably good, but asking him to be home promptly tomorrow. But Mr Churchill wished to be away tonight; he saw no cause to delay. He had his own reasons, perhaps.'

'Perhaps,' said Jane, quietly.

She took her tea to the window and looked out upon the gloaming as it stole upon the vicarage garden. So that was it. He would not call on her tomorrow. He would not try to win her back. She did not know if she would have accepted him. He had about him that degree of charm and earnestness she found hard to resist. But no. It was better this way.

Presently she said, 'Mrs Elton, I have changed my mind about Mrs Smallridge's offer. I shall accept it.'

Great was the astonishment of Miss Bates and Mrs Bates at this sudden and unprecedented change of heart, and yet they could not but agree that the situation was such that one could not feel oneself justified in declining.

'I shall write to Colonel and Mrs Campbell in the morning, and Rowena also,' Jane said, as they walked through the moonlight back to their home. 'It is the shortest night, tonight. I need not wait many hours until I begin my task; four or five will accomplish it I think before the dawn gives me the light and the clarity I need.'

Mrs Bates pressed her hand and Jane promptly burst into tears.

Chapter Forty-Five

Highbury

June 24th

Dear Colonel and Mrs Campbell

I write to you out of turn to apprise you of a development that will perhaps surprise you as much as it has surprised me. The prospect is one I have long anticipated and is therefore no source of wonder, but its coming now is earlier than looked for. Indeed, I have not looked for it, and yet it has presented itself to me and herein lies its most astonishing feature.

My acquaintance Mrs Elton, wife of the vicar of Highbury, has excellent and respectable connections in Bristol and through them I have been given the opportunity of a position as governess to a family called Smallridge. Mrs Elton speaks highly of the family, and the situation seems to offer all—indeed far more—that one could desire. I will not enumerate the manifold benefits of the family, their home and its environs, the children whose education I am to supervise or the remuneration. Suffice it to say that these are all unexceptionable and that as my aunt and grandmamma see only good in the opportunity and commend me to accept it without delay, I have been guided by them and by my own inclination to do so. We always thought, did we not, that my twenty-first year would be the opportune time? What must be done eventually had better not be delayed.

Mrs Smallridge requires my presence in Bristol within the next fortnight and there is no reason why I cannot oblige her in this. Consequently, my ability to meet you at Bute Square on your return from Ireland is now in doubt.

My dear—parents, I wish to write, for so I have long thought of you both. How can I begin to thank you for your care and affection to me? Since I was eight years of age, I have walked along a velvet-lined path of pleasure and plenty due to your generosity and Christian kindness. No blessings such as the ones you have bestowed on me could have been expected, much less deserved, for a girl situated such as I was when you found me. My consciousness of my shortcomings is acute. Who was I, and what was I, then? Nothing and nobody. But you lifted me from obscurity and showered me with good things I did not merit and still do not merit. Indeed, if you only knew how precipitately I have fallen short of what is due to you, you would disown me, I am sure.

Now I must step from the easy road you have laid before me and begin to earn my bread. I am not afraid and in fact the prospect of passing on in my turn what wisdom, ability and knowledge I have received through your good offices is a pleasing one to me.

Thank you, thank you, from the very bottom of my heart.

I shall write to you from Bristol when I am settled, and enclose in this packet a separate letter for Rowena that I beg you will place into her hands when they are at liberty from tending the precious babe.

I hope to remain

Your very dear

Jane.

Dear Mrs Smallridge

I thank you most cordially for your kindness in offering me the position of governess to your children and am delighted to tell you that I accept.

Mrs Elton speaks highly of your family and your situation. She assures me that you are aware that this will be my first situation; I have, through various acquaintances, had much intercourse with children but I have never had the sole management of them. Nevertheless, I am confident that with your supervision and the co-operation of my charges I shall soon understand and execute my responsibilities as you would wish.

I propose travelling to Bristol on 8th July where I beg you will arrange to have me met and conveyed onwards.

I am, madam, your obedient servant

Jane Fairfax.

Dear Mr Churchill

I write to you to establish beyond any degree of doubt or misunderstanding that the engagement that has existed between us is now terminated. Our conversation at Donwell on 22nd and the unmistakable inference of your remarks at Box Hill on 23rd persuade me that your comprehension of this matter is the same as mine; the engagement has been a source of repentance and misery to each of us and so it is dissolved.

I think it better that we do not meet again, therefore I request you to return by post any of my letters that you have kept.

Jane Fairfax[xxxii]

Chapter Forty-Six

Frank returned to Richmond from Highbury earlier than necessary, very angry with Jane and with himself. That she was unreasonable seemed very apparent to him; she had placed him in an impossible position again and again—with his aunt and amongst the people at Highbury. How was he to confront his aunt with their engagement without risking her displeasure? She *would* be displeased, *seriously* displeased; nothing was more certain. Perhaps he had overstated his ability to win her round—*that* he was reluctantly willing to concede—although he still thought that, in time, he might succeed in doing so. In the meantime, Jane's insistence upon utter secrecy had caused more difficulties than it had solved. What would it have mattered if a few very intimate acquaintances, or indeed a large number of people wholly unconnected with either of them, should have discerned an attachment between them? So long as the Churchills did not find out, the risk was small. But Jane had been adamant; nobody, *nobody* must construe the truth. And so, he had come up with the splendid diversionary scheme of making love to Miss Woodhouse. Who would believe a man capable of courting one woman whilst he was engaged to another? It had taken him a very short time to detect that although Miss Woodhouse enjoyed his flirtatious banter, she was not ensnared by it; he gratified her vanity without endangering her heart. In paying attentions to the mistress of Hartfield he had pleased his father and humoured his stepmother. Most importantly it had put every more perspicacious observer off the scent. But Jane was jealous; she did not like to see him paying court to another even if it was a façade. And she had feared for Miss Woodhouse. Ridiculous! When Miss Woodhouse had never cared a fig for her.

But then, he supposed, he would not have liked to watch Jane courted—toyed with—by another. Look how jealous he had been when he had seen her with Mr Mosley in Weymouth. No, he supposed it could not have been easy for Jane. Her care for Miss Woodhouse was only part and parcel of her care for everyone. Was that not what he most loved about her? Her generous heart? Her disinterested soul? Her desire to put everyone's happiness before her own? The truth was that Jane was day to Mrs Churchill's night, light to her dark, the antidote to her poison. The worse his aunt behaved, the more splendid and desirable did Jane become.

It did not take Frank the duration of his journey to Richmond, or even half of it, to persuade himself that he was still very much in love with Jane Fairfax and that his determination to make her his wife had not diminished. Nevertheless, he bridled. Her words on Box Hill had stung him deeply; she had called him weak and irresolute. *That* would take some time for him to forgive. He *would* forgive it, however, as soon as ever she wrote to him.

The next day but one[xxxiii] he found her letter on his breakfast tray. It was thin, one sheet of paper only, and as he opened it, he could see that the lines were few. It did not matter. Three words, 'I am sorry,' would have sufficed. The words he read astonished and panicked him. He leapt from the bed disturbing his breakfast and spilling tea. It was insupportable! Impossible! It could not be over. Life without Jane was unthinkable. She referred particularly to their quarrel at Donwell and his behaviour at Box Hill. Of course, of *course* she was right about everything, He *had* been weak and irresolute; their argument had been all of his making; because he had been hot and cross with his aunt, he had been insufficiently compassionate at what *she* endured. How could he have spoken to her as he did? And at Box Hill—his heart quailed. He was ashamed to think of his behaviour. He had been neglectful and insolent. No woman of sense could have endured it. He was a dog who did not deserve her.

He was resolved. He washed and dressed and went in search of his aunt.

He found her in a sunny sitting room that overlooked the gardens. She, too, had breakfasted on a tray but she had not breakfasted well; her toast lay untouched and her tea was but half drunk. The years had not been kind to Mrs Churchill. Great beauty she had never possessed although she had made up for the lack with a great deal of air, elegance in dress and a scornful manner that dared anyone to call her ugly. But now, in the harsh, bright light of morning, in her dressing wrap, her hair still untended, it was hard to see anything other than a bitter, self-absorbed old woman with a sharp nose, a cruel mouth and eyes that looked disappointment and daggers at everything she saw.

'Good morning, Aunt,' said Frank, bending to kiss her cheek. 'I hope you slept well. I hope you were not too much troubled in the night?'

'I was very much troubled,' Mrs Churchill complained, 'but I am the last to bore others with my complaints.'

'Sir Lester seems to think that your symptoms, while distressing, do not bode ill. He was sanguine, I thought, when he was here last.'

'You do not know the half of what he says,' Mrs Churchill replied. 'Ring the bell and have these things cleared, will you? It makes me sick to look at them.'

Frank did as he was bidden and when the maid had gone, he was careful to close the door behind her.

'My uncle has gone into town?'

'Yes. He meets some acquaintance at his club. Come and sit beside me and keep me company. You will not desert me, Frank?'

'Not today,' Frank replied, taking his seat and lifting his aunt's hand to his lips. How thin her hand was in his, so bony and claw-like. Jane's hands were very soft, he recalled, and always warm.

'You do not return to Highbury?' Mrs Churchill asked, in a carking tone.

'My plans are not fixed. I *may* do at some point in the near future. I am welcome at any time. But I have no absolute engagement.'

'Mrs Weston is close to her confinement?' It sounded as though the enquiry were dragged from her; she really had no interest in Mrs Weston.

'Yes. It wants a month, or less, I believe.'

'Hmmm.' Mrs Churchill closed her eyes. 'When they have their own child, they will not require you so frequently perhaps. You will be usurped. When a woman has her own son, she does not care for another woman's child.'

Frank took a deep breath; how shallow she thought the Westons, how little she supposed they cared for him. He summoned patience and said, 'I do not quite agree with you, Aunt. I cannot believe that if you and my uncle had been so fortunate as to have children later in life, *I* would have been any the poorer.'

'The poorer?' She turned sharply to face him. 'Indeed, you *would* have been poorer. *My* son would have had all that now falls into your lap.'

Frank felt as though he had been slapped, but he swallowed hard and said, 'I chose my words unwisely, Aunt. I was not referring to material gain. I meant, I suppose, that even if you had your own child to love, you would still have loved me.'

'I see,' she said, looking hard at him. 'Is that what you meant? Pull the blind, will you? The sun hurts my eyes.'

Frank adjusted the shades and, rather than regaining his seat, took a turn or two around the room. 'Yes,' he said at last, puzzled and more than a little hurt that she had not offered the assurance he had sought. 'You know, Aunt, a person likes to be loved for who, not what, they are.'

'I do not understand you,' his aunt intoned.

'No,' Frank replied quietly. She had no comprehension of love. How was he to make her understand? He ploughed on. 'I am my uncle's sister's child. That is *what* I am, and in the absence of your own children you made me your heir. But *who* I am is something quite different. I am Frank. I hope I would be loved because of that, regardless of any other children you may have been blessed with.'

That is how Jane loves me, he thought. She has no care for my wealth or position. She loves me for myself. He was getting closer to the point and it aided him to keep Jane in the forefront of his mind.

Mrs Churchill was silent for a while. Frank almost held his breath. If he could wring from her a confession that she did love him unconditionally, it might be something. But she shook her head.

'It is nonsense to speak like that,' she snapped. 'I have no other children. You are all I have and, I may say, I am all that you have. We must make do.'

'No, Aunt,' Frank burst out. Her coldness, her obtuseness was disgusting. 'In point of fact, there is another.'

'Your father?' Mrs Churchill turned her head to look at him, her expression sneering and cruel. 'Oh! I have told you. *He* will throw you off when he has his own child.'

'I do not believe he will,' Frank replied hotly and with more confidence than he felt. Mr Weston might well disown him when he found out the truth about his secret engagement. But no, his father had proved his faithfulness in the past. Shock and hurt there would be, and in considerable measure, but he would not renounce him. 'And Mrs Weston has shown such kindness to me. She is gentle and good and cares a great deal. She is the kind of mother …' he stopped abruptly. He must not be cruel.

'She is nothing like your *real* mother, then,' Mrs Churchill spat. '*She* thought only of herself. But Mrs Weston sounds like a perfect ninny, a milksop of a woman. Weston finds her easier to handle than Louisa, I'll be bound.'

'I have never heard him compare them,' Frank said. 'That would be ungentlemanly. But you mistook me, Aunt, when I spoke of another. I did not mean Mr or Mrs Weston.'

'Oh?' She turned a withering gaze upon him.

Frank quailed. He found his hands were trembling and he clasped them behind his back. Now he had come to it. He had gone too far to turn back now. 'Yes,' he said, as firmly as possible.

'I hope you are not going to disappoint me, Frank,' his aunt said, picking up her reticule and bringing out a handkerchief and a small vial. 'Do not make me ill, Frank.' She fiddled with the cap of the little bottle. 'Oh, I feel a strangeness coming upon me. How you heap troubles on my poor head. Go away, Frank. You are cruel and vicious. Look how ill I am! Can you not see how you wound me?' Indeed, she did look very pale. Her eyelids fluttered and Frank feared she would faint.

He squatted at her side and took her hands. They were cold and, he was surprised to find, they, too, were trembling. 'I do not wish to disappoint you, Aunt. I never wish to be the cause of trouble to you. But I must own the truth to you; I am in love and I wish to marry.'

'In love?' Mrs Churchill screeched, at a volume and with a power that belied her apparent frailty. 'What nonsense! You will not marry for love. You will marry for position and title and power. I will not have you throw yourself away on a love match.'

'I cannot choose who I love,' Frank remonstrated.

'No, perhaps not, and neither can you choose whom you marry. *I* shall choose.'

'Forgive me, Aunt, but you will not,' said Frank gently. 'I mean no disrespect, indeed I do not, but on *this* I must insist on having my own way.'

'On this? On *this?*' Mrs Churchill roared. She got to her feet with astonishing energy, her handkerchief and *sal volatile* falling forgotten to the floor. Frank was toppled from where he crouched and found himself akimbo on the rug. 'Everything that has been done since you came to us a snivelling wretch, has been to suit you,' Mrs Churchill shrieked, looking down at him with ire. 'What sacrifices I have made! I cannot even begin to enumerate them. And this is how you repay me? Oh,' she clutched her chest, 'you will kill me, Frank, with your ingratitude.' She stumbled a little and seized at the arm of the chair.

'I hope not, indeed,' said Frank, getting to his feet and standing to face her. He reached his hand to her shoulder. 'I pray you would be seated, and let us talk reasonably.'

'You are a stranger to reason,' she replied, straightening with a snap and marching across the room with energy. 'How can I be reasonable when you are so cruel?'

'I do not mean to be cruel,' Frank stated. 'Only, I must be truthful.'

Mrs Churchill found herself in that part of the room where a glazed cabinet stood, displaying nick-nacks and curios. In a fury she wrenched open the doors and began raking her hands amongst the china and porcelain, dashing many items to the floor and cutting her skin on the broken fragments of the rest.

'Aunt! Aunt Churchill!' Frank cried, running to restrain her. 'You must not! Indeed, you must calm yourself. Oh, you have made yourself bleed. Come, come, let me staunch the flow.'

'Get away from me,' his aunt screamed, hurling figurines at him. 'Do I frighten you, Frank? I hope I do. I hope I terrify you into obedience. I will teach you to flout my will.'

The door of the room opened a crack and the petrified face of the maid peeped through. Frank waved her away and she withdrew.

'No, Aunt,' he said, finding that it was true; he was not afraid, he felt only pity. 'I am not frightened of you. And as a grown man I think I can be my own master. I owe you duty, but, on this matter, not obedience. I feel sorry for you.'

A look of calculation crossed Mrs Churchill's face. She will throw herself to the floor, Frank thought, she is conjuring a fit. But, in fact, what Mrs Churchill did next was more shocking because it was unexpected. Her body went limp and she crumpled, like an empty sack, to her knees. Her shoulders sagged as though weighted by boulders. She put her head in her hands and began to cry. Blood from her cut knuckles, mingled with tears, dripped down her hands and began to soak the sleeves of her robe. Frank was dismayed, perplexed and rather embarrassed but quickly perceived this development to be in direct correlation to his previous statement. She had decided that if anger would not subdue him then pathos might.

'Oh! Oh! You are cruel,' she sobbed. 'Look at me! Look what a thing you have reduced me to.'

'I am being truthful,' he repeated, gently but with adamantine firmness. 'Can we not discuss this together Aunt? It may not be as bad as you fear.'

'Unless you have engaged yourself to a viscountess, at the very least, it could not be worse,' Mrs Churchill gulped out. 'You will tear my heart out with your unkindness.' A beady eye peeped from between her gnarled fingers to assess the effect of her tirade.

Frank allowed himself a little smile. Her histrionics were a façade, he thought, as he had always suspected. The woman was as strong as an ox, as calculating as a snake.

He drew himself up. 'I have the honour to be engaged to Miss Jane Fairfax,' he said.

Mrs Churchill scrambled to her feet, her tears forgotten. 'What?' she spat out. 'That chit? That *nobody?* She is without family or fortune, she has no name, no connections, nothing whatever to recommend her beyond a tolerably pretty face.'

'Be careful, Aunt,' Frank said in a voice that trembled with anger.

'Oh, Frank how could you have been so taken in?' Mrs Churchill came and stood before him. Her tantrum and her tears were both forgotten. Now she was only adamant and angry and looking for a door at which to lay the blame. 'She has ensnared you. A confederacy, I surmise, between those dreadful people at Highbury. Your father has engineered it, no doubt, to spite me, in league with her impecunious relatives. No! No! I will not permit it Frank.' She looked up at him, all fire and energy and resolve. 'I suppose the Campbells purposed it from the beginning. I distrusted them in Weymouth.'

This time Frank laughed aloud. The woman was ridiculous. 'You cannot have it both ways, Aunt. *Either* the Westons *or* the Campbells. So far as I know the two have never met one another. They cannot very well have plotted and contrived as perfect strangers! As it happens, neither party has the least suspicion of our engagement. *You* are the first to receive the happy news.'

'Cynical, ungrateful boy!' she scorned, her eyes narrow with spite. 'It will not be happy when you are living in poverty. I shall disown you. I will cut you off without a shilling. How will you like that? How will *she?*'

'I shall not like it,' Frank admitted. 'Not because we shall have no money, but because it will pain me to be divided from you. As for Miss Fairfax, she cares nothing for money. But perhaps my uncle will be of a different opinion. Where you are inflexible, I think he will be indulgent. After all, *he* married for love.' He gave her a straight look. Whatever riposte she had been preparing died on her lips. Her mouth flapped uselessly. His point was unanswerable. I have done it, he thought, I have bested her at last. He felt no triumph in it, only sadness, that she should have made it necessary. He should have confided in his uncle in the beginning, he realised. He had put Jane through torment for nothing. 'I think,' he said coolly, 'if you will excuse me, Aunt, I may ride to town to speak to him. I shall find him at his club.'

Mrs Churchill threw herself onto the floor and began to writhe and thrash. Her eyes rolled in her head, she drooled foam and spittle. Frank looked down at her for a while, detached and unmoved. He had seen this before; it was nothing, a charade. Like the swoon, like the violence, like the tears, it was specious, manufactured to deter him from his object. But he would not be deterred. He would write to Jane first and tell her that the deed was done, and then he would saddle his horse and follow his uncle to town. He left Mrs Churchill where she lay, rigid and pale, noting that she had managed to fall on a convenient rug. He left the room and closed the door softly behind him.

'Mrs Churchill is resting,' he told a servant who loitered in the hallway. 'She does not wish to be disturbed.'

He returned to his room and wrote his letter. It took him some time and several drafts; he could not express with sufficient humility and passion his remorse for the way he had behaved, his continuing and increased love and respect for her, his relief at having told Mrs Churchill the truth. At last, he had got the lines into a semblance that he felt would appease and soften her when a knock at the door caused him to lift his head.

The maid, very white, with a voice that shook, said, 'Excuse me, Mr Churchill, sir, but you had better come. The mistress ... I fear ... but you had better come.'

Chapter Forty-Seven

It was earnestly to be hoped that the final severance of ties between Miss Fairfax and Frank Churchill, the end of despicable secrecy and the consequent removal of the burden of shame would have a beneficial impact on the lady's health and mood, but it was not the case. She suffered still, she suffered greatly; the following ten days deluged her in a misery unequalled by anything that had gone before. *Then* she had acted contrary to all her sense of right and felt the punishment for her misconduct to be only justified. But her pain at doing the right thing *now* was unexpected and doubly cruel.

Her heart was broken—crushed and damaged almost beyond her ability to endure. Frank's love had been the sole possession of her life that was not to be shared with even the most deserving friend. It was to have been in a permanent fixture, a treasured belonging that need never be given up. His love had been disinterested, undemanding, such a relief after the sometimes oppressive neediness of Rowena. He had recognised and applauded her independence of spirit. How glorious and inspiring had all this been to her! But it was lost. Of course, he had his failings—a character that was too easy, a reckless streak that courted danger—but these had been the perfect counterbalance to *her* reserve and caution. His defection removed the balance she felt he had provided and she felt bereft and out of kilter, a sensation that was, at times, quite physical; more than once did she stumble and almost fall.

His love was not hers to cherish and she missed it; he loved her no longer. It was a cruel truth to endure.

Her opportunity at Mrs Smallridge's establishment should have provided some comfort. There was no denying that it was indeed a superior situation. But because she had not found it herself, because it was Mrs Elton's recommendation that had secured it rather than her own qualities and because it had come upon her unexpectedly, unlooked for and, truthfully, undesired, Jane did not embrace it. It was one thing to go in search of a situation, to apply for it and be successful, at a time of one's own choosing. It was quite another to be manoeuvred into it and as Jane prepared her things, she found that resentment, and not gratitude, predominated.

How bravely she had spoken, in the past, of taking this step. How she had set her mind to it and even relished it. With what specious calmness she had contemplated it. Such self-deceit and blindness! She despised herself.

And Oh! How Mrs Elton crowed with insufferable complaisance, and congratulated herself on her cleverness; there were times when Jane had to restrain her own hand for fear she would slap the smugness from Mrs Elton's face. And how her aunt fluttered and fussed, like a fly caught against a window, and said again and again how glad they were that dear Jane was to be settled, that an opportunity such as this could not have been looked for and what a boon it was, while all the while dabbing her eyes and showing with every gesture that she doubted the wisdom of it very much. And how many interminable visits would she have to endure, with a rictus smile upon her face, while Mrs Cole and Mrs Perry and every other person in Highbury told her what a wonderful thing it was, while her head ached and ached, her eyes burned, her heart dissolved and all she wanted to do was cry, and lie down, and die. But suffer it she did, to the last vestige of her strength. It was only Miss Woodhouse could she not countenance; Miss Woodhouse, who called and invited and offered her carriage, who sent arrowroot and other delicacies that it would have sickened Jane to touch. Insufferable, gloating, triumphant Miss Woodhouse, who smiled at the prospect of Miss Fairfax so reduced, and who would marry Frank Churchill in her stead. No. No, it could not be borne.

No one in Highbury knew what Jane had lost. How could they know her grief, her shame or her disappointment? But she felt the weight of what they did not know with an acuteness that bore her down. She stayed indoors until she thought she would go mad, and then went out into the countryside where she could bawl and cry without fear of witness. Often and often did she go to the little copse where she and Frank had trysted, but the stones and trees offered no comfort.

Then, when it seemed that wretchedness could not be more acute, or despair more crushing, news was received of Mrs Churchill's death. The intelligence, as unexpected as it was cruel and untimely, undid Jane. Naturally she could not explain it, and the deterioration in a condition already giving serious cause for concern was marked. She sank under it alone and, without a creature to confide in, she sank deeply indeed.

'I think Mrs Smallridge must be written to,' Miss Bates whispered to her mother. 'I do not know how it is, but Jane grows worse and worse. She cannot travel to Bristol in this state. She cannot possibly embark on her duties. She is very ill, Mama. Her condition reminds me—oh but it is painful to recall, and painful to make the comparison—but does not her condition remind you of her dear mama, *our* Jane, when she returned from abroad? Was *she* not brought low in just this same way? Were not *her* spirits similarly depressed? I am anxious, Mama, extremely anxious, as I am sure you are. Mr Perry shall be called. We shall not think of the expense.'

Mrs Bates nodded sagely, and Mr Perry was summoned, but no diagnosis could he pronounce, no assurance and no remedy. Miss Fairfax was ill. Yes, she was very ill indeed.

One afternoon Jane rose up from her bed where she had lain listless and inert for most of the day. A tray by her bed contained temptations to the appetite that she knew her aunt could scarcely afford; it was untouched. Every so often during the course of the day her door had been opened a crack and an anxious head had peered in, but Jane had feigned sleep.

Now she drew out from beneath her bed a small velvet bag, and shook its contents onto her coverlet. Frank's letters, carefully preserved, often read over. She wrapped them in some brown paper and appended a note.

Highbury

5ᵗʰ July

Dear Mr Churchill

I offer you my sincere condolences on the death of your aunt.

I must say that I have been extremely surprised at not having had the smallest reply to my last letter. Silence on such a point cannot be misconstrued, however, and as it must be equally desirable to us both to have every subordinate arrangement concluded as soon as possible I now send you, by safe conveyance, all your letters. I request you to send mine to Highbury within the next week, or if you cannot immediately command them, to send them as soon as possible to me c/o Mrs Smallridge, Little Bower, Bristol.

Jane Fairfax

Chapter Forty-Eight

Frank, in his turn, had had much to bear. Of course, it was not nearly so much as Jane, but for a man such as him, it was good deal. His aunt's death had been shocking and terrible, and not the less because in his secret heart he suspected that he had caused it. The doctor might pronounce that the seizure had been sudden, and of a different nature from anything foreboded by her general state, but Frank recalled the awful episode in the sunny sitting room and quailed. It was sobering indeed, especially to a man not given to temperate, solemn contemplation. Perhaps in *that* period he experienced something of what Jane had endured for months past; terrible guilt, a conviction of wrong-doing, a feeling that serious and long-term consequences could ensue. He waited with a sense of impending doom for one of the Richmond servants to mention the raised voices, the sound of breaking china and the general disorder of the room following Frank's interview with his aunt, but they remained silent.

Once his uncle had been found and brought back from town Frank had little liberty to ponder it, and this was a relief as he disliked facing disagreeable facts and avoided doing so whenever he could. There were many letters to be written, logistical arrangements to be made and his uncle to support as best he may. But in the time he did have to go over it in his mind, with a great effort of concentration and truthful acknowledgement of his own culpability, Frank came to the clearheaded conviction that *this* was a secret that must be preserved always. His uncle, Jane, his father, no one at all must ever suspect what Frank knew in his heart to be true. There was a certain justice about it, he thought; it was no more than he deserved. He who had wantonly kept secrets, who had delighted in subterfuge, now had a real and pressing burden of knowledge that would dog him until his dying day.

Mr Churchill was saddened by his wife's demise, and took himself to task for deserting her in her hour of need. Death, especially one that is unlooked for, has the tendency of smoothing out any little imperfections of the departed in the memories of those left behind, and so it proved here. Mrs Churchill, who had been a spiteful, selfish and censorious harridan in life, was remembered in death as being so long-suffering and admirable that it is doubtful that she would have recognised herself in the eulogy delivered at her funeral. All was done for Mrs Churchill that could be done; a service with full rites, eight black be-plumed horses, a cohort of sober attendants and as many mourners as could be press-ganged to be present by heart-felt appeal or the promise of a superior buffet of funeral meats. Only once all this had been achieved did her cortège depart on the long journey to the family mausoleum. Mr Churchill and his nephew had observed deepest mourning and spoken in respectful and even loving terms of the dead until it was over. Then they gathered themselves, closed up the house and removed with relatively cheerful hearts to Windsor, where an old friend of Mr Churchill's, very dear to *him* but perennially disliked by Mrs Churchill, had long been urging him to come and look over his collection of botanical specimens.

Here it was that Frank received the packet sent by Jane. It surprised him very much. He *had* replied to her letter, hadn't he? For a while he raved at the blunders of the post but then, bethinking himself of the day he had last written to Jane, and the circumstances that had immediately followed, he summoned his writing slope and discovered to his horror that the letter he had written and re-written while his aunt had been in her death throes was still within it. *Then* he raved at his own blunder. He saw Jane's design, saw it immediately and with clarity. He recalled the name of Smallridge—she had mentioned it on the day of the Donwell picnic—and instantly knew what she had been doing. It was thoroughly in accordance with her character and her delicacy that she should have neglected to mention her intention in her previous letter; she would not for the world have seemed to threaten. But here she was on the point of throwing herself away, within a day or so of departing Highbury and believing herself entirely dissevered from him. What must she had thought, when no word in reply to hers had been received? What agonies and disappointment? What anger?

Frank paced around his room, opening at random and re-reading snatches of the love letters he had written to her over the previous months. Here, he had called her an angel. Well, she *was* an angel. Here he had declared himself unable to contemplate life without her by his side—and so he *still* felt. Here, and here, and here again he had promised to speak to his aunt. What a treacherous reprobate he had been, to promise and promise again but do nothing. He must have tried her patience. He knew he had. On the question of Miss Woodhouse he censured himself severely. It had been despicable of him to behave to her as he had done; he was a coxcomb, a scoundrel. But to have done so in Jane's sight and hearing! There could not be another woman in England who would have borne it. What was certain to him was that he could not ride to Highbury—or to Bristol, if necessary; indeed, he would ride to Constantinople if Jane were there—unless he had his uncle's sanction. His uncle must be spoken to, he must be apprised of the whole—*almost* the whole history of their attachment.

He found Mr Churchill in the glass houses that appended his friend's property in Windsor.

'Ah, my boy,' Mr Churchill said genially, when Frank came between the rows of exotics towards him, 'we could have nothing like *this* at Enscombe, I think?'

'No, indeed, sir,' Frank agreed. 'Even if the wind did not continually break the panes of the orangery, the sun does not appear frequently enough to encourage such luxuriance.'

'No,' his uncle nodded sagely. 'But, to be truthful, I am not minded to return to Enscombe with any great alacrity. There are too many memories. The place is austere—there is no gainsaying it. I wished to make improvements but your aunt differed. And now …'

'I am quite of your opinion, sir,' Frank interjected. 'Better to stay away for a long time. In fact, if you do not wish it, we need never return there at all. A tenant could be found, I suppose? *This* is a pleasant area. I am sure we could find a comfortable house with extensive gardens that would be convenient. Then,' he indicated the plants that surrounded them, 'you could begin your own collection.'

'You have no desire to return to Yorkshire, Frank?' Mr Churchill asked, bending over a brightly flowered shrub to examine it more closely.

'No indeed, sir, and, to tell the truth, I have pressing reason *not* to do so.' Frank hesitated fidgeting, while his uncle withdrew a small notebook from his pocket and laboriously wrote down the name of the plant.

'Mmm? Oh?' Mr Churchill said at last.

'No, sir. I had not intended broaching this subject with you. It is too precipitate, even indelicate, given the circumstances. But intelligence has come to light that means that I cannot delay it.'

'Well then,' Mr Churchill said, straightening up and putting his book away. 'Let us sit together on that seat between the *ananas comosus* and the *hippobroma longiflora* and you can tell me what is on your mind.'

The story was long in the telling and at the end of it Mr Churchill pondered deeply before saying, 'And you really love Miss Fairfax?'

'Oh yes, sir,' Frank burst out, 'more than I can properly articulate.'

Mr Churchill nodded. 'So it is, with love. I have always wanted you to marry for love, Frank, so I am satisfied. I would not have had you hurry into it, however.'

'I do not think anyone could accuse me of that,' Frank said.

'No, but from what I understand that has been more due to Miss Fairfax's caution than to yours.'

'She … we both …' Frank began, but Mr Churchill held up his hand.

'I fully comprehend the impediments that seemed to stand between you,' he said. 'They would *not* have done, if you had come to *me*. On that score I cannot commend your behaviour. A covert engagement, be it never so secret and confidential, can be ruinous to a lady's reputation, just as much as one that is publicly known but that fails to culminate in matrimony. These things have a habit of escaping into the public domain. Your mother's experience should have taught you that much.'

'My mother's experience?'

'Oh, but I am forgetting, you were not fully informed about it. Your aunt's doing. She meant well, no doubt, but *I* am all for openness.'

'As shall I be, from now on,' Frank averred, pressing to the back of his mind the truth about his aunt. He was curious to know to what his uncle referred, and determined to quiz his father about it one day soon. But not *too* soon. Frank had no leg to stand on when it came to the topic of secrets.

'As to Miss Fairfax,' Mr Churchill continued, 'I liked her very much when I met her in Weymouth. I was predisposed to do so because I had liked her mother. She is everything I would wish for in a daughter. I wish you joy, Frank.'

'I fear sir, that manifold as her qualities are, she has no … that is to say, she *brings* no …'

'Yes.' His uncle nodded.

'The family is unobjectionable. Her father was a gentleman. Her grandmother and aunt are gentlewomen but in reduced circumstances.'

'That is of no consequence, Frank,' Mr Churchill waved an impatient hand. 'You must impress that upon Miss Fairfax. It could not matter less.'

'You are all generosity, sir. And with that in mind I ask leave to ride to Highbury immediately. For all I know Miss Fairfax is already gone from there. But I can ride faster than a messenger and I have pressing reason to seek a personal interview. May I tell her that we have your blessing?'

Mr Churchill stood up. It seemed to Frank that his uncle had never seemed kinder or wiser than he did then, or more the friend he should have turned to in the beginning.

'You may, my boy,' Mr Churchill replied. 'Give Miss Fairfax my kindest duty, remember me to her fondly. I wish that you may find at least as much happiness in the married state as I did, or,' with a flicker of the eyelid that might have been a wink, 'even more. Here.' He withdrew from his smallest finger a gold ring with an emerald embedded within it. 'Give her this as a token of my blessing. It shall serve until your aunt's jewels can be retrieved from the vault. Then Miss Fairfax will have something more fitting.'

Frank thanked his uncle most heartily, and with a tear in his eye.

Then Mr Churchill said, 'Go now, and secure the lady.'

Chapter Forty-Nine

Frank rode towards Highbury with hope and fear in his heart—but more of hope, since he was sanguine by character and trusted that, beneath Jane's anger and pain, he would find a sufficient residue of love remained that he would take pleasure in reviving.

The Bateses had just finished dining when he was announced. Patty cleared the dishes in a fluster while Miss Bates helped her mother to her usual fire-side chair, removed some mending from another seat and bade Mr Churchill sit down in it, all the while speaking a torrent of words that would barely have been intelligible to a man more rational in his mind than Frank was at that moment. Where was Jane?

'Oh Mr Churchill! Such an honour as we did not expect! How are you sir?' (Not giving him time to reply), 'but I had not understood that you were expected in Highbury. Is Mrs Weston quite well? Mother and I have received no intelligence from Randalls. Perhaps you are more forward in the news. Although Mrs Perry did promise to inform us if Mr Perry was called for. How disappointing the weather has been of late! I declare our trip to Box Hill was quite the zenith of the summer. Hardly a dry day since! The farmers despair of their harvest; the crops quite sodden. Abbey Mill was almost flooded at one point, the water quite within an inch of the door, Mrs Hopley tells me. Highbury has been very quiet since you were last here. Mrs Elton pondered the idea of a garden party for some time. The vicarage garden *is* delightful. She hoped it would induce the Sucklings to come. It did not, however, and the idea was abandoned. Mr Knightley has been away. He went to visit his brother in London. Such a charming family, the John Knightleys. I believe I was amongst the first to know of their engagement, you know. I recall the day very clearly. We were at the vicarage *then,* although, of course, in those days Mr Paling ministered. It was before Mr Elton came amongst us. You have been to Hartfield, I suppose? Miss Woodhouse has been *most* attentive to us, I must say. We are so blessed in our neighbours. Nothing too much trouble! Everything put at our disposal! Dear Jane …'

'How is Miss Fairfax?' Frank interrupted desperately. 'I heard, that is, I was informed that she is to go away?'

'Oh yes. Such a situation as one could not have hoped for. All Mrs Elton's doing. A Mrs Smallridge in Bristol. So now …'

'Now?' Frank urged. Would the woman *ever* say *anything* to the purpose?

'Now, well, let me see. It would be wrong to say that the scheme is abandoned.'

'She has not gone, however?' Frank almost shouted. 'Forgive me, Miss Bates, but please let me understand correctly. Has Miss Fairfax gone to Bristol?'

'Oh no,' Miss Bates replied, 'she is too unwell. *She* would have gone tomorrow, as arranged, but mother and I would not allow it. Mr Perry was of our opinion; Jane is unequal to such an undertaking, at present. I wrote to Mrs Smallridge myself. Even that was beyond Jane's capability.'

'Ah,' Frank sat back in his seat and took his handkerchief from his pocket to mop his brow. 'She remains here, then.'

'Oh yes, Mr Churchill, she remains here. This is her home, you know.'

'Of course,' Frank said, swallowing hard, 'and, if I may enquire, Miss Bates, where is Miss Fairfax *at this moment?* I would ask the honour of a few moments' private conversation with her.'

'Oh,' said Miss Bates, 'well. I do not know. That is, of course, I *do* know where she is. But I do not know if it would be proper to allow you to see her. She is ill. Perhaps I have not been clear. She is unwell, Mr Churchill.'

'Hetty.' A low voice issued from the chair occupied by Mrs Bates. 'Let Mr Churchill see Jane.'

'Mother!' said Miss Bates, leaping to her feet. She lifted her gaze to the door of Jane's bedchamber. 'Do you think it quite proper?'

Mrs Bates nodded, but spoke no more.

'Oh,' Miss Bates hesitated, 'perhaps I should just go in and see if she is awake.'

At that moment Jane's bedroom door opened with a creak and Jane herself appeared in the gap. She wore a nightdress loosely covered with a wrap, her hair was undressed and fell around her shoulders, her face was very pale. Her feet were bare, very small and white on the floorboards. It was this last circumstance that seemed to discompose Mr Churchill the most. He stood, blushing and gulping and mashing his hat in his hands, and stared at them very hard.

'Miss Fairfax,' he choked out, very agitatedly, 'oh, Miss Fairfax.'

Jane held out her hand to him. 'Come in, Frank,' she said.

What transpires in a lady's bedroom should never be the subject of general conjecture, let alone description. Only the dullest mind, however, would not ponder the interview that took place that July afternoon between Jane Fairfax and Mr Frank Churchill.

That the gentleman was aghast beyond his ability to articulate at the altered looks, thinness and debility of the lady is unarguable, and much can we assume he railed at himself for so reducing her. Often and often would he have clasped her fleshless hands and stroked the tumbling hair from her careworn face, and ardently would he have importuned her to forgive him. He may have wept; what man with even half such a heart as he possessed could have refrained? Whether he allowed his tears to fall or not it is inconceivable that she should not have read in his appalled expression, and heard in his words, the abject shame and remorse that finding her in such a state had provoked in his heart.

The malign effect of too much heat; the frustration of a nine-mile ride; veiled remarks and cutting reposts made in the pique of jealously when plain conversation is impossible; letters written but not sent; the interference of others both well-meaning and malevolent. All these might have had their passing share of the conversation, but after all they were but distractions from the principle matter. *He* was constant, his love undiminished, his desire and determination to make her his wife more fixed than ever, if only she could bring herself to forgive him.

And what about the lady? After the days of torture she had endured, the misery of believing that he was lost to her forever, that life, from then on, must be a weary drudge through loveless days, what reversal, what resurgence of hope his coming must have stirred! Here was the cure to all her ills. The heart that had been wrenched from her was hers once more. Anger and pain she undoubtedly felt and other women may have withheld for a time that forgiveness that *she* was all too ready to grant. One scruple only would she have had, and on that question the uncle's ring, brought forth from an inner pocket and placed on her wasted hand, would have been sufficient assurance.

Hearts re-opened, fears assuaged and love renewed. Forgiveness begged and received. Assurances made, obstacles removed. All these we can be sure of. An hour later Mr Churchill emerged from Miss Fairfax's bedchamber, his habitual smile playing about his mouth. He bowed low to the two ladies anxiously waiting without.

'I must go to Randalls,' he said. 'Not a moment must delay me, but I go there, I assure you, a happier man than I was when I came *here*. Miss Fairfax will explain it to you better than I can. She is better now. I think you will find her much improved. I find her so, even after only this short time. In her health, I mean. In herself, I find she is not to be improved upon by any measure you might name. She is perfect. Good day, ladies.'

He swept from the room and the women looked at each other. Much confusion there was on one side if there was quiet satisfaction on the other.

'Oh Mother!' Miss Bates burst out. 'What can have occurred? Can you guess? I cannot fathom it at all. We must ask Jane, I suppose. Shall I go in? Will you accompany me? I confess I almost fear to see what we shall find. He *said* she was better. But I doubt. It seems improbable that Mr

Churchill can achieve what was beyond Mr Perry's powers and the efficacy of your prayers, not to mention mine. Perhaps we should have tea. I did not throw this morning's leaves away. We could see what can be wrung from them. Jane shall have fresh, of course. Oh Mother. I am all of a dither! I am sure something has occurred, but I cannot think what.'

Mrs Bates raised a wry eyebrow that said as clearly as any words, 'Can you not?'

Chapter Fifty

Frank rode directly to Randalls and an awkward interview did he have there with his father and stepmother before hurrying back to Windsor. He did not wish to leave his uncle for many hours and he did not know when he would be able to return, but he promised a letter in due course that would supplement the sketchy but unequivocal information he had provided to them; he was engaged to be married to Miss Jane Fairfax and *had* been since the previous autumn.

Much dismay, some anger and not a little embarrassment did he leave behind him. The wicked hypocrisy and practiced deceit of their son was hard to assimilate in and of itself, regardless of the consequences to others. Of those others, Miss Woodhouse, the darling of both, was their first concern and until they could assure themselves that her heart was in no manner damaged, they could not be easy. Mr Weston, therefore, undertook to bring Miss Woodhouse to Randalls without delay. With much anxiety did he do so, but at last he was reassured. Frank had trifled with her, but he had not wounded her, *this* was her assertion, although she thought Frank greatly to blame. The Westons thought so too, but such had been Frank's agitation, and so very manifest his dismay at finding Miss Fairfax so ill, that they could not doubt his sincere attachment to the lady. With Emma's heart secure they began to think that Frank's attaching himself to one of the loveliest and most accomplished young ladies in England was the very best thing he could possibly have done, however underhand and bizarre his method of going about it.

Highbury in general took longer to forgive their prized orphans. Highbury disliked secrecy and surprises and here were both practiced beneath their noses. They questioned each other closely about it. Who had seen what? Who had suspected anything? But all declared themselves so wholly deceived that they concluded that the secret engagement was a fantasy made up to tease them. In any case the couple's acquaintance in Weymouth could only have been a precursor; they belonged to Highbury and only Highbury itself could have produced the romance that had always been their destiny. Mrs Cole was particularly unhappy—her hopes of securing Jane as wife to one of her sons, and gaining thereby free tutelage of her daughters, were dashed by the news. Mrs Perry lamented very much that Jane's health should have been so damaged by the affair but harboured hopes that the bill for Perry's attendance might *now* be settled.

Mrs Elton was at first very offended by the intelligence that her particular friend and protégé had concealed her true circumstances; it was shabby and insincere of her. But Mrs Elton was not the kind of woman to own that she had been tricked; she declared she had suspected something as early as March, which, in point of fact, was impossible since she had not arrived in Highbury until April. But a little empirical evidence was not to stand in her way and before long she was congratulating herself on having found out Jane's secret, of being quite in her confidence and party to all. The only mystery was that, knowing, she should still have exerted herself on Jane's behalf with the Smallridges, but no one in Highbury was disposed to question Mrs

Elton closely on that point. Mrs Elton was the intimate friend of Miss Fairfax who would now become Mrs Churchill of Enscombe. It was debateable, a very controversial question, but it was arguable that Enscombe stood higher in esteem even than Maple Grove. What was without doubt was that *both* were a great deal better than Highbury, and Mrs Elton became increasingly convinced that Highbury, a small town with small ambitions, little elegance and negligible real society, was not her natural milieu. Elton was wasted on it; more to the point *she* was wasted on it. What could a woman, be she ever so blessed with resources, do in such a place? There must be suitable livings to be had elsewhere; Bath, Cheltenham, Brighton—any of these would suit. She was not particular, but superior society she would stipulate for, music of course, and a vicarage that would accommodate the Sucklings and—when they were at liberty—the Churchills, in comfort.

Miss Woodhouse declared herself very happy for the engaged pair but *she* was not a woman to be outdone by Miss Fairfax and soon secured the hand of Mr George Knightley. He was not as wealthy as Frank Churchill, nor as amusing. In looks he was only tolerable but he was squire of Donwell and other than the upstart lawyer William Coxe or the yokel farmer Mr Martin he was the only single man in her reach. He had always taken a paternal interest in her and his anger at Frank Churchill's cavalier treatment of her awoke her to the possibility that he might think himself in love. All in all, it was a convenient arrangement. As much influence and prominence as she had enjoyed as the premier lady of Highbury, how much more would accrue to the mistress of Donwell? The Claytons of Clayton Park and the best ranking families of Kingston would now be within her sphere. Oh! There would be no limit to her ability to meddle and interfere, to patronise and to gloat, to have much more of her own way even than she had ever enjoyed in the past.

Frank wrote his letter to Mrs Weston and a lengthy, full and frank account it was of all the events, the rationale—however flawed—the difficulties and despair that he and Miss Fairfax had undergone. He chastised himself but vindicated Miss Fairfax in every particular; he was to blame, if blame were deserved. She was only to be admired, praised and cared for.

He was forgiven.

Miss Fairfax, daily improved in health, appetite and looks, at last agreed to a visit from her prospective mother-in-law. Even if Mrs Weston had not been notified by Frank's letter that Jane lived in dread of the meeting, she would have discerned it by the diffidence of Jane's manner and the hesitancy of her speech. Miss Bates' fidgeting and fussing made unreserved converse impossible and at last Mrs Weston suggested a carriage ride. Once in the fresh air of the countryside and away from the well-meaning interference of her aunt, Jane's demeanour improved. Mrs Weston encouraged her, by focussing her remarks on all the good that would accrue from Jane's engagement and marriage to Frank.

'I am not acquainted with the elder Mr Churchill,' Mrs Weston said, 'and I am sure he mourns his late wife very sincerely, but the addition of a *different kind* of lady to his household can only be a consolation he anticipates with great satisfaction.'

'Oh yes,' Jane agreed. 'He has written. He is all generosity.' She lifted the ring that she wore on a ribbon at her neck. 'It is too large for my finger,' she explained, 'but he sent it in token of his affection. Frank says there will be more. Indeed, he says we shall have *everything*. It is too much, I am sure it is far more than I deserve.'

'What happiness it will be,' Mrs Weston remarked, 'to have the means in your power of improving matters for your aunt and grandmamma.'

'Whatever capacity I have in that way, it shall all be directed to their comfort,' Jane said earnestly. 'I want nothing for myself at all. I am worthy of nothing. But if they can benefit in any manner that I can facilitate, you can be sure that they will do.'

'You must not denigrate yourself, Miss Fairfax,' Mrs Weston averred gently, taking Jane's hand in hers as though she were a small child. 'You must look forward to what will be. You have suffered, I know …'

'Oh!' Jane burst out, the floodgates on all the remorse, self-blame and misery she had endured on Frank's behalf opening at last. 'Pain is no expiation. I can never be blameless. I have been acting contrary to all my sense of right; and the fortunate turn that everything has taken, and the kindness I am now receiving is what my conscience tells me ought not to be.'

'Let others be the judge of their own behaviour,' Mrs Weston advised. 'If they choose to absolve, to understand, you should not argue with them. You seem to me to judge your own conduct severely enough, *too* severely indeed. Let that suffice. Do not allow your rosy future to be shadowed by what has gone before.'

At last Jane lifted her eyes and Mrs Weston read in them what Jane was too delicate to express; the *cause* of all her suffering—her great and incontestable love for Frank Churchill. Mrs Weston understood it however, and assured her with gentle looks and pressing compassion that *this,* in time, would conquer the remorse and recrimination. They would fade, and only love would remain.[xxxiv]

Thankyou

Thank you for reading this book. I really hope you enjoyed it. As a self-published author I don't have the support of an agent or a huge marketing department behind me. I rely on my readers to spread the word about my books. Please would you consider returning to the platform where you purchased the book and leaving a short review? Just a few words to accompany your star rating would mean so much to me.

You could connect with me via Facebook or visit my website at www.allie-cresswell.com where you will find details of my other books and have the opportunity to sign up to receive news and special offers. If you don't live too far away from me I would be happy to visit your reading club, WI or creative writing group to give a short talk or a reading.

I can supply questions to guide your reading group discussions about any of my books.

Bibliography

Of course, Jane Austen's *Emma* has been my main inspiration for this trilogy of Highbury novels.

In addition, I benefitted from the wealth of information in:

The Georgian Seaside by Louise Allen

Weymouth, an illustrated history by Maureen Boddy and Jack West published by The Dovecot Press Limited

Acknowledgements

Thank you to my beta readers Lona Manning, Sallianne Hines, Helen Pryke-Domi, Kath Middleton and Helen Clark. Your patient and accurate reading and helpful suggestions made this book so much better. Thank you to Tim, who listened while I read the manuscript aloud, and picked me up when blue eyes turned brown.

About the Author

Allie Cresswell was born in Stockport, UK and began writing fiction as soon as she could hold a pencil.

She did a BA in English Literature at Birmingham University and an MA at Queen Mary College, London.

She has been a print-buyer, a pub landlady, a book-keeper, run a B & B and a group of boutique holiday cottages. Nowadays Allie writes full time having retired from teaching literature to lifelong learners.

She has two grown-up children, two granddaughters, two grandsons and two cockapoos but just one husband—Tim. They live in Cumbria, NW England.

Dear Jane is her ninth novel.

You can contact her via her website at www.allie-cresswell.com or find her on Facebook

Also by Allie Cresswell

The Talbot Saga

The Talbots: a family with a shady past, a glittering present and an uncertain future.

The Talbots' country house: a place that uncannily shares its owners' fates.

The Talbot Saga begins at the turn of the nineteenth century and follows the family and their mysteriously secluded Yorkshire home through two hundred years of British history.

Notes

[i] Mr Weston's history and situation can be found in Chapter Two of *Emma*.

[ii] The scant information we have on the Bates' past is to be found in Chapter Three of *Emma* and later in Chapter Forty Three when we hear that 'it would have been an honour for [Miss Bates] to notice [Emma].'

[iii] Jane Fairfax's history and situation can be found in Chapter Twenty of *Emma*.

[iv] The version of Cinderella which Miss Woodhouse and Miss Fairfax would have been familiar with.

[v] Chapter Nineteen of *Emma* makes clear the disparity in personal beauty between Miss Campbell (by then Mrs Dixon) and Jane Fairfax

[vi] Calculating the respective ages of Jane Austen's characters has been tricky but vitally important to get at least approximately right. Jane Austen gives us only a few numbers to work with.

We know Emma is twenty one at the beginning of Jane Austen's book, and Miss Taylor has been at Hartfield sixteen years, making Emma five when she arrived. We can presume that Miss Taylor was employed when Mrs Woodhouse died.

Jane Fairfax is a similar age to Emma. We are told in Chapter Twenty of *Emma* that Jane's mother died when Jane was three, that at aged five Colonel Campbell began to interest himself in her and that she went to live permanently with the Campbells 'before she was nine years old.'

George Knightley is sixteen or so years the girls' senior, described as thirty seven or eight at the commencement of Jane Austen's novel.

Frank Churchill is described as being 'three- or four-and-twenty' in Chapter Eighteen of *Emma*, so some two or three years older than the girls.

We are not told how much older Isabella is than Emma but as *Emma* begins she has five children and we know she has been married seven years. If she married at nineteen this would make her twenty six or seven so, five or six years older than her sister, which seems reasonable.

Likewise, apart from being the squire's younger brother we are not told the age difference between George and John. I have chosen to place Mr John Knightley closer to Isabella's age than George's. In *Mrs Bates of Highbury* young George is eight years old, his brother not quite two.

Mrs Bates of Highbury and *The Other Miss Bates* take place over the years 1780 and 1781. This places the commencement of this novel nineteen years later, in 1797. *Emma* was published in 1815 and Jane Austen gives absolutely no real-world reference to help us place it accurately in time, but it seems reasonable to me that she would have set her book at some period in her relatively recent past.

[vii] To read the story of Jane Bates and Lieutenant (later Captain) Weston, read *Mrs Bates of Highbury* and *The Other Miss Bates*.

viii This incident is described in *Emma* in Chapter One

ix This is the Miss Bickerton who will later abandon Miss Smith to the gypsies.

x I wanted to introduce Harriet Smith and Mr Martin to each other!

xi This family is mentioned later in connection with Frank's being allowed to visit Highbury. It is implied that Mrs Churchill does not like them.

xii A loud and unruly dance or gathering likely to end in a brawl

xiii This accords with canon. We know that when Jane does arrive in Highbury next, it is two years since her last visit

xiv Frank was right! See chapter Two of *Emma*

xv Chapter Nineteen tells us that Jane caught her cold on 7th November

xvi See Chapter Fourteen of *Emma*. This circumstance is mentioned in the letter which Mr Weston shares during the Christmas Eve dinner at Randalls

xvii See Chapter Fourteen of *Emma*

xviii This is the letter that Emma escapes hearing when she calls on Miss Bates in Chapter Nineteen of *Emma*

xixxix From this point onwards I turn detective, trying to see the events described in *Emma* from Jane and Frank's points of view and describing the illicit encounters and whispered asides which they must have shared while Emma blunders on, centre-stage.

xx See Chapter Twenty One of *Emma*.

xxi See Chapter Twenty Three of *Emma* for Miss Austen's account of this

xxii See Chapter Twenty Four of *Emma*

xxiii As reported in Chapter Twenty Five of *Emma*

xxiv See Chapter Twenty Six of *Emma* for an account of the Coles' dinner party

xxv A huswife is a small case containing needles, pins, thread, scissors etc, used by a lady for running repairs to her attire. Jane Austen mentions that Miss Bates has one in Chapter Nineteen

xxvi This is the scene I imagined took place between Frank and Jane before his visit to Hartfield to say farewell to Emma. Something had moved him to confide in Emma. See Chapter Thirty of *Emma*

xxvii This unlikely excuse is the one he comes up with. See Chapter Thirty Seven of *Emma*

xxviii She did! See Chapter Thirty Seven of *Emma*. Emma perceives Frank's spirits to be flustered and describes him as 'restless.'

xxix We know from Miss Bates' own lips that she slipped away before supper to put her mother to bed, leaving Jane unchaperoned. This coincided with the flurry of interest which followed Mr Elton's snub and Mr Knightley's rescue of Harriet. I feel certain that Frank and Jane would have taken advantage of these events to have a tête a tête. See Chapter Thirty Eight of *Emma*.

xxx See Chapter Forty One of *Emma*

xxxi We know that Frank encountered Jane as he rode towards Donwell. Later, it transpires that they argued.

xxxii Chapter Forty Four tells us that Jane spent all the morning writing letters and we later find that one of them was to Frank

xxxiii In his letter to Mrs Weston (Chapter Fifty of *Emma*) Frank mentions that Mrs

Churchill died on the 26th. Much of the tone and some of the actual words here are taken from Frank's own letter.

xxxiv Wisdom which this writer can attest to be true.

Printed in Great Britain
by Amazon

83192951R00294